PRAISE FOR

HARBINGER

"Romance, banter, and all the yearning? I'm obsessed."

—#1 *NYT* bestselling author **REBECCA YARROS**

"Stunning. Just stunning—the world, the magic, the romance. This will be your new addiction from the first page."

—#1 *NYT* bestselling author **ABIGAIL OWEN**

"Deliciously dangerous and savagely sexy, Geneva Lee's *Harbinger* delivers swoons and suspense in this intoxicating new world ruled by the stars . . . I couldn't turn the pages fast enough!"

—*NYT* bestselling author **RACHEL HOWZELL HALL**

"An original and fascinating take on Romantasy. Bishop and Arden are truly written in the stars!"

—#1 *NYT* bestselling author **TRACY WOLFF**

"Fast-paced and action packed, it grabbed me from the first page and didn't let go. I devoured this and am eagerly awaiting the next book. This is an absolute must read!"

—Amazon bestselling author **ALEXIS CALDER**

"Geneva Lee always writes my newest favorite escape. She never fails to craft rich worlds packed with characters you love and desperately miss the second you finish the last page."

—*NYT* bestselling author **MOLLY LEE**

"*Harbinger* is everything I crave in an epic romantasy. Unique magic, plenty of twists and turns, and a dark and dangerous love interest that will have you fanning yourself. Geneva Lee weaves magic and mystery into an unputdownable story that's written in the Stars."

—*NYT* bestselling author **NISHA J. TULI**

HAR
BIN
GER

HARBINGER

GENEVA

NEW YORK TIMES BESTSELLING AUTHOR

LEE

RED TOWER BOOKS™

Entangled Publishing, LLC
644 Shrewsbury Commons Ave., STE 181
Shrewsbury, PA 17361
rights@entangledpublishing.com
Red Tower Books is an imprint of Entangled Publishing, LLC.
Visit our website at www.entangledpublishing.com.

Edited by Liz Pelletier
Cover design by LJ Anderson and Bree Archer
Original 3D bird model by BreathTime
Edge and case design by Bree Archer
Edge image by Lazarev/Getty Images
Case images by musalim/Getty Images and Taufik Ramadhan/Getty Images
Original constellation illustration by Geneva Lee
Original endpaper illustration by Juho Choi
Original map illustration and design by Elizabeth Turner Stokes
Interior design by Folio Book Production LLC

HC ISBN 978-1-68281-673-8
Signed Edition HC ISBN 978-1-68281-850-3
Ebook ISBN 978-1-68281-677-6

Printed in China

First Edition September 2026

10 9 8 7 6 5 4 3 2 1

To S—

My darling, I can't wait to read your book someday.

Remember, astra inclinant, sed non obligant.

*

ANTARES
THE WEEPING SISTERS
WINTOUR
ISOLDORO
FLORENTIA
STYGIA MOUNTAINS
VENNARO
WOLF'S KEEP
THE BELLATORUM
ASTROLATORY
MIRADORES
BARON SEA

THE RUINS OF CALVERA
JOURNEY'S END
THE EASTERN OUTPOST
DAMALIS
THE CINDERWALD
ARDERMARE
N
S
E
W
N-E
N-W
S-W

CONTENT WARNING

Harbinger is a pulse-pounding romantasy about power gifted by the Stars—and the mortals who will do anything to gain that power. The story features elements that might not be suitable for all readers, including violence, blood, death of people and creatures, grief, injury, perilous situations, graphic language, suicide and suicidal ideation, burning, poisoning, alcohol use, and sexual activity on the page. War, large-scale death, and loss of family are discussed. Readers who may be sensitive to these elements, please take note, accept this dagger, and prepare for the Kindling . . .

ONE

Out the window, the full moon hangs low and heavy, as if it doesn't quite belong among the stars above or here at the palace below. That makes two of us.

I shift my weight, last in line to exit the rear vestibule and head to the Royal Astrolatory. Only initiates, nobles in their twenty-fifth year, will be allowed to enter tonight. That hasn't stopped my older brother, Broderic, from escorting me all the way to the door.

In front of us, a tall young man with a shock of red hair steps forward. The guard swings the door open, hitting us with a frigid blast of air before the initiate races out and he closes the door again.

I turn to Broderic, raising an eyebrow. He refused to bend the rules and let me take a coat.

He opens his mouth like he might offer some advice or encouragement. Instead, he pats my arm. "You're an Icaros. Act like it."

I'm not sure if he's making a threat or giving me the world's worst pep talk.

I nod quickly, and the guard opens the door again. With a deep breath, I wrap my arms around my chest and step into a howling swirl of snow. Cold gusts bite through my gown, a flimsy ceremonial scrap thrust at me upon my arrival at the palace. It's meant to show the Stars my devotion—because nothing says dedication like suffering.

At least they allowed us undergarments. Small blessing.

The other initiate is already halfway across the snow-laden gardens, so I pick up speed. The Stars don't like to be kept waiting.

A row of heated aviaries lines the garden path, birds of every size and variety little more than restless shadows behind the iron bars of their cages.

My breath fogs in front of me as I trudge through the snow, the wind stinging my cheeks. I'm told the weather here is like this nearly the entire year. Now I understand why they named the city Wintour. Back home, the leaves haven't even begun changing colors. Here, the evening would be better enjoyed under heavy blankets with a mug of hot tea.

Instead, *I* have a ritual to attend.

Past the last sweep of garden hedges, the astrolatory rises from behind a stone wall and spins upward in a spire of stone and glass to kiss the night. It perches at the brink of the Weeping Sisters, twin waterfalls that tumble to the sea below. Inside the sanctuary, scholars and disciples study the sky above. Some watch the Stars for omens. Others search for new ways to harness their magic. Each serves the king. Most never leave the tower, their lives bound as much to the Stars as to him.

But tonight, for the first time in five hundred years, its doors will open to initiates from every order. Including me.

It's a great honor—according to *everyone* I've *ever* met. But on the city's northernmost bluff, the bitter cold is so sharp it circles back to burning and feels more like a punishment.

The initiate who left before me is nearly to the gates already. My heart races to catch up, but the snow deepens with each step, sucking at my boots and forcing me to slow down so I don't lose them altogether. My mother used to say I'd be late for my own funeral. Arriving late to my Petition is roughly the same thing.

But when I reach the wrought iron gates, a sentry holds up a hand to stop me. He points to the squat stone wall running alongside us, separating the hallowed space from the rest of the palace complex. "Leave your boots here."

Looking over, I find a line of abandoned footwear. I blink a few times like they might disappear. When they don't, my jaw loosens—along with my tongue. "You can't be serious."

The astrolatory's entrance is still a couple hundred yards away. The dress is bad enough. Going barefoot will be torture.

He resumes his rigid stance without another word, which is answer enough.

Tradition always favors the sadistic.

I grumble under my breath, mixing in a healthy dose of curse words, as I fumble with numb fingers to loosen the stiff buckles of my new boots. I nearly fall over twice before I get the first one off and drop it at the end of the line. Even new, their sturdy brown leather, tanned in my home village, looks shabby and utilitarian next to the finery of the others. The second comes off more easily. Snow bites into my bare feet, the chill spreading until it reaches my bones. I turn and glare at the guard.

"One lamb to the slaughter," I grit through chattering teeth.

I swear his mouth twitches as he shifts aside to let me pass. I take a single excruciating step and decide to abandon my dignity as well. Gathering the skirt of my dress into my fists, I run the final distance to the stairs of the astrolatory's limestone portico. Tall columns line the entrance, offering little shield against the wind, but I climb quickly, my feet screaming at contact with stone that's somehow even colder than the fucking snow.

Most of the others stare, like running implies I've lost my mind, except for a pair of initiates who offer sympathetic nods. Both share the same black hair, the woman's cascading in a glossy sheet past her shoulders but the man's shorn to just below his ears. They blink similar warm brown eyes at each other—probably cousins or siblings—then move to offer me a space between them.

Their compassion tells me they're likely descendants of Order Leontia, the healers who use their steady magic to patch the rest of us up. I take the spot because I'm alone as the only initiate from my province this year. But mostly I do it for the warmth.

Another initiate paces nearby, her rich, olive skin unflushed despite the cold. She pauses for a moment, turning back, face entirely unreadable as her dark eyes sweep over the group before her. No one moves to offer her a place, and I realize she's alone, too. I shift to give her space, but the woman to my right mutters, "Marius."

And for a second, I go still like the rest of them.

With no wars to fight, Order Marius focuses most of its time on border skirmishes with pirates and raiders from the Lost Continent and the lands beyond, lands who covet our magic. But it's what those from Marius do inside Antares that makes us all pause: ferreting out unlicensed magic and then executing anyone involved with ruthless indifference.

Her eyes fall on me for a moment, like somehow she knows I don't belong with anyone here, either. Nothing changes on her blank face, but guilt floods through me. I nudge back to make more room for her, but the Marius initiate squares her shoulders and strides to stand next to a marble column by herself. She's brave enough to be from the military order, I'll give her that. Especially since a spray from the curtain of waterfalls below us finds its way past the columns. I shiver harder as droplets of ice-cold mist settle on my arms and face.

No one speaks as we huddle in small clusters near the massive oak door. Half of us are just trying to stay warm. The other half are sizing one another up.

We all hail from the five noble bloodlines of Antares, but some orders are more . . . *cooperative* than others. So, while we may technically be allies who need one another's magic to survive, we're all rivals. Even now, most of the initiates have splintered off with their bloodline rather than move close enough to share body heat.

"This will be worth it when we receive our birthright tomorrow." The young man next to me breaks the silence like he senses that everyone needs a pep talk and he's nominated himself Team Captain. "We're very lucky."

A few others nod. I manage half a smile. Luck has nothing to do with it.

Before we governed magic, the Stars chose randomly, picking who to bless with little regard for merit or morality. Witches and gods walked the world then, if you believe the old stories. They gave us nochtimetry—the sacred art that harnesses the magic of the Stars.

They also gave us war.

Endless, brutal war.

But we mere mortals fought back, annihilating them in the Last War. The general who led the defeat was named king, and he elevated the most powerful families that fought alongside him to patrons, tying each bloodline and its descendants to one of the powerful constellations that determine our fates. These noble families became the pillars of our society, each learning, governing, and controlling an order of magic for the good of all of Antares.

That's the history, anyway, and since I hail from one of the original patron families, I'm not supposed to question it. None of the nobility would dare. Not when it means we're among the few that will inherit the responsibility of wielding that magic.

Normally, we accept this birthright at our home astrolatory in front of our families and a few close friends. But not this year.

This year is the Quincentennial, the five hundredth anniversary of the day our illustrious ancestors decided to lay down their weapons one final time and give peace a chance. And, of course, now the new king wants to celebrate like this was somehow all his idea.

So, he's summoned every noble coming of age this year to receive their birthright at court.

Or die of exposure.

Whichever comes first, apparently.

Team Captain turns to me when no one else responds to his words of encouragement. "Where are you from?"

Before I can answer, the wooden door creaks open to reveal the dimly lit entry. A vesper, one of the astrolatory's cloistered scholars, appears in the open doorway. The gray streaking her long, dark braids matches the shimmering, embroidered fabric of her robes. Part priestess, part oracle, and part scientist, her life is dedicated to studying the Stars above.

We move toward her in a herd, eager to warm ourselves by the heating stones within. But the vesper doesn't invite us inside. Her gaze sweeps across each initiate in turn, assessing us like we're books to catalog instead of people.

"It is a great honor to pass through these doors and give your life to the Stars," she explains in a clear, strong voice.

Forget honor. I'll take a coat. But I nod dutifully along with the others.

"Tonight, you will each face your Petition, the first step required to receive your birthright," she continues. "Which of you will go first?"

For a moment, no one moves as it hits us. The ritual is private, a showing of loyalty to the Stars. Before we receive our magic, we're meant to stand beneath their canopy and prove we're ready to leave our old lives behind—whatever that means. But if we're doing this *one by freaking one*, and she's blocking the door, the rest of us will wait *outside*. I lift my hand to volunteer, but Team Captain shoots forward and bows.

"It would be my honor," he announces, puffing his chest like he's accepting a medal. Someone in the group across from us whispers to his friends, and they all snicker. Arrogant enough to mock someone in front of a vesper? What order are they from?

The vesper stares Team Captain down. "Name and order?"

"Ren Sata, Order Leontia."

He's a healer, like I thought. Although his ambition is a surprise, since his order prides itself on being self-sacrificing. Then again, he probably sees it as his duty to go first and show us we have nothing to worry about.

The vesper gestures for him to follow. They disappear inside, the door closing behind them.

Thick, uncomfortable silence descends again among the rest of us. With Ren gone, I'm exposed on one side. I wrap my arms around myself as the wind picks up.

"He better not take too long." A blonde with wide-set eyes across from me flexes her hands. Her nose is upturned at the end, reminding me of my favorite cat from back home. "I feel like I'm going to lose a finger."

The man beside her has the same green eyes and tilted nose, though he stands at least a foot taller. Twins or very closely related. He catches me studying him and winks. "That's not the appendage I'm worried about."

I almost find it funny. But his pants look a lot warmer than the silk dresses given to the women, so I dislike him by default.

"Would it kill them to let us wait inside?" I mutter, earning a few nods of agreement.

Unfortunately, the blonde takes this as an invitation to complain more. "This is why I hate visiting the capital. It's always so cold in Wintour."

In other news, water is wet.

I focus on warming up my hands, but another initiate takes her bait and asks, "Have you visited here before?"

"We travel *all* the time. We're second cousins of Patron Calix." She flicks a finger at her brother, brightening like the bragging is warming her up. "My father imbues armories, so we've been to nearly *every* province."

My father always said Calix is the one family no one can afford to cross—and the gleam in her eyes tells me she knows that, too.

Because Calix is the only order that can make steel indestructible . . . or as fragile as glass. Even my family's magic isn't enough to keep crops alive if our Calix-supplied equipment breaks. But they *also* control the entire black market. If it's magical and convenient, a Calix has figured out how to sell it.

That's not a problem for most of us, except Order Marius, who are stuck dealing with the forbidden magic. I guess after five hundred years of peace, it gives the military *something* to do.

"Wow," I say, if only to keep my lips from freezing shut. This conversation isn't worth wasting energy better spent on maintaining the last of my body heat. A few of the other initiates manage more enthusiastic responses, and she begins spewing stories about her family's trips to nearly every corner of Antares.

"Where are you from?" her brother asks me, eyes twinkling.

First a dick joke and now this? Somebody's here for more than their birthright.

Still, I admire his ability to flirt under these conditions, so I answer with a forced smile, "Damalis."

"Damalis?" his sister repeats with a slow blink, like she's just realized I have two heads. "I've never met anyone from Order Icaros before."

Probably because agricultural magic requires sticking close to the land. Even though my father was a patron, he only traveled to the royal city once a year. My older brother took over those business trips when he got sick, but we couldn't afford to send anyone else. The Quincentennial might be my only chance to see something other than farmland in my lifetime.

The blonde must be thinking the same thing, because she says, "Farming must be so boring."

My throat knots, heat rising to my cheeks despite the weather. From irritation, not shame. She might look down on me, but I bet she likes to eat.

"It's not so bad. I know how to butcher a cow." This time, I don't smile, and she moves closer to her brother.

Agriculture isn't the most glamorous magic—or the most lucrative—but it's still necessary. And unlike *Miss Second Cousin*, I hail from a patron bloodline, one of the original founding families of modern Antares. Only a handful of the other initiates can claim the same, if any.

She's moved on to describing her home estate when the ancient door opens again, and the initiate from Leontia staggers out. His tan skin is paler than before, and he steels his face like he's trying to keep tears from leaking out of his shining eyes. His hands are clean and empty, but he wipes them on the hem of his tunic over and over, like they're covered in something. He doesn't look at anyone as he pushes past us, hurrying away from the astrolatory and disappearing into the night.

"Are we supposed to just . . . *leave* like that?" the blonde asks.

"I don't think so," I murmur with another shiver. Not that they gave us a rule book.

The vesper reappears in the doorway. Her silver robes billow as she lifts her hand. "Next."

But no one moves forward. A few people even back away, the cold forgotten following the first initiate's hasty departure.

Tomorrow, we will all witness one another's Kindlings, the ceremony when we receive our inherited power from the Stars. The Kindling doesn't just hand you magic, though. That's why it's customary to undergo the night before alone to show proper reverence. Whatever that means. Broderic only told me: *what happens tonight is between you and the Stars.* That I should show I'm prepared to shed who I am and be what they need me to be.

That didn't scare me before. Now I wish I'd badgered him for more information.

Because the Kindling only stokes the magical ember in our blood. It smolders unseen, waking on its own schedule over the months that follow, if ever.

Until it manifests fully, any nochtimetric patterns we attempt are pretty much useless in our hands. Or worse, they backfire. Maybe that's why duty and responsibility have been drilled into my head since I could understand the concepts. I'm only half convinced I even want my magic to wake up at this point.

But *anything* is better than standing out here a minute longer. I'm nearly frozen to the stone, but I manage one step forward and then another, pins and needles stabbing the soles of my feet.

The vesper studies me, and her eyes narrow slightly. "Order?"

"Icaros." I raise my chin and clench my jaw to keep my teeth from chattering.

Her gaze settles on me like she can see the dirt that's usually under my fingernails. "Name?"

"Arden *Icaros.*" My breath curls around my name like fog.

"Follow me, Lady Icaros." The vesper steps to the side, nodding permission for me to enter.

"She's from a patron line," someone whispers behind me, sudden interest dripping in their tone. My family name changes the math.

For them.

I don't turn to see who said it. Even if part of me wants to see Miss Second Cousin's face. Instead, I square my shoulders and march inside, ignoring how my body protests the sudden movement.

I might not be beautiful or rich like the other initiates, but what I do have is enough common sense to get out of the fucking cold.

The sluggish warmth of the floor's inlaid heating stones rewards me. It seeps into my numb feet and spreads across my skin before settling into my tight muscles. The vesper closes the door and latches it, locking the others out—or me in. Ren seemed pretty eager to get out.

Nope. Not going there.

"This way." She breezes through the vestibule toward a bend in the corridor.

I'm not even half thawed, so I can barely keep up with her brisk pace. I still try, since the others are stuck out in the cold until I finish. It would be a shame to send Blondie back home with only nine toes.

I make it a few steps before I stop in my tracks. This time to stare.

Moonlight spills through the astrolatory's glass ceiling—glass so the vespers can watch the Stars, and so the Stars can watch back. Torchieres flicker with captured starlight that illuminates the hallway. Their faint glow catches gold shards embedded in the floor to make the dark stone look like the night sky.

Our astrolatory back home is open to every citizen in the province of Damalis. Unlike this one, it is rustic and plain, little more than stone walls and a paned, sheet-glass roof. Dad used to tell us that the more gold there was inside an astrolatory, the less soul it had.

Which makes the Royal Astrolatory the most soulless place I've ever set foot in.

Either the black marble or the gold set into it could probably pay off our estate's entire debt and fund our family for another century or two.

When we reach a series of alcoves carved high and shallow into the building's stone wall to our right, she slows, allowing me time to study each one.

Constellations are carved into the recessed walls, their dots and intersecting lines painted with gold leaf. One each for the original patron orders of Antares: Velesont's many-headed hydra, the gentle lioness of Leontia, Calix's overflowing chalice, the horned wolf of Marius, and my own order's pegasus. As we pass a blackened sixth alcove, I avert my eyes. So does the vesper.

The corridor ends with a staircase that spirals up, floor after floor stacking in tiers on top of one another toward the heavens.

We pass doors on each level inlaid with gold and jewels that connect in patterns more complicated than any I've ever seen. Each is more intricate than the last until we reach the top. The final door is a slab of stone, unadorned save for a simple knob.

There's nowhere else for us to go, but she doesn't open it. Instead, she reaches into her robe, and my breath snags. The first initiate looked devastated when he came back. Now it's my turn to be traumatized.

And to think I begged my brother to send word that I was sick, so we could skip all of this.

But she only withdraws a small bottle filled with a thick, milky substance that lingers on the sky-blue glass. Smiling at my confusion, she uncorks the lid. "The crown's observatory is a sacred place," she explains, dipping a finger into the oil. "Bow."

I squat into a graceless curtsy, too nervous to do it properly as my eyes drop to the floor. She draws a line across my forehead, then another that bisects, then another, and another. The oil warms on my skin as she murmurs in the strange, melodic language I've only heard a handful of times before. During weddings and other rituals. When our local vespers bless the fields before seeding. At my father's funeral.

"It's a great honor to enter this chamber," she says, stepping away. "Only those willing to dedicate their lives to the safeguarding of magic should do so."

Straightening, I nod. Rites and ceremonies have never been very important to me. Working the land requires practical magic, not ancient superstition. But even in Damalis, there are plenty who believe the Stars expect our devotion and that they'll punish those who neglect to show it. It's why every year we perform a fertility ritual in the fields before any magic is done. It's also why no one says anything if the crops fail anyway.

However, since I'm here as a guest of the king, I can't risk offending anyone in the royal city. Not if Broderic is going to secure a wealthy wife and, along with her, our family's estate.

The vesper slips the bottle back into her robes. But when her hand reappears, it's not empty.

My stomach sinks as I stare at the slender dagger. She holds it out, and I fumble taking it. There are stars and lines engraved on the silver blade. Its gold hilt is studded with sapphires and diamonds, all connected by more etchings. It's utterly ridiculous, but the dagger is light, almost dainty, and it fits in my palm like it was made especially for me. I turn it over like I'll find instructions written on the other side.

"What am I supposed to do with this?" I ask, still studying it while I process what's happening.

I'm standing in the Royal Astrolatory.

Where a less-than-talkative semi-priestess anointed me.

And she just handed me a knife.

The pit in my stomach grows.

"Do what needs to be done," she murmurs.

I think of the initiate wiping his clean hands. Of what little information my brother gave me about tonight. But it's the haunted sadness in her eyes—the same look that my father got during the seasonal slaughter—that tells me exactly what needs to be done.

Fuck this.

And fuck my brother for acting like this was a simple rite of passage.

A girl should be warned when knives are going to be involved in the evening's activities.

The vesper gestures to the door in front of us but doesn't reach for its knob.

I'm being tested.

I have to open it this time. *I* have to walk inside.

Or I could turn around. She can't stop me. Not while I'm the one holding the knife.

"I'm not . . ." I swallow back the words.

She places a gentle hand on my shoulder, guiding me forward. "Remember who you are, Arden *Icaros*." She emphasizes my family name like I did outside the astrolatory—as if I need to be reminded. "Then do what needs to be done."

You're an Icaros. Act like it.

I clutch the dagger, Broderic's words nudging me toward the door.

No wonder that initiate nearly ran from the astrolatory. Raised to heal his entire life, then given a dagger at the door. Order Leontia has always felt the most like ours.

Until today.

Today, I see the difference between us. He probably didn't know why she gave him this knife. I do. But something sour pools in my stomach. It clenches and twists as I touch the door. The heavy slab swings open with a hiss and a rush of cold air. I don't dare look back to see if the vesper follows me inside. I don't turn when the door closes with a soft but ominous *thud.*

After the gold-flecked marble and extravagance of the rest of the building, the observatory is depressingly sparse, though the circular stone room with its flaming torches feels more like my home astrolatory. Damp air prickles my nose, the scent of musty stone and faded incense mingling with something metallic that sticks in the back of my throat.

I know that tang, but there isn't a speck of blood to be found.

I choke back a cough rather than break the heavy silence. Centuries of rituals have worn the limestone floor smooth against my bare feet. An icy breeze drifts toward me, catching my hair and raising goose bumps all over my body. Looking up, I find endless night. There's no ceiling above the circular chamber, not even glass, to separate this space from the Stars. They're so close that my fingers itch to reach up and pluck one from the sky.

But that's not why I'm here.

I drop my gaze, my eyes adjusting to the dim firelight, and find an altar. But it's the tall man standing on the other side of the chamber who catches my attention. Tightness laces my chest, constricting more with each breath I take. He isn't alone, but somehow, I only see him. He doesn't move or speak, but his presence is as demanding and damning as the sky above me.

He is a column of shadow against the dull stone in his black uniform. The only color in the room is the red cloak that falls from his broad shoulders to the straps of his thick-soled boots.

Only bishops, the highest-ranked officers of Order Marius, wear that color. It's a position so revered—so sacred in its duty—that many second-born nobles from their order train from the time they can walk in preparation to claim it. Few manage, but when they do, they give up everything—

marriage, children, even their own names as proof of their unwavering dedication to protecting the people of Antares—and become simply *Bishop*.

There are only a handful that carry this rank in Antares. Each travels the continent, maintaining the law with little oversight from anyone save the king and the high vesper.

When I was little, one came to Damalis, but it was so long ago that my recollection of her is more feeling than concrete memory. A pit in the stomach. A sense of being small and insignificant. A tugging alarm in the chest that's impossible to ignore. All wrapped in scarlet.

This bishop's hood is drawn, obscuring his face even more in the dim room. I take a step in his direction like he holds some invisible thread that I can't resist pulling. He tilts his head, and the hood shifts just enough to see one corner of his mouth curve slightly, like he knows I'm walking toward him and no one else.

The movement breaks the spell. I stop, remembering that we're not alone.

Two others flank him, dual weapons ready to strike. The silver embroidery on their uniforms marks them as knights, the highest rank someone without noble blood can achieve.

The first knight's face is all sharp lines and brutal angles, like her skin was hewn from the black stone that makes up the Stygia Mountains. And with the sword strapped to her back, she looks as beautiful and deadly as their uncrossable peaks. The other knight is handsome despite the pale web of raised scars that mars one side of his tanned neck and continues to his cheekbone. His eyes keep flicking to the door with a restless energy that suggests he can't wait to get out there and add more damage to his otherwise perfect face.

"Pretend they're not here," the vesper says behind me, and I almost jump out of my own skin. I'd forgotten about her. "They will only observe your ritual."

Observe. The single word crashes into me. To my audience, I'm little more than a woman holding a knife pointed at the stars—and they're waiting for me to use it. I force my attention to the altar. It's a simple stone plinth that is empty save for a black silk cloth draped over the shape of a bird's cage.

The vesper walks over and tugs the cloth off of—yes, a golden cage.

And inside it: an offering to the Stars. A sacrifice to earn their favor. Proof I've left my old life behind.

That I'm worthy of their magic.

The black bird tries to stretch its wings, sidling on its perch as it searches for room that isn't there. It's too large to be an ordinary raven. I take a single step, and it tilts its head, two beady black eyes zeroing in on me with unnerving curiosity. There's something almost human in the way it stares, and a chill races down my spine.

The cage's moon-shaped clasp is studded with pearly stones, and the bars don't curve into a bell. Instead, they intersect like a trellis.

Not an ordinary cage. Not an ordinary bird.

And it's still watching me.

When I was a child, my mother spun stories of witches who transformed into oscens. They flew to the heavens as the giant black birds to listen to the Stars whisper their secrets. When I was only a bit older, Broderic told me the witches turned into birds to steal children from their beds. I had nightmares for weeks. Mom made him sit up with me as punishment. She said they were only stories. Only birds.

Still, oscens have been hunted to near extinction. People believe they're a sign of bad luck. I never thought I would see one.

I really wish I wasn't seeing one now.

A cold sweat breaks across my skin, making me shiver in the night air. My palms grow slippery, and my grip on the knife falters. I catch it as it slips down without thinking and gasp, the blade slicing open my palm. I pass the dagger to my other hand. The wound is just deep enough to spill blood. Nothing serious, even though it stings like seven hells. I clench my hand tightly to stop the bleeding. I'll deal with it later.

There's a rustle of red cloak as the bishop shifts forward. He doesn't come any closer, but heat blooms on my cheeks. Having an audience is only making this worse.

Get it over with.

I feel eyes boring into me as I inch toward the altar. It hardens my resolve, even though my stomach is still churning.

I'm not afraid to get my hands dirty. I've held a lamb while my father slit its throat, felt it thrash for survival, go still, and then helped cook it to feed our family. Before that day, we provided and cared for it. It didn't know not to trust us when we came for the slaughter. But we made its end swift. A kind but necessary death. Everything about *this* feels wrong.

It's a crime to cage a wild thing.

My chest tightens, trying to confine my racing heart like it's inside that golden cage.

Trembling, I unlock the hinge with my injured hand and clutch the dagger behind my back in my other.

The clasp pops open with a slight hiss of released magic. Opening the door, I will the oscen to fly away, but it continues to watch me like it's here to observe me as well.

"I'm sorry," I murmur and reach inside.

The bird bumps its beak against the blood that's now smeared across my whole hand.

What comes next is easy. Or it should be. I don't even need the knife. Grab it by the neck like a chicken. A quick twist. Fast and clean.

That's all I need to do.

But the oscen climbs onto my wrist, claws scraping my skin. Not the behavior of a wild animal, but one that's been tamed.

Broken.

Something cracks inside me as I draw it out of the cage. I tighten my hold on the dagger's hilt, feeling every unnecessary jewel dig like teeth into my palm. Such a beautiful weapon for such an ugly deed. No wonder the man from Leontia kept wiping his hands. Some stains aren't visible outside one's own soul.

The Petition demands evidence I'm ready to step into my new life. Apparently, by taking another life.

Do what needs to be done.

The vesper's words echo in my head. Instructions that feel like a curse.

Resolve blazes through me until I'm sure I'll combust, and I move my arm, drawing the bird closer, looking into its curious eyes.

There's no other choice.

I know what's expected of me.

I know what I must do.

I move on instinct.

"Fly," I whisper and fling my arm up.

Wings stretch. Beat. Soar.

I drop the dagger on the altar with a *clang* as the oscen surges toward the stars overhead and disappears through the opening. Relief washes through me.

One of the knights makes a choked noise that I'd almost swear was a laugh, but my gaze stays on the clouds drifting over the constellations above. I don't look away until I'm certain the creature is gone, and then I look at *him*.

At the twin swords strapped to his back and peeking over his broad shoulders. A shiver races down my spine. His hood still shadows his face, but the smirk from before flattens into a grim line.

"You were expected to kill it." His voice is low and raspy, each word drawn out like an executioner delivering a slow death.

Fear climbs up my throat, but I swallow it back. Lifting my chin, I shrug, the movement braver than I feel. "I decided not to."

I brace for punishment. For refusing to make the sacrifice. For speaking like that to a man like him.

But the bishop turns his face away from me, and my cheeks flame. It's a subtle dismissal, and it cuts to my core. I'm not even worth the effort of a reprimand.

I don't hear the vesper approach, and I startle when her hand rests gently on my arm. "You're done here."

Yes, I probably am.

We descend the stairs in silence, our feet carrying us more quickly than before. Part of me wants to slow down. Nothing good awaits me on the other side of tonight. But I also need to put distance between him and me. The thought of the bishop chases me down the stairs until my head is spinning. The vesper matches my pace, clearly ready to be rid of me. She doesn't look at me once as we wind our way to the exit.

I botched my ritual, but there's no blood on my hands. Apart from my own. Still, something unspoken and oily churns inside me. It spills out when we reach the door.

"I know I failed, but—"

"The Petition isn't a test," she cuts me off. Finally, she looks at me, but she might as well be wearing a mask. "You can't fail it. You only had to make a choice."

Maybe it's meant to soothe me. It doesn't.

I glance at the stairs. "Is that why he let me leave without making the sacrifice?"

She doesn't need to ask who I mean. "You aren't the only one capable of mercy."

A pit hollows in my stomach, any lingering relief leaking away as her fingers close over the door handle. She yanks it open, blasting us both with cold night air. It whips my cheeks raw as I step out to find the other initiates gathered at the edge of the colonnade, shouting and gesturing to the sky.

"Use that mercy wisely, Arden Icaros," she whispers before continuing toward the steps to claim her next victim.

I follow her to the others, and the blond from Order Calix turns to me with shining eyes. He points to a black shadow circling overhead. "It's an omen!"

The oscen flies higher, rising to a black swath of night not even the Stars dare to breach. I'd thought nothing of the row of caged birds as I approached the astrolatory. They'll just send for another bird. My chest tightens with the urge to run and set them all free.

"Wish me luck," he says as the vesper shepherds him toward the door.

The words stick in my throat, so I nod before he disappears into the astrolatory.

We're all here because the king wants a spectacle. I didn't expect to be the one to give it to him. I stare into the night with the others as the wind kicks up. It rips through my thin gown and bites into my bare skin.

But I'm no longer cold.

TWO

My younger sister storms into the breakfast room, still in her dressing gown, and yanks the velvet drapery open. Morning light spills through the floor-to-ceiling windows across from me, watery and sullen—not unlike Isidore's current mood.

"They put us in the oldest wing," she announces, glaring at the opulence around us like she expects the walls to crumble imminently. "A girl from Velesont told me."

"So?" I shrug.

Last night, my siblings were asleep when I dragged my half-frozen ass in from my Petition. They were still in bed when I visited a Leontian healer at dawn to mend my wounded hand. But I knew the peace wouldn't last. Not when they started smelling coffee and bacon and the dozen other scents currently torturing my stomach.

Isidore spins toward me, hair swirling like ink over her shoulders. She's wearing one of the new dresses our brother bought us, but the neckline is a good two inches lower than mine. "We're in the worst rooms in the palace, *Arden*. It's an insult." She aims her glare at me. It falls on the necklace I'm wearing, and she grimaces. My sister shakes her head, staring at the shabby locket like it's worse than the walls. "I can't believe you put that on."

Ignoring her, I pile as much as I can onto a gold-rimmed plate, hoping the delicate porcelain doesn't break from the weight. There's enough food to feed half the conscripts in Order Marius. Then, I pour coffee into an equally delicate teacup that's decorated with a gold-leaf crown—the constellation of the royal line of Augustus. Lifting the cup, I inhale the rich aroma, steam tickling my nostrils.

Coffee is the one crop we rarely get to keep back home. It's too valuable.

Most of our fields need to remain devoted to food, not luxuries, and the last few years, my family's magic needed to grow the beans has been fickle. What we manage to harvest is sent here or collected by Order Velesont to sell in shops in Antares's largest cities—along with nearly everything else we grow.

"The other orders think they're better than us," Isidore says, her voice catching.

She's not going to let it go.

I drop into an upholstered chair at the table. It creaks in protest. Even the furniture is offended by our presence. "Let them."

I nearly tell her about last night, nearly ask her if these are people we want to impress. Something stops me. Something in her ever-changing hazel eyes. Something *hungry*—that has nothing to do with the food in front of us.

"It's . . . it's . . ." Her lower lip trembles.

She doesn't have to explain. I might ignore the feeling, but it's still there. The feeling that everyone else is on a pedestal, staring down at us. Sighing, I push my cup toward her. "Try this."

Isidore is a few years younger than me, so I know she's never tasted coffee. That's how long it's been since we could justify keeping any. Her eyes light up as she takes it, but her nose wrinkles with the first sip. "That's disgusting." She shakes her head but takes another drink. "People like this?"

For twenty-two, she's still such a child.

But at least now she's a distracted child. I reach for it. "Give it back."

She rolls her eyes and keeps drinking. "There's plenty here. Get another cup."

I admire her determination to take full advantage of the opportunity—even if it means suffering.

"Are you ready for tonight?" She taps the porcelain between sips.

I shrug and cram a bit of a buttery crescent-shaped pastry into my mouth, scattering flakes all over the pristine linen tablecloth. There's nothing like this back in Damalis. Our food is simple but plentiful. Roast meats, fresh vegetables, bread when one of us bothers to make the dough. Food to survive. This food tastes like sin. I'm going to need larger clothing when we return home, because I plan to hunt down every pastry in the royal capital before we leave the city. "I haven't really thought about it."

That's a lie. I stared at the ceiling last night, listening to Isidore snore in the bed next to mine while replaying what happened over and over again. Every noble-born enters an astrolatory for the rite that prepares them to receive their birthright. Even Broderic did it four years ago, although not in front of a bishop. No one really talks about their rituals. Now I understand why.

Still, I can't be the only one who refused the sacrifice.

"I wish it was me," Isidore says dreamily before frowning at the coffee.

"It's enough that you're here, and you got a new dress," I remind her.

I'd thought the same. That it should be Isidore, the more charming of us, who got the chance to be presented at the royal court, where they would appreciate her beauty. Long-limbed and slender, rather than compact and curvy like me. Her hands don't have calluses from long hours doing the work that magic doesn't. She's exactly what's expected of a noble-born daughter, devoting her time to volunteering in the village and keeping house. She would be the better initiate—except she's never culled a herd or flock. I bet Broderic would have warned her better, because if she'd been handed that knife . . .

Then I remember the hunger in her eyes. Do I really know what she's capable of? I push the thought away and reach for another pastry.

Before she can snap back at me, a blur of elbows and knees vaults into the room and nearly crashes into the table. Andreas, our youngest brother, grins up at me from under his mop of curly brown hair.

"I bet I could climb out that window," he says, glancing toward its latch with the reckless ambition of a boy who has never been in a room this high from the ground.

I arch an eyebrow. "You'll break your neck and stain the stone below. And *then* poor Broderic will have an aneurysm."

Andreas scowls, as if falling to his death were preferable to another hour of confinement indoors. He's twelve and has yet to break enough bones to learn this lesson. Not that he hasn't been trying his hardest.

"Why do we have to be here?" he whines. "Arden could have done the ritual at home."

"Because the king is bored and enjoys watching the children of dead patrons embarrass themselves." It slips out before my brain catches up with my mouth.

They both fall silent like they do whenever someone mentions our parents in the past tense. Mom's been gone longer, but it has only been a year and a half since Dad died, and they still don't know how to talk about it.

Neither do I, apparently.

The silence hangs for a moment before Isidore mutters, "Why was I worried that Andry would embarrass us when you're here to do it?"

I consider arguing with her, but she's not wrong.

But Andry isn't so easily deterred. "Why can't we go into the city?"

"Because you will get lost," someone booms from the door, "and miss all the fun tonight."

My little brother barrels toward the familiar voice, and Kieren, our personal guard during this trip, catches him. His broad shoulders strain against the too-small uniform he borrowed from a retired city guard who lives near our estate. His position has always been honorary. We've never needed security in Damalis.

I want to laugh every time I see him with his black hair slicked back and tucked behind his ears, trying to look the part for the sake of our family's reputation. A year younger than me, he's far from intimidating.

We released our remaining household staff last year. Arriving without a single attendant would have been noticed, so Kieren stepped up like he always does. All he's done so far is mediate when we start bickering—and stay by my older brother's side to boost his status.

"Please," Andry begs. "I won't get in trouble."

"When have I heard that before?" Broderic asks as he enters the room next, giving Andry a stern look. My brother is a couple of inches taller than Kieren, though not as broad-shouldered and muscular. He's dressed for the day in a velvet morning coat cut to his trim figure. The rich emerald fabric draws attention to the green hues in the hazel eyes we all inherited from our mother. But he is the only one of us with her copper hair. This morning, it falls across his forehead in a sweep of soft curls. I suspect that he'll catch the attention of plenty of noble-born daughters today. He gives our little brother a stern look. "Did you go into my room?"

"No!" Andry says a bit too quickly to believe.

Kieren tuts, flipping Andry upside down and shaking him until the gold astrolabe that belonged to our father falls out of his pocket. "There you go."

Broderic scoops it off the ground and pauses like he might lecture Andry. Instead, he shoves it into his jacket. "Why don't you go play in the snow?"

Andry is moving the minute Kieren deposits him onto his feet.

"Don't stray too far from the palace, or a heart collector will get you," Isidore calls after him.

Andry races out of the room like he's been given a challenge, and my older brother smiles, but it doesn't reach his tired eyes. The exhaustion is nothing new. Not since Dad's illness took a turn and Broderic became patron overnight, only to discover how much our father's treatment from Leontia had depleted our accounts. Deep down, I'd hoped that this trip might give him a chance to rest.

That was before he announced his intention to use the Quincentennial to make connections. Something our family has never been very good at.

So, while I was off making bad impressions at the Royal Astrolatory, he'd been out with Kieren doing just that in a desperate attempt to shore up the estate by any means necessary.

"Did last night go well?" I ask. The circles under his eyes are darker, like he didn't sleep, either.

"Fine," he replies in a clipped tone.

Kieren catches my attention from behind Broderic and draws a finger across his neck. A warning to let the topic die.

But Isidore doesn't see him do it. "Did you meet anyone?"

"Yes." He slumps into a chair by the hearth, bypassing the platters of food and coffee, and stares at the fire.

Isidore opens her mouth, but Kieren cuts her off. "What about you?" He shifts the conversation to me. "How did it go?"

Both my siblings turn to hear my answer.

I'm going to kill him.

I paste a smile onto my face. "I still have all my toes."

"What does that mean?" Isidore frowns.

"Never mind."

"It's done. That's all that matters," Broderic says, still staring at the flickering fire like he's hypnotized.

For once, I'm grateful for his moodiness. Because I don't want to talk about it. I don't even want to think about it.

Isidore pushes up from her seat, muttering under her breath, "I'm going to bathe."

"You've done that twice already," Broderic says.

"The king has plenty of hot water," she says over her shoulder, already halfway down the small corridor that leads to the attached bedrooms.

Kieren's eyes track her movement across the room. They've tracked her since the day our father brought him home half-starved and told us to treat him like a brother. A command we've all followed, even—most unfortunately for Kieren—Isidore.

Broderic doesn't notice. He never has. I pretend not to for the sake of my best friend's pride.

But this morning, Kieren isn't the lovesick fool I'm worried about. I pour my brother a cup of coffee. He takes it without a word.

"You never get me coffee," Kieren teases, snatching a slice of cake studded with dried berries from my unguarded plate.

"You can get your own coffee." I shoo him away from my food. "*You're* not heartbroken."

Broderic straightens with a scowl. "I'm not heartbroken."

Kieren and I share a look, and he mouths a single word: *Don't.*

But ignoring the situation isn't an option. Am I supposed to sit back and watch my oldest brother ruin his own life to save the rest of ours?

"Have you spoken to Miranda?" I ask.

His frown deepens, making him look older than his twenty-nine years.

"That's over. It has to be." His steely tone tells me that this conversation is over, too.

Because that's part of his plan. Before Dad's death, Broderic intended to marry Miranda. He held on to that delusion as long as he could. But marriage is mostly transactional among nobles, and there are plenty of potential matches from the wealthier families where the bloodlines extend out to distant cousins too far down the pecking order to stand a chance at inheriting control of their own provinces. For them, an heir is an heir—even if they're from Order Icaros.

He'll marry to shore up our finances, and I'll spend the next two years learning the sacred nochtimetric magic entrusted to our order—precise patterns that connect the Stars' magic to enrich our soil or call in rain. And together, we'll keep everything from falling apart.

Hopefully.

Still, with Velesont swooping in to sell our crops and livestock to the kingdom through their shipping network, we have little control over how much we earn. And without connections, we might never get them to pay us fairly. But I can't stomach the idea of letting him marry for money or clout any more than I could stomach the idea of sacrificing that oscen.

Kieren catches my eye and shakes his head. He usually knows what I'm thinking.

"Why?" I ask, ignoring his warning again. "You love her."

"You know why," Broderic grumbles, his gaze not bothering to meet mine as he tosses another log into the fire. "We need money."

"Why not ask the king?"

My brother blanches as if even suggesting this makes him nauseous. He settles back into his chair and glares at me. "I am a *patron*. Order Icaros is a pillar of Antares. We do not beg, especially not from the king."

"So, you're just going to whore yourself to some insipid heiress who only wants your title? Dad wouldn't have wanted—"

"Dad can't want anything," he says flatly. "He's dead."

Unlike my younger siblings, this reminder doesn't shut me up.

"There has to be another solution." If only he'd talked to me before he broke things off with Miranda, we could have found a way. But it's not too late. "We can barter with Yonas to—"

"Enough." He cuts me off again. "This isn't up for discussion. I'm head of household. This is on me. I don't expect you to understand the importance of duty yet. Once you've been initiated . . ."

But I can't hear him past the ringing in my ears. He's determined to shoulder the entire burden of our family's needs. No matter the cost. Even if it's eating him alive.

"And what happens if you become ill, too?" I say softly. "You aren't sleeping. You aren't taking care of yourself. Neither did Dad."

"I'm not him," he says through gritted teeth. "This conversation is over, Arden."

"But—"

"Enough!" he snaps, and my sympathy vanishes. I hate it when Broderic gets into his I-Know-Best attitude. "You receive your birthright tonight. You should get ready." He shifts back to face the fire, the coffee still untouched, and flings a verbal knife at me. "Too bad you won't be able to properly wield for years. Not that it would help much anyway."

I stare for a moment, my chest heaving as a dozen retorts, ranging from cutting to devastating, jump to my lips. It's not my fault inherited magic wakes when it wakes. That it could take months before it even stirs and then still requires years of training to actually wield. Or that with each generation, the magic seems to grow weaker, as though the well were running dry. Sometimes it doesn't manifest at all. Throwing it in my face isn't fair. I open my mouth to tell him he's being a dick, but what's the point? He's unreachable in this mood.

In the end, I stomp out of the room without another word.

I don't bother stopping in the sleeping chamber I'm sharing with Isidore. The last thing I need is for her to start on me, too. She hasn't even tried to talk him out of it. Neither has Kieren. Maybe if they would, Broderic would see what I've been trying to tell him all along. Maybe we could find another way together.

I grab my new coat from a hook by the door and head out, determined to find my way through the maze that is the royal palace. I need air. I need to breathe. I'm going to suffocate under the weight of words like *duty* and *birthright.*

I wind through corridors, pretending to look at the tapestries and oil paintings while checking for exits. There are so many turns and twists that it's like the castle doesn't want me to escape.

Rounding a corner, I spot a group of last night's initiates. I duck back behind the wall before they see me. Talking with them is the last thing I need right now.

"That's what happened," one says in a hushed voice.

"No member of Velesont would ever do that." Her companion shakes his head in disgust.

My pulse ratchets faster with each word. They aren't talking about me. They can't be. How would they know what happened during my Petition? I peek around the corner, careful to stay hidden in the shadow of the alcove.

"I knew the second I saw her." It's the blonde from last night, her nose impressively high in the air. "I can't believe she's actually from a patron line. How embarrassing."

That pretty much seals it. I don't want to hear the rest. Not after my own brother was so condescending. That's enough for one day.

Pressing my body close to the wall, I sneak around the corner and discover the front hall. I dash toward the door, not slowing until I'm outside.

Cold air crashes into me, flurries dancing on the wind. I consider heading back to where it's warm. Instead, I swivel on the top step and stare at the city stirring to life below. The palace complex sits at the top of Wintour like a crown. A dense fog blocks all but the tops of the buildings: roofs and spires, glass domes and chimneys pumping plumes of smoke.

I gulp down a deep breath, but my frustration lingers. I don't care about the stories people are sharing. But I do care that Broderic is acting like the events of this weekend will save us all. Well, at least *his* actions.

Money troubles are one sort of prison. Arranged marriages are another. It doesn't matter which you choose, you're still a prisoner.

I'm so lost in my own thoughts that I don't hear the front entrance open. A moment later, Kieren is next to me.

"You couldn't let it go." He shakes his head. "You're lucky he didn't bite your head off."

I start down the steps before he can drag me back to make nice with my brother. "Broderic is being silly. Our accounts are low, but we don't need to be rich."

There's a difference between self-sacrifice and martyrdom. Not that Broderic is in a mood to hear that, nor am I in the mood to explain.

"He just wants to take care of you," Kieren says softly after we reach the bottom of what feels like a hundred steps, sadness tracing the words as he follows me down the wide stairs.

I wish that mattered to me.

"I can take care of myself." I nearly slip on the fresh snow dusting the paved private drive. The soles of my new boots—another unnecessary expense for this trip—are still slick.

Kieren sees but doesn't comment. "Should I go back inside, then?"

I sigh. Kieren always gets stuck in the middle of our battles. "No, stay."

"Come on." He crooks his arm. "We're going to explore Wintour."

I stare at the iron gates that separate the palace grounds from the outside world. They are a different kind of cage. One I can choose to open. One I can escape—for a little while, at least. "Is that allowed?" I tease, wishing I felt as light as my tone. "I wouldn't want to get lost."

"Ah, but you are not ten years old." Kieren grins at me. "And since tonight you officially become *Lady* Icaros, I think you're permitted."

I grimace at the title. "Please never call me that."

"Of course." He gives a solemn nod before tacking on, "My lady."

I push him into the snowbank.

THREE

The trouble is that an Icaros never goes down without a fight. And Kieren is an Icaros in spirit. He snags my ankle as he falls, and I shout as we go down in a heap. It's still early in the eleventh month, and there's already enough powdery snow to nearly swallow us.

A sentry stationed at the base of the stairs hurries over, frowning at Kieren. The guard offers me his hand, eyes darting around like he shouldn't risk the distraction of helping me up. "Allow me to assist you, my lady."

Indignity upon indignity.

I force myself to thank the sentry anyway while Kieren laughs in the snowbank. The guard quickly returns to his post, his gaze sweeping the grounds for signs of real threats.

Kieren is still howling when he makes it to his feet. He brushes snow from his coat, then the flakes dusting his dark hair, his brown eyes crinkling at the corners. "Why does he get to call you—"

"Don't finish that question," I warn him.

He holds up his palms. "I surrender." His mouth twitches like he wants to tack on my future title again. "Shall we?"

His restraint is a small miracle.

"There are posterns throughout the city." He points to an arched opening carved into the stone wall near the gates, a swirl of blue light emanating from inside. "I hear there are a few needing repair, but we can take any working one wherever you want to go."

I wrinkle my nose. Of course Velesont would create plenty of the connected portals in a city this size, but I've never liked the way postern travel feels—like being doused in ice water so cold it seeps all the way to your bones. "Let's walk."

Kieren doesn't argue with me, even when one of the guards at the gatehouse begs us to reconsider. Given how long she takes to open the gates, and the fact that coaches have fallen out of fashion except for formal events, I suspect the woman doesn't remember how to operate them.

The castle gates open to a spacious avenue of private estates, each building featuring the same black marble exterior with lines of gold and stars etched into the stone leading up to its domed glass roof. Mansions with columns and fences and fountains glare down at the city below, each the size of an overinflated ego. Sentries are stationed at each of their gates, their uniforms bearing a horned wolf, the sigil of Order Marius, as if the wealth past the wrought iron deserves to be protected to the death.

Wind nips my cheeks as I stare at the estates, and I fluff the fur trim of my coat to sit higher. "They're nearly as big as the palace."

"Homes to lesser royals," Kieren whispers so the nearby guard can't hear. "The ones the king needs to keep an eye on."

But doesn't want living in his own residence. They aren't mansions. They're gilded cages for royal hostages.

"Is everyone in Wintour rich?" I know I'm staring, but I can't help it.

"Hardly." He snorts. "But the king has plenty of favorites in the other orders."

"I can't imagine leaving Damalis for this," I admit.

"It's considered an honor to live here at his request," he says gruffly. His calculating gaze falls like dominoes on the sprawling estates lined up before us.

Being given a house like that is the kind of honor that might catch the attention of my otherwise oblivious sister.

I frown. "You wouldn't actually move here, though."

His head snaps to face me. "No."

But he *would*. We both know my sister would prefer to live in the capital. Why do people always try to change for love?

Some of the houses bear the symbols of other orders. We pass ones marked with the sigils of Calix, Leontia, even Marius.

"Are we the only patron line that doesn't have an estate close enough to kiss the king's ass upon demand?" I ask as we reach a gate bearing the hydra of Velesont.

"Unfortunately, yes," he says.

A few streets farther down, the stately homes give way to rows of elegant town houses lined up like trophies. Each still features a dark exterior to honor the Stars, but the black marble has been exchanged for stone, actual gold for paint. The entire capital is cloaked in darkness, broken only by gilded lines and domes of glass. The effect is a city that feels trapped in endless night, even at midday. It's nothing like the simple wood buildings and limestone estates in Damalis. Although in both cities, we use heavy draperies and shrouds to protect the sky from our light pollution. A sign of respect to the Stars.

Guards stroll the streets. There's less security here than near the palace, but I can feel them assessing us.

Kieren fiddles with a carved bit of bone as we walk, his thumb tracing the pegasus etched into it out of habit. He chatters away as I drink in the city, sharing everything he knows about the capital. Which apparently is a lot. He visited with Broderic last year when my brother attended his first annual council meeting as patron.

Kieren points out the way the city is stacked like the towering astrolatory at its peak, descending in tiers of power. The vespers sit at the top, because whoever reads the Stars first has all the leverage. Followed by the palace and the king himself to control the vespers and what they know. Then the aristocrats, the rich and the businesses that cater to them, and, at the bottom, the poor souls truly responsible for keeping it all running.

"Shouldn't the astrolatory be for everyone, at least?" It seems unfair.

"It's strategic," he says, leading me toward a bustling city block. "The Weeping Sisters prevent attacks by sea."

I roll my eyes. That's why I nearly froze to death last night? Because the waterfalls serve as added security for what's already the most inaccessible point in Antares? "No one has attacked us since the Last War."

Of course, that's usually the case.

A shadow passes over his face, but he shrugs and it's gone.

Past the wealthy residential district, the city opens into the wide High Street lined on either side by shops and cafés. Shoppers spill out their doors, loaded down with packages wrapped in brown paper, bags hooked on their arms.

The morning sun catches the jewelry displayed in the nearest window.

Poison rings with their delicate clasps opened to reveal hidden compartments, their designs refined for court but lethal at dinner parties. Next to them, a jewel-encrusted cane showcases its hidden dagger.

Maybe this is why Broderic doesn't want any of us going into Wintour alone to explore. Beautiful things feel deadly here. Even the jewelry is made for those with too much money and even more enemies.

Although I suffer from neither problem, I still shiver as I drink it all in. I've heard stories—everyone has—about the mysterious or sudden deaths that seem to plague particular bloodlines. Mostly Order Calix, even if Velesont seems to be similarly afflicted. I suppose when you control all the commerce and transportation, you make plenty of enemies—even ones related to you.

The next shop is less dangerous, only hawking the latest fashions. Velvet overcoats with matching embroidered gloves, leather breeches, lace gowns with high necks that are far from modest.

By the time I'm forced to drag Kieren away from a display of corsets and frilly undergarments, I've relaxed a little, despite the prickling at the back of my neck that feels as though we're being watched by the sentries posted on every city block.

"Look at that." He stares longingly at a new astrolabe, one with a dial that sends and delivers messages. His is so old that it can only send a simple summoning signal.

I lean closer to read the attached price tag, my fingers brushing the few silver crowns in my pocket, but I nearly choke at the eye-watering price. "You could buy one of the houses outside the palace for that!"

"So, I won't find it in my boot on Twelvetide?" he teases.

"Maybe in two or three hundred years." Because that's how long it would take me to save the money for it, but he just laughs.

"There's Icaros." Kieren jabs the glass, pointing at a model tucked in the window and shooting me a wide smile. "Just think, by this time tomorrow, you'll bear that mark."

The words dig a pit in my stomach. The models are three-dimensional versions of the constellations I saw etched into the Royal Astrolatory's alcoves last night. My mark will look more like those engravings, the Stars choosing where to brand it into my flesh. If I didn't fuck up my chances of receiving it last night. What if the Stars refuse to endow me like I refused to kill the oscen? I shake the thought off. No sense dwelling on what's done.

"Let's keep going." I tug his sleeve, wanting to fill the hole my nerves have carved into my stomach. "I'm hungry."

His eyes widen. "You can't possibly be hungry already."

"I'm gastronomically ambitious." And a total stress eater.

He snorts, then scans the street before grabbing my hand and dragging me toward a nearby coffee shop. We get into the short line of customers waiting to place an order. The man in front of me shifts on his feet, twisting his hands like he might panic before he gets a chance to order. His partner brushes a soothing hand down his arm, then laces his fingers through his. The others in line seem equally on edge.

I look up at the menu and balk. It's not simply coffee. They're using nochtimetry to infuse each drink with a slight dose of magic. And the price reflects it. No wonder we're required to send our entire crop for distribution.

"Is this legal?" I whisper to Kieren, watching the woman behind the bar spoon grounds into a muslin-lined pot. Its ceramic exterior is painted with intersecting lines and shapes in a beautiful, intricate pattern.

He shrugs, still studying the options on the menu. "It is if they have a license from Order Calix. If there's money to be made off magic, they'll approve it."

It seems a trifle extravagant to use magic to make coffee, but the shop is brimming with people willing to pay. Someone chooses a brew infused with clarity. Another, a drink that claims it calms the nerves.

I shake my head. "This is a waste of money."

Kieren raises a brow. "You sure you don't need something to calm *your* nerves?"

Leave it to Kieren to know me well enough to spot that something is off today.

"I'm just anxious." It's a bit of an understatement. "Why did I have the bad luck of coming of age during the Quincentennial?"

"It must be your destiny," he teases, but his smile slips when I don't grin back. "Hey, don't worry. The chances you fall on your face in front of every noble in Antares are nearly zero."

"Nearly?" I widen my eyes, suddenly queasy. "I wasn't worried about *falling*."

Until now.

My stomach rumbles from that fresh hit to my nerves. "Let's go. I'd rather spend my money on food. *Regular* food. Please."

"Fine." He holds up his hand in surrender. "We'll find food and try to fill that bottomless pit you call a stomach."

As soon as we step out the door, my panic settles to a low hum.

"Where are we going?" I ask as Kieren leads me away from the High Street.

"You'll see."

I poke him in the ribs. "I better see food."

He starts to walk faster. My best friend is well-versed in what happens when I don't get fed quickly enough.

I glance over to offer a quick smile, but he's too focused on steering us through the crowd. His jaw is tight, his eyebrows drawn together as he sweeps an arm out to keep someone from bumping into me. A beautiful woman in a high-necked dress offers him an interested look, but he doesn't seem to notice, and her face falls a little as she passes.

She's not the first, but Kieren has only ever had eyes for Isidore.

He guides us deeper into the heart of Wintour, where the buildings start to shrink. The storefronts and businesses sit closer together on streets half the width of the High Street. There are more people here and even more Marius guards.

Kieren hurries us along, unconcerned as we walk toward a glass-domed market that looks like it takes up several city blocks.

"What is that?"

"I'm pretty sure you'll think it's heaven," he says, stepping aside to give a young mother room to pass with her pram.

I'm not sure my idea of heaven is plastered with posters and bulletins or guarded by men with swords. But at least it's busy here.

A wooden sign hangs over the entrance with the words The Grand Arcade painted in sweeping letters. Next to it, the Civicus, a large, ever-updating notice board, delivers news. It's twice the size of the one in Damalis, because it displays stories from all over Antares as well as job postings and announcements.

A call for dock workers in Isoldoro posts as we pass, sandwiched between a story about a murder on the western shore and an advertisement for a dress shop we passed only an hour ago. Kieren pauses to read the job listing, nonplussed by the gruesome illustration of the crime next to it that I can't bear to look at. More proof that tonight's celebration of peace is overlooking a few things. I finally pull him away before he gets any wild ideas about running away to be a sailor, something he's always fantasized about thanks to an old pirate novel he was given years ago.

The Arcade has none of the leisurely energy of the High Street and its aristocratic shoppers. People are here to do business. While permanent storefronts make up the Arcade's outer perimeter, the center is crammed with tables of goods, selling everything from Ardermarian spices to bolts of silk and wool to trinkets for children. The briny scent of the ocean wafts from a stall where a fishmonger hacks the heads off still-flailing tuna. Sprinkled throughout the chaos are makeshift stalls hawking every type of food imaginable. It's overwhelming enough that for a moment, I forget about tonight's ceremony.

Customers bicker and barter with vendors, haggling over the fairness of prices. Regardless of whether they're wearing the sort of fine clothes we saw in shop windows earlier or simple pants and tunics made from homespun fabrics, everyone is trying to get the best deal for themselves.

But I'm here for the food.

We step up to the first food stall we see and study the various options. We both settle on hand pies filled with tender chunks of roast chicken and potatoes. The crusts are so flaky, and I want another immediately, but with our meager coffers and plenty to eat waiting at the palace, it seems like too much of a waste.

That doesn't keep me from drooling over the noodles in broth and grilled lamb skewers in the next two stalls.

"Go ahead." Kieren motions to the skewers, and I give in and purchase one, nibbling on it as we continue to walk. At least everything here is gloriously, temptingly cheap.

I finish the last bit of tender meat and drop the skewer into a nearby rubbish bin. "When I die, bury me here."

Kieren laughs, although he knows I'm not joking. "Noted."

He digs into his coat pocket and frowns, withdrawing his astrolabe.

I know that look. The giddy, floating sensation that's been growing in me for the last hour starts to leak away.

"Ignore it." I'm not ready for this adventure to end.

"It's your brother. I can't." He spins the summoning dial to reset it, but it instantly rotates back to its previous position. Kieren sighs. "And apparently, whatever he needs is urgent."

My stomach twists. "It's probably nothing."

"We should take the postern on the next street back," Kieren says, ignoring me.

I grimace. I don't want to return and sit in the palace, watching the clock tick closer to whatever mistake I'll make tonight—*this* time in front of the entire court. "Why don't you do that, and I'll walk?"

"Arden, I can't just leave you here."

"Why not?" I press. "I'm twenty-five . . . which is a year *older* than you. Plus, like *you* said—there are guards everywhere."

Not that I find them comforting. The sense of being watched snakes down my spine even now.

But Kieren shakes his head. "It's your first time in the city."

"I know the way." I lower my voice. "Just walk until I hit the palace." Since the palace is visible from nearly every street in the city, I can't get lost.

Kieren holds my gaze, then lets out a long sigh. Bending over, he fiddles with something in his boot. When he straightens again, he's holding his sheathed dagger and its leather strap.

"I don't need that," I protest when he tries to pass it to me. Why does everyone keep trying to give me knives?

"Seven hells, you don't." He forces it into my hand. "And be back in time to get dressed for the feast or your brother will hand me my ass."

I try not to grin and fail.

He doesn't return the smile. "Seriously, promise me."

"I swear. I won't get lost. Or be late. Or do anything stupid." I draw an *X* over my heart. "How would I live without you?"

"Be late tonight and you'll find out, because your brother will murder me." He takes a deep breath but doesn't turn to leave.

I roll my eyes. "Technically, I could *order* you to leave without me."

He gives me a look that says one thing: *try*. But he almost grins as he shakes his head. "Already abusing your position." He backs away before adding, "My lady."

He's around the corner before I can yell at him.

I shove the dagger into my coat pocket with my last silver crowns, cursing him quietly when I find at least twice as many as I had when we entered. Enough money to take a starsforsaken postern. Kieren will be getting those dumped on his head as soon as he's asleep tonight.

I slip back into the bustle of the Arcade and wander among the tables and noise for a few minutes, trying to work up the will to climb the steep streets back to the palace.

Instead, I find myself heading out the opposite exit and onto a muddy, roughly cobbled road. There are no guards stationed on this side of the Arcade, as if no one in this part of the city has to worry about thieves or safety.

Or maybe no one here cares.

The sound of striking steel rings through the smoke-filled air. Here, the closely clustered homes and businesses rely on wood fire rather than expensive heating stones. A small gang of children runs in front of me, almost colliding with a man dragging a cart behind him. The smallest pauses to squeak an apology, showing off a gap-toothed smile that makes me grin back. Everywhere I look is a curious mix of dirty and clean. A house with flowers planted in a window box next to a grimy pub with a smoke-stained chimney. I walk carefully to avoid holes and loose stones in the street, but something in me relaxes.

It's simpler here, more like our village in Damalis, only busier. No shops selling the latest magical innovations, no gilded signs and glass storefronts, no expensive coffee or diamond jewelry. I've found the backbone of the city.

Halfway down the block, I stumble across a pleasure house, men and women with painted cheeks hanging out the windows. They're laced in low corsets, biceps and breasts spilling out as they call to everyone passing by on the street. My cheeks must be as red as theirs, because a girl who can't be a day older than me takes a step from the door and looks me up and down. Her skirts are hiked so high that I can see the garters holding her stockings.

"This is not your street, dove," she whispers in a kind voice. "Best head back where you belong."

I nod, a lump forming in my throat, and head toward the first side street I see. She calls out again, but I don't turn back to see if it's meant for me or for a potential client.

I dart down the narrow alley, catching a few people looking at me as I pass. When our eyes meet, their gazes drop guiltily to the street. Glancing down at my new dress—one of three Broderic scraped the money from Stars know where to buy—I realize how I must look. I'm dressed as a lady. My clothes aren't quite as elegant or expensive as those on the High Street, but they're not the working garments of the people around me. I don't belong here, but I don't belong at the palace, either.

And now I sense eyes watching me again, the feeling like a stone in my shoe that I can't shake loose. Clipped but distant footsteps echo behind me. They fade in and out. One second, I'm sure I'm imagining them. The next, it feels like I'm being followed.

I quicken my pace, looking around like I'll find the right place to land, but I might as well be stretching my wings in a cage. There's nowhere for me to go. The walls close in, the alley tapering and my chest constricting along with it until I can't quite catch my breath. I'm sure that I'm going to pass out, but then the passage twists slightly. I steady myself against the wall as I stagger a few more steps to a hidden square.

In the open air, the tightness around my heart eases—until I look at the sign hanging from the nearest eave: The Sixth House. The name isn't as concerning as the skull and bones crudely drawn under it. Its windows are blacked out, as are the ones in the shop next to it. That one doesn't even have a name, just a painting of a heart impaled on a knife. Somehow, that's advertisement enough.

Dread skitters down my neck like a dozen tiny legs. Something tells me that I won't find any Calix-issued licenses in these shops. No chalice-stamped documentation that the magic inside is legal. The door to The Sixth House groans open, and I find myself sidling toward the only normal storefront I see: a bookshop with thick, leather-bound tomes piled in the window.

A bell jangles as I enter and swiftly close the door behind me. The little shop is so cluttered that I immediately knock into a table, sending a cloud of dust into the air. I steady the table, barely stopping its heaped books from hitting the floor, as a well-dressed woman appears from some hidden pocket in the back.

Her dark hair is cut bluntly at her chin, and it swings just above the tall collar of her neatly tailored wool jacket. She looks at me and blinks, her blue eyes shutting and reopening as slowly as a drowsy cat.

"Can I help you?" The question is colored with doubt, like she already knows the answer.

"I'm . . ." I pick up the first book I see. "Browsing."

Her mouth twists, but she inclines her head. "Of course you are. Fiction is on the east wall." Boredom replaces the doubt as she rattles off my options. Then she pauses and studies me for a second before slowly adding, "The *specialized* texts are past poetry, upstairs through the curtain."

I don't know what she means by "specialized," although her tone gives me some idea. Everything else in this square suggests the forbidden. I don't want to know what's up there, but I'm sure it's equally scandalous, if not outright illegal. I inhale, swallowing my pride. "Thank you, but I'm just browsing."

"Take your time." She sweeps one more look at me and disappears into the back again.

Opening the book in my hand, I'm relieved to find it's only a history of the Last War, the foreword proclaiming an honest and accurate depiction through personal stories. Aside from whatever waits upstairs, the books seem relatively innocent, if a bit dusty. I shove it back on the shelf and make my way to the poetry corner, studiously ignoring the heavy curtain that leads to parts unknown. A few minutes to calm my nerves, and then I'll head down that crooked alley and back to the Arcade.

I reach for a book of sonnets, but my hands are still trembling and I nearly drop it.

"I'm twenty-five. I know the way." I mutter my own words to Kieren under my breath, each minute making me more embarrassed than the last.

Just as I'm about to put the book back and leave, the bell over the entrance jangles again. I peek through the empty space on the shelf, and my breath catches when I see a red cloak, dark as blood in the shop's dim light.

The bishop stands in the doorway.

FOUR

His hood is down, but his face is angled away, revealing only a hard jawline and the muscular bands of his strong, lightly bronzed neck. Thick, silver-blond hair, the top half tied with a leather cord and the rest brushing against his shoulders, brings out the olive undertones in his skin.

I never actually saw his face in the astrolatory, but I know it's him.

It's something in the way he holds himself. Something in the set of his broad shoulders. The way he stands with such casual confidence and still exudes a lethal, almost primal threat.

My body moves before my mind catches up, some base instinct screaming at me to hide, run, *escape*.

He's blocking the door, so my feet carry me in the opposite direction, and I bump into the curtained-off stairs on my right. I duck behind the draped fabric and find a narrow staircase, made narrower still by more haphazard stacks of books. I test the first step, flinching when it creaks slightly under my weight.

For a second that feels roughly like eternity, I stay rooted to the spot, waiting for the curtain to be thrown open, for the bishop to seize me by my hair and drag me out into the gloomy square.

He tracked me here.

It's the only explanation. The footsteps in the alley. The constant sense of being followed. The fact that this entire area reeks of forbidden magic and yet, he's in here. With me.

But he doesn't whip back the drapes. I hold my breath until I hear the low murmuring of voices. I can't make out what they're saying past the blood roaring in my ears, but there's a tug at my center—that invisible thread being pulled again—and I know he's the one speaking.

Maybe he did follow me but didn't see where I went. Maybe he's asking the shopkeeper if she saw me.

My eyes travel up the staircase. Sanctuary waits there. Or the closest thing I'll find with *him* between the door and me. The shopkeeper will never suggest I'm there. She'll never send a bishop to a room that's full of illicit texts.

I tiptoe along the steps, sneaking like I did as a child when I wanted to avoid either chores or lessons. I slip behind the curtain at the top and pause, some of my panic ebbing enough that I finally catch fragments of the conversation below.

The bishop's deep voice floats toward me. Most of his words are still lost, but a few drift up the stairs. ". . . the usual arrangement."

"Of course, my lord." Her higher pitch carries more clearly, but there's something different in her voice now. There's no amused boredom, but rather something careful and practiced. "The second floor is yours, as always. I'll ensure you're not disturbed."

My heart shoots into my throat. *The second floor.* The floor I'm currently standing on, surrounded by whatever fucking *specialized* texts she hinted at earlier.

The floor shakes when his heavy boots hit the first step.

The sound slaps me like a bucket of ice water. I pivot, frantically searching for somewhere to hide. A maze of tightly crammed shelves fills the left side of the room, and there's a worn table tucked in the opposite corner. The space is even less organized than the shop below—books are piled on the floor, crammed onto shelves at odd angles, stacked in precarious towers. Some have fallen, spreading across the floor like an avalanche.

And the books themselves . . . I catch glimpses of their spines as I pick my way toward a gap in the towering bookcases. The symbols stamped on their covers make my skin crawl—geometric patterns that seem to shift under my gaze, words in languages I don't recognize.

I nearly trip on an open book, and I glimpse an illustration as I steady myself: a human grotesquely contorted, arms and legs at odd angles, back bowing into a hump. These aren't scandalous books.

They're *dangerous* ones.

The footsteps grow closer, and I weave quickly through the bookcases, wedging my body in the narrow gap between the farthest one and the wall. My hip bumps the shelf, and a book topples down. I slide into a crouch and catch it with my skirt before it hits the floor. Clutching it to my chest, I pull my skirt with me behind the bookcase and peer through a small gap just as the bishop steps inside. He stops and glances around, and for one brief, horrifying second, I'm certain he can hear my heart pounding.

I glance at the book still in my hands and bite back a gasp at the illustration on the jacket: a raven engulfed in flames. Beneath the illustration, an ash-black diagram sprawls across the cover—elegant, deliberate, and unfinished, its lines intersecting but not ending so much as disappearing into the dark.

The fallen constellation?

The one now blacked out in the sixth alcove in the Royal Astrolatory as a warning against hubris.

The order our five families joined General Titus to fight when they began abusing their magic. We almost lost to their power. Forced to regroup in the south, we begged the Stars to help us defeat them.

And the Stars answered.

Despite the sixth bloodline's access to the deepest magic in Antares, there was no sign. No warning. No time for them to run when the Stars sided with our families against them, and the volcano that had quietly loomed on the northern edge of their province shook the earth.

No member of the sixth house survived, as if the Stars had reached down a hand and wiped them from existence. When the smoke and ash cleared, the entire population was gone. Only ruined land remained. Their constellation fell from the sky, leaving behind the Night's Scar, a swath of endless black without a single surviving star in its void.

A book about it shouldn't be hidden in a shop. It should have been destroyed generations ago. Anyone caught with texts about the fallen constellation faces—

Death. They face death.

My tongue turns to sandpaper, sticking to the roof of my mouth. If I'm caught here, with this book in my hands, no amount of noble blood will save me. Suddenly, what I did last night feels like nothing, and tonight's ritual is the least of my worries. I'll be lucky if I make it to sunset.

I press deeper into my hiding spot, not daring to breathe. My leg muscles scream in protest as they strain to maintain the awkward position. Sweat beads across my forehead. I can't risk moving. If he finds me . . .

I can only see his lower body as he strides forward and grabs a book from a stack under the single, grimy window in the room. Then he picks up another one, turns, and sits down at the ancient table, shoving the piled volumes out of the way and opening the first book.

He's not here for me. He's here to . . . read?

Either the sadistic prick knows I'm here and he's toying with me, or he's looking at a book full of forbidden knowledge.

I could reveal myself. Step out now and claim ignorance. Admit that I'm lost and ask for his help. But the book in my hands damns me. Even holding it is probably a crime. And I didn't make the best impression on him last night.

It's getting harder to stay upright, crouched on my heels like this. At any moment, I'm going to topple like those haphazard books that have fallen all over the floor.

Maybe he would be merciful. That's a laughable thought. No matter what the vesper said last night.

No one attains his rank through *mercy*.

My legs start to give out, and I brace myself harder against the wall. It doesn't matter *why* he's here. It matters *who* he is. If he's reading something he's not supposed to, he'll kill me for discovering his secret. If he's doing something for the crown, he'll kill me for holding this book. For me, all roads end in him breaking my neck on the spot or hauling me in front of an inquest, which will most likely end in a public execution.

Either way, my family will be ruined. If they aren't executed alongside me. Steadfast Broderic. Proud Isidore. Reckless Andry. Loyal Kieren. They'll all die because of me.

The bishop rises again and walks straight toward the bookcase I'm behind. I try to close my eyes like he won't be able to see me if I can't see him, but they refuse to obey.

He reaches for a book directly above my hiding spot, so close that his sleeve brushes against the wood mere inches from me. The shelves block the top half of his face, leaving only his full, sculpted lips and cleft chin visible.

He lifts his hand to his mouth and yanks his glove off with his teeth, letting it dangle between them. Even in the dim light, I can see that he wears the gloves for more than warmth.

A silvery scar runs the length of his hand. The markings are too precise, too intentional to be from a wound. The lines look more like a brand, or maybe—my stomach does a small flip—like they were carved purposefully into his flesh. It's nochtimetric, but it's not the mark of his birthright. Not the symbol of the horned wolf of his order. It's not *any* pattern I recognize. Maybe it's a strength spell, the kind meant only for Order Marius? The other orders don't carve magic into their skin, but it might be different for the military.

A drop of sweat runs into my eye. It burns. I bite down on my lip to keep quiet. Each second feels like an hour.

The bishop runs his scarred hand along the shelf, fingers ghosting over spine after spine until they finally stop. The dark leather binding seems to drink the light as he draws it free so decisively that I only glimpse two foiled letters as he flips it over.

S and *C*.

The book falls open in his hands, and he flips through several pages. He traces a passage with his index finger, his lips moving silently as he reads before closing it with a *thump* that echoes in my heart.

And then he slides it under his red cloak.

He pulls his glove back on, covering that unsettling scar. Something eases in my chest until he pauses, and his head tilts slightly, revealing a glimpse of a strong, slightly aquiline nose. His nostrils flare like a predator scenting the air, and I forget to breathe.

But then he turns and strides away, shoving aside the curtain and tromping down the stairs at a heavy clip. The shop bell tinkles distantly, but I remain frozen.

I count thirty heartbeats, then sixty, then a hundred. Pins and needles shoot through my numb legs, but I don't move. My breathing goes ragged from the exertion, but still I wait.

My body gives out before my willpower, and I topple forward, the book thudding open on the oak floor. I don't bother picking it up.

I pretty much fall down the steps, my legs too numb to cooperate. I'm forced to catch myself on the wall twice to keep from tumbling headfirst down the staircase.

Bracing myself for a trap, I peer from behind the second curtain and find the shop empty. The shopkeeper doesn't appear, and something about her absence unnerves me further. I flee through the front door, not caring if anyone sees me leave. Just hoping that *he's* gone.

I bolt along the alley, no longer scared of the narrow passage and its shadows. I stop where it bends and press my body against the rough brick. Drawing a breath so deep it burns my lungs, I peer around the corner, looking for any sign of that red cloak.

But the bishop is gone.

Forcing myself forward, I count my steps, my heart rate ratcheting up with each one. The sky overhead has dulled to a shade of gray that suggests a storm is coming. Probably a fucking omen. A chill floods my veins as I reach the alley's mouth and the first snowflakes hit.

I have no idea what time it is. I can't remember whether I turned right or left before. Biting my lip, I take a chance and head left. After a few blocks, I realize I've chosen incorrectly—there's no sign of the pleasure house.

I'm about to retrace my steps when a door bangs open behind me and a man stumbles out, a sour reek wafting off his filthy, wrinkled clothing. He weaves unsteadily toward me.

"Well, well," he slurs, his eyes lighting up with interest. "Look what the Stars dropped on my doorstep."

I dodge him, picking up my pace, which is more difficult as snow begins to collect on the uneven cobblestone streets.

"That's not very friendly," he calls, some of the drunken thickness ebbing away. "I just want to talk."

Speeding up, I glance over my shoulder to find him sure on his feet. It's a trick. He's not drunk at all. My hand slips into my coat pocket, feeling for the dagger Kieren gave me. I hesitate, weigh my options, and turn at the next marked street.

Only to find myself staring at a crumbling brick wall with a rotting barrel stationed under a drainpipe, no windows low enough to reach. A dead end.

"This is better," the man says, stepping behind me and dropping his act completely. There's a calculated edge to his gaze that makes me wish I'd come out from behind that bookcase and begged mercy from the bishop. "There's only one reason that a person of your . . . *breeding* . . . bothers to crawl to our part of town."

Acid shoots up my throat, but I swallow, shaking my head. "I was lost, but I think I see the street I missed. If you'll excuse me . . ."

I dare one step to the side. He mirrors the movement.

"Lost?" He laughs, drawing closer. There's no sour scent of wine on him now. Even his clothes look cleaner. It's like he's a different man altogether. "You're not the first lady to sneak out of your prison up on the hill and come looking for a good time."

He reaches out, and I jerk back, but he only twists a strand of my hair between his thumb and forefinger.

"Don't touch me," I whisper hoarsely.

"Jumpy, aren't we?" His gaze drops to the simple silver locket at my throat. "Maybe we can come to an arrangement."

"It's worthless," I say too quickly. Interest gleams in his eyes. "It's tin. The silverplate is nearly gone. See?" I flip it over to show him the back, where the plating has worn thin enough to reveal the base metal underneath. "The clasp barely stays latched. I don't even carry a portrait in it."

All of this is true, except it's not worthless. Not to me, anyway. My mother wore this for almost twenty years. It was a gift from my father on their wedding day. It used to hold a portrait of him, but it fell out. It's the most precious thing I own.

"If it's worthless, then you won't mind parting with it. Consider it a contribution to the local economy." He flourishes a hand down his own chest.

"I said no."

He clicks his tongue. "But *I* say yes."

I back away, my hand slipping toward my pocket again and the dagger inside it. But he doesn't advance on me. Instead, his fingers flick the air like he's conducting a symphony. It takes me a second to realize that he's tracing a pattern. At first, nothing happens, but then the air glimmers, momentarily mesmerizing me.

The locket lifts from my neck like it's been caught by a gust of wind. The loose clasp falls open, and the necklace floats between us before dropping into his open palm.

I'm too stunned to move. That is *definitely* unlicensed magic.

"My sincerest gratitude." He gives me a mocking half bow. "It's been a pleasure doing business with you, my lady."

The taunt snaps the shock leashing me. My fingers curl tightly around the dagger. It's out and unsheathed before he's finished turning around. Lunging, I wrap my arm around him from behind and dig the blade's tip in at an *uncomfortably* low position.

The thief stills, except for his head, which tips down to look at the dagger pointed at his dick.

"Let's try this again," I hiss. "You're probably thinking that you are bigger and stronger than me. Maybe you're calculating if I'll actually do it."

"Interesting negotiation technique," he says through gritted teeth, eyes still on his prize. "Odds are you won't."

"Want to bet?" I flatten the edge of the blade against his balls, and he yelps. I extend my other arm out, palm to the sky. "Here's my counteroffer. Something precious for something precious. You give me back my mother's locket, and maybe you'll still have children one day."

He starts to pant, daring to shake his head. "You're bluffing."

I press it in another fraction of an inch, just enough to make my point. "Have you ever castrated a pig? I have. Would you like a demonstration?"

We remain frozen for a moment, no longer sure which is predator and which is prey. Then, slowly—as if his life depends on it—he opens his hand. The locket drops into my waiting palm, still warm from his grip.

"Pleasure doing business with you." I spit his words back at him. Stepping away, I keep the blade angled between us.

He spins toward me, a small snarl curling his lip as his eyes narrow on the dagger. I thrust it in his direction. But he jumps back, the knife slashing only air. His hand captures my wrist, twisting it until my bones protest. "I'm not a pig."

"Could have fooled me," I say, the words as strained as the joint he's pinned. My heart is hammering so hard it might crack my ribs.

He tightens his grip, and I whimper.

"But *you* are a bitch," he mutters, "so be a good dog and drop your toys."

It's the only sensible thing to do. It's also definitely the stupidest. But I'm out of options. I relax both my fists, the dagger and the locket clattering to the stone. He doesn't so much as look down at them, and he doesn't release me. Darkness glints in his eyes, and he yanks me close, breathing heavily into my face. I thrash against his hold, sweeping a knee toward his groin as I scream, but he shoves me to the ground like I'm little more than a rag doll.

"Worthless necklace." He stomps on the locket, crushing it under the heel of his boot. Then he bends down and picks up the dagger. He flips it between his hands with alarming dexterity. "Nearly as worthless as you."

The malice on his face sends me scuttling back, my breath seizing in my throat. My palms scrape against the slippery stone. I'm dimly aware of dirt and grit and snow, but they fade, instinct taking over. Blood pounds in my head as my eyes dart around us, looking for a way out.

A cobble shifts under my hand, and I dig my fingers beneath it. It comes free with a grinding squelch of brick and mud. I heave it at him.

And miss.

He waves the dagger in admonishment. "Stop fighting. You've already lost."

No fucking way. My fingers dig for another loose stone.

He flips the dagger one more time, its hilt landing neatly in his palm, and lifts it to strike. I don't look away. I won't give him the fucking satisfaction. A shadow falls over us, long and dark despite the afternoon sun barely peeking over the top of the buildings.

A sliver of hope cracks through my bleating terror when the thief turns toward the newcomer, giving me a window of opportunity. I seize it, flipping over and pushing myself up. My feet tangle in my skirt, and I trip forward. At the last second, I throw myself in the opposite direction, collapsing to the side of him and the stranger.

A sob wrenches out of me, my shoulders caving into a protective hunch, my hands flying up to cradle my head.

"What do we have here?"

My heart recognizes the low, raspy voice and skips a beat.

"Bishop." The thief addresses him like he's saying a prayer, and I wonder which one of us he's here to save.

I squint up in time to see my attacker backing toward the dead end, color draining from his face.

"She was lost," he says, eyes skittering like a trapped animal. No hint of the predator now.

Bishop strides toward him with lethal calm. His red cloak stirs on a gust of wind, lifting like a billowing stream of blood. Two long swords peek over his shoulders. Hidden but within reach.

He pushes his hood back, revealing the kind of beauty the old stories warn about. Dazzling and cruel and made for vengeance. Winter-blue eyes, slightly gray and stormy like the sky overhead, are set above high cheekbones as sharp as the blades at his back. His nose is long and straight save for a crook that suggests it's been broken more than once. And that full mouth . . .

"And you were offering your assistance?" Bishop says coldly. He points to the dagger in the thief's hand, and the man drops it.

"My lord." The thief's voice cracks, and he continues to back away like he's afraid of being so much as within the reach of Bishop's shadow. "This is a misunderstanding. If you allow me a moment, I can explain—"

"Are you harmed, Lady Icaros?" Bishop's question cuts through the man's pleading, but the warrior's gaze doesn't leave the thief.

"Ic-ar-os," the thief stammers. His eyes widen as it hits him, and he begins to shake. He falls to his knees. "Please. I didn't know who she was."

Bishop's glare softens at the edges, but his tone remains steely. "Do you honestly believe her rank is what matters?"

The thief understands at the same moment I do. It's not mercy softening Bishop. It's comprehension. Like he sees the man in front of him for the scum that he is and knows exactly what to do.

Bishop towers over the thief, who's been reduced to blubbering and wringing hands. The man bends forward, reaching for Bishop's boots as the air begins to shimmer in the space around him—just like when he stole the necklace right off me.

"Watch out." The warning leaps from my tongue as the thief's back arcs unnaturally.

Bishop steps away, a stony mask descending over his face. It's a curious combination of disinterest and disgust that seem to cancel each other out in favor of . . . boredom.

Maybe if he were the one covered in scrapes and bruises with a torn gown, he'd be more invested. But even without my injured pride, this is new to me. Horror floods through me as the thief's body contracts. Bones snap like the illustration in that forbidden book and transform with wet, grinding sounds that make my stomach heave. Dirty brown fur sprouts across his shrinking shape, and his nose elongates into a pointed snout, wiry whiskers shooting underneath. His clothes pool on the ground, and where the man begged on his knees a moment before, a rat now crouches.

For a heartbeat, I can't move or breathe. I can hardly think.

"Nice choice," Bishop says dryly like this is all perfectly fucking normal. "It fits."

The rat darts over my feet. Tiny claws scrabble on the wet, loose stones as it races toward the back of the alley. It scampers up the side of the rain barrel, racing toward the drainage pipe. He's going to get away. A cry escapes me as movement blurs in the corner of my vision.

The dagger flies so fast, I don't see it before it sticks its target with a wet *thwap*, pinning the rat to the barrel's wooden side. A thin squeal escapes the creature, sounding somehow horribly human, and then its tiny body goes limp.

I shake my head as if I can make my brain process all this faster. "He . . . he . . ."

Bishop crosses to the barrel and plucks the knife free. The rodent's body falls to the stones, its blood dripping down the weathered wood. Grabbing the edge of his cloak, he wipes the blade clean on the fabric before returning it to some unseen spot underneath. Must be where he hides all his contraband books and deadly weapons.

"He broke the law." His voice is firm, leaving no room for argument. "That kind of magic is punishable by death." He turns the full weight of his icy stare on me like he's daring me to question his authority.

I bite my lip to keep the wrong response from spilling out. I'm not sorry the thief is dead, especially not when he was going to kill me. But I have roughly a dozen questions about what I just saw. All of them pale in comparison to the ones I have for Bishop himself. Why here? What about all the unauthorized magic happening in that secluded square we were just in? Why didn't he punish those people?

He might have an explanation for those, but then I would have to explain how I know about those places. And I can't do that without outing myself, which means I'll never uncover what I want to know most of all: Why was Bishop in that bookstore? Why did he take that book with him? Where is it now?

He extends his hand to help me up. There's a splash of blood on his glove. But I take it anyway, carefully keeping my gaze on his face for signs that he knows where I've been and what I was up to. He scans me, eyes narrowing like he's contemplating queries of his own. "You're unusually quiet."

I blink. "How would you know?"

"I saw enough last night." He wrenches me off the ground with the same care he took removing the dagger from the dead rat. "You don't strike me as the strong-and-silent type."

And you don't strike me as the type to read illicit books. I swallow the retort and grimace at my scraped palms. The bleeding has mostly stopped, but the raw wounds are peppered with sand and dirt. "It's been a rough day."

He takes my hands, frowning as he examines them. "At least you have something to look forward to tonight."

A laugh escapes me, startling him from his inspection. Our eyes meet, his wide and surprised. Up close, his irises are rimmed with a silver that glints like starlight. I lose myself for a dangerous second.

"What's funny?" he asks, and I crash back to reality.

"I thought you were joking." I pull my hands free of his grasp.

But he's still staring at me. "You're not anticipating the Kindling?"

After last night and this afternoon? Not even a little bit. All I want is to go home to Damalis.

"Just nervous." I'm starting to believe my own lie at this point.

"Is that why you tried to fight him?" he asks. "It would have been better to run."

"He took my mother's locket." I keep my voice soft, so it doesn't break in front of him.

"I hope it was worth it."

"It would have been." I swallow as a knot forms in my throat. Bending down, I scoop the locket off the ground. It's crushed beyond repair, the cheap tin no match for being stomped on.

He cocks his head to the side, studying me from a different angle. But the chill is back in his voice when he speaks. "The king won't appreciate theatrics."

Heat blooms on my cheeks. "I'll take that into consideration."

"Don't consider," he says in a low voice, stepping so close that I smell a waft of leather mingling with something warm and smoky. *"Behave."*

Somehow, he turns the command into two words. A warning meant only for me.

Like *he* behaves? Sneaking around in back-alley bookstores? I clamp my mouth shut and brush my filthy hands over my equally filthy skirt. "I should be going."

"You need to see a healer." He nods toward the street beyond. "I'll escort you to the palace."

An entire walk of broody judgmentalism? I'd rather take my chances with the thief. "What about him?" I hitch a thumb toward the barrel. "Shouldn't you inform his family or . . ."

The words die on my lips as I look over my shoulder and discover he's in human form again, blood puddling on the stone street. His back is split open, and bits of pearly spine bulge through like the wound transformed along with him. My hand flies to my mouth in an effort to keep this afternoon's meal in my belly.

"He's dead." Bishop shrugs. "Men like that don't have families."

"All men have families," I say quietly. I don't care that he's dead. Not after what he planned to do to me. But no one needs to be left waiting for someone to come home. A mother or a friend. Maybe even a child . . . left waiting.

A shadow dims Bishop's shrewd eyes, but it's gone in an instant, like a cloud passing over the moon. "You can't let them all go, Arden."

Surprise that he remembers my given name bolts through me, but I smother it. "I have a long walk back to the palace. Thank you for your assistance."

But he takes my elbow. "I have no idea why you're this far from . . . civilization—"

Says the man just as far from civilization as me.

"—but you aren't leaving palace grounds unattended again."

"I didn't. I had an escort," I huff, jerking away from him.

His forehead jumps an inch. "And what befell him?" He glances around mockingly. "I have no idea why you're out here alone, but I will speak to your brother—"

"And then maybe you can spank me?" The words leap out before I can swallow them. Seven hells, why can't I keep my head around this man?

He simply stares back, eyes lingering on my mouth without comment. Between the blood and daggers, I didn't take him for a gentleman.

"Perhaps, if I thought it would be effective, I would," he says dryly, flourishing his arm toward the street. "Shall we go, *Lady* Icaros? You need to clean yourself up. King Ophelian is eager to meet you."

Okay, not a gentleman. Naturally. But the mention of the king is a dagger to my own chest. So, Bishop told him what he observed during my Petition. I lift my chin and dare to hold his gaze longer. "I suppose you'll tell him about this, too."

And probably my brother, who will yell at Kieren, who won't let me out of his sight until we've safely returned to Damalis. But Bishop's eyes skim down me, his gaze lighting a trail of fire in its wake. He pauses when he's reached the torn hemline of my dress where my freshly scratched boots peek out.

"It is my job." He doesn't even blink. "We can't have nobles being murdered in the streets. It would be twice the mess to clean up for me."

"Well, I wouldn't want to cause you trouble." I summon my most withering glare and march forward, pausing only to drop the mangled locket in a street cart piled with rubbish. I don't dare look at the actual mess behind me. Last night, I freed a bird. Today, I watched a man die. So much for exploring the city. The Kindling can't be over soon enough. Not even the pastries could cage me here.

Bishop catches up in two long strides and glowers down at me from his self-righteous pedestal. "Maybe I'll just keep an eye on you myself."

And then he falls back a step, already making good on his threat.

FIVE

Isidore's fingers work through my hair with methodical proficiency. Although she tugs harder than necessary as she hits a tangle.

"Sorry," she says too sweetly when I wince.

"I didn't mean to ruin the dress." I've apologized a dozen times since I returned with my clothing in tatters this afternoon. I don't give a shit about the gown, but I can't stop thinking about the locket. Isidore didn't even notice it was gone.

My family bought my fib—that I'd fallen on an icy patch on my trek back from the Grand Arcade. Isidore did *not* accept my apology for wrecking my new outfit, which, clearly, she'd planned to steal as soon as we returned home.

"I know it was an accident," she says while pushing a pin into my hair so hard that it nearly impales my skull.

Yes, she's not upset at all.

If she knew the truth, she would forgive me. I know that. But telling any of them about what happened means explaining where I was this afternoon—and who I was with. Getting turned around and winding up in a shady part of the city? That might happen to anyone, but if I say something, Kieren will be in trouble. Making a wrong turn and warding off an attacker? That will definitely work Broderic up even more. Telling them Bishop saved me? Embarrassing. Maybe even humiliating. Especially after he marched me back to the palace like a lost child. But what happened in that bookshop keeps me silent.

Bishop has a secret.

Or maybe his position allows him to read about prohibited magic. If I confess the wrong thing, it will raise questions I can't answer—and I have plenty of my own questions already.

So, I let Isidore fume over the dress instead. Never mind that there is no place back home for her to wear such ornate clothing. Most of our closet is worn and threadbare. We so rarely purchase new things that I can't blame her for coveting them.

"You can have my gown from tonight when we get home." I doubt I'll ever find occasion to wear it again. The annual Harvest party we throw for the village is the closest thing to a formal affair that I attend, and the dress is far too extravagant for that.

Isidore perks up instantly regardless. "As long as you don't mind."

But her gaze travels to the shimmering gown lying on my bed and lingers like it's a carrot on a stick.

"The other families probably have entire teams of maids." Isidore sighs, securing another curl. This time without blunt force injury to my head. "Lady Carrera—"

"We manage fine on our own," I stop her. Because at the end of this, we must keep managing without servants, whether my sister likes it or not.

She huffs a little as she begins weaving silver ribbons through my hair, creating an illusion of wealth that's as delicate as spider silk—it will only hold until someone ruins it.

"Remember when Mom used to do our hair?" Isidore's voice fades like she's stepped back in time. "She had to tell us stories so we would sit still."

"Yes." The memory aches like a bone bruise, the kind of pain that you learn to live with but that never seems to fully heal. Some days I can't even remember my mother's face or her laugh. She's been gone so long now that I mostly remember how she *felt*. Gentle and patient. Not rushing between duties like I always am, not trying to be sister and servant and substitute parent all at once.

"I wish I could remember her stories," Isidore says softly.

So do I.

She clears her throat and takes a step back. "You're finished."

And just like that, the reminiscing is over, replaced by the usual call of duty.

My sister gathers the gown into her arms as I slip out of my robe. She fusses with my hair as she helps guide the dress over my head, clucking when I snag it on a pin. Silk and chiffon whisper against my skin, but she tugs and adjusts straps and fasteners into submission. Every time I reach to help, she swats my hand. I give up and let her treat me like I'm her doll.

Finally, she steps away, eyes gleaming. "Arden, look."

I turn toward the mirror and freeze when I find a stranger staring back.

Her cheekbones are higher, and the freckles that dust the bridge of her nose have been softened under powder, making them look more like flecks of gold than the smattering of dots I've always resented. She's elegant, the kind of person who belongs in the palace, not tramping through muddy fields.

Light catches the silver ribbons in my dark hair, making them twinkle like captured starlight. And the dress . . .

I'm having second thoughts about giving it to Isidore. When I tried it on in Damalis, I felt nothing. Now I see why my sister pushed me to choose it. The dress is the color of moonlight, and every inch of it, from the plunging sleeveless neckline to the sweeping skirt, is embroidered with tiny golden crystals. I hadn't paid attention before, but now I see the gems form constellations in a subtle tribute to the Stars that will honor me tonight.

"I look—"

"Beautiful," Isidore finishes. "Mom would be proud."

Her words close my throat. I haven't bothered with mirrors much lately. There's too much else demanding attention, too many responsibilities that don't care how I look or what I'm wearing. But tonight, for just this moment, I'm a person in a pretty dress with her whole life ahead of her.

Who miraculously did not die in an alley today.

Maybe I should be celebrating.

Isidore places a floor-length cape around my shoulders and fastens its gold chain across my collarbone. "You look like you belong here." The admission is so soft that it feels like a secret.

But I know it's a lie. I could never belong here, regardless of our family name.

"We're running late." Isidore blinks rapidly, but a single tear leaks out. She swipes it away. "The boys are waiting."

We make our way down the hall, our shoes barely registering on the palace's expensive rugs. Voices drift from the sitting room, muffled by the thick oak door, but even stifled, I can hear Andry jabbering away, interrupted every few seconds by Broderic's steady tone or Kieren's warm interest. All three fall silent when we enter.

Broderic's mouth drops open, his expression cycling through surprise, pride, and something protective that hits me squarely in the chest with a pang.

"Well," he finally manages slowly, "I might need to bring my sword after all."

"Sword?" I blink. My brother has never carried a weapon in his life. "You don't even own a sword."

"Then I'll borrow Kieren's." Light finds his face again, and he breaks into a teasing grin. "To fight off all the potential suitors. They'll be circling you two like vultures. Andry might have to help."

Andreas groans and slumps in his chair. "You look okay. For people stuck wearing dresses."

"Careful, or all the flattery will go to our heads," I say dryly.

Kieren remains quiet, but he's not looking at me. His gaze is fixed on Isidore, something soft and hungry and hopeless in his eyes. This is nothing new, but for the first time, her cheeks go pink like she's actually noticed.

Broderic glances between them, his smile sliding into a scowl.

I step quickly in front of her. "Can we leave? The sooner we go, the sooner this will be over."

Broderic turns the frown on me. "Stop acting like you're on a death march." He stands and smooths the wrinkles from his woolen dress jacket. "Receiving your birthright is a privilege, not a punishment. Not everyone is lucky enough to inherit magic. *Right, Kieren?*"

Kieren flinches as the barb strikes but collects himself quickly. "Of course."

For a moment, I'm too stunned at the obvious slight. Collecting myself, I reach for Kieren's arm, if only to reassure him that he is still part of this family, but Broderic intervenes.

"I think it will be best if I escort you," he says to me, but the words are directed at our surrogate brother. "There will be no need for security with the palace guards and Order Marius in attendance. Kieren gets the night off." Broderic tips his head to Andry and Isidore. "We better get going. It's up to the *four* of us to represent Damalis."

Isidore shuffles past with her head down and hurries into the hall. Andry grumbles about stupid parties and follows. But I can't make my legs work. I look at Kieren, trying to find the right words, but Broderic moves between us and offers his arm again. "We're going to be late."

Kieren forces a smile. "Good luck."

"She doesn't need luck." Broderic stares ahead as he sweeps me toward the hall. "*She* is an Icaros."

I can't bring myself to glance back at my best friend, but as soon as we're around the corner, I smack Broderic's shoulder. "How could you treat him like that? He's our brother."

"He is our *ward*," he corrects me, lowering his voice as our siblings come into view ahead of us. "And he needs to remember his place."

"His place?" I repeat. "Don't be a snob."

But Broderic ignores my reprimand. "How long has this been going on between them?"

"Nothing is going on." But there's a ringing in my ears. An alarm warning me to defuse this situation. I'm just not sure how to do it.

"That look was far from *nothing*." Broderic shakes his head, a muscle twitching in his jaw. "How could you keep this from me?"

"I wasn't keeping anything from you." Laughter and muffled conversations float toward us as we approach the ballroom. We're nearly there. Once we're inside, he'll be too distracted to think about this, which will give me time to come up with an excuse for Kieren.

But Broderic stops, his gaze focused ahead of us. "Maybe not, but you suspected."

"I have eyes, unlike some of us," I hiss, pleased when this time, he's the one who blanches. "It's nothing to worry about."

Broderic finally turns, his brows drawing together. "Of course I worry." His tone is caught somewhere between sadness and rage. "One of us has to."

The words suck the air out of me, stealing my ability to speak. How can he think that? How can he act like I've been lounging in our sitting room with my feet propped up while he does everything? No one asked me what I wanted. I didn't choose to be born into Order Icaros. It's not like I'm passionate about crops or weather patterns or livestock.

"What does that mean? Is this because you think I'm treating my birthright like a punishment?" My voice cracks around the anger building inside me.

"Yes, because you are," he says firmly. "Your birthright is a responsibility."

I finally realize what I heard in his voice a moment ago. Not anger. Not sadness. *Resentment.* This isn't about me at all. Well, it's not entirely about me. But I'm not the one who chose responsibility over love. I swallow, trying to keep myself from snapping back. I don't want to make this situation worse.

"Perhaps it's time Kieren joins the conscripts like the other orphans," he adds.

The world shifts on its axis, my knees wobbling as I try to stay upright. "You wouldn't . . ."

Broderic turns away from me. "We can't afford a match like that."

Afford? And suddenly I see how he's calculated all of this. "Like we can't afford the clothing on our backs? Like we can't afford to drink the coffee we grow? Like you can't afford to marry the girl you love?" I want to walk away from him, but people are arriving behind us—and I'm sure we can't *afford* for me to make a scene, either. "Are you going to sell us off to the first rich noble who will buy us?"

"I would never force you to make that sacrifice."

Bullshit.

I look him directly in the eyes. "No, only you're that much of a fucking martyr."

"And you don't understand. That's the price of power," he says in a clipped tone. "Aren't we the lucky ones?"

He extends his arm. I take it limply, mind swimming with the truth as he guides us toward our fates. I'm so preoccupied I barely notice the guards stationed at the door. Broderic leads us through a wide archway into the ballroom, and I gasp, my worries replaced momentarily by awe.

The palace's grand hall opens before us like a jewel box, every surface designed to remind lesser mortals of their place in the hierarchy. Crystal chandeliers drip from the painted ceiling over a long table rising from a dais at the far end of the room. Beneath it, a shining oak floor is surrounded by circular tables covered in shimmering lace. Most of the tables are already full of nobles and their families, except for one that hosts a six-tiered cake. A layer for every patron order, each decorated to reflect our patron constellations, and one for the king reigning over them all. Our tier is on the bottom. Later, when all of this is finally over, there will be celebrating, and, more importantly to me, dessert.

Isidore is waiting for us near the left side, clutching our younger brother by the collar. "Finally. You two took forever. I've barely been able to keep Andry away from that cake."

"Can I at least taste the wine?" Andry pleads. "Isidore tried coffee."

We all ignore him.

After the ritual, there will be drinking and dancing. Probably too much of both, since the first always leads to the second. For now, an attendant shows us to our designated seats. The centerpiece of our table is a curious mix of candelabra and sculpture, the gold shaped to resemble a pegasus. Its flickering candles are staggered at various heights, so that the individual flames take the shape of the Icaros constellation.

Our table is positioned close enough to the royal platform to mark my lineage as significant, but sufficiently far that I might avoid the king's eye. It's bad enough that Bishop told him about my ritual. If he mentioned what happened this afternoon . . .

Isidore preens at our placement, practically vibrating with satisfaction over tonight's carefully choreographed dance of who sits where, who speaks to whom, who gets served first. "We're seated closer than half of Order Calix."

"Because we are here with an initiate from a patron bloodline," Broderic reminds her. "If any of our cousins had been invited, they would be in the back, too."

Isidore's mouth puckers like she's accidentally bitten into something sour. "They only invited us, but every other order . . ."

"Can buy their invitations." Broderic dares a glance at me. "Power is expensive."

Apparently, our fight isn't over. I resist the urge to scream at him, but only barely. Is this what this evening's about for him? For *all* of them? Taking my place in some ruthless food chain? No wonder they gave me a knife on the very first night.

I scan the rest of the room for proof that he's telling the truth. There are at least a dozen tables glowing with the chalice sculptures of Order Calix. The most in the room. Since controlling every magic-imbued good sold makes them wealthier than nearly all the other orders combined, that tracks. Velesont is in second, with almost half as many, thanks to controlling all our posterns. Leontia has modest representation, but they rarely act flashy even if they're the ones keeping us alive. No other table boasts a pegasus. We're all alone. But there's one more notable absence. "What about Marius?"

"They have better places to be." Broderic shrugs. "I'm sure the king prioritized guarding our coastline, and they only have one initiate this year."

"Soldiers have more important things to do than get married and attend tea parties," Andry chimes in, reaching for the wine.

Like follow people through crowded cities.

Isidore rolls her eyes as she catches his wrist. "Don't even think about it," she warns him, "and who told you married people have tea parties?"

He blinks up at her. "I asked Kieren why anyone would want to get stuck with a wife, and he told me that grown-ups like stuff like that, playing house and tea parties."

Both Isidore and I smother laughter, and even Broderic's mouth twitches. My older brother meets my gaze and sighs, shaking his head in a familiar, conspiratorial way that makes the tightness in my shoulders relax. He was upset earlier, but he'll see reason eventually. He would never actually send Kieren away. Or force Isidore or Andry or me to marry for connections. He's just scared. So am I. But we have each other, and that has to be enough.

Isidore moves the wine safely away from Andry and pours herself a glass before offering it to our older brother.

But Broderic stands. "Not yet. I need to present Arden to the king."

"You need to do what?" I blurt out. *That's* what Bishop meant when he said King Ophelian was eager to meet me?

I didn't expect it to be quite so literal—*or* so soon. Then again, I wasn't given any warning about the ceremonial sacrifice, either. Everyone is just full of surprises.

"You are here at his invitation," Broderic reminds me.

"So, then he already knows who I am." I can't face the king, especially with my brother at my side. Bishop made it clear he'd told the king about my Petition, and if Broderic finds out what I did . . . I haven't allowed myself to consider the consequences. That sometimes the Stars skip generations. "Let's not waste his time."

"If she won't go, I will." Isidore perks up, her eyes darting to the royal platform. The hunger is back. My sister is pretty enough to enchant the king, but she'll have to fight her way through every noble hoping to catch his attention.

"No. Just myself and Arden," Broderic says, crushing her hopes. "She's the one receiving her birthright."

"Let Isidore go," I insist. Will I shamelessly throw my weight behind my sister's cause to save my own ass? Apparently. Then again, the king is just as likely to say something to Broderic if I'm not there.

"I could introduce myself," Isidore suggests. "I don't want to be rude."

"You can wait until after the Kindling, like everyone else," Broderic says.

I latch on to the idea. "Maybe we should all wait." They both ignore me.

Broderic stares pointedly at our sister. "And stop looking at him like he's a trophy to claim."

She gasps. "I'm not—"

"You are."

I watch them bicker with a strange detachment that only comes when one is completely and utterly doomed. My sister wants to marry the king. My brother wants to maintain our dignity. Andry wants to taste the wine. I want to hide under the table until the void swallows us.

I foresee a lot of disappointments in our collective future.

"We should hurry," Broderic says. "They'll serve the first course soon."

I scoot my chair back reluctantly. There has to be a way out of this. "What if I just wave? He can probably see me from here."

My brother's expression could frost glass. "Arden."

So much for a truce. Refusing will result in another fight, and I can't risk that. Not with Kieren's fate on the line.

"Fine. Lead the way." It's only my funeral.

I follow Broderic through the maze of carefully spaced tables, humming a dirge under my breath.

The royal family's table looks down at us from its silk-draped pedestal as we approach. We may share magic in Antares, but the real power in the room rests on the shoulders of the man seated in the middle. I've only seen the artistic renderings of King Ophelian that they send out with royal bulletins; he looks younger in person. In the pictures, they give him shrewd eyes and sharp, hewn features, but his dark-brown cheeks are round as a baby's. He laughs at some private joke, and there's something almost boyish about his easy smile.

The sight lessens the anxiety gnawing a pit in my stomach. He doesn't look dangerous. Maybe that's why his mother sits on his right side, like she's not quite capable of trusting the twenty-six-year-old with the crown. To her left, jewels drip from the necks of her daughter and the princess's consort, their dresses lavishly beaded with even more sparkling gems. A few advisors and distant family members fill nearly every seat, save for an empty chair to the king's left.

I almost trip over my skirts when Bishop ascends the platform, clad in a scarlet dress uniform. Its tailored jacket fastens high on his throat with gold clasps, a horned wolf mid-snarl embroidered across the chest. His leather gauntlets have been replaced by white gloves, and his twin swords traded for a single saber worn at his side.

"Why is *he* here?" I ask without thinking.

Broderic follows my gaze, brows drawing together. "The king's left hand is a position of honor." He sighs. "I hadn't heard Bishop was back from the Lost Continent."

My eyes widen as pieces fall into place, revealing what I should have seen all along. Not just anyone would observe last night's ritual. Few people travel to the wild, magicless lands across the Baron Sea willingly. Coming back is even less common. I can only think of one person who might regularly do so. And how many people would risk looking at forbidden texts? Only someone totally beyond the reach of the law.

My stomach twists into knots. If he's important enough to sit next to the king . . . "What's his surname?"

"Marius," Broderic says, confirming my fears.

My gaze flies back to Bishop, watching him bow rigidly before taking the open seat by the king. He's not just any noble who's risen to this rank. Not just any bishop.

He's Bishop Marius.

The *patron* of the most ruthless order in Antares, my savior, *and* the current thorn in my side. Who says men can't multitask? The information dashes any lingering hope I had that he kept quiet about my encounter this afternoon. Order Marius lives by the sword, rooting out any and all unlicensed magic in the kingdom with merciless brutality. Somewhere in the back of my mind, I hear the sickening wet sound his dagger made when it pierced the thief's animal form. No wonder he hates me for freeing that oscen. Men like him don't just need to possess magic, they need to control it, *especially* who has access to it.

"But bishops don't marry." My confusion gets the better of me and begins spilling out. "He can't be patron. He won't have an heir."

Not a legitimized one, anyway.

Broderic nods. "I can't believe he remained a bishop after his family died. His cousins must be thrilled, but what kind of a man sacrifices his bloodline's birthright to keep more power for himself?"

Patrons answer to the king, but a bishop's duty is a divine calling from the Stars themselves to shepherd those losing their way and cull those already lost.

"How do you know him?" Broderic asks, drawing my attention back to him.

"Um, I don't. Not really." Is facing two life-and-death situations together enough to *know* somebody? Especially if everything about Bishop, including his family name, raises more questions than answers? Definitely not. "He observed my Petition."

Broderic studies me for a moment, but he doesn't pry.

I, on the other hand, can't stop myself. "Is he always so full of himself?"

"I suppose that's the hazard of being the youngest patron." Broderic shakes his head in disgust.

"I thought you were the youngest?" I blink up at him.

"I'm the newest," he corrects me. "Two years ago, Bishop became patron a year after receiving his birthright. He probably only knew half of his order's magic when he came to power."

My eyes widen. Most new initiates spend their first year just learning to wield the basics of magic.

"And now he's sitting at the left hand of the king," I say. I can see why Broderic is annoyed. He rushed to finish his studies while our father was dying.

"Heirless," Broderic mutters like it's a slur, shaking his head in disgust.

"He's probably filling the king's head with more nonsense about seizing the Lost Continent."

At a dinner to celebrate the last five hundred years of peace, no less. "We won't really invade a—"

But Broderic shushes me as we reach the head table.

We aren't the first family eager to address the king, so we're forced to wait in a line of impressionable young nobles and overly enthusiastic parents. The king could probably request each of them brought to his chamber at midnight, and their parents would deliver them wrapped in bows.

The line moves slowly, each person taking up as much time as the king will allow.

"Can't they just bow, pucker up, kiss his ass, and get on with it?" I grumble under my breath.

"This is a chance for them to make an impression. For *you* to make one," Broderic whispers like he's disseminating trade secrets. "The right impression can impact the rest of your life."

It's a little late for that. I'm guessing the wrong impression can as well.

Broderic clears his throat as we shuffle forward a few steps. "About earlier. I should not have—"

"No, you shouldn't have." I don't need him to apologize. I swivel to face him. "You can't force Kieren to join Order Marius. He belongs with us. He's family."

A muscle works in Broderic's jaw. "I will never allow him to marry Isidore," he says in a low voice. He holds up a hand when I start to protest. "Not only for her sake. For his. Isidore . . ."

He doesn't have to explain why it would probably never work. I take a deep breath and nod. "Kieren knows that, too. He's never made a move. He's never even spoken about her to me. You really don't need to worry."

Broderic looks unconvinced, but he continues to shuffle forward in silence.

When we reach the front of the line, Broderic bows deeply before taking my hand. "Your Majesty. May I present my eldest sister? We're honored that you invited us to receive her birthright before the Eternal Throne."

I've read shorter books than his speech, but I force myself into the curtsy our mother drilled into me before she died. Back straight, head tilted just so, one foot behind the other in a graceful sweep that makes my silk gown pool around me like rippling water.

When I rise, the king is grinning at me.

"*The* Lady Icaros I've heard so much about?" he says, and I flush. Even his voice sounds young, still touched with the careless humor of someone who doesn't grasp the extent of his power. He glances at Bishop, who nods in confirmation. Bastard. "So, *you're* the one who lost my bird."

Lost? Doesn't he know why the bird was there?

Royalty doesn't face the Petition. They're bound to the Stars at birth.

Broderic's hand tightens around mine hard enough to hurt. Everyone surrounding us falls silent. No one turns, but I know they're all eavesdropping. Even those seated at nearby tables seem to be listening. Bishop might as well have nailed me to the table with a dagger.

"What *exactly*," Broderic says through barely moving lips, "is he talking about?"

What happened to the ritual *not* being a test? Because I sure as hell feel like I failed. I force my mouth into a smile and meet the king's eyes. Behind the laughter, there's something darker that nearly sends my knees buckling. "You're mistaken, Your Majesty. I saved your bird." I can't help glancing at Bishop. He's not hiding behind a hood tonight, but his expression is so unreadable that he's basically wearing a mask. "I was expected to kill it."

The king's amusement deepens. "Then I suppose I'll be in your debt . . . if we ever find the creature."

I hope they never do. I swallow and incline my head, trying to keep my mouth shut.

"We can always catch another," Bishop says in a gravelly voice that sends a shiver dancing down my neck.

King Ophelian beams at the most dangerous man in the room, looking like a small child about to pat a rabid dog.

My gaze flicks back to Bishop's. He's only slightly older than the king, but he holds himself with the vigilance of a warrior. Even now, Bishop seems to be bracing for a fight. The king, on the other hand, looks like he's never seen one. There's something so innocent in his shining eyes that I can't stop myself.

"If I can be so bold, I might be more careful with my next pet if I were you." The warning slips out of me.

"Indeed." His face lights up like I've delivered another joke, and he almost laughs before catching himself. "I look forward to attending your ritual tonight, Lady Icaros. Thank you again for *saving* my bird."

He tips his head to signal he's done speaking with us.

Broderic steers me away swiftly, his grip on my hand still painfully tight. Behind us, laughter spills from the royal table, and my cheeks burn even hotter than before. We pass the first table of nobles, and they lean toward each other, murmuring in lowered voices. But every one of them has their eyes on me. It's the same with the next table and the one after. It seems Petitions aren't really private. Or about responsibility. Or whatever other bullshit they've swallowed that justifies exchanging cruelty for power.

I lift my chin and focus my attention straight ahead, trying to ignore the whispers. Part of me wants to walk right out of this ballroom, say fuck tonight's ritual and fuck them all, especially Bishop.

Our family's magic has waned so much in the last few generations that honestly, I probably do more in the fields to feed the kingdom than my brother does with his nochtimetry.

I hold my head high, refusing to look at any of them. It was all a game to the king, and why wouldn't it be? It's easy to sit on a throne and sacrifice what you claim to love when the world conspires to give you whatever you wish. What is one dead bird when another can be caught?

Broderic drags me away from the crowd before leaning in to snap in a low voice, "You let it go? There's only one task in the Petition, and you didn't perform it?"

Until now, I hadn't allowed myself to believe Broderic had known about the sacrifice—let alone performed it himself. I stare at my brother, afraid that I'll never see him the same way again. I shake my head, searching his face. "Why kill something just because you're holding a knife?"

"To prove you can follow orders, Arden!" He pinches the bridge of his nose like one of his headaches is forming.

It probably is. My siblings and I are usually the leading cause of them.

"I was told to do what I had to do." Perhaps our instructions were different. Maybe all of this is just a big misunderstanding. "Killing a bird wouldn't show the Stars I'm ready for my magic."

Broderic's face softens. "Sometimes unpleasant things must be done for the greater good."

"You really made the sacrifice, didn't you?" I ask softly, unsure I want him to answer.

He takes a deep breath. "Yes, Arden." His gaze sweeps around the room. "We all did. No one wants to anger the Stars."

It takes me a moment to realize the sadness in his voice isn't over what he did. It's for me—for my failure.

My nerves wind tighter as neither of us speaks until we finally make our way back to our table, but the whispering continues in our wake.

"What did you say to King Ophelian?" Isidore asks as I take my seat. Broderic cuts her off with a single sharp look.

The first course arrives—delicate arrangements of things I can't identify. I'm dimly aware of Andry groaning and Isidore chastising him. But my thoughts are far away from here, circling somewhere distantly like that bird in the night sky. When I finally force myself back to the present, force myself to smile, force myself to eat despite the churning in my stomach, I can't help but look at the king's table to find him and the rest of his table casually feasting like all of this is normal. All of them but one, that is.

Bishop Marius is watching me.

SIX

News travels fast, but gossip travels faster, and dinner from two hours ago now turns in my belly. I swallow back bile as I catch snippets of what the others are saying while we wait to be led into the throne room.

Every initiate is talking about me. About how I let my sacrifice go. How I refused to make my Petition. How I think I'm better than everybody else.

They cluster in small groups, whispering behind their hands while shooting glances in my direction like I might suddenly sprout wings and fly away.

I'm this close to trying when a vesper appears, wearing a white robe embroidered with the royal constellation. He clears his throat. "If I can have your attention."

The conversations stop, every initiate shifting to face him. I'm just grateful for the momentary reprieve.

"You may prepare." He clasps his hands and waits.

I take a deep breath before reaching for the gold starbursts at my shoulders. I pinch, and the chain draped across my chest slackens, allowing me to remove my gown's delicate cape. Cool air brushes the bare skin of my back, tickling down my exposed arms. Without the additional layer, the gown's neckline seems to plunge even farther, and the long slits in the shimmering skirt allow my legs to slip through.

The woman closest to me slides out of a fur jacket. Underneath it, she's wearing a cropped top that hugs her breasts but leaves her midriff bare. The man next to her strips to a loose vest that's little more than two pieces of fabric tied with a length of leather cord, putting his sinewy arms on display along with glimpses of a hewn slab of abdominal muscles.

The other initiates disrobe in similar fashion, slipping off coats and jackets to reveal more flesh for the Stars to burn their mark into.

I hug my arms across my chest, wondering where the Stars will brand me. *If* they will.

"When the doors open, you will form a single line leading toward the well in the center. Please wait for your name to be called." He rattles off instructions, my peers hanging on his every word, but I'm only half listening.

Stand here. Walk there. Bow to this person. Bleed into that place. And don't forget to smile. The pageantry of it all makes my teeth ache.

When he finally shuts up, the girl closest to me whispers, "Did you really release your sacrifice?"

I'm almost impressed she dared to ask—if she weren't maintaining her distance like my rebellion might be contagious.

I stare back at her. "No, I taught it to dance."

She shifts farther away, nose wrinkling. A few others edge closer, spurred on by her bravado, and I grit my teeth.

The doors swing open, saving me from their curiosity. We file in with theatrical slowness. I'm near the rear of the line, and when I finally make it inside, I understand what took so long.

It's like time stopped here centuries ago. The Eternal Throne commands the room. Carved from obsidian, it surges up in jagged, angular lines from a dais situated on the far wall, the entire pedestal a physical constellation of black stars. There must be a mile of nochtimetric patterns worked into its surface. Each line is etched and filled with shimmering resin that seems to glow in the dark room. The throne and this room are the oldest part of the palace, the only things to survive the Last War. Everything else was rebuilt around it.

There are no plastered walls or polished marble floors. But the space isn't barren like that room at the top of the Royal Astrolatory, and thankfully, no sacrificial bird is waiting. The only offering we'll make tonight is a single drop of our blood as a gift to the Stars.

The domed ceiling rises impossibly high, the glass so clear that it might be mistaken for open sky, if not for its impressively thin copper foiling. The night spreads above us, constellations surrounding the black void of the Night's Scar, each star burning so brightly it's as if they've gathered to watch—just like the audience of nobles seated a respectful distance behind the throne in a gallery wrapping around either side of it.

Too much blood was spilled in the name of claiming that throne by people desperate to believe their power could be eternal, too. I swear I hear them: a thousand years of ghosts calling to me, crying out, desperate to be heard. But I force myself to follow the procession and take my place.

The vesper begins to chant, and I lower my gaze to the floor. The stone has been carved with deep channels to create a labyrinth of connected patterns that form the shape of every patron constellation. I search for the pegasus of Order Icaros, its wings spread wide in eternal flight. Instead, I find the remnants of a different pair of wings. Like always, their etched lines are filled in with mortar as a warning.

The fallen constellation.

Suddenly, it's like I'm back in that bookstore. The knot in my throat tightens until it's hard to breathe. This can't end soon enough.

I search for my family among the tiered rows of spectators. Andry is up on his knees in his chair, craning for a better look. My sister has one hand on his tunic to keep him from toppling over. Andry waves at me, grinning from ear to ear, and I wave back, glad that at least one person doesn't care that everyone is talking about me. Because judging by Broderic's rigid stance, he's noticed, too, and *he* cares.

The woman beside him leans close, her hand touching his arm as she whispers something in his ear. She's beautiful in a calculated way—brown hair arranged in perfect ringlets, a dress that suggests everything while revealing nothing, and enough jewels to assume she'll fulfill my brother's only criterion for a potential wife. Velesont? Calix? I can't tell from here. But the way she positions herself—the casual ownership in how she touches him—sends my heart leaping only so it can plummet.

Another sacrifice in the name of responsibility.

The sinking sensation continues when the doors to the throne room open again and Bishop Marius enters with the king and a contingent of guards in black dress uniforms. His knights position themselves in front of the exit. With the royal family and most of the nobility in attendance, the knights aren't here to observe. They're here as security.

Bishop scans the initiates with the same cold, assessing look he wore in the alley. When his gaze reaches mine, it pauses for just a moment longer than the others. Then he takes a place by the main door, hands clasped behind his back, eyes tracking King Ophelian as he makes his way to the throne.

The vesper from the astrolatory trails behind him, holding a bloodred pillow with an ornate box resting on top.

The king stops before the throne, and a hush falls over the room.

"Five hundred years ago," he begins, his voice carrying through the space, "our ancestors faced a choice: submit to the darkness that threatened to consume our world—or stand against it together."

A few nobles shift in their seats. Some of the older ones mutter to each other. More than a few look at the fallen constellation's blackened mark like it's marring the floor.

"They chose unity," the king continues. "Five bloodlines joined with mine to bring an end to the fighting. Five stood here after the last blood was shed. Five swore it would never happen again. And those five bloodlines—*your* bloodlines—entrusted my family to guide us into a new era where magic was granted not by luck or chance but to those who were worthy of it. To those willing to take up the responsibility of governing it for all of Antares."

A laugh bubbles in my throat, but I swallow it down. And five hundred years later, we license magic to anyone with a large enough bank account. We marry to steal the secrets of other orders and secure our family fortunes. We whisper behind one another's backs. It's not exactly the unified front he's describing. I suppose *we all secretly hate each other but pretend otherwise for political gain* doesn't sound quite as inspiring.

"Tonight," the king says, his gaze sweeping over us, "you join that sacred trust. Tonight, you take your first step toward sharing the great responsibility of protecting our kingdom. Tonight, you become guardians of Antares's future."

My feet ache as the speech drags on, the straps of my shoes digging into my skin. I shift my weight carefully as he drones on about duty and the future, trying to ease the pressure on my pinched toes.

He finally winds down—thank the Stars—and nods to the vesper. She steps forward, bowing her head as she lifts the pillow to present the box. The king reaches inside and draws out last night's dagger, its jeweled handle glinting in the starlight.

With a dramatic flourish, he raises the knife and says, "Come forth and claim your birthright."

This part is usually over quickly. At least Broderic's was, four years ago in Damalis. The ceremony itself had been fast and to the point. A boring knife and a tiny bowl on an altar. At least tonight's pomp and circumstance gives people something to stare at besides me.

Broderic received his mark without complaint, and we celebrated with a cake Isidore baked that afternoon. Something tells me that my own Kindling won't be so simple, since tonight there is a line of initiates waiting to step forward and make their offering to the Stars.

But I will survive, and, in a few days, we'll be back in Damalis, where I've never been robbed or attacked, there's no need for brooding soldiers, and people are too busy to bother with forbidden books.

The attendant calls the first name: Lucian Carrera. He strides forward, chest puffed, displaying the confidence of someone who's never doubted his place in the world. His family probably bought the first spot in line to prove his importance. At the well, he picks up the ceremonial dagger and pricks his finger without hesitation.

A single drop of blood falls into the basin.

For a second, there is only the silence of held breath. Nothing happens. Almost like the Stars refuse to answer. Like the magic is stuck. A few whispers ripple through the audience, and even my chest threatens to cave in.

But then, silver light races through the channels in the floor, rushing along them like water finding its course. Relieved gasps fill the room as above us, the stars of the hydra constellation brighten until they're nearly blinding. Lucian gasps and staggers back a step, like something hit him. His hand flies to his wrist. I lean forward, holding my breath.

When he raises his wrist, his mark shimmers there—the hydra in miniature, etched into his flesh in lines of glowing light. The magic is still new, still settling, but as we watch, it fades into a silvery scar that marks him as Order Velesont.

Applause erupts, and I nearly jump out of my skin, our audience forgotten in the presence of true magic. Lucian grins, rejoining our line with even more swagger than before.

They continue calling names. Each ritual follows the same pattern—

blood, light, constellation, varying degrees of wincing followed by a mark—but the locations vary. The Stars mark a girl named Ellena on the back of her neck, the brand hidden beneath her hair until she lifts it to show everyone the lines of a chalice. The first initiate from the Petition gets his on his palm, the lioness symbol roaring silently every time he flexes his hand. The sole initiate of Order Marius receives hers on her upper thigh. One of the knights whistles loudly as everyone claps. I can't resist peeking over at Bishop to see what he makes of that, but he's staring sullenly ahead like just being here is a chore.

By the seventh initiate, my earlier awe has worn off. By the tenth, I'm actively fighting back yawns. The mystical ceremony becomes routine. Even the gasps from the audience grow more perfunctory. Several of the elderly nobles have dozed off, chins dropping to chests and mouths hanging open. I count the remaining initiates—five, four . . . Looks like I'm being left for last. What a surprise.

My feet throb. The straps of my gown chafe against my skin. I'm fantasizing about ripping it off when the attendant calls, "Arden Icaros."

Murmurs run through the crowd, the audience instantly interested in the pomp and circumstance again. I can't bring myself to look at Broderic to see if he notices. Not with hundreds of eyes watching me so sharply that it's like knives stabbing me in the back.

A heavy weight settles across my shoulders as I take the first step toward the well and nearly stumble because of my pain-numbed feet. I catch myself, but the heel of my shoe hits the stone sharply, and I cringe as the sound echoes through the chamber. I can't mess this up. It's only a drop of blood, a light show, a mark on my skin somewhere, and then I can take off these damned shoes forever.

The ceremonial dagger waits on the fat rim of the basin. Dried blood speckles the blade from the other initiates. No one wanted to ruin their fancy clothes by wiping it off. I pick it up, its weight familiar in my sweating palm. The hilt is warm from all the hands that have held it tonight. Using the same knife is symbolic for the others—proof of the sacrifice they made. For me, it's a pointed reminder. Then again, how many ceremonial daggers do they have lying around?

I prick my finger with the tip of the blade. It's quick and sharp, and I barely register the sting. I've had worse injuries from thorns. A perfect red pearl beads on my fingertip. One drop of blood in exchange for a lifetime of power. It hardly seems fair. But I hold my hand over the well.

The drop falls.

And nothing happens.

My heart pounds in my chest. Did I really fuck up that badly last night?

I did what needed to be done. There was no reason to kill the oscen. The vesper told me it wasn't a test. My hands shake as I set the knife back onto the edge of the well.

Why aren't the Stars binding me? The audience begins to whisper, breaking the uncomfortable silence and filling it with something much worse. Everyone else received their Kindling. I'll be the only one who doesn't.

And they all know why.

Dread pools in the pit of my stomach as my eyes dart around the room. Until they snag on Bishop. His posture still screams boredom, but his gaze drills into mine.

I square my shoulders, refusing to turn away like I did something wrong. Fuck him. Fuck all of them.

If killing an innocent creature without purpose is the only way to earn the privilege of magic, I don't deserve it.

None of them do.

Bishop leans forward, eyes narrowing slightly. Probably debating throwing me out of the palace. If the Stars rejected me . . .

The ground begins to tremble beneath my feet, and I gasp.

I grab the basin's rim as the floor actually shakes, like something deep below has awakened. All of a sudden, there's movement in the corner of my eye. Murmurs ripple among the audience as the silver light races through every etched channel like the magic can't decide which path to choose.

Pain slices along my skin so sharp and sudden, I almost pass out. A scream claws its way up my throat, but I clamp my mouth shut. If this is the Stars' punishment, I won't give them the satisfaction of hearing me break.

Instead, I cling to the basin, eyes flying around the room so quickly that everything is a blur until I look up at the night sky, searching for my own constellation. For the stars that mark the tips of its wings, the ones that make up the line of its body. But the pegasus of Order Icaros doesn't flare with recognition.

Please.

The twinkling starlight dims, and relief floods through me. But before I can pry my fingers from the well, the sky goes black. Like every star is rejecting me at once.

I close my eyes, hoping that I might open them and find myself in bed. That this is just a nightmare brought on by nerves and too much wine.

"Look!" someone shouts, and my eyes snap open again to find a single star blazing overhead . . . in the center of the Night's Scar.

Wrong. This is all *wrong*. Beneath me, the silver light diverges from the normal channels toward the unthinkable. Mortar cracks in the floor as it carves its way into the lines of the fallen constellation. I step back, instinct telling me to run, but white-hot agony erupts across my chest. Not on my wrist or palm or neck like the others. My hands fly out, lifted by some unseen force as red light sears the skin over my heart, burning lines like fire. There's no way to stop it. I can only watch as a new pattern forms.

One I've only seen in a blackened alcove, cracked into the mortar under my feet, illustrated on the cover of a banned book in a shop. One in the shape of a bird—the fallen constellation that disappeared five hundred years ago. The one that only exists as a warning.

Except it's burning itself into my skin right now.

A hush falls over the room, the kind of silence that hits before a storm.

And then a single word rips through the air. "Harbinger!"

SEVEN

The pain in my chest intensifies, tendrils of fire rooting under my flesh as the magic claims me. The pain ebbs, and under it . . . nothing. There's no stirring sensation like everyone describes. Not even a faint fluttering. But I still can't breathe, can't think, can't do anything but clutch my chest as chaos descends in the throne room.

Chairs scrape against stone as people leap to their feet. Some rush forward, others back, torn between attacking and fleeing. Everyone is shouting, and I want to cover my ears with my hands.

"Not possible—"

"It's the burning raven—"

"Kill her before—"

"Get the high vesper!"

Strong hands close around my upper arms, and I look up to find Bishop staring down at me. How in all seven hells can he look so fucking calm right now? A group of knights surrounds me, and panic grips me even more tightly than the man holding me. I try to pull free—of him, of the fear—but neither releases me.

"I didn't do anything." I tug harder. "Let me go."

He ignores me, barking orders to his people as he drags me toward the exit. "Secure the royal family. Make sure no one leaves until *I* say."

I can't let him take me away. Shoving against him, I search for Broderic in the havoc. He won't let this happen. But my older brother is nowhere to be found. I spot Andry pushing his way toward me. Isidore, wide-eyed with tear-stained cheeks, is right behind him. I shout their names, stretching my arms in their direction.

Bishop blocks me, seizing my wrists and pinning them behind my back.

He leans down, his breath hot against my ear. "If you want to make it out of this room alive, you'll let me walk you out of here."

I have no reason to trust him. In fact, I have multiple reasons *not* to trust him. But I catch sight of a group of men talking quickly, heads bowed toward one another, hands balled into fists. One glances up and meets my gaze. His lip curls into a sneer, a hand moving to the sword sheathed at his side.

I press into Bishop, allowing his solid body to form a shield between me and the violence I glimpsed in the man's eyes.

"Good girl," Bishop mutters, and I instantly regret my decision.

But I'm out of choices, especially as more nobles begin to form groups, some inching closer like they might risk rushing Bishop and his knights. We're nearly to the door when a young man wearing a thin shirt steps into our path. His round face is familiar, and it hits me. He's not one of the nobles from the audience. He's an initiate from Order Calix. I think his name is Dimitri. Something glints in his left hand. Horror floods through me when I realize he's holding the ceremonial dagger.

Bishop places his arm in front of me. "Try."

The single word carries enough threat that Dimitri hesitates, his knuckles going white as he grips the knife. A second later, it clatters to the ground. Dimitri backs away from the door.

"You won't last the night, witch," Dimitri shouts when we reach the exit.

Bishop's finger pauses on the handle. There's a flash of movement, the glint of steel, and a second later, Dimitri's shirt hangs open, the fabric shorn completely through.

"If anything happens to her," Bishop says in a low, measured voice, "I'll split you open and see how long *you* last." He pushes open the door, nudging me through it. Two knights follow—the ones who were with him during my Petition. "Stay here," he orders them. "I'll send word when she's secure."

Secure. That's a nice word for what probably means imprisoned.

But Bishop doesn't grab hold of me again. Instead, he nods toward the corridor. "I'll be right behind you."

I manage a few steps before the tears hit. There's no point trying to fight them. Instead, I let them fall fast and hot down my cheeks. I make it a few more steps before I stop in my tracks.

"There's no time," Bishop growls as I bend over. "What are you doing?"

"Speeding things up," I say through gritted teeth. I yank my shoes off one by one. For a second, I stare at the pretty heels, my toes sinking into the plush rug that lines the hallway. Isidore picked them out. I couldn't be bothered. No wonder they're too small. They're *her* size. I don't even think—I just turn and chuck them as far as I can. They land at the feet of the scarred knight. He looks down at them, then back at me with a blink. "Get those to my sister."

My voice breaks, my heart already knowing that I won't see her again. I won't see any of them again.

And then I'm running.

The soles of my feet protest the change in altitude and circumstance, but I ignore them, pushing myself faster until my muscles burn, until I'm gulping down air but unable to catch my breath. I don't stop until the hallway splits.

Doubling over as I drag in long breaths, I stare in the direction of my family's assigned quarters. But all I can see is that initiate holding the knife. Going back to my room isn't safe for my siblings.

Bishop catches up to me, never having picked up his own pace. He glowers at me for a second. "Were you headed somewhere?"

"Away." I don't bother saying more. He wouldn't understand. He has a place here. A place within his own order. He knows who he is.

An hour ago, I thought I did, too.

But I straighten and meet his eyes. I'm not foolish enough to believe I can fight him. Not when he's twice my size and trained to be lethal. But whatever he plans to do with me, I will not hang my head in shame. I will not beg for mercy. I will not go easily.

Silence stretches as we measure each other up.

"Are you going to run again?" he finally asks.

I tilt my head and meet his eyes. "That depends. Are you going to hurt me?"

There's a slight tug on his lips—that smile of his that never seems to fully materialize—but his silvery blue eyes remain shadowed. "If I planned to hurt you, you would already be dead."

Well, that's comforting.

He can claim whatever he wants, but we both know that it's not entirely true. He wouldn't bother with me if he didn't see a threat.

"You heard what they said." I swallow, trying to soothe the ache in my throat. I will not break down in front of him. He might not be my enemy yet, but he's deadly. "They called me a harbinger."

The stuff of stories and legends. Plenty still believe in omens, still study the night for them. Even the astrolatories devote resources to searching for signs of fortune and fate despite our ability to tap the power of the Stars and bend it to our needs and whims.

"And you believe that nonsense?" He shrugs, but something in his voice betrays him. Bishop Marius—lethal, ruthless, *and* superstitious, apparently.

"It doesn't matter what I believe." There's no point in hiding from the truth. "A lot of them *do*."

"That's why I'm taking you somewhere safe, so we can sort this mess out."

A hollow laugh rattles from me. *Mess* doesn't begin to cover this situation. I'm fucked, and we both know it. "A holding cell, I presume?"

We're in a palace. There must be a dungeon.

"I said somewhere safe." He gestures in the opposite direction. "Not the first place they'll look for you."

And it would be, given that Bishop himself escorted me away from the throne room. "What did you have in mind?"

"It wouldn't be any fun if I told you." His tone is drier than the Burning Sea of Ardermare, not even the slightest hint of amusement coloring it.

"I guess as long as you're not planning to kill me." I hide my shaking hands within the folds of my skirt and start down the hall. Each step I take feels like it's carrying me miles away. Even if I turned around, would I ever find my way back to that throne room? To myself?

We bypass staterooms and parlors, all empty. So much wasted space. Away from the throng of visiting nobles, there's so little life in the palace. Under the beauty and wealth, there seems to be only loneliness.

Bishop guides me away from all of it to a cramped staircase leading to an upper level. My heart constricts. Maybe he lied. Maybe a tower cell is waiting for me after all. But it's not like I have a lot of options. Bars work both ways—and I'd rather have some between me and those people ready to murder me down there.

I start to ask him why he's helping me, but something holds my tongue in place. Judging by our every interaction, I won't like the answer.

The staircase empties into a hall devoid of any decoration. The plaster walls are unpainted. No rugs line the worn oak floors. There's not a single hint of the palace's grandeur.

Bishop stops at an unmarked door. My stomach tumbles as he unlocks it.

The room beyond is nearly as empty as the corridor that led to it. A bed sits under the window. Its sheets are tucked in crisp, tight lines. A massive trunk waits at its footboard. There's a small table and chair in the corner, and a simple armoire against the wall. That's it.

"Whose room is this?" I stare at the bed.

He hesitates, which doesn't fit with what I know about Bishop. "Mine."

I spin to face him. "This is *your* room?"

Now I understand his reluctance. What in all seven hells possessed him to bring me to his room? I start backing toward the door, but he blocks me. Panic flares in my chest, my eyes darting in search of another exit.

"You'll be safe here." He holds up his hand like I'm a horse he's trying to steady. "It's the last place anyone will look for you."

The expression on his face begs me to understand.

He's right. No one in their right mind will look for me in Bishop's private quarters.

"I'm not sure this is a good idea." Actually, I'm quite sure it's a *terrible* idea.

He crosses his arms over his broad chest, still carefully positioned between the door and me. "Are you worried that people will question your virtue?"

That doesn't even rank on the list of things worrying me.

"What era do you think this is?" I roll my eyes, panic giving way to stabs of annoyance. "It's *your* reputation that I'm worried about."

That threat of a smile ghosts over his lips before it fades to a scowl. "I can send for someone to look at your mark." His eyes don't dip lower than my chin. He doesn't even glance at the savage birthright branded into my flesh.

I swallow. "It doesn't hurt." *Anymore.*

Not physically, at least.

"Very well." He tips his head slightly as if he understands what I've left unsaid. "I'll station Vessica at the door."

"Am I allowed to leave?" I ask.

His jaw works for a moment. "You are not a prisoner, Lady Icaros. You are allowed to leave, but I would advise against it."

"You shouldn't call me that," I murmur. "The Stars marked me as . . ."

I can't bring myself to say it.

He does it for me. "Ravenell."

The name hangs between us. It's the first time I've ever heard it spoken aloud.

Shadows move like omens in his eyes. "The Stars can be wrong."

Does he actually believe that, or is he trying to trick me into saying something that will condemn me? "That's damn near heresy."

"That is reality." But something unreadable flashes across his face. Still, he shrugs and crosses to the armoire.

Finally leaving the chamber door unguarded.

I glance at it. Chances are slim that I can outrun him—if I even make it to the hallway. Stars know what might be waiting for me if I manage it. But trusting him . . .

"I wouldn't," he says in a low voice, and I turn to find him strapping a sheathed dagger around his thigh. He reaches back in the wardrobe. I brace myself for more weaponry, but he only pulls out a red cloak. His eyes never leave mine.

"I wasn't going to."

He lifts an eyebrow but doesn't press the issue. Swinging the cloak over his shoulders, he starts toward the door. "A word of warning," he says when he reaches it. "Vessica is less charitable than I am."

Less? I choke back the response, managing a quick nod before he leaves.

He's been gone for all of ten seconds before I realize that he's left me facing the real danger: being alone with my own thoughts.

That seems like a pretty bad idea at the moment.

Better to distract myself with something. *Anything.* Given that his room is fittingly austere for someone in Order Marius, I come up with *nothing.* Nothing that tells me anything about the man who sleeps in this bed. No pictures. No letters cluttering the desk. Not even a shirt wadded up and left on the floor.

My body takes over, wearing a path back and forth through the room as I try to outpace my thoughts. But there's no escaping them. My mind and I are pretty much a package deal.

What does he actually do in here? Even sleeping seems impossible on that thin, narrow mattress.

My heart squeezes. It's been mere hours since I explored the capital with Kieren. He probably doesn't even know what happened, and I'm not sure Broderic will tell him.

I shake off that thought. Of course my brother will. And even if things continue to be strained between them, it's not like Kieren won't hear soon enough. Along with everyone else in Antares.

So much for avoiding thinking.

"Tell me there's a bottle of wine stashed in here." I rifle through his armoire, then his desk. No flask. Not even a pen or piece of paper. Right now, I'd settle for a book. Not that he has one of those, either.

But Bishop *does* have a book. I saw him steal it. And while I might not want to answer questions about my own fate, I'd be willing to dig up some dirt on his.

There are very few places he could be hiding it. It's definitely not on him, given the way his dress uniform is tailored to flaunt the brutal, muscled lines of his body—and remind everyone that he's a killer. Nope, the book must be here. At least it won't take long to search for it.

I know the desk is empty, but I check the armoire again. There's a second cloak. Up close, it's splattered with faint stains that send my stomach lurching. It's the one he wore this afternoon. I take a steadying breath and run my hands over it. There are no pockets inside. Nowhere to hide a book. I search the other articles of clothing half-heartedly, but they're all freshly laundered, cotton pressed and leather oiled. Most are so pristine, I'm not certain they've even been worn. How many uniforms does he have? Stupid question. If you're expected to dress to intimidate, you need a threatening wardrobe for every occasion.

That only leaves searching the trunk. The most obvious place and the one that I already know is a dead end, judging by the nochtimetric pattern etched onto its lock.

I sink onto the floor in front of it anyway. A bolted trunk is the perfect place to hide a forbidden book. I study the pattern for a moment before I trace a few lines in quick succession. The metal scorches my fingertip, and I rip my hand back. That's definitely not the right combination. I try another, this time earning a stinging pulse. Not it, either.

I lean back on my palms and glare at the lock. "I can do this all night. I have nowhere to be."

And now I'm talking to inanimate objects. I just need something to do. Something to focus on. Something to help me forget that I am trapped in a stranger's room, waiting. But for *what* exactly? It's the not knowing that risks driving me mad.

Shifting onto my knees, I try the lock again. This time, I don't mind when it burns me.

I've lost count of the number of times I've tried when the etchings on the lock start to glow. I move closer, heart shooting into my throat. The lines continue to glow for a moment before fading into a blank metal square—a fail-safe enacted after too many attempts to access it.

"Fine. Be like that." I push up with my palms, the stiffness of my legs telling me that I've been at this longer than I thought.

And no one has come for me.

A pang of disappointment hits me, but I ignore it. Who do I hope will come? A rabid crowd intent on flaying me alive? The savior who casually killed a man in front of me this afternoon? My brother who is probably trying to act like he has no idea who I am to save his own reputation? Broderic is smart enough to keep the rest of my family away. It shouldn't hurt, but it does. Maybe I'll just stay locked in here while everyone pretends this never happened.

I move to the window, staring at the sky above. The stars have reappeared. I study each constellation, carefully avoiding that new star blazing brightly in the dark swath of the Night's Scar. My gaze dips to the courtyard below to find a half dozen uniformed guards stationed underneath the window. Two of them are staring directly at me, and I stumble a step back. There are no bars on the window, but this might as well be a cage.

Looking down, I take in my own skin for the first time since I left the throne room. The mark of Ravenell is starting to settle into my flesh. But even now, unlike the marks the other initiates received, it doesn't glow with silvery light. Instead, there's a fiery red tinge to each bisecting line and star-tipped point, making the wings of the raven look like they're burning. It's fitting, given how Ravenell was destroyed.

I don't know why the Stars chose it for me. I don't know why they cursed me. But my hands move toward it, palms trying to smother that flaming light. The mark doesn't hurt when I touch it. Whatever caused the pain during the ritual—the pain that seemed so much more pronounced than it did for the other initiates—is gone. Despite the mark's fiery lines, it's just part of me now.

And I don't want it. I scrub at my skin. "I am Arden Icaros. I live in Damalis. My family works the land. We have for five hundred years." My voice cracks as I whisper, "I'm sorry."

For letting that bird go. For thinking my birthright was pointless. For all the harsh things I said to Broderic tonight and over the years to Isidore and Andry.

But no matter how hard I try to wipe it away or how many tears fall or how many apologies I make, the guilt doesn't fade.

A soft knock interrupts my prayers.

"Enter," I call as measuredly as possible.

The female knight from earlier, rows of dark braids pulled back now with a band, steps inside, gaze moving quickly over me. An assessment of her charge. Her attention lingers for a moment on my red-rimmed eyes, but she doesn't comment.

"I thought you might need something to eat." There's no friendliness in her tone. Each word is clipped and purposeful. As though everything about her adheres to the strict order of the military. She crosses to the desk and places a plate of food and a folded dress on it. "And something to wear."

"Thank you," I manage despite the lingering rawness in my throat.

She doesn't seem particularly moved by my gratitude.

"What's going on out there?" I hitch my thumb toward the window.

"The sentries Bishop ordered to stand guard?" She crosses her arms. "I would think that's obvious. No one wants you to escape."

"Do they really think I'm going to jump out the window?" It's been a rough night. A terrible night. A night I would be very happy to wake up from and discover was only a bad dream. But seriously?

"No. They think you're going to fly away." She doesn't even blink when she says it.

But my mouth drops open. Jumping is at least a *rational* expectation. "They can't really believe that. It's impossible."

"And yet a hundred people witnessed the impossible tonight." Her eyes pin me, and she taps her chest to remind me what's on mine. "The king ordered Bishop to station them throughout the courtyard and around the perimeter of the palace."

Food, clothes, quickly dashing any hopes of escape. What else is on her agenda? Then again, maybe she's one of the people who actually believes that I now have access to Ravenell's lost magic.

"You know it's only superstition, right?" I say coldly.

A smirk lifts a corner of her mouth. "Superstition kills more people than magic."

"Is that a threat?" I ask.

"It's a warning." There's no amusement on her face now, her dark eyes narrowing. "Stay put."

"I was just getting comfortable." I drop onto the bed and pat Bishop's pillow. "Think he'll mind?"

She huffs and turns away. "If I were you, I would change. It's better if you cover that mark up."

She grabs the dress off the desk and throws it at me so quickly that it hits me in the face. I'm too stunned to respond before she leaves, locking the door behind her.

I dream of liquid flame and black feathers falling. People wailing under a crimson sky. I can feel the end approaching, and it's hotter than the fire of all seven hells. Welts blister my skin. Smoke clogs my throat until I can't breathe. I wake gasping. My hands fist the clean, white sheets, screams still echoing in my ears.

Only a dream, but I swear I taste ash on my tongue.

The shouting grows louder. But I'm not asleep. I fly off the bed and look out the window to find the guards yelling at each other. A few rush out of sight as lights blaze to life in the courtyard below.

A muffled scream from beyond the door sends me spinning toward it.

Something's happening *inside* the palace.

Fear winds through me and tightens like a noose. I turn back to the window and find an oscen roosting on the closest turret, its large, black body nearly blending with the night. It stretches and takes flight, only to land on the wall that joins this wing of the palace to that tower.

"No one is watching the window now," I mutter like it can hear me. Ignoring my churning stomach, I unlatch the window and study the battlement. It's wide enough that I might make it across—or fall to my death. But if they're coming for me, I'd rather die trying to escape than wait around for them to kill me.

I plant my hands on the sill, wishing Vessica hadn't brought me a dress. This would be much easier in pants. I boost my knee onto the windowsill, refusing to look at the ground below as I clutch the framing to pull myself up. Wind blasts me, sending my hair whipping into my face, but the battlement is only a short drop. I just have to let go and jump down. That seemed a lot easier before I was hanging out of the window.

The oscen squawks, somewhat impatiently for a fucking bird.

"I don't have wings," I snap at it.

But my fingers loosen as the door flies open behind me, and I sway dangerously, my foot tangling in the hem of my dress. I barely manage to regain my grip before a hand grabs the back of my borrowed clothing along with a good bit of hair and hauls me back inside.

Bishop slams me against the wall, his cheeks mottled red now. He's not the one I expected to hunt me down, but he certainly looks capable of killing me at the moment.

I aim an elbow at his throat. He doesn't expect it, and he stumbles back a step, gagging as I squirm free of his hold.

But he's between the door and me. I throw myself toward the window.

"Don't you fucking dare," he growls, moving with unnatural speed to block me. "Are you a witch?"

"You really think I'm a *witch*?" I spit the last word at him. "Maybe your friend is right. Maybe superstition kills more people than magic."

His eyes narrow like he doesn't believe me. "Why are you trying to climb out the window?"

"I'd rather greet death with open arms than sit here and wait for it," I say through quick, ragged breaths, darting a step in one direction, then the other as I try to find a way around him.

But he goes utterly still.

"You were going to jump?" he asks so quietly that I pause, too.

"Like you care." But I shake my head. The denial breaks him out of his momentary daze.

"No one else is dying tonight." He turns and latches the window. "Not on my watch."

Ice filters through my veins. No one *else*. "What do you mean? Who died?"

I can't bring myself to ask him more. My brothers, my sister, and my best friend are all in this palace. If someone was looking for me . . . if someone found one of them . . .

But he remains silent, which feels like answer enough.

EIGHT

"Who?" I repeat, my voice trembling, as Bishop unlocks the trunk. He lifts the lid and then tosses me a pair of boots. "Put these on."

I don't ask him where we're going this time. I pull the boots on, not bothering to fasten them. They're too big anyway. I tug at the high collar of my borrowed dress. Vessica and I aren't going to be best friends anytime soon, but I owe her for thinking of that.

Bishop waits by the open door. "After you."

He sounds as put out as Broderic when he got stuck babysitting me when we were kids.

I don't give Bishop the satisfaction of a passing glare as I stride out of his room.

He moves into step beside me in the corridor. "You aren't going to ask what happened?"

"Do I want to know?" I snap even though my heart is pounding. "Would you even tell me?"

He huffs in response. How illuminating.

"Someone died?" I ask anyway. "Is that why people are screaming?"

"Yes." He shoots an incredulous look at me. "The king has been assassinated."

King. Assassinated. Each word is harder to process than the last. My steps slow until I come to a complete stop. "Someone killed the king?"

Harbinger.

I push the thought away.

"And cut out his heart," he says grimly.

The ground seems to slip from under my feet. Miraculously, I stay upright.

"A heart collector," I say breathlessly. The stuff of fairy stories our mother told us. Boogeymen meant to make us behave.

Or so I thought.

"Now who's the superstitious one?" he asks.

There is something dismissive and slightly arrogant in his tone that thaws my shock, and I march forward. "Spoken like someone who let a killer walk straight into the palace and murder the king."

Of course he's above the old childhood fear written into every generation. He's been forged into something meant to *strike* fear, not yield to it.

His gloved hands curl into fists, but his gaze remains straight ahead of us. "Remind me why I keep saving your life?"

His guess is as good as mine.

"How can someone just get inside the palace and do that?" I ask without thinking. A second later, it hits me, and I halt in my tracks again, my stomach pitching. "You think I had something to do with it."

That's why he asked me if I was a witch. I wish I could change shape, could slip into the night, could leave all of this behind.

"No, I don't think that, because I had eyes on you all night," he says in a low voice.

The reminder is a stab to the chest. The king is dead, and I am alive. For some reason, that feels backwards. Mostly because now I suspect the man who should have been protecting him was protecting *me*.

Uneasiness ripples through me in waves of fire and ice until I'm covered in a cold sweat.

Every guard was watching *me*. Everyone was focused on *me*. An innocent man is dead, and it's my fault.

My knees buckle, and I brace a hand on the wall, pretty sure I'm about to vomit.

"No time for that now." Bishop grabs my sleeve and pulls me back to standing. "I'd summon some of that self-righteous recklessness if I were you."

"Self-righteous?" I consider shoving him down the stairs. Since I'll probably be blamed for the king's murder, what's one more?

"Oh, for fuck's sake." He rolls his eyes up like he's imploring the heavens themselves for patience. "I don't know if you're courageous or incredibly reckless, but whatever it is that keeps getting you into trouble, you're going to need a lot of it."

The pit in my stomach grows. "Where are you taking me?"

"Are you sure you want to know?" he asks.

I swallow before nodding. "Tonight hasn't been full of good surprises."

He finally smiles, but it's gone in an instant. "The queen wants to see you. She's called for a meeting of the patrons."

The woman sitting a few seats from King Ophelian at dinner isn't just his sister anymore. Now that she's queen, my fate is likely in her hands. But the patrons are what worries me.

Because that means that Broderic will be there.

I *really* need to vomit.

"What are they going to do to me?" I ask, my voice ragged.

Bishop hasn't lied to me yet. He won't pull punches. No, whatever gruesome fate awaits me, he will lay it out in simple, factual terms like a healer setting out his instruments.

He takes a deep breath before he answers, "That will largely depend on you."

Somehow—and it amazes even me—that's the worst news of the night.

"I thought you told me to be reckless," I grumble. "How is that going to help me?"

"No." His voice drops as we approach a corridor swarming with nobles. Half of them are drunk, and the other half are in their nightclothes. "I told you to be brave."

"It's not quite the same thing, don't you think?"

He snorts. "Trust me, there's not much of a difference."

A noble at the end of the hall catches sight of us and elbows his companion. Panic cinches my chest like a vise as we continue toward the gawking men.

"What do I have to do?" I ask.

"Convince them you didn't have anything to do with it."

"Half of them think I'm a witch," I remind him. Seven hells, even Bishop accused me. I tear my attention from the men and turn it on him. "They're not going to believe anything I say."

A muscle works in his jaw. "You won't have to convince *all* of them."

Does that mean he's on my side? I'm about to ask him when someone touches my shoulder from behind. A shriek jumps to my lips before I realize it's Broderic.

"Are you okay?" My brother's arms wrap around me before I fully process that he's here.

I dissolve against him. "Yes."

Not even a little.

Broderic pulls back just enough to study my face. "I'm not going to let anything happen to you," he promises, and warmth floods through me. "We'll be back in Damalis before you know it."

I find myself nodding. Broderic steps away, his arms falling to his sides, and I resist the urge to rush at him like I'm ten again. Like he'll catch me, lift me, make me fly. Like he'll always keep me safe.

"I'll see you inside." He nods quickly to Bishop, some silent understanding passing between them, before continuing down the hallway.

This is what Bishop meant. I have at least one ally in there. If Broderic can sway only a few of the other patrons to his side . . . Hope flutters in my chest, its fragile wings tickling my rib cage.

My brother won't let anything happen to me. That fact is enough to help me face this.

Bishop escorts me the rest of the way, and for one horrifying moment, I think we're walking toward the throne room. We bypass it, turning into another large room across the hall instead. Broderic's already taken a seat at the round table along with the rest of the patrons. He glances at the others, all of whom are decades older. My stomach sinks again. Icaros is the least influential order. If my father were here, we might have stood a chance. If we had money, we could buy some clout. But we have nothing to bargain with.

Bishop points me toward an empty chair next to my brother before settling into the one closest to the door.

An old man leans toward him, his face and hands creased with age. "I trust the palace is secure."

Bishop doesn't bother to look at him as he answers, "I have it under control, Patron Velesont."

"Do you, heirless one? I wonder if you should be here after—" He shuts up when Bishop finally glares at him.

I have the same question. I'm not sure having Bishop here works in my favor. Although he's had ample opportunities to kill me in the last twenty-four hours, so maybe he'll take my side.

Before anyone else can question Bishop's methods, a retinue of guards marches into the room. They part to reveal the newly minted queen.

She looks smaller than she did at dinner, as if the weight of everything that's transpired is already starting to chip away at her. The chamber's dim light catches on the deep brown tone of her skin, and her coiled curls are pulled tightly back. A few have come loose, feathering her temples, but there's nothing but grim determination on her face.

The man accompanying her has a nose nearly as long as his pallid face, with brown hair shorn closely as if he can't be bothered with it. A few lines crease the corners of his eyes, but otherwise, he seems too young to be accompanying the queen. The sash draped across his shoulders is embroidered with stars, his robe marking him as a vesper. Most of the patrons gasp, bowing their heads like somehow he's more important than the queen. I shoot a puzzled look at Broderic, but he's too busy gawking.

Velesont's patron rises to his feet and bows deeply. "It's a privilege, High Vesper."

He's not what I expected. Then again, nothing in Wintour has been what I expected.

"What's going on?" I nudge Broderic beneath the table.

My brother leans closer and whispers under his breath, "The high vesper only leaves the Royal Astrolatory if the Stars demand it. He must have noted a sign."

I guess the king getting his heart carved out would qualify under that heading.

He can't be here because of me.

The high vesper gives us a gentle smile before placing one hand on the queen's shoulder. "I'm only here to support Selestina during this difficult time."

Her throat slides, but she maintains her poise. The high vesper guides her to the large armchair positioned on the other side of the table, lingering behind her once she's seated.

"Thank you for coming." Squaring her shoulders, she glances at each of us in turn. She pauses when she gets to me, and I drop my head dutifully.

Better to save the recklessness for later.

"Has the culprit been caught?" a man with salt-and-pepper hair but smooth, light-brown skin demands like he's speaking to a child. A silver chalice glimmers on the back of his hand. Order Calix. Naturally. Control enough things people depend on, and you think you control them, too.

Queen Selestina shakes her head. "The grounds have been swept. There are guards at every entrance. It's unclear how the assassin escaped or how they got in at all."

Patron Calix glances toward me, his eyes narrowing. "Isn't it, though?"

"What are you saying?" Broderic asks, planting his hands on the polished tabletop.

Patron Calix's thin lips curl into a vicious smile, revealing large, uneven front teeth. "Do you mean to claim the witch?"

"If you mean my sister—" Broderic stops himself. He drags in a deep breath before continuing with a more measured tone. "What does my sister have to do with the king's assassination?"

"He was killed with the dagger from the Kindling." Patron Velesont draws out each word, his eyes narrowing on me. Dread coils tightly beneath my ribs. "Your sister was the last one to use it."

"It's also missing," Patron Calix adds, as though stealing the weapon might be a worse crime.

"Seriously?" I blurt out, and my brother kicks me under the table.

"Are you accusing my family of stealing a *ceremonial* dagger? Really?" Broderic scoffs, but he shoots me a sideways glance.

"What would we need it for? Tilling the soil?" I ask, and Broderic kicks me again. Harder this time.

Patron Calix leans forward. "It *is* covered in jewels."

"And?" Broderic asks, his eyebrows shooting up.

He hasn't figured it out yet, but I have. Because it's always there, lingering under the surface. We might as well hang a sign around our necks.

We're poor.

"Talk to your family," I spit back at Patron Calix. "Your initiate Dimitri tried to kill me with it." I turn a furious glare to Bishop. "Tell him."

But Bishop's face remains a stony mask as Calix snarls, "No one in my family would—"

"How dare you," my brother cuts him off, pounding on the table like he's finally taken offense. Nice of him to catch up. "You're accusing my family of killing our king for some bloody *jewels*, you—you—"

"Gentlemen," Queen Selestina interjects. "There has been enough ugliness tonight. We are equals here. Let's act like it."

Next to her, the patrons of Leontia and Velesont share a meaningful look, but they don't say anything.

"I'm merely pointing out the obvious." Patron Calix swivels his attention to the queen. "The Stars tried to warn us." He jabs a bony finger in my direction. "We've seen an increase in raids on our southern border. You've seen the reports. The Stars marked her as a harbinger to warn us war is coming."

"They marked her as a Ravenell," Bishop corrects.

For a moment, Patron Calix hesitates, like he's unsure whether or not to risk contradicting him despite the fact that Bishop is half his age.

"Yes, well, Ravenell or not," the queen says, "Bishop is right. Order Icaros would not have stolen the dagger."

I bite my lip. Not a thief. She didn't say anything about murderer.

"But they cursed her, my queen. No one has been marked by Ravenell in more than five hundred years." He shakes his head, glancing at the others for support. "We all know the history. And now the king is dead?"

The others begin to murmur, and Broderic shifts nervously in his seat.

But Queen Selestina raises a hand to silence the room. "It's not for us to question the Stars."

"Of course you're right, Your Majesty." Patron Velesont inclines his gray head, already attempting to slither into her good graces. I guess you don't get to his advanced age without knowing exactly whose ass to kiss.

"Why now?" asks Patron Leontia, her brown hair still plaited into a long silky braid like she came straight from bed. She spares a sympathetic glance at me, ever the healer. "I'm not saying it isn't strange, mind you. But for *all* of this to happen in one night seems . . . convenient."

Honestly, I agree with her.

I'm not about to say that out loud.

"The only explanation is that it's a sign of the return of—" Patron Velesont starts.

"It's hardly the only explanation." Bishop cuts him off. "And I'll remind you, not all of us are patrons."

He means me. I'm not a patron. I sit up a little straighter, wondering what Patron Velesont was about to let slip.

"It could be someone from the Lost Continent," Broderic suggests. "Maybe they heard the rumors that Antares plans to build settlements."

"If that's the case," Patron Calix says with a sneer, "it *is* an act of war. And that *still* makes her a harbinger." He flicks a finger at me again, and my control slips.

"It's not polite to point," I say through gritted teeth. This earns me everyone's attention. Broderic clears his throat, but I ignore the warning. "Why are you so worried about an omen? People think they see them all the time."

But Patron Calix is unruffled, his beady eyes squinting at me. "They must not teach history in Damalis."

"I guess I skipped the day we studied ancient superstitions." If I'm going to be condemned, it's not going to be by a man like him.

Bishop hesitates, then says, "A harbinger foretold the coming of the Last War."

"And there hasn't been one for five hundred years," Patron Leontia says calmly. She reaches over and pats the queen's hand. "The rumors can be squashed before this reaches a head. What happened tonight is a tragedy, but we do not have to allow more violence."

"An execution is hardly violence," Patron Velesont says, stroking his thumb over his cane's rounded handle.

Execution. My mouth goes dry as I suddenly understand what we're *really* debating.

Patron Calix nods in agreement, a rabid gleam in his dark eyes. "If we do nothing, that sends a message."

They both want me dead. I clutch my armrests to stay upright. Two of the patrons will vote to execute. Even if Bishop sides with Broderic . . . I shake away the thought. I won't fear two greedy old men suffering a bout of irrationality.

"And what message will executing her send?" Bishop leans back in his chair, crossing his arms over his broad chest, his blue eyes stony.

This time, Patron Velesont doesn't shrink from him. Instead, he whacks the handle of his cane on the table. "That we take security seriously. I should think that's a message *you* would be eager to send."

The certainty I've been clinging to cracks, and something inside me wavers—just for a second, but it's enough.

"What are you implying?" Bishop arches a brow.

"Perhaps being patron *and* bishop is too much responsibility. If Order Marius isn't up to the task of protecting our king, even . . ." He taps his cane again, smiling like he's already won.

The little snake waited to strike, but Bishop shrugs a shoulder. "Your concern is noted. Perhaps we could alleviate some of the strain on *my* troops by removing the ones stationed in Isoldoro."

The older patron stills, the strike landing. Velesont's province is a cluster of wealthy islands that oversees all trade in Antares. If enemies from the Lost Continent or beyond attack, they'll likely be hit first.

"Not with a war about to begin, if it hasn't already," Patron Velesont backtracks, clearly realizing the same thing. He looks toward the queen, his knuckles going white around his cane, but his gaze travels past her to the high vesper. "What do the Stars say?"

The high vesper places his hands on the back of the queen's chair and meets my eyes. My pulse stutters as he measures me. Wisdom reflects back at me, ancient and patient despite his age, as though the years spent in that spiraling tower with the Stars have prepared him for this precise moment. "No cycle has begun."

"But she is marked a Ravenell. She will cause another war," Patron Calix says, lifting his bushy eyebrows.

The high vesper looks down his long nose at him. "That remains to be seen."

"Isn't that what you're doing up there?" Patron Calix needles him. "Seeing these things? You're saying that you didn't see that star in the Night's Scar?"

Queen Selestina flinches, wincing slightly like the words sting. "Enough." Her chin quivers. "The high vesper has spoken."

Relief leaks through me.

And apparently, that's that—until Patron Velesont taps his cane loudly on the floor. I really hate that fucking cane. "Her magic hasn't manifested yet. That is precisely why we act now. A Ravenell with fully awakened magic . . ."

He pauses like he's giving us time to remember every terrifying story we've ever heard about the witches. "Executing her may be the *only* way to stop the cycle from beginning. Are you willing to risk that?"

The words land like a punch to my gut. I should have known it wouldn't be as simple as one person's verdict. I glance around the table at Patrons Calix and Leontia, even the queen, and for the first time, all of them look nervous. Fear floods through me, and I turn toward Broderic.

The panic in his eyes is somehow worse than anything on their faces. As if he's watching someone slam a door he can't reach in time.

Something inside me gives way, threatening to drag my body down with it. My shoulders sag as it hits me.

I'm not leaving Wintour with my family.

Not alive, anyway.

"Harbinger or not, the Stars *chose* her," Bishop counters, then hesitates before adding, "and executing her might *begin* the cycle."

What is this starsdamned cycle? I turn to ask, but Patron Velesont grunts, "That's a risk I'm willing to take."

"No one is executing my sister," Broderic says with quiet firmness.

"*That* will be up to a vote," Patron Calix says, one corner of his mouth turning up cruelly. "Her magic won't stay quiet forever. We don't know *what* she'll become. I'd rather end this while we still can."

I should be running or fighting or throwing my chair through the window. But my body won't move as I listen to them discuss the relative merits of murdering me for participating in their stupid ritual. I stare at my hands on the table. There's still dirt under my fingernails from this afternoon. That alley and the thief seem like a lifetime ago. I fought then. Why am I just sitting here now? Why does it feel like all the forces of the heavens have strapped me to this chair and cut out my tongue? *Speak.* But I don't know what to say.

Hey, I promise to not become mad with power and nearly destroy the world? I don't think they're going to accept that on my word alone.

My eyes lift, and I find myself looking directly at Queen Selestina.

She gives me the slightest smile, wiping it from her face before anyone else can see. "There has been enough death today." The finality in her tone suggests that even she knows we are *not* equals here. She is the queen, and we are beneath her. The high vesper leans down to whisper something in her ear, and she nods. "We will not presume to understand what the Stars intend. Not until we've studied them. In the meantime, Lady . . . *Arden* will be protected."

"We'll leave for Damalis first thing in the morning," Broderic says, rising to his feet.

"You can't think she'll be allowed to leave with you." Patron Calix shakes his head. "She stays here—in custody—where people can keep an eye on her."

Broderic slams a fist onto the table, so hard that the wood groans. "She has done nothing wrong."

"Then she has nothing to fear," Patron Calix says with a smile that doesn't reach his eyes. "Can you be certain that she's not a witch? She's marked by their order."

"You forget the witches stood with us once," Patron Leontia says quietly. "None of us would be here without them."

"You know as well as I do that they—"

"We know very little about what happened to them," Queen Selestina interrupts. "Perhaps we should ask Arden what *she* wants." She gives me a subtle nod.

I want this nightmare to be over. Next to me, Broderic relaxes slightly. Leontia. The queen. They're on our side. But Calix and Velesont? They're not looking at me anymore. They're watching my brother.

"I want . . ." What do I want? I shoot a panicked look at Bishop. "What I want is . . ."

"She wants to come home, obviously," Broderic says impatiently.

"Do you really think that's the best idea?" Bishop asks him, his eyes on mine.

He's not asking my brother. The question is meant for me. It's his job to see the violence in men, to anticipate it. Or maybe it just speaks to what runs in his own veins. He nods slightly as if he knows what I'm thinking. He is not my friend, nor my ally. He is an instrument of justice. He is a wolf with teeth that will protect me until he's ordered to bite.

"Arden?" the queen prompts.

And suddenly, I know what I have to do. The decision slices into my heart like a knife. Whatever future I'd dreamed of for myself was traded when I set that oscen free. But I won't let it take away anyone else's.

I can't go home, if Damalis *is* still my home. We have no security. Kieren isn't even really trained. He can use his sword but only because it is sharp. And men like Patrons Velesont and Calix have means. They never cared about a vote. They decided my fate in the throne room.

I don't have a choice. Not really. Not if I want to protect my family.

"Arden," Broderic whispers. "It will be okay. No one in the village will care."

What a beautiful, hopeful delusion.

I hate the other patrons for making me do this. I hate Bishop for forcing me to see the truth. I hate the Stars for cursing me. Mostly, I hate myself for what I'm about to say. But if I don't burn this bridge, Broderic's stubborn pride might get all of us killed.

My eyes shutter, and I take a deep breath. "I'm not an Icaros. Not anymore." The words shred me, more painful than when the Stars doomed me to this moment. But I take that pain and transform it. I reach for its darkness, and in its shadows, I find something useful. *Rage.* I let it flow into my voice, let its fire transform me into something brutal and unyielding. "I don't belong in Damalis. You all saw the truth. The Stars have spoken."

"Arden, of course you belong with us. We're your family." Broderic reaches for me.

I shake off his touch and turn my anger on him. I twist it into something cruel and smug and pray that my voice doesn't break. "I never asked to be born to Order Icaros." No, that was a gift I no longer deserve. "I never asked to be shackled to a farm, cleaning up pig shit and digging in the dirt." Making things grow. Spending the afternoon with the sun on my back. Chasing down cattle with Kieren and then scolding Andry for leaving a gate unlatched.

Broderic shakes his head. "You don't mean that."

No. No. No. Take me home to Damalis. Erase this mark from my skin. Let me pretend this never happened. That's what I want.

But that's also what I can never have if I'm going to keep *them* safe. For him, for all of them, I have to do this. If I don't, my brother will fight to keep *me* safe—with his last breath.

"I don't want to be a poor nobody." I say the things I saw on his face before the feast. I channel the resentment I heard in his voice. "Go home, Broderic. I'm sure the Stars have better things planned for me."

"You can't possibly believe—"

"Of course I do." *Stop talking me out of this.* "You said it yourself earlier. I acted like my birthright was a punishment, because I thought it was. I thought it was going to force me to stay there, to live a life stuck in the middle of nowhere."

Broderic flinches, his head shaking slightly. He opens his mouth.

So I deliver one final blow. "And now I won't have to marry someone for their money."

The look on his face—it's the same as the day Dad died. I force myself to keep staring at him until he turns away.

"Well," Queen Selestina says quietly, "I suppose that's settled."

"Is it?" Patron Velesont asks as he leans forward on his cane, but there's something new gleaming in his eyes. It's as wicked as before, but it makes my skin crawl in a different way, like I've walked through a spider's web and the silk is still clinging to my skin. "Where will she go?"

"Planning to adopt her?" Bishop asks him gruffly. "How charitable." But he shoots a look at the queen.

She hesitates just long enough for me to see her determination waver. "She will stay here, for the time being," she tacks on like the thought unnerves her. Then she rises, and all the patrons quickly follow. "If you'll excuse me, I'd like to rest. I have a funeral to arrange in the morning."

The high vesper moves beside her, whispering with a comforting smile as they leave the room.

My legs are unsteady as I turn to leave, but I'm unable to resist glancing at Broderic. He's staring at the floor like I broke him. Something cracks in my chest, threatening to spill out, and I take a quick step away from the table.

Bishop appears at my side and grips my elbow, guiding me toward the door. I wait for my brother to follow.

He doesn't.

"He believed you," Bishop whispers when we're out of the room.

"Maybe because I was telling the truth." I can only sell the lie if I'm willing to keep pretending. This is the price of my birthright. Maybe I *am* the harbinger. Maybe I was sent to destroy everyone, starting with myself.

NINE

The grounds are busier than usual this morning. Flags are still lowered to half-mast, like they've been for three days now.

Three days that I've counted with the rise and fall of the sun, ever since Bishop dumped me in his room after the council meeting and vanished. Vessica is the only one who's bothered to come, but only to deliver meals with little more than a grunt to acknowledge my existence.

Fine by me. After my last words to Broderic, I'm not in the mood for conversation.

The springs squeak as I push off the bed and walk over to stare out the window.

Gray clouds hover as if the heavens also know it's time for the funeral. I keep far enough from the sill that no one spots me watching the constant stream of deliveries. Only the damn oscen continues to show up to perch on the battlement. It's the only one that seems to care that I'm here.

The things I said that night to Broderic play on a loop in my head. I can't escape them any more than I can escape the palace.

Coaches begin to arrive midday, hauling the city's wealthy either for show or from overly delicate refinement. Because who can be bothered to walk the few steps up the royal drive and risk ruining their shoes in the snow?

A knock startles me from my thoughts. I glance at the clock on the desk, one of the few amenities my new room has to offer. I've already eaten breakfast, and supper is hours away. No one has bothered to acknowledge my existence for any other reason.

The change in schedule is enough to make me pause at the door before opening it. At least a murder attempt would break up the monotony.

Vessica is on the other side. She holds out a fresh set of clothing. "These are for you."

It's the first time she's spoken to me since the king died, and her expression says she's not enthused to be breaking her silence.

I flap open the shirt, and a pair of fitted breeches tumbles to the floor. I expected another dress. The black shirt I'm holding has a high neck with a tightly fitted bodice. The material is expensive—soft and thick—but practical, with the subtle silver embroidery that marks it as military-grade. It will be by far the most comfortable thing I have worn since I arrived in Wintour. "What are these for?"

"To wear." Vessica gives me a bored blink, her dark-brown eyes betraying nothing as she passes me a pair of boots. That's a definite upgrade from the oversized ones Bishop gave me. Maybe this is her version of an olive branch.

"Look, I feel like we got off on the wrong foot," I begin, but she's already walked back out the door.

Okay, maybe not.

No one knows what to do with me. Maybe they're just hoping I will start developing Ravenell's powers and give them a reason to lop off my head.

Yeah, things are getting dark.

Perhaps because I can't stop remembering the looks on the patrons' faces in the council room. I haven't felt even a hint of magic since the Kindling, but too many people already see me as a threat.

I lean over to scoop the pants off the floor before dropping the new items on the bed. Stripping down, I change, eager to be out of a skirt for the first time in almost a week. Particularly since this week feels like a lifetime. I've just fastened the last buckle of the boots—which are stiffer than the ones I purchased in Damalis—when the door swings open. Bishop strides in wearing his usual scowl.

He's not in uniform today apart from a single sheathed sword. There's no sign of his signature red cloak, and the woolen black coat buttoned tightly at the neck is devoid of any insignia. Its hem extends to his knees, giving him plenty of room to hide weapons and stolen books and whatever else he usually conceals under his cloak.

"Don't you knock?" I spring up from the bed, pleased to find the boots are unexpectedly comfortable despite their newness. "I could've been naked."

"But you weren't," he says like this settles the matter.

"If you're going to keep me locked up in here, maybe it's time we get a few things straight." I've been rehearsing this speech, just waiting for a moment to deliver it.

But Bishop waves me off. "It's your lucky day. You're finally getting out of here, so why don't we skip the lecture?"

"Getting out?" I repeat, heart stuttering. "Why now?"

"Things have changed," he says, adjusting his gloves.

Ice slides down my spine, freezing my muscles in place. "Changed in a good way?"

His silence is answer enough. I'm fucked.

I take a deep breath. "Where am I going?"

"I'm sure you've noticed there's a funeral this afternoon." Bishop glances toward the window.

My stomach bottoms out so fast, I feel dizzy. He can't be serious. I take a slow step backward, shaking my head. The black shirt with its high neck to cover the mark of Ravenell—the bastard wants me to go to the king's funeral. "You can't expect me to go . . ."

"To the funeral?" He raises his eyebrows. "Everyone else expects you to be there. You are a noble-born daughter of a patron line."

"That's a terrible idea." I continue to shake my head like it's come loose. "It will be a spectacle."

It will draw attention not just to me but to my family as well. Broderic may not have come to visit, but I have no doubt he's still in the city. He'll attend the funeral out of duty despite the humiliation I've caused our family. He's too proud to do anything else.

"I'd rather stay locked up." Please and thank you very much.

"Too bad. As I said, things have changed." He flourishes an arm toward the door. "After you."

He's actually making me do this. Maybe Bishop *does* want me dead.

I shuffle toward the hallway, grumbling under my breath, "Are you going to follow me around for the rest of my life?"

"Your life will be a lot longer if I do."

My guts twist as we descend the staircase, my anxiety building with each step. Maybe that's what the outfit is about. It's hardly a fashion statement. I'll blend in. Perhaps people will mistake me for one of his conscripts. But what changed that Bishop needs to drag me to the king's funeral?

We reach the landing for the main floor, and the sconces on the wall gutter, winking out like the stars did that night.

I freeze as if it's an omen, but Bishop gestures to keep heading down.

I glance toward the sounds of muffled chatter. "Where are we going? Isn't the funeral up here?"

"It's not for another hour," he explains. "But if you want to go and make small talk with the early arrivals, be my guest."

"I do not," I say quickly.

He nods like he agrees with my position on the matter. "Then follow me."

We descend into the bowels of the castle, which are teeming with staff and servants rushing about and making the final preparations for whatever lavish luncheon is to follow the burial. Bishop carves a path through the chaos with the ease of someone who knows his way through every passage in the palace. A few people pause and curtsy when they see him. Most immediately shift direction, not daring to get in his way. They're so focused on my brooding guardian that they don't notice me, and my nerves ease a little.

Unlike the upper floors, the spaces below are utilitarian, connected by a labyrinth of cramped corridors and low doorways. The air carries the sound of clattering dishes and the smells of roasting meats and baking breads. Bishop opens a back entrance and leads me into a small courtyard. It's not the extravagant one viewable from my window or the snow-covered gardens beyond that. Waste bins line the squat brick walls enclosing the space; crates of empty wine bottles are stacked next to the refuse. Bishop continues through, heading for the stable complex.

"Wait." I stop in my tracks, tugging on his arm. "Seriously. Where are we going?"

"Keep asking," he says dryly and continues walking. "It's endearing."

I refuse to move and toss at his back, "I thought we were going to the funeral."

Bishop doesn't break his stride. "You said that was a terrible idea."

"Yes, but you didn't agree with me." I rush forward when it becomes clear that he's not going to stop.

"Oh, I agree with you." He heads into a carriage house. "Like I said, everyone will be at the funeral."

Before I can ask him what the hell is going on, there's a laugh from somewhere deeper in the building, followed by distant footsteps.

"What a way to start a war," a male voice sneers.

My heart jumps into my throat, but Bishop is already backing closer, his arm extended protectively in front of me.

Another voice answers, "I'm just glad it's no one important. No one will miss an Icaros."

"Don't you mean a Ravenell?" The following laugh sounds closer. So do the footsteps. "I just hope the queen is more ambitious than her brother."

"Doubtful, or she'd have been the one to hire us."

A slight gasp escapes me, and a second later, Bishop has me pinned against the wall before I can draw another breath, one palm covering my mouth, the other braced beside my head. There's nowhere for me to go.

"Don't say a word," he breathes.

Leaning closer, he angles his face over mine, his silver-blond hair falling like a curtain to shield me. The conversation continues, but I'm no longer listening. Bishop slides his hand from my mouth to the back of my neck, settling there like he's anchoring me. Holding me exactly where he wants me. Even in the carriage house's dim light, the silver rimming his blue eyes sparkles as his gaze dips to my mouth, the intention there unmistakable. He smells like leather and smoke and the faint hint of soap from his morning bath. I close my eyes, half in dread, half in anticipation.

His forehead grazes mine, breath warm against my lips, our bodies almost touching. He stays there, never letting his mouth move closer.

My heart races as the voices near. It has nothing to do with him. Even if he's so close that I can almost taste the mint lingering on his breath. My skin heats, suffocating under his massive body.

Someone whistles behind us, and I know we've been *caught.*

"Sorry to interrupt," one of the strangers says.

Bishop lifts his hand off the wall and flips them off.

"Move along. I'm not putting on a show," he growls. Despite that, he dips his head lower. I arch instinctively, and his lips brush my throat without meaning to, blazing a trail of fire. Jerking away, I bury my face into his shoulder. Hopefully, our audience just thinks I'm shy.

"Enjoy yourself," the man says, and I can hear the smirk in his voice. I hold my breath, counting their footsteps silently until I hear the door creak open.

As soon as it slams shut, Bishop backs off, palms raised. But even with the space between us, my skin still burns.

"What was that?" I demand, trying to shake off what just happened.

"I'd think it obvious. Those men are planning to kill you."

Not pulling any punches today.

I scowl at him. "Yes. I figured that out. What did you think *you* were doing?"

"Saving you *again*," he grits out. "Some people might say thank you."

"Saving me? You're leading me right *to them*. If people are planning to kill me at the funeral—"

"Yes, I've been keeping you alive for days simply because I was waiting to deliver you to just the right assassin," he deadpans.

"You're an ass," I say, glancing around us. "What happened to the queen's protection?"

He pauses, eying me sidelong. "She's young. Some of the patrons are . . . not. They see that mark on your skin as a threat. I hate to ruin your day, but you aren't safe in Wintour, even with her protection."

Day officially ruined. Not that it had been going that well before. "Then tell me what the fuck we're doing."

"Well, we're obviously not going to a funeral," he says, and my eyes widen.

My gaze travels to the collection of coaches. Some are from visiting nobles desperate to add a little pomp and circumstance to today's morbid pageantry. Others look like they've been collecting dust for the better part of this century. "We're leaving."

"She gets there eventually," he says and moves toward a coach in the royal collection. It looks like it's been cleaned up recently. "People will be in and out all day."

Coming and going, everyone too busy making a show of their grief to realize that neither of us is in attendance.

Opening the door, he pushes back the velvet curtain and offers his hand. "I'll go see what's taking Taliesin so long with the horses. Wait in here."

I don't move. My heart is still racing in my chest.

"I can't leave," I blurt out. "My family . . ."

I need to say goodbye. Even if I can't admit the truth. Even if I can't take back what I said that night. They need to know I might not ever see them again.

"Your family knows." His tone is measured but filled with unmistakable pity.

It's worse than if he'd kissed me.

"How?" My voice shakes.

He raises one brow. Of course Bishop told them. That almost hurts more.

My family knows I'm leaving, possibly forever, to Stars know where, and they don't care. Aren't coming to say goodbye. And I can't even blame them.

I grab hold of the coach's handle, ignoring his offered hand, and climb inside, blinking back tears. I refuse to cry in front of him. Again. The last thing I need is Bishop Marius feeling obliged to take care of me. He's a means to escape this shitty situation so I can figure out what I'm going to do next. Nothing more.

Bishop closes the door and nods toward the curtains. "Draw those. Don't come out until I return."

I yank them swiftly shut before the tears begin to fall. Hot and angry. Fat and sorrowful. Each one an accusation aimed directly at myself. I did this. It's what I chose. Knowing I had to do it does nothing to soothe the jagged ache growing inside me. Maybe it was to protect them, but now I'm imagining what Broderic told Isidore. Told Andry. He might not have told Kieren anything, given how things were between them the last time we were all together. I did it for them, but I'm the one who has to survive this pit of despair—and I haven't even stopped falling into it yet.

The coach door opens again, and I quickly swipe my eyes, turning to hide the evidence of my weakness from Bishop.

But it's Kieren's relieved voice that says, "Thank the Stars."

He drops into the seat next to me.

"Oh." The word is too small for what I'm feeling, so I throw myself at him, not bothering to hold back a fresh wave of sobs as I bury my face into his broad shoulder.

Kieren holds me, feeling so solid and warm and real that for a heartbeat, I almost believe things will be okay.

"What are you doing here?" I manage after a moment, my voice cracking in my aching throat.

"I've been trying to see you for the last three days." His arms tighten around me like I might slip away. "Broderic wouldn't tell us what they did with you. Isidore has been asking around. Andry too."

This only makes me cry harder. Not abandoned. They've been looking for me. I pull away and draw a shuddering breath until I'm able to speak. "Did Broderic tell you what I said?"

"He told me what you said, what you decided," Kieren says quietly. "But he lied to Isidore and Andry and said the queen won't let you go home."

Broderic was protecting them. I was protecting them. That's how it's always been. We protect each other.

"I didn't mean it." It's a confession I can only make to my best friend.

Kieren forces a half-hearted grin. "I told him that you were full of shit, but he never believes me."

There is an edge to the words that tells me all is not forgiven between the two of them.

And I won't be there to fix it, to help them put the pieces of their relationship back together.

"Broderic finally told me that you were leaving Wintour. I couldn't let you go without . . ." He trails away like he can't bear to say the words, either. "Is it true? What they're saying about your mark? About the king?"

"Some of it." I can't manage more than that without falling apart again. But Kieren seems to understand. He always does.

I bite my lip. What in the world happened between when the queen offered protection a few nights ago and the city filling with assassins? I've had too much time alone for a thousand questions to form about what it means to be marked as a Ravenell. About whether all the old stories are true. Or what will happen when my magic finally manifests.

"Where are they taking you?"

I swallow around the knot in my throat. "I have no idea," I admit. "I was only told I'm leaving a few minutes ago. Bishop is sneaking me out of the city. He says people will be distracted by the funeral." I don't mention the sudden need to leave the capital. Mainly because Bishop hasn't bothered to share what "things changed" other than the obvious. I'm a threat that needs to be managed.

"I was thinking the same thing about the crowded ceremony." He glances down at my pants. "Good. You're already dressed for riding."

My chest tightens. *That's* why he's here. Not to say goodbye . . .

"We don't have much time." He grabs my hand and tries to tug me off the seat. "Let's get out of here while we can. We can reach the coast in less than two days."

Something splinters in my heart. Something I know will never fully heal. The part of me that wants to leave with him. The part of me that believes we can do it. The part of me that was foolish enough to hope I could outrun consequences.

That girl is gone now. I sacrificed her in place of the oscen.

"There's nowhere for us to go," I say quietly.

"The Lost Continent," he says without missing a beat. "We can sell the horses we take when we reach the nearest port. It should be enough to buy us passage—"

"I want to, Kieren. I really do." I shake my head, continuing quickly when he opens his mouth to object. "But I'm sorry. I can't go to the Lost Continent." Not with people hunting me.

"I agree," Bishop's gravelly voice cuts in. He pushes open the curtains, his gaze narrowing on mine. "Patron Velesont will be expecting that."

And they control the ports. We wouldn't even make it onto a boat.

I turn my gaze back to Kieren and reach for his other hand, holding them both like they need to carry more weight than ever now. "You're the only security our family has," I whisper.

He scoffs. "I'm hardly security. I'm not even trained." His eyes turn pleading. "Arden, I—"

"You're strong and can use a sword. That's more than Isidore. More than Andry." Each broken piece of my heart sharpens into resolve. "You have to protect them. They're not safe now."

He stares at me like he's looking at a stranger. "Broderic can do it."

"And who is going to watch out for him?" Why does this have to be so hard? "I need you to watch out for him until . . ."

I can't bear to finish the sentence.

"She's right." Shadows mask Bishop's face. "When people realize that she's left Wintour, they will come to Damalis."

I want to vomit.

"Who will come?" Kieren asks. "No one's ever cared about the Icaros patronage. They just think Arden is some stupid omen."

There's so much he doesn't know.

"And they will come looking for her in Damalis. I've already ordered troops to be stationed in the province. It will take them a few days to arrive." Bishop nods to Kieren. "It's best if someone travels with your family."

I squeeze Kieren's hands tightly. "Stay with them," I beg. "Stay with *her*."

His mouth presses into a firm line as I hit his biggest weakness. Finally, he tilts his head. "If that's what you want."

But I don't want this. I want him to come with me. I want to go with him. I choke that desire back along with the rest of my tears. "I do." I nod. "I promise I'll let you know when I'm settled."

Bishop's mouth twists, suggesting this promise will be up for discussion in the near future.

"I'll give you two a minute," Bishop says, then backs completely into the shadows.

"This is for the best," I murmur, willing myself to believe it. "Stay with them. Keep them safe."

Kieren doesn't say a word.

"And tell Isidore how you feel." This time, my voice breaks.

He releases a heavy sigh. "Then Broderic will kill me."

"Regret will kill you faster." I muster up a smile. "Besides, her marriage prospects just diminished significantly."

Neither of us laughs.

"I'll do this," he says before lowering his voice. "But once the troops arrive and I can get some money together, I'm coming for you."

And then he'll never be safe. "Kieren, you belong in Damalis with your family."

"*You* are my family," he corrects me.

"But the others—"

"I'm nothing to them. *Nothing*." He slumps back in the seat, his head falling forward from the weight of his confession. "You're the only one who's ever really seen me as family."

I don't know what to say. Don't know how to convince him otherwise. Not when it's clear he believes it.

"That's not true," I say weakly.

"We both know it is." His answering smile is soft and resigned. But he squares his shoulders and reaches for the door. "Send word."

He ducks out of the coach, and an emptiness spreads through me. He's gone before I realize we didn't say goodbye.

My hands shake as I cross them in my lap, fighting the urge to wrap them around my waist. I know now that I'll never go home again. Not really. No matter what happens. Because home won't be the same. I'll see Broderic's resentment. Remember Kieren's confession. And they will both look at me as the one who abandoned them.

I can't bring myself to move from the spot. Even when the carriage shakes as horses are hitched to it. Even when Bishop confers with someone in a low voice.

I'm still sitting in numb silence when he reappears by the coach door. "It's time to go."

I look out the other window.

Bishop groans. "Come on. We don't have much time."

"I'm not stopping us," I snap, still refusing to look at him.

"But we're not taking the coach." He holds the door open.

This gets my attention. *"What?"*

"No. Time," he repeats, like somehow it's an answer.

I force myself onto my feet. It's not as though I have a lot of options. "What *is* the plan exactly? Or do you even know?"

"Your confidence is inspiring." He doesn't bother to offer me his hand again as I climb down the steps. "I would have told you, but you were occupied."

He's actually annoyed. Like letting me have a few final moments with my old life is a huge sacrifice. Heartless bastard.

The other knight—the one with the scars on the side of his neck and face—grins at me from the coachman's seat. "Sorry, it's my fault," Taliesin says, winking at me as he lifts a hood over his head. His dirty-blond hair is short but long enough on top to flop to one side. "I told some jackass from Calix you and I would be leaving around noon."

The coach is just another distraction.

Eyeing Bishop, I realize he *does* have a plan—and he's not going to share it with me.

Bishop checks the horses' harness before turning to him. "No one will attack until you're outside the city limits. Be prepared—"

"To fight?" Taliesin's smile widens. "I'm looking forward to it." He snaps the reins and urges the horses forward. He lifts a hand when he reaches the exit. "See you in hell."

Charming.

Bishop moves to close the carriage house doors.

"Before you ask where we're going again," he says, picking up a pack from the ground. He rummages in one of its side pockets before pulling something out. "I should warn you that I'm not used to answering questions."

Probably because he's usually giving orders. The kind that no one dares to question.

Maybe I should have gone with his knight.

"Will you really send those troops to Damalis?" I ask.

He looks up from the small object he's fiddling with in his hands and frowns. "You have my word."

"And that's good enough?" I cross my arms.

His face darkens. "Are you questioning the word of a bishop?"

"Maybe I wouldn't if you gave me some idea what you're planning."

This earns another groan. I'm shaping up to be his favorite person.

"I'm taking you somewhere no one will dare to look for you."

Well, that sounds familiar. "You said that before." I shrug. "Shouldn't I just stay in your room here if that's the big plan?"

"No one would *think* to look for you there," he corrects me. "That's what I told you. I said no one will *dare* to look for you where we're going." He stops playing with the gadget and stares me down. "But if you want to take your chances, so be it. So far, there are only three assassins in the city who have been hired to kill you. Decent odds, if you're up on your sword work."

Point fucking taken.

I sway slightly at the idea that three people in Wintour are out to kill me. How many more want me dead?

"Take your time deciding," he drawls. "It's your life, not mine."

I grit my teeth. "And how are we getting to this untouchable location if the coach already left?"

He lifts his hand and drops what he's holding. It's a disc of obsidian engraved with lines that catch the faintest light and split it into hundreds of starbursts. The device hits the ground with a *thud* and sputters before a shock wave of light streams around it to form a glowing blue pool.

"What is that?" I ask slowly.

"A postern," he says.

I step away from it, suddenly afraid I'll accidentally fall through it and land Stars-know-where. It's not like any postern that I've ever seen, but that's not the problem.

"Velesont controls the posterns," I say. If I can't take a ship from a port, a postern has to be even easier for them to track.

"Not this one." He extends a gloved hand. "This one is special."

That sounds like code for *risky*.

"Is it safe?" I ask.

But he laughs at me. "The trick is knowing what's on the other side."

TEN

There are a hundred reasons why this is a terrible idea, starting with the fact that I hate posterns. But trusting that Bishop knows what's on the other side—trusting Bishop at all—that's my real problem. Still, if he wanted me dead, I'd already be a smear in some palace hallway.

"Ready?" he asks. It doesn't sound like a question.

I am not remotely ready. I came to Wintour with my family, with my best friend. My future was laid out neatly, the rest of my life prescribed into a series of events with little room for deviation. It wasn't exciting, but I was safe. Now? I'm stepping into a portal with no idea where I'm going, with a man who might be ordered to kill me later.

I already miss *safe*.

But I nod and take a small step toward the pool of light circling the ground that leads to my uncertain future.

Or a trap. These days, a girl can't be sure. Not with assassins prowling the palace.

"You go first," I blurt out.

Bishop shoulders his pack higher and scowls. "And trust that you're going to follow?"

"And where would I go? Worried I'll track down those assassins and offer my head on a platter?" I twist my fingers, darting glances at the shimmering portal. A regular postern is bad enough. I can't imagine what one that appeared one minute ago will feel like. And then there's the question of whether or not it's even stable. "Just . . . go first."

He draws a breath, then shakes a finger at me. "Don't make me come back here after you," he warns.

I cross two lines over my racing heart.

Bishop hesitates for only a moment—like he's questioning his own sanity—and then he steps through the postern. One second, he's there, and the next, I'm standing alone in the carriage house. It's a testament to my hatred of posterns that I consider marching back to throw myself at the mercy of Queen Selestina. Assassins be damned. But I don't doubt Bishop will keep his word and return just to drag me away.

It's better to do it on my own terms. I close my eyes, count to three, and step into the shimmering ring.

Mottled light burns my eyelids as a wave of cold blasts up from the ground. The sensation hits like shards of ice, stabbing through my skin to the bone. I clamp my mouth shut to stop my teeth from chattering *and* keep my breakfast from making an encore appearance.

I force myself to look at where I'm going as a thousand needles of light prickle my eyes. I'm blinking through tears when I stumble forward, my foot catching on nothing, and suddenly I'm falling into the roaring silence of the void. A scream lodges in my throat, unable to escape in this strange bottomless nothing. I collide with something solid on the other side, careening to the ground as I realize it's Bishop. Something splashes my hands and shirt, and he curses underneath me as he shifts.

Strong arms haul me upright, Bishop's grip almost bruising, but I'm too busy trying to reassemble my insides to care. The world spins once, then twice, before clicking into focus.

Bishop is *covered* in mud. It's splattered across his coat, sword sheaths, hands, neck—even his hair. He flicks some off his hands, glaring at the sodden puddle of dirt underneath us, and despite the nausea still churning in my belly, something far more dangerous bubbles in my throat. I barely hold back a giggle. If he doesn't want to kill me for sending him into that muck, he might if I laugh at him.

I stagger a step, but Bishop catches me again, keeping me from face-planting into a half-rotten log.

"Give yourself a second." He grimaces at his ruined clothing but doesn't release me again.

For once, I don't argue. I sway, the ground still rocking beneath my feet.

"It's not as smooth as your typical postern," he admits. Concern flickers in his eyes and vanishes in an instant. "But it's effective."

"Effective for what?" My mouth is so dry that the words try to stick to my tongue. "Making me vomit?" I step free of him.

He hovers like he doubts I'll stay upright before he finally drops his pack on the log. "A little discomfort is better than finding a knife in your back."

I question his metrics, but I brush dirt off my knees and finally take a better look around. "Where are we?"

We're standing in a clearing surrounded by oak trees, their branches already disrobing for the coming winter. The damp scent of rain hangs in the air as the wind catches piles of ruby leaves and sends them scattering. I listen for signs of life, but there's nothing beyond the faint rustling sounds of autumn. A few feet away, the portable postern—now just a dull black disc—sits abandoned on a patch of grass.

"Just outside the southern border of Florentia, near the Stygia Mountains," Bishop says, gesturing with his chin. I follow his gaze to a range in the near distance. The mountains are a jagged line of darkness against the horizon, their white-capped peaks piercing through a heavy shroud of mist. The forest blocks a direct path to them, and there are no roads, no houses, no hint of life except for the slow, predatory circling of a large bird overhead.

I shiver despite the thick wool of my borrowed coat. "So, we traveled to the middle of nowhere? We couldn't have chosen somewhere with a roof?" I ask, trying to wipe the lingering mud off my hands. "Or a bath?"

"Nowhere equals no one," he says, like it's no problem that everything from his clothes to his hair is covered in mud, too. He just walks over to the postern and kneels, running his gloved finger over it until the portal retracts back into a disc the size of a coin, then picks it up and pockets it. "It's not powerful enough to take us very far without replenishing its magic, and it's safer to avoid any cities."

He's right, but I cross my arms, fingers digging into my ribs for warmth. "You just happen to know the setting to use on your secret escape hatch that leads to places like this?"

He looks up, face utterly unreadable. "It's my job."

"I thought your job was to protect the kingdom." The words are out before I can stop them. My heart gallops in my chest, but I force myself to keep my chin up, to meet his wolfish stare head-on. "Not sneak around it."

He stands, wiping his hands on the small patch of his pants that didn't get ruined. "Stealth is considered an asset by Order Marius. It got you out safely, didn't it?"

"You have to have better things to do than be stuck escorting me to . . ." I trail away, hoping he'll take the bait and tell me where we're going.

"Maybe I do." He almost smiles. "Or maybe I just enjoy your company."

I can't help snorting. "That's the worst lie I've heard in days, and I've been surrounded by patrons."

I expect him to snap back. Maybe give me one of his signature growls. He's a patron, after all. But he shrugs. "You don't know me well enough to judge my lies, Lady Icaros."

Truth and a warning wrapped in one. I should probably heed both, but it's the use of my family name that sticks. I clear my throat. "Arden," I correct him. "Please call me Arden."

"Arden," he repeats with a nod.

Our eyes lock, and warmth floods through me, pooling somewhere low and unwelcome. I don't need Bishop Marius to understand me. I certainly don't want him to be kind to me. Not when I can't risk letting my guard down. I turn away from him, the sudden heat dissipating just as quickly in the cool air, and scan our surroundings, cataloging the features of the clearing enclosed by woods: a tangle of brambles at the base of a nearby tree, a shallow dip in the earth where rainwater collects, a half-collapsed cairn that looks old enough to be a relic of the Last War. There's no shelter apart from the trees.

"How long do we have to stay here?" Not that I'm eager to take the postern again.

"It only holds enough magic for one trip." Bishop's tone is flat. "It needs to draw power from the stars for another, but it should be ready again by dawn." He crouches beside his pack, extracting a canteen and a tightly rolled blanket from its main compartment.

A night alone in the woods with Bishop sounds about as appealing as smashing my face into one of the cairn's loose rocks.

"We'll camp here tonight." Bishop tosses the blanket at me.

I catch it on reflex. The wool is stiff and scratchy, but it will keep me warm.

He pulls out a knife—one of a dozen, I'm sure—and bits of rope and wire. "I'll set up some snares and try to catch us dinner."

My stomach rumbles at the reminder that I haven't eaten since nearly dawn. Out here, the flaky, butter-soaked pastries feel like a lifetime ago. "Can I help?"

"Gather some branches, logs if you can find them. We'll need them for the fire."

I set to work. Not because I'm enthusiastic about our plan, but because I understand this. Working. Doing. Moving. I might prefer four walls at the end of the day, but I'm not afraid of doing what it takes to survive.

Bishop and I fall into silence as we carry out our tasks. He doesn't comment when I drag a large fallen branch into the clearing, dig around in the pack for a small axe, and begin hacking it into firewood. He disappears deeper into the woods, always returning just when I'm beginning to worry that he won't. By the time the sun drifts halfway to the horizon, I'm coated in sweat and grime, but I've gathered enough wood to last us through the night.

"Anything else?" I ask, plucking at the bits of dried leaves caught in my hair.

"There's a lake about a hundred yards past that tree." He jerks his thumb toward an oak on the far edge of the clearing, a foot-worn trail leading through the undergrowth past it. "Wash off and try not to drown."

"You're not *that* lucky."

He grunts. Or maybe it's a laugh.

"And stick close to the path to avoid the wolves," he adds, then goes back to work.

I stare down at him. "*Wolves?* Please tell me you're joking."

"I don't joke about things that could kill me." He doesn't stop what he's doing. "Don't go too deep into the woods, and they'll probably leave you alone."

"Probably?" I choke on the word and still don't move. "Are you sure there's not a village nearby? I grew up in the country. I can blend in."

His look is long and slow. "No, you can't."

"What does that mean?" Heat rushes to my cheeks, and I plant my hands on my hips. "Florentia is Leontian territory. Surely they don't want to kill me."

"You're a target, even here. You could hide under a cloak, charm the pants off every local villager, and I guarantee that within an hour, even in Florentia, someone would be trying to sell your location to the highest bidder."

And the highest bidders are probably the ones who paid those assassins.

I want to argue, but the words die in my mouth. Maybe he's right. I was in the capital city for less than a week and managed to piss off the entire power structure of Antares. I guess I'm not great at winning others over.

But right now, I'm not sure if I'd rather face the wolves or paranoid villagers.

"Interesting," he mutters, mostly to himself.

My eyes narrow. "What?"

"I didn't take you for a coward." He shrugs. "If you're too afraid . . ."

I'm halfway to the tree before I realize he's won this round. I hesitate, slowly coming to a stop.

"Problem?" he calls from behind me.

I stomp along the trail without looking back.

"Lake" is an overstatement. It's little more than a depression in the land. The glassy black water is choked with reeds, and insects buzz around the shore despite the crisp autumn air. In two months' time, the surface will probably be frozen solid. Florentia is still northern enough to experience a true winter. I kneel at the lake's edge and splash my face with the cool water. The late-afternoon sun is warm enough that I strip off my thick shirt and wash up, scrubbing at the dried mud caked on my palms and under my fingernails. The water ripples slightly with the movement of small white fish, but even with the distortion, the surface is dark enough to reflect my face. To reflect the mark on my chest that seems to glow red even days later.

A twig snaps behind me, and I jerk upright, nearly falling into the lake. Bishop laughs. I grab my shirt, clutching it to my chest as I turn to find him standing with folded arms at the edge of the clearing. The sun burns a halo through the trees behind him.

"Done daydreaming at your reflection?" Bishop asks.

I wrench my shirt back on. "I wasn't daydreaming."

"Then can I take a turn?" He nods to the lake. He's still covered in mud from me crashing into him, his normally silver-blond hair a mess of brown clumps at the ends.

"Be my guest." I scramble to my feet.

Bishop doesn't move closer, and I realize he's waiting for me to leave. Apparently, only one of us gets the privilege of modesty.

My stomach grumbles again. "Did you catch anything?"

"You can check. I set the snares about twenty paces from the edge of the clearing." He looks back at the trees. "Sorry, I forgot that you're too scared to go into the woods."

My throat tightens as I picture teeth flashing in the dark. For one treacherous second, I almost say I'll wait. Almost let him *protect* me. But he smirks, and pride sinks its claws deeper than fear ever could.

"Fine." I hold out my hand. "Give me a knife in case there's something in the traps."

He winces, squinting slightly in the afternoon sun. "Are you sure that's a good idea?"

Of course he won't arm me. "Never mind. I'll take care of it myself."

"Look," he starts. "Let me know if you find something, and I'll come to—"

But I'm already stalking toward the tree line, ignoring the rest of his instructions. Stepping into the trees feels like walking into a mouth that might snap shut. My breath shortens, palms slicking with sweat. But I refuse to turn back and let him think he's right about me.

The snares are empty, except for one. It's been sprung, but whatever was caught chewed its own leg off to escape. I stare at the bloody tuft of fur for a second. The creature will still die, and I'll go hungry. A thin blood trail leads away, and I follow it, ignoring the tingle of warning that grows with each step I take deeper into the woods, the need for food winning out over my fear.

But there's no animal at the end of the trail. The blood simply stops. I'm still looking for where I went wrong when leaves rustle behind me. I whirl toward the sound, my heart slamming hard enough it might crack my ribs. A form explodes through the underbrush, branches snapping as something heavy barrels between the trees. Why the fuck didn't I demand that knife?

I stumble back a few steps, tripping over a fallen branch as the crashing sounds grow closer. Shoving myself to my feet, I run toward the dappled light breaking through clustered trunks. I burst past them, boots skidding on fallen leaves as I reach Bishop. He's washing up in the lake, back turned to me and his tunic and armor on a rock nearby. I force enough air into my burning lungs to yell, "Wolf!"

He startles, water flying around him as he moves with the instinct of a warrior toward me. He looks larger stripped of his coat and armor, all hard lines and power, like nothing about him is meant to yield. The sun is lower on the horizon now, turning the water to molten gold, and the light catches on a network of scars on his chest. The sight of them makes me freeze, makes me forget why I'm running.

No. Scars don't look like this.

These lines and patterns connect and intersect, shimmering like the starlight of a patron's birthright.

"Do you mind?" he snarls.

I turn quickly away as he snatches up his tunic. Void swallow me. He caught me staring. He probably thought . . .

I resist the urge to look at the marks again as he yanks on his shirt.

I don't know why I'm so rattled. I've seen a man before—but never one marked like that. As if every line on his chest is a record of something survived, and the sum of them is a story I can't begin to understand.

"Stay here," he orders.

My eyes fly open to find him prowling toward the woods in his pants, his now slightly damp shirt and gloves on again, holding his sheath.

"You're not actually going after it!"

But he pulls out his sword, tossing the sheath to me. "Will you sleep tonight if I don't?"

He stalks through the trees, not waiting for an answer. I drop the sheath next to the coat he's left behind, and, against all reason and common sense, follow him. "Bishop, let's just find a village. Take our chances."

Turning toward me, he tucks his sword behind his right arm. "Trust me. It's safer to face the wolves."

The sound erupts again, the crashing closer this time. The footfalls are frantic and uneven. Bishop's sword slices through the air in an elegant arc as he spins toward the sound. He raises it at the approaching predator as a white-spotted fawn ambles from behind a tree and freezes.

Bishop lowers his sword slowly. "That," he says flatly, "is a deer."

"I know what it is," I say through gritted teeth, cheeks already burning.

But he's still glaring at me. "You screamed *wolf* like we were about to be torn apart."

"I thought we were!"

"It has spots, Arden."

"Forgive me for not pausing to inspect its coat while it was charging at me!"

His jaw tightens. "If you're going to panic every time a leaf rustles, you're going to get us both killed."

"Oh, I'm sorry," I grit out. "Next time, I'll let whatever it is chew on me first, so I don't inconvenience you."

I turn on my heel and march back into the trees, jaw clenched to keep my humiliation from turning into tears that I refuse to let him see.

I rest against a tree, trying to keep myself together.

A soft, choked noise comes from ahead. I push off the trunk and creep forward, afraid to startle potential game. A small, gray rabbit is caught in a snare, its paw twisted at an unnatural angle. It's still alive, twitching as it struggles to free its trapped leg.

I crouch beside it and run my hand gently over its fur, whispering the way I used to when Andry came with me to slaughter dinner.

"It's okay," I say, stroking it. "Let me help you." It settles a little, although I feel its tiny heart beating a frantic rhythm.

I break its neck as cleanly as I can, then carry it back to camp. Bishop is waiting by a pile of logs, sharpening his knife. He looks up when I arrive, anger lingering in his eyes. I toss the dead rabbit at his feet. He blinks as he lifts it by the ears to inspect my handiwork.

"You broke its neck," he says, turning it in his hands. "Most people couldn't do that."

I brush my palms on my thighs, ignoring the dip in my stomach. "I'm not most people."

"No, you aren't." He studies me long enough that my heart jumps. I swallow, and he tears his attention away, slicing the pelt open with two quick flicks of the knife. He guts the rabbit, hands moving with practiced indifference.

I'm not letting him off the hook so easily. "You aren't surprised after I ran from a wolf?"

"You ran from a deer." He tosses the entrails onto the logs.

I cross my arms. "I thought it was a wolf."

He mutters something I can't hear, then says, "At least you have some survival instinct. But to answer your question. No, I'm not surprised."

"But I didn't kill that oscen."

"You weren't hungry then." He laughs. The sound is as brief and sharp as the knife in his hands. "Mercy is a privilege the starving can't afford." He spears the carcass on a stick and holds it out to me. "I'll start the fire."

I glance at the sky darkening overhead. Clouds roll across the rapidly setting sun, a heavy dampness thickening the air. "It's going to rain."

"It won't be more than a drizzle," he says, continuing to brace logs as the first misty drops hit my skin.

Without a fire, cooking might be a privilege we can't afford, either.

But instead of a match, Bishop traces a nochtimetric pattern in the dirt with a stick. Nothing happens, and he curses, erasing the lines with the toe of his boot. I don't know what he expects from damp soil. But when he draws it again, the lines flare blue, then white, and the wood bursts into flames even as the rain picks up a little.

"How?" I lean to study the markings.

"Military grade," he explains. "Burns in any weather, but it can take a few tries. The magic is tricky but necessary. You'll understand when we reach Vennaro."

The name lands like a stone in my stomach. "That's where we're going?"

We're already on the border of Florentia, close to the Stygia Mountains. I'm not sure why it didn't occur to me that he's taking me there.

"It's the only place no one will dare come after you."

But I snort. "Easy for you to say when you're not the one being hunted."

His eyes flash. "You think I've never been hunted?" For a moment, we just stare at each other until he adds, "You'll be safe there."

Because it's his territory. The only way inside Vennaro—if you weren't born there—is to volunteer for military service. The region is nearly impossible to reach from most of Antares due to the deadliness of the mountains. Its coast is fortified with Marius strongholds to deter any threat coming from the Baron Sea. And then there are the troops, trained like soldiers but guarding the territory like they're little more than packs of the wolves embroidered on their uniforms. There will be no mercy for anyone who trespasses on his land.

I stare at the flames, watching the fat pop and sizzle as the rabbit roasts. "Have you ever had the privilege of mercy?" I ask him quietly.

He's silent for so long I think he's going to ignore me. Then: "Once."

I wait, but that's all he gives me.

"Let me guess, you let the mosquitoes bite you at the lake," I say, rolling my eyes, "without swatting them."

"When I stopped hunting down the man who killed my parents and brother." He doesn't look at me, but there's a rawness in his voice that tells me the grief is still there.

And now I feel like the asshole.

"Any other questions?" he adds quietly.

Not about that. But if I don't get some answers, I'll be killed, too.

"Why does everyone want me dead?" I ask, finally working up the courage. "What changed since the council meeting?"

"Everything," he says.

Well, no shit. I grind my teeth and try again.

"Look, I'm sure people hunt you all the time, but it's new to me. So, I've got a few questions. Like what the seven hells this mark means." I thump my chest for emphasis. "It's not even doing anything yet. I don't feel any different than before. I need—"

"I know exactly what you need," he interrupts. "You want to know what happens when your magic awakens." He pauses. "So does everyone hunting you. That's why I'm taking you somewhere you might find the answers."

My eyes widen. Was that really so hard for him to share?

Apparently so, because he doesn't add more. I debate needling him until he tells me what he thinks it all means, but my shoulders sag with fatigue. Tomorrow is soon enough to face how fucked I really am.

We split up the rabbit, devouring it in silence as night falls. The moon is lost behind a bank of clouds, but the stars are bright enough to burn holes in the night.

Bishop rolls his shoulders. "Get some sleep. We'll leave at sunrise."

But I stay by the fire a little longer, watching the flames eat through the last of the wood.

Maybe Vennaro is where this ends. Maybe it's where I finally learn why Bishop Marius is helping me. Or maybe it's where I disappear forever, leaving nothing behind but rumors and whispers. Either way my magic is still sleeping like it has all the time in the world, even if I don't.

I glance at Bishop, but for once he isn't watching me. He just sits staring into the distance like he's alone. Like I'm not right next to him. He doesn't move when I finally climb under the blanket.

If I were braver, I'd ask what happened to him. I'd ask about the patterns on his skin, the book he stole, the things he doesn't say.

But I don't. I stare up at the star burning brightly at the center of the Night's Scar.

I close my eyes, listening to the fire crackle and wind sing through the trees. I wait for sleep to drag me under. When it doesn't, I whisper to the night, "Are you really going to keep me safe?"

"I don't break my word."

For the first time, I believe him.

But that doesn't mean I trust him.

ELEVEN

The sky is still dark when I wake to Bishop organizing his pack, and I'm immediately certain my toes are going to snap off from cold. The fire from last night is little more than a blackened ring in the dirt, wisps of smoke crawling up to nothing. Even the embers look tired.

I sit up and flex, wincing as pins and needles stab the soles of my feet. "Did you pick the coldest camping spot in Antares?"

Bishop doesn't look over. "You're alive, aren't you?"

"Debatable," I mutter, dragging myself upright. My hair actually crunches when I touch it. The air nips at any exposed skin, and I wrap the blanket around me tightly. I'd kill for a cup of something hot—even the herbal tea from home that tastes like boiled weeds and regret.

Bishop digs into his coat and pulls out an astrolabe, its brass rings faintly humming. He twists it until it silences.

"Not now." He mutters a few curses that tell me exactly how he feels about the device and drops it into his pack. He roots around for a minute, then stands and tosses me the last bit of rabbit that we left on the fire overnight. "Eat."

It's practically jerky now, dry and smoky, but I'm too hungry to complain. I hate how quickly it disappears.

The postern's lines glow faintly when Bishop picks it up and studies it. "It's powered up just enough. We'll need to be quick."

"Wonderful," I say, dread pooling in my belly as I realize there's something I hate more than posterns. Half-powered posterns.

Bishop traces a pattern over the disc with a gloved finger. Lines glow under his touch, forming a constellation.

"What about Velesont?" I ask in a quieter voice. "Will they know if I go through this?"

"Yes, but that's the point." He draws another smaller pattern, and the postern flickers with soft blue light. "They'll know exactly where you are. No other order will dare breach Vennaro. Stay put, and you'll be safe."

"Is that a threat or a promise?"

He actually considers. "Why not both?"

Safe as long as I stay where he wants me. I cross my arms to hide the tremor in my hands. "Fine. After you."

But safety also means I'll be able to figure out what the hell is going on.

He vanishes into the ring of blue light as soon as his boots hit the postern's threshold. I grit my teeth and brace for that gut-emptying cold, but this time I manage not to stumble, reaching out to rest a hand on a nearby wall. We've travelled to a room. I take a single step into it, and the swirling light fades, erasing all signs of the postern save for the slightest trace of an arch. It blends into the wall so well, I can barely tell where it is now.

The air inside is warm, the rug thick beneath my feet, and straight ahead is a hearth so massive I could walk into the fire and not touch either side. Mismatched chairs are scattered about, some so tall they look like thrones, others squat and inviting. A long oak table looks comfortable but regal. Ceiling beams arch overhead like wooden ribs, and the windows are barred with iron so that only the fading twilight can get through. The room sprawls wider than my family's entire estate. The horned wolf is everywhere—in the woodwork, on the banners, even carved into the mantel. Despite the size, the room feels lived in, not imposing. The scent of woodsmoke and the hissing of the fire are our only welcoming party.

Bishop shakes off his coat, then picks up the coin-sized disc again, and his shoulders relax. He looks around, and I catch a flicker of relief crossing his face.

He strides to the hearth and throws another log onto the fire while I stand slack-jawed.

"Is this your house?"

He shrugs. "My family's."

"You just . . . brought me to your actual house?"

First his quarters. Now this? Bishop has no boundaries.

"Is that a problem?" He lifts a brow like I should have figured this out already. "You're safer here than anywhere else."

"I'm surprised you trust me," I admit.

"Trust?" He chuckles, shaking his head slightly. "Let's not go that far. Should I be concerned you're going to burn the place down?"

I glare at him, but my adrenaline is already dropping, replaced by exhaustion and something dangerously close to gratitude.

I'm in the heart of his world, and he's the only thing standing between me and everyone who wants me dead.

It's a terrifying kind of safety.

A woman barrels into the great room like a force of nature. She's plump, with cheeks as round as apples and nearly as red. Her gray-streaked hair is tied back with a blue scarf, and her apron is dusted with so much flour, it looks like she wrestled a bag of it and lost.

Her eyes land on me, and her mouth forms a perfect *O*. She swings an accusing look at Bishop. "Oh, for the love of Stars, why didn't you tell me you were bringing a guest?" she says, hands on hips. "I don't have supper prepared."

He shoves his hands in his pockets. "You always have enough food around for a battalion, Lenora. I didn't think you'd mind." He looks at me. "Lenora keeps everything from falling apart."

"I'm just the housekeeper," she says, rolling her eyes, but I can see she's pleased by his flattery. She shakes a finger at him. "What's done is done. But one of these days . . ."

Bishop has the sense to look sheepish.

Lenora turns to me, her appraisal quick but thorough. "You look like you've walked through the gates of all seven hells. Come, come, let's get you situated. I'm sure I can scare up something to eat."

She steers me to a chair near the hearth, grabbing a thick woolen blanket on the way. Wrapping it around my shoulders, she tucks it under my chin as if I'm a child. I let her fuss, too tired to resist.

Bishop leans against the mantel, watching the scene with a blank expression.

She whirls and points at him. "Don't just stand there like a statue. Wash your hands and come help me fetch some food."

He makes a faint sound—almost a groan—then pushes away from the fireplace and disappears through a side door.

Lenora's eyes crinkle as she smiles at me. "He knows better. Sometimes he just needs a swift kick to the . . . well, you know. What's your name, dear?"

I hesitate. "Arden," I say. "Arden Icaros."

The name hangs in the air like a lie, but Lenora only squints like she's trying to get a better look at me. "An Icaros, huh? He's not brought an Icaros home before. Well, welcome to Miradores. The only thing you need to worry about in this house is eating too much."

"I don't think that's possible." My stomach is already grumbling at the promise of food.

She gives my arm an approving squeeze before heading for the kitchen, singing under her breath. *"Black wing, black wing, don't beat so fast . . ."*

The tune is familiar, like something my mother used to hum, and an ache grows in my chest.

"The night is long, the die is cast . . ."

Maybe all caregivers' songs sound the same when they're putting the world back in order.

I settle into the chair, lulled toward sleep by the soothing song. But when Bishop returns carrying a large tray, he's not alone.

TWELVE

So much for a moment of peace. Bishop's knights from Wintour are already here. Clearly, they used more efficient means of travel, and *I* haven't even caught my breath. I start to drop the blanket Lenora wrapped around me but think better of it. They weren't huddled in the woods freezing their asses off an hour ago.

Bishop deposits the tray on the table, and I shuffle over, still wrapped in the blanket, to study the small feast Lenora scrounged up: several cheeses, some fruit, a bowl of olives, and a basket of split-top rolls with a plate of freshly churned butter beside them. Given my current level of anxiety, my first impulse is to dive into the rolls and eat until my stomach explodes. I drop into a chair and reach for the bread.

Lenora reappears with two mugs of steaming coffee. She sets one in front of me. "Would you like cream?"

But I'm already gulping it down, ignoring how it scorches my throat. Lenora glances at Bishop, but he just shrugs. So much for manners. One day in the wild, and I'm acting like an animal.

"Can I get some?" Taliesin asks her, still watching me.

"Get it yourself," Vessica says and tosses her long braids over her shoulder.

But Lenora waves a hand. "Of course. I'll be right back."

I put down my cup and glance around, realizing the estate is awfully quiet. "No other staff?"

Bishop shrugs. "Fewer people, fewer problems. I don't need coddling."

"Don't listen to him. He could use some coddling," Taliesin says, popping an olive into his mouth and talking around the pit. "He's getting grumpy in his solitude."

"And yet, the more company you keep, the more trouble you get in." Bishop swipes the bowl of olives from him.

Vessica watches them with wary eyes, like she's tracking two wolves circling a fresh kill. But Taliesin grins before spitting the olive pit with remarkable accuracy into a little silver dish by his elbow. "We haven't been properly introduced yet."

Like I'd forget someone who gleefully lured assassins away on my behalf. "Taliesin, right?"

"You remember." His smile widens. "But everyone calls me Sin."

Vessica shakes her head. "No one calls him Sin," she says to me before turning on him. "Stop trying to make that happen."

"I'm not a quitter." Taliesin winks at me.

I can't help laughing, even though it feels reckless when half the world wants me dead.

"And stop flirting," Bishop says, the blade of his knife flashing in the firelight as he cuts a hunk of cheese. "You aren't as charming as you think you are."

Taliesin claps a hand over his heart. "I am trying to lift her spirits." He slings his feet off the chair and shoves his thick blond hair out of his eyes as he leans forward, elbows on the table. "How are you doing, Lady Icaros? Need company? I can be bathed, powdered, and sent to your room."

I nearly choke on my roll.

"Smooth." Vessica rolls her eyes and settles into a tall chair across from me. "Bishop is right about your charms."

Taliesin ignores them, his gaze still pinned on me, and lifts his brows like he genuinely wants an answer. I'm not sure what he expects. For me to spill my soul to him? Maybe to cry? Crack a joke? Actually consider sleeping with him?

He's definitely good-looking—and knows it. The scars on the side of his face only add a roguishness to his questionable charm. He even looks roughly the same size as Bishop, which is also impressive. But I'd rather focus on not dying than him, no matter how much he flirts.

"Leave her be," Bishop says in a quiet voice. "She just got here. Stop picking at her like she's carrion."

I force myself to finish the roll as slowly and delicately as possible. Then

I pile cheese and fruit onto my plate. I swallow and smile at Lenora when she delivers a pot of coffee and more cups. "Thank you for the food, Lenora. Bishop's a lousy hunter."

Taliesin cackles, smacking his knee as he leans back in his chair again.

"That's what I get for sharing my rabbit," Bishop mutters, picking at our impromptu luncheon. Considering he's twice my size, I'd expect him to be hungrier.

Lenora must have read my mind, because she scolds him. "You need to eat."

"I'm fine." He points at the cheese still sitting on his plate.

Lenora shakes her head. "Don't come sneaking into my kitchen when you're hungry later."

"I won't," he promises. "I'm going to Ardermare on business tonight. Your kitchen is safe."

She frowns at this news as she pours more coffee into our mugs.

Bishop is leaving town so soon? Curiosity flares in my chest. "Where are you going?"

"The king's assassin needs to be brought to justice." He crosses his arms, still not bothering to eat.

"We'll catch them," Vessica adds in a somber tone.

But Taliesin only grimaces. "Will we? Whoever it is got in and out of the palace undetected."

I butter another roll, hoping they've forgotten I'm here and will keep talking. I might actually learn something. Maybe if the king's killer is caught, and it's not an omen of war, the rumors that I'm some harbinger will die down and people will leave me alone. Or stop hiring assassins.

"Most of the troops think it's a heart collector," Vessica says.

I drop the roll. It splatters butter-side down on the table.

The others look at me. Bishop blinks and returns his attention to his friends. "Most of the troops are superstitious fools."

"So, there's really no such thing as a heart collector?" I ask despite my better judgment. He made his thoughts clear at the palace.

But Bishop still meets my gaze. "No."

Liar. It's an instinct that I can't explain, but the look Taliesin and Vessica share confirms it.

I stare at my roll, my appetite gone. What does he gain by lying? It doesn't make sense. Then again, not much about Bishop makes sense.

"And the rest of them think your guest of honor did it," Vessica continues to Bishop.

But she's talking about me. If news has already reached here . . .

I look to Bishop again, but when our eyes meet, something dark flashes in his before he looks away.

"That's enough," Lenora announces and beckons me to stand. "Let me show you to your room. You need to rest. I'll bring up some proper clothes while you have a bath." She shakes her head at Bishop. "Making a lady wear clothing meant for a soldier."

He leans back in his chair, amusement tugging the corners of his lips. "My mother wore the same."

"I don't mind," I say. Although the idea of something clean is tempting. "I don't want to cause trouble."

"Since when?" Bishop asks, earning a swat to the back of the head from Lenora.

"I'm sure that if she caused you any trouble, you asked for it," she says, but her eyes gleam as she leads me toward the hallway.

"Not the western wing," Bishop calls after us.

Lenora sighs, grumbling under her breath. "Off-limits."

We're just out of the great room when I hear Taliesin say, "She's feisty. Maybe you're wrong."

"Without him, she'd be dead in a week," Vessica says flatly. "I wouldn't put it past Calix to come after her, even here."

"That would start a war," Taliesin replies, not sounding the least bit perturbed. "Maybe she *is* the harbinger."

He says it like I'm a fuse that's already been lit.

"Come along, Lady Icaros." Lenora ushers me away before I can hear Bishop's response.

"Arden," I correct her. Hearing my family name is too painful, even if I'd rather be Arden Icaros than whatever the Stars chose for me. "If you don't mind."

"Of course, Arden," she says softly.

Lenora points out every room we pass, her pride evident. "That's the library. Don't let him catch you in there after dark; he's particular about his books. I don't even bother going in there anymore."

I take note of its double doors. Libraries hold answers. It's worth checking out.

"The armory's down there." She nods to an iron-barred door. "If you need anything sharper than a kitchen knife, just ask."

I sincerely doubt Bishop plans to arm me, but I nod. It never hurts to know where to find a sword.

Lenora continues cheerfully. "Oh, and the music room is by the front door, not that anyone uses the piano since . . . Well, it's been too long. Do you play?"

"No." There was never time for lessons.

We climb a grand staircase that empties into a long, narrow gallery where the windows change from stained glass to something else—clear but with lines etched into the surface. At first, I think it's decorative, but then I see the patterns. Nochtimetry.

I trace a finger along the windowsill as we pass. "These are wards."

"Miradores is full of them." She nods. "This house is built to withstand a siege. Or worse."

What could be worse than a siege? I'm not about to ask.

She moves on, but I linger to study the lines. The entire estate is beautiful but also intimidating—and the nochtimetry feels like it's there to keep people in as much as out. I'm not sure which applies to me.

When I catch up, Lenora is waiting in front of a heavy wooden door. She opens it and ushers me inside.

It's at least twice the size of my bedroom in Damalis. My heart squeezes at the thought of my old home, but I ignore it. Painted pale blue, the suite is feminine in a way that's at odds with the rest of the estate. The bed's canopy is trimmed with lace. Perfume bottles rest on the desk, and a low settee waits near the fireplace.

Lenora heads straight to the claw-foot tub in the attached bathing chamber and starts the water. Its brass tap is shaped like a wolf's head, the horns labeled *hot* and *cold*. Towels are stacked on a stool next to it along with a basket of soaps wrapped in paper and tied with silk ribbons. The floor is tiled in moonstone that catches the light of a gold leaf chandelier.

"This is a very . . . nice room," I say, failing to come up with a better word.

"It was decorated when one of the princesses visited decades ago." Her brow furrows like she's trying to remember which one as she starts tidying the already neat room. "We used to host guests all the time. Now we only entertain on Twelvetide, but I try to keep it up. Just in case."

"In case Bishop shows up with a woman?" I ask, gliding my hands down one of the bed's smooth posters.

"In case someone needs it." She tugs at a corner of the duvet that's wrinkled. "It's been quiet since the tragedy."

"Oh?" I try to sound casual, even though Lenora keeps piquing my curiosity.

But she forces a smile. "I wouldn't have dreamed of Bishop showing up with a lady. I suppose anything can happen."

Indeed.

"There's a view of the gardens." She fluffs one of the many pillows on the bed.

I wander to the window and pull the curtain aside for a better look. There's enough light left to see the garden is a riot of tangled branches and dead leaves. Vines have seized control, creeping across the path and winding around a moss-covered fountain.

"It's a little wild." Lenora moves beside me, sighing. "No one's tended it in a spell. My knees don't appreciate all the stooping."

"There's no gardener, either?" An estate this size with the wealth of Order Marius should have more than one.

"Bishop prefers his privacy."

The lack of household staff doesn't make sense, *unless* my family isn't the only patron line struggling. It's hard to imagine the king wouldn't reward Marius better for their service. Then again, he's ignored our troubles for years.

"And Lord Marius is gone half the time. He's always traipsing to some far corner of the world for Stars-know-what reason." Lenora shakes her head like she can't fathom the idea of travel. She plants her hands on her hips and surveys the room for anything she's missed. "I'll bring up some fresh clothing. There's paper in the desk in case you want to write home." She pauses. "Will you be staying long?"

I bite my lip. "I'm not sure."

She nods as if that's answer enough. "If you need anything, just ring," she says, pointing to the old-fashioned bell cord by the fireplace. "I'll find what I can for you to wear and leave it in the wardrobe. I'm afraid it will be out of fashion. You'll have to go into Wolf's Keep for the rest."

"Wolf's Keep?" Just the name sends a shiver down my spine.

"The village." She nods toward the bathing chamber, where the tub is still filling up. "Enjoy your bath. I'll leave those clothes for you."

But after she's gone, I rest my forehead against the window, the glass fogging under my breath. The garden is beautiful in a ruined sort of way, clinging to life even in the midst of so much death.

This place is full of secrets. I can feel them pressing in, crowding out the silence. But mostly, the house feels lonely, as if even the walls would trade their ghosts for company. I thought Bishop had a secret before. Now I'm sure. I don't know why, but I'm certain that secret is somehow connected to why he's protecting me. This is where he's hiding it, and I'm going to find out what it is.

My life depends on it.

THIRTEEN

A storm wakes me at midnight, rattling the windowpanes and sending flashes of light skittering across the ceiling. Between the wind and rain pelting the house, sleep feels impossible. I pull the quilt to my chin and lie there, willing myself back to blissful unconsciousness, but every roll of thunder drives me further from it. Eventually, I give up and shove the covers aside. The fire in the room's hearth has dwindled to embers, and I grab a crocheted shawl from my stack of new clothes, shivering.

The hallway outside my room is even colder, the old stone floors like ice under the thin soles of my borrowed slippers. I listen for any sign someone else is awake, but there's nothing except the howling wind.

My fingers trail the wooden banisters as I tiptoe down the stairs, my eyes never leaving the head of a horned wolf mounted above the landing.

Miradores feels like a labyrinth in the dark. Each wrong turn leads to some cold, windowless passage and a dead end or down a narrow staircase that I swear doubles back out of spite. Finally, I find my way to the great room.

The kitchen beyond the swinging door is empty, but there's a candle stub burning in a lantern, wax puddled around its base. It's just enough light to allow me to search for something to eat. I settle on a heel of bread and a wedge of pale cheese, afraid to upend Lenora's breakfast plans. I nibble at them, watching as lightning splits the sky and casts monstrous shadows in the overgrown garden.

Another flash illuminates the grounds, and for a split second, I see two figures. My heart jumps into my throat, and I back away, nearly dropping the last bit of cheese. I sink into a shadowy nook, eyes never leaving the window as I wait for another lightning strike. I'm not sure I want to know who—or *what*—is out there. But when the next one comes, the garden is empty.

Now I'm seeing things. Because this week couldn't get any better.

The back door creaks open.

". . . not as simple as you think," Bishop says, shaking rain from his hair.

Taliesin follows him inside. "If she's the harbinger, it's *exactly* that simple."

I push myself flatter against the wall. I could show myself. It's not like eating cheese at midnight is a crime. But they're talking about me, so I stay where I am to hear more.

Do these people have nothing better to talk about than me?

They pause long enough that I'm sure they've heard me. My heart hammers against my ribs until I hear the wet squelch of muddy boots being pulled off.

"I hate to say it, but if what's written is—" Taliesin continues.

"Don't finish that thought." Bishop's voice is quieter now, like he doesn't want anyone to hear, not even the walls.

But Taliesin sighs. "You're the one who dragged her here. Lied for her."

"I didn't lie," Bishop says. "I kept her alive."

"Was that the wisest course of action? Because now she's here."

"That's my problem."

Something heavy lands on the prep table with a dull *thud*, followed by the scraping of chair legs on stone.

Fantastic. They're getting comfortable. How many times can I get stuck in a dark corner hiding from Bishop Marius?

"Do you want a bandage for that?" Taliesin asks.

"It's fine."

It's the middle of the night, and one of them is bleeding—why am I not surprised?

"That's what you always say." Taliesin sounds close to shaking him. "If you would just carry your astrolabe—"

"I hate those things." He's grumpier than usual.

Taliesin sighs like he's lost this argument too many times to bother again. "So, what are you going to do with your *guest*?"

"I don't know yet," Bishop admits.

"You brought her all the way here, and you still have no idea?"

Bishop doesn't answer, and silence stretches between them, punctuated by the rattling wind.

"She's dangerous," Taliesin says, softer than I've ever heard him. "If she really is—"

If she really is. Even Taliesin won't finish the thought. Like just saying the name Ravenell might wake the terrible powers still dormant inside me.

"If she is, then the only ones in danger are the people trying to kill her."

Taliesin snorts. "You actually believe that?"

"I don't have a choice," Bishop says. "Not until I know more."

A chill settles over me, as brittle as the fear in my veins. I need to know what they're talking about.

Finally, Taliesin clears his throat. "And if she tries to escape?"

"She won't," Bishops says. "She hates the postern, and she'd never survive the mountains."

"Desperation makes you do reckless shit," Taliesin warns him. "Now that she's able to leave her room, I'll keep an eye on her."

I bristle at this, but I don't dare to move. As if I've done something worthy of attention. As if I committed a crime instead of the Stars marking me.

"She seems very interested in heart collectors," he continues.

"Isn't everyone?" Bishop sounds tired. I hold my breath, hoping they'll say more, hoping he'll admit the monsters aren't real. "Come on. I want to show you something I read about scions."

My eyebrows shoot up. What the hell is a scion? And why does it warrant study in the middle of the night?

"Now?" Taliesin groans. "It's nearly one."

"I had no idea it was past your bedtime." A chair pushes back. "Come on. It's in the library. I want your opinion. It might be what's messing with the magic in Florentia."

"Vessica is the smart one," Taliesin says.

"So smart that she's in bed. I just want a . . ." Bishop's voice fades into the corridor. I resist the urge to follow, too haunted by what I just heard. I take the narrow staircase near the rear entrance instead, cringing every time it creaks.

Bishop doesn't know what to do with me.

And they both think I'm dangerous.

• • •

I am not sitting around waiting for Bishop to murder me.

A breakfast tray is at my door, and I devour most of it while I change into one of the old uniforms Lenora left, ignoring the dresses she also found. Mostly because the uniform includes a high-lacing collar that covers where the very top of my mark's wings peek. The shirt is embroidered with intersecting lines in a delicate silver thread, so fine that the patterns it creates catch the light one moment and disappear the next. Likely some type of protection magic woven into the garment itself. Paired with the thick military-issue pants and boots, it's clothing fit to explore the estate, both inside and out.

Bishop will have been up with the sun. That's one thing soldiers and farmers have in common. My family will have been dressed and off to work hours ago.

Ignoring a twinge of guilt, I arm myself with the letters I wrote them last night when getting back to sleep proved impossible. I creep into the hall. If anyone catches me snooping in the wrong place, I'll claim I'm looking for a spot to post them.

As soon as I step out of the bedroom, I pause to listen for nearby activity. But the house is quiet save for the distant chime of the astronomical clock that seems to give up halfway through its count of the hour.

My first stop: the off-limits western wing. Places are only forbidden if there's something worth hiding inside them.

It's situated on the opposite side of the estate from the room I've been given, and the security isn't subtle. The double doors are barred with a black iron lock. There's no keyhole, only faint nochtimetric lines like the ones I tried to thwart on Bishop's trunk in the palace. I jiggle the handle anyway, just in case luck is on my side.

It isn't.

Leaning in, I press my ear against the smooth wood.

Why bother telling me the wing is off-limits if Bishop has it locked up like a dungeon?

I could try to guess the pattern—because that worked so well with his trunk—but I don't want to get caught before I know what I'm looking for.

Time for plan B.

Thanks to my late-night escapade, I know something in the library might have answers. Or just raise more questions. But I'll take either at this point.

Lenora warned me not to visit the room after dark. Luckily, the sun is shining. But as I reach the stairs, I see its doors closing behind someone. It has to be Bishop.

Apprehension hits me as I approach them. Like nearly every surface in this place, a horned wolf is carved into each, both snarling like they know exactly why I'm here. I swallow, wishing I'd pocketed a pastry to nibble on for my nerves.

Maybe Bishop collects forbidden books. Maybe he's stolen half the ones inside. Even if I don't find answers, I might gain leverage to use against him. If someone is in there, I'll make up an excuse, but my fingers tremble as I reach for the knob.

The sound of approaching footsteps sends me flying back a few steps.

"What are you up to?" Bishop asks.

Taliesin is by his side.

If they're here, who just went inside the library?

"Lost," I lie.

Bishop tilts his head, studying me, but Taliesin grins and gestures to my outfit.

"I like you in uniform," he says. "You look like you could punch a man in the throat and no one would even question it."

Tendrils of suspicion twist through me. I don't trust that smile. Not anymore. But it's not like I can call them out without admitting I overheard them in the kitchen. I glance at Bishop, then pin a bland expression on my face. "I'll keep that in mind."

Taliesin leans closer to him but doesn't bother to lower his voice. "I think she wants to punch you." He straightens up. "All I ask is that I'm there to witness it when you do."

I force a laugh. He can keep charming me, but we'll never be friends after last night.

"Taliesin is going to give you the tour," Bishop tells me, starting down the corridor.

"What?" I follow him, shaking my head. "I don't need a—"

"I don't mind," Taliesin says. "I'm more than available."

As if *that's* my concern.

Bishop looks at him, the edge of a smile ghosting his lips. "Can you try to have better manners than last time?"

"Which time was that?" Taliesin asks. "The last time you asked me to show someone around, or when I got punched in the throat last?"

"Why can't *you* show me around?" I ask Bishop, not wanting to be left in the care of his two-faced friend. I must be fucked if I prefer Bishop's grumpy ass.

"I have a meeting in Florentia."

"But you just got back." Panic spikes my blood.

"It's part of the job," he reminds me. "Don't worry. Taliesin will take care of you."

I bet he will.

"And I only bite when bitten first," Taliesin promises as we reach the great room.

Bishop grimaces. "I should have asked Vessica."

My gaze darts in the direction of the library. Maybe she's who I saw going inside. "We could find her."

"She's already in Florentia." Bishop studies me. "Lenora went shopping in the village, but if you'd rather stay here alone . . ."

No one else is here, so who went into the starsdamned library? Something icy chases my lingering panic.

"No." Not if there are fucking ghosts in Miradores. That's the last thing I can handle today. "Maybe I should come with you."

I'm not looking for answers in a haunted library.

"You can't. I'm meeting with Patron Leontia." He pauses and lowers his voice. "Is something wrong?"

I could tell him what I saw. Seven hells, I probably should. But something holds me back. Probably my complete lack of trust in him. "I'm fine."

He nods, but suspicion clouds his eyes. "I'll be back in a few hours. Try to stay out of trouble."

There's a weariness in his voice that suggests how unlikely it is that I'll listen to that command.

He's right. Trouble might be the only way out of here.

Bishop pauses to give Taliesin a few more instructions before he crosses to the secret postern and activates it.

"Off with you," Taliesin says when Bishop hesitates on its threshold. "I'll look after her."

It sounds even less convincing coming from him.

Bishop steps through, leaving the two of us to stare at each other.

"I'm sorry you have to put up with me," I say through clenched teeth.

He shrugs. "Could be worse. You're better company than Vessica, and you don't try to stab me when my back is turned."

"She stabs you in the back?" I can't hide my surprise. Vessica seems so direct, unlike the man standing next to me.

"Only literally. She calls it a *training exercise*. Just sneaks up behind me and—" He mimes a stabbing motion and shakes his head before offering me his arm. "I think she just likes the idea of seeing me bleed."

That makes two of us. "And you aren't afraid of me?"

"Why?" He escorts me into the hallway. "Because of the Ravenell mark you're hiding under that shirt?"

Yep, I definitely want to see him bleed.

I don't buy the act. Not after last night. But I know what he's up to, and knowledge is a weapon.

Time to use it against him.

FOURTEEN

Taliesin walks with a speed that suggests he knows exactly where he's going.

Since we're heading toward the front door, it's information I'd prefer he share.

"I thought you were taking me on a tour." I start to slow down, but he continues, dragging me along. "Or are you just going to flirt with me until Bishop gets back?"

"I don't know. Is it working?" he asks. "Come on. We're going on a field trip."

"Where?" But I plant my feet as he reaches for the handle.

"I promised the grand tour." His smile widens as he opens the door. "You've had a couple of hours to snoop around here. I figured I'd show you the rest of your new *home*."

Alarm bells go off in my head. The way he says *home* sounds more like *prison*, but that's not what makes me sputter.

"Snoop?" Maybe I should have been more careful when I tried to get into the western wing earlier. Did Bishop see me? Is that why he pawned me off on the knight? I square my shoulders and hope my voice doesn't tremble. "I have barely—"

"Relax," he cuts me off. "It's the first thing any self-respecting person would do in your shoes. Let me guess, you didn't find much?"

I cross my arms and glare at him.

"I'll take that as a no." He tilts his head toward the door he's still holding open. "I thought you might want to see the Bellatorum and some of the grounds."

"So I can snoop around?" I bite back.

"Exactly." Taliesin winks at me. "It will make your inevitable escape attempt go more smoothly."

My mouth falls open. "Why would I try to escape?"

"Well, let's see. Curiosity. Recklessness. Boredom." He counts each reason off on his fingers. "I already mentioned self-respect. And, of course, there's always the simple, well-intentioned, but ultimately doomed sense of self-preservation."

Taliesin thinks he has me all figured out based on whatever Bishop's told him. Fine. Maybe we should get to know each other.

I walk through the door, refusing to look at him. "And where would I go?"

"That is the question, isn't it?" He follows me outside. This time, he doesn't offer me his arm. "It's only a short walk." He sniffs the air. "But it's probably going to rain. We could take the postern by the gate."

Despite the clouds, the sun is shining. "No postern," I say quickly, my stomach lurching just at the thought of it. I'd much rather get caught in a downpour.

Taliesin nods. "Might as well get a lay of the land while you figure things out."

Maybe he doesn't want to kill me. Maybe he *wants* me to escape.

Or Bishop does.

Either way, they're right about one thing—I need to figure out what I'm going to do next. I can't just hide in Bishop's home forever.

I scratch at the mark on my chest but change the subject to something safer. For now. "Does it rain here often?"

"We pick up most of the storms off the sea. Rain can't seem to make it over the mountains, so it all gets dumped on us. Some sun in summer and fall, but once winter hits . . ."

"Vennaro must be mostly mud, then." I know from experience that while rain is a blessing, too much of it can be a curse.

"And fog. The mist gets so thick some days, you could get turned around just walking into the garden." He glances at me, eyes twinkling. "But I expect you'll find your way."

It's definitely like he wants me to run.

"Careful," Taliesin advises as we start toward the gates of the estate. Wild grass shoots through cracks in the path, and the dead leaves scattered across the broken stone crunch under our feet. "Some of these need replacing."

Quite a few, actually. Nearly half are cracked past the point of repair, and several are so loose that I nearly trip. But when I try to avoid them, my boots sink into the muddy spaces between stones.

The grounds between the house and the gated entrance are in the same shape as the garden. Towering evergreens stand sentry along the drive. Some are so overgrown that their branches droop from the weight of their own ambitions. Others show signs of disease, their brittle, brown needles clinging to scraggly branches or dumped at the base of their trunks. Brambles have sprung up between them, edging so close to the walkway that they tear at my sleeves as we pass.

My family's estate in Damalis is just barely in worse shape. Although Lenora is doing a better job keeping up the actual house than we have.

"There's really no one to tend the grounds?"

"Are you volunteering?" Taliesin moves a low-hanging branch out of our path.

"Me and what army?" I shake my head. This is too much work for a single person. "Or can I borrow yours?"

"Bishop has never really cared about the grounds." He shrugs, stepping over a giant puddle. "His father did, but now that he's gone, it's not a priority."

I consider asking him more about Bishop's family but stop myself. People die. It's an unfortunate fact of life, and one I know all too well. But, unlike my family, Order Marius should have money and means.

Beyond the gardens, set high on a rocky rise, a narrow tower cuts into the fog, its domed crown catching the light like a watchful eye.

"That tower," I say, nodding toward it. "Is that the Bellatorum?"

Taliesin snorts. "That's the astrolatory. It's a couple of miles' hike *up* from the Bellatorum."

"That seems a bit hard to reach." The remote location would be more fitting for a military fortress. "How does anyone visit it?"

"No one really bothers with rituals or watching for omens here." There's a note of judgment in his voice. "Bishop thinks any real threat will come from the sea, not the Stars."

Most people build their lives around the Stars. Bishop tries to ignore them. I swear the mark on my chest twinges like it's itching to prove him wrong.

I press a hand over it to smother that feeling. It's nothing more than a phantom ache, a hit of fear followed by a sickening rush of relief.

When we reach the wooden bridge that connects the estate's spit of land with the main territory, I'm relieved to see it's well-maintained given the choppy water below. White-capped waves roll and crest before crashing into the rocky shoreline, and gusts of wind knock into us as we cross. But on the other side, even the solid ground beneath my feet feels shaky.

Taliesin tells me stories as we walk, each slightly more improbable than the last.

"I was considering settling down until she tried to poison me," he says after filling me in on his most recent failed love affair.

"Did you deserve it?" I ask.

"Oh, absolutely." He grins. "But she was still worth it. Best three weeks of my life."

"It seems like a lot of people want to hurt you."

His smile only widens. "Bishop says I bring out the violence in people."

For once, I agree with Bishop.

We only walk a few minutes on the mainland before we reach a split in the road, marked by a column carved with directions. Unfortunately, the directions are written in the ancient tongue. Taliesin continues toward the right-hand path, which slopes at such a steep angle I wonder how close we are to the mountains. I lag behind him a few steps, staring in the other direction.

"That way takes you to Wolf's Keep," he says, noticing my interest.

I recall Lenora mentioning it in passing. "The village, right?"

He nods. "Probably your best chance at finding a way out of here."

"I'm beginning to think that you want me to escape."

"Honestly? I'll be a tad disappointed if you don't try."

Probably because it's his best excuse to off me. Still, I can't stop myself from asking, "Why?"

"You let the oscen go." His voice drops so low that it's almost lost in the wind. "No one does that."

No one except the girl Bishop dragged halfway across Antares and dumped in his lap.

"That's what my brother said, too," I grumble, and Taliesin laughs. But thinking of Broderic—even in passing—makes my chest tighten. "If I'd known how much trouble it would cause . . ."

"You wouldn't have released it?"

For a second, I feel the weight of the dagger in my hand. My fingers close reflexively but find only air. There is no knife. No bird. No second chance. I shrug. "It doesn't matter now."

Taliesin pauses, his forehead wrinkling. "Yes, it does. Would you let it go again?"

I resist the urge to roll my eyes. I hadn't expected today to include exercises in personal morality. Especially considering my companion. But I mull over the question as we walk. I could have made it quick. Painless. I can only imagine how the other initiates botched their sacrifices. And maybe if I had killed the oscen, I wouldn't be here now, having this pointless conversation. Maybe the symbol of Order Icaros would be seared into my skin somewhere far less conspicuous than the mark I bear now. Maybe King Ophelian would even be alive.

The trouble is that dwelling on my choices won't change anything.

And I know with certainty that my hands would have never felt clean again. I would have spent my life like that initiate from Leontia, trying to wipe off blood no one else could see.

"Yes," I answer finally.

Taliesin doesn't press the issue, but something that looks suspiciously like approval glints in his eyes.

We continue in silence, each lost in our own thoughts, but as we reach the point where the road crests, the Bellatorum comes into view.

There is no fortified wall. No heads on iron spikes. It's actually . . . elegant.

Somehow, the Bellatorum is larger than the royal palace in Wintour. It sprawls across the foothills of the Stygia Mountains in a curious mix of old and new, half built from the ruins of something that feels ancient.

The gates are open and unguarded apart from a pair of enormous stone wolves, mottled by moss and time. A black bird perches on one of their horns, wings tucked tightly against its body. Its beady black eyes don't blink as we approach.

Taliesin doesn't seem to notice, but I look down as we pass through the gates. It can't be the same bird. I'm just seeing signs where there are none. Another victim of Antares's deeply rooted superstition.

Ivy strangles the walls of dormitories and various structures, so thick in places that it looks like the building is being pulled back into the ground. Some of them are situated around a grassy knoll, although most are built on the fringes of a collection of stone arenas that seems much older than anything else around. We pause at a postbox so I can drop my letters before Taliesin leads me to the closest building.

"Home sweet home," he says.

"You don't miss your real home?" I ask, staring at a statue by the door. It's so battered by time that its face is nothing but a few vague dents.

"I was dumped on the Bellatorum steps when I was about four."

He says it so cheerfully that his words hit a beat too late. "You were abandoned?"

"It's how most conscripts wind up here." He pushes open the door and almost collides with a gaggle of children wearing various mismatched armor.

My heart lurches. How many of them were abandoned, too?

Taliesin yanks me toward the wall as wooden swords continue to swing. We've clearly interrupted something. "Stay here," he orders me before striding into the fray. The effect of his presence is instantaneous. The wooden weapons hit the entry rugs with dull thumps as the children come to attention. Only a handful keep fighting, too caught up in their game to notice his arrival. Taliesin raises two fingers to his lips and looses an ear-splitting whistle. I wince, but it works.

"What have I told you about fighting in the foyer?" He winds his way through the kids, a single brow raised.

One of the littler ones lifts his chin and shouts, "If we break something, we'll have to walk to Miradores and explain ourselves to Bishop." He swallows like the thought horrifies him before squeaking, "Sir."

Just his name is enough to spark the reaction, but it's not fear on the boy's face.

It's respect.

"At least you remember that, even if you can't seem to remember the rules." Taliesin takes a deep breath, his face the definition of disappointment. He nods toward the door. "Take it outside."

A chorus of *yes sirs* echoes as they grab their swords and rush out. The fight resumes as soon as they hit the top step, and I bite back a smile. Taliesin follows behind them, shaking his head and shouting more commands before he closes the door.

"So, this is where your love of fighting started." It's beginning to make sense. Although, it's dangerous to imagine him as a boy with a wooden dagger, especially since I'm pretty sure he wants to kill me. "How many times did you make that walk to Miradores to explain breaking something?"

"I still hold the record," he says with a smirk. "It's a miracle that there's anything left to break."

That, I believe.

"This is the Commons," he says as we pass a dozen open doorways, every room full of people of all ages. Some in uniform, others in everyday clothing. The whole place hums with energy. A boy no older than Andry races down the corridor, chased by a girl his age wielding a fireplace poker. People cluster around tables in one room, playing cards in front of them. In another, groups of conscripts pore over books.

"I thought this was a military base."

"It is," Taliesin says. "But no one fights all the time."

He sounds a little sad about it.

It's not what I expected. Neither is Taliesin, if I'm being honest. But I keep my guard up. A few lighthearted stories and a walk don't absolve him from what he said to Bishop last night.

He leads me through a back exit into a large courtyard that looks over the rest of the complex. He points to a dormitory choked with ivy. "That's where the youngest ones live."

"How young?" I ask, remembering what he told me about how he wound up here.

"We don't have anyone under five, last I checked."

"Five? That's too young for conscription." I know what he told me before, but seeing it—knowing families abandoned their own children to a lifetime of fighting—is different.

"It's not really conscription. Classes start when they're six. No one starts training until they're twelve. Before that, it's all books and games and learning how to not be a jackass."

He must have missed some of those lessons.

There are three more dormitories, several other buildings devoted to education, a gymnasium, and various training facilities, both indoor and outdoor, all teeming with activity. I strain to watch a sparring match happening in one of the distant arenas carved from stone ruins. But Taliesin directs me into the dining hall. Rows of tables and chairs are set up in precise formation. Banners hang from the rafters, each bearing the symbol of Order Marius.

Only a handful of people are eating at this hour. Heads turn as we pass. Some stare, others whisper.

"Your reputation precedes you," Taliesin says. I can't quite tell if he's teasing me or warning me.

He waves to a woman in the kitchen, who responds by pelting him with a bread roll. He catches it one-handed, tears it in two, and offers me the bigger half. "Best bread in Antares."

I accept it but wait for him to take a bite first.

"It's not poisoned," he says, ripping into it with his teeth. "I'd never waste good bread on an assassination attempt."

That makes two of us. We really might get along if it wasn't impossible to trust each other. But I try it. He's right. It's perfect—soft and warm and sweet. I don't stop him when he charms the kitchen into giving us each another one.

We visit a few classrooms next, each more impressive than the last. Walls are lined with maps and diagrams. Shelves sag under the weight of books.

"Everyone takes classes?" I ask, peeking into a room of young adults frantically jotting down notes as a man in uniform lectures from a pulpit.

Taliesin nods. "Math, reading, how not to blow yourself up the first time you're trusted with Marius magic," he whispers. "The younger you arrive, the more education you receive, but everyone is expected to be literate before they join the ranks."

In the next classroom, a girl is reading aloud to a cluster of younger kids. Her voice is soft but clear, and every pair of eyes is glued to her.

"Don't look so surprised," Taliesin says when he catches me staring. "We can't ask them to fight without making sure they know what they're fighting for."

"That's probably easier to do when there hasn't been a war in five hundred years," I point out.

A shadow moves over him. "There are plenty of dangers facing Antares, even without war." He pauses, his eyes darting back to the room full of children. "But they'll be ready when war comes."

I hear the resignation in his voice, as though war is inevitable. I wonder if he felt this way a month ago. A year ago. Or if my presence is responsible for the haunted look in his eyes. I push the thought away. Once the king's assassin is caught, once people know the truth, this talk of war will die down. It has to.

I change the subject back to Taliesin's favorite topic: himself. "I thought you fought because you liked it."

"I do." He winks. "But between us, I hate the idea of them fighting."

Part of me wants to believe him. Part of me *longs* to. But belief leads to trust, and trust is the last thing I can give anyone who wears the symbol of Order Marius.

The last stop is the dormitory for senior conscripts—the ones who will soon be given a rank. It's quieter here, as if to prove the years of training and discipline actually work. A few people pause to salute Taliesin before hurrying off, eyeing me over their shoulders with curiosity. This might be a tour, but I get the distinct impression that in this building, I'm the one on display.

Taliesin takes me to another common room, where a group of conscripts is playing a frantic game, tossing cards face down and grabbing more off a stack. All while shouting at one another. Silver crowns are scattered in the center of the table. We linger in the doorway and watch the chaos.

"People are always playing Liar's Hand," he says.

"My parents used to play with friends, but I never learned," I admit, feeling a slight pang.

Someone slaps the table, laughing. "Call it. Liar's Hand or not?"

This sets off a passionate debate.

"You don't win by having the best cards," Taliesin whispers as they argue. "You win by convincing everyone else that you do."

He motions for me to follow him inside. But as soon as we step into the room, the conversation dies.

A tall woman about my age, brown hair pulled into a low ponytail, looks me over, then scowls. "Who is this?"

"A friend," Taliesin says without missing a beat. Maybe he should be playing their game.

A bearded conscript holds up his fanned cards. "Care to join us?"

"You can't afford to play me." Taliesin smiles, teeth flashing.

"Not if you won't give me a chance to win my money back." The conscript glances over at me. "What about you?"

"I didn't bring any money." And the last thing I need is to risk making any actual friends here.

"Taliesin will spot you," the one with the ponytail says. She gives him a look that suggests she knows him well enough to expect this.

Taliesin pales slightly, but he shakes his head. "Sorry, we can't stay." He grabs my arm and tugs me away.

"Sooooo," I say as soon as we're far enough from the door, "is she the one who poisoned you?"

"I'd rather not say." He glances behind him like he might find her standing there.

I make a show of pretending to turn around. "On second thought, maybe I do want to play."

"I beg you . . . *no*."

I laugh but follow him out.

We make our way back through the main corridor and, for a moment, I forget that I'm supposed to be watching for the trap to spring. For a moment, I almost feel like I've spent the afternoon with a friend—until I remember he wants me dead.

But then we step outside, pass a bathhouse, and enter a training arena, and the illusion shatters.

It's little more than a pit surrounded by splintered plinths, wooden benches, and the remains of a few toppled statues. The stone floor has been battered by centuries of rain and salt air, worn down in spots to patches of muddy gravel and sand. The thick clouds overhead cast a gloomy shadow on a nearly empty rack of swords. Most of the weapons are already in use.

A dozen conscripts are lined up in two rows at the far end, watching as two of them battle. The pair's swords clash, slicing through the air, metal clanging and ringing as they advance and retreat.

Taliesin points to a nearby bench a safe distance from the sparring. "Want to watch?"

Something tells me this is why Bishop sent me with him.

The fighters move so fast it's hard to track. Each movement is graceful, precise but brutal. Blood sprays as one of them lands a blow to the other's shoulder. The wounded woman barely flinches, just grits her teeth and keeps swinging. Her red hair is short, curling on the ends as it frames high cheekbones, her freckled skin boasting a sheen of sweat and dirt. This feels like more than practice. It feels like survival.

I wince, my fingers instinctively going to my own shoulder. "What happened to the wooden swords?"

"These are the proving grounds. The soldiers here are training to be knights. That's Shea," he says, pointing at the one with the bleeding shoulder. "She'll be one by the end of the year."

The highest position a conscript could rise to, since other ranks are reserved for those with Marius blood. I study her, the way she moves, the way she keeps fighting despite the pain. I wonder if I could do the same.

A thought suddenly occurs to me. Given only those of Marius blood have a Kindling and inherit magic . . . "Are you related to Bishop?" I ask.

Taliesin looks serious for once. "Not by blood."

"But I thought knights were the ones who studied magic?" If he's not related, how can he have magic?

"We do. After we prove ourselves." He gestures to the pit. "If they make it out of the proving grounds, Bishop will knight them, granting them some of his family's power, and they can begin their studies."

My eyes widen. "I thought only Order Calix could imbue magic."

Taliesin laughs. "That's what they want you to believe. But it's possible to gift magic if someone's willing to give it up."

Someone giving up power? That's even harder to fathom than imbuing magic.

I glance around the room, at all the soldiers fighting for a piece of Bishop's birthright.

"They get access to magic if they're the best fighters?" That doesn't feel like much of a bar.

"*We* get access to magic," he says pointedly, "if we prove that we're loyal. The sparring matches are only part of it."

Loyalty. That's what this is really about. Not only here but in Wintour, too.

Shea manages to parry *while* bleeding *without* losing her balance. Because she has to. She wasn't born to power. None of them were. This is all they have—a chance to fight, survive, carve a place in the world with a sword. I was handed a ceremonial knife, and I flinched. I doubt I would last a day here.

Taliesin watches, studying the fighters like he's up next.

Blood soaks Shea's uniform, but she doesn't slow down. It's only when her opponent's weapon clatters to the ground that she presses a palm against the wound to slow the bleeding. Then she bends and retrieves the fallen sword. Her opponent bows his head, and she tosses it to him, her lips quirking up. The pair stagger back toward their cohort, teasing and mocking each other. They fall silent as a new match begins. Taliesin tracks their movement the entire time.

"You miss this," I say softly.

He tilts his head, something distant and thoughtful shining in his eyes. "Sometimes. It's simpler at the Bellatorum. Fight. Win. Don't accidentally get yourself killed." His grin is crooked. "The rest of life is messier."

"Tell me about it," I mutter.

"I'd rather show you." He stands and extends his hand.

I drop mine into his, panic building in my chest as he pulls me to my feet. "Show me what?"

But he walks to the rack of swords and picks one up. He turns it over in his hand. "What it's like."

I hesitate, but the challenge in his voice is unmistakable. Watery fear churns in my stomach—I'm the one who needs to prove myself. That's why he brought me here, and now he's armed. I could run, but he'll catch me. I stand a better chance with a sword in my hands.

"Fine," I say, crossing to the weapon rack. "Show me, but if you're going to kill me, make it quick."

I'm only half joking.

"I like a girl who keeps things interesting." He steps to the side and allows me to choose a sword. They all look roughly the same. Basic, unadorned apart from the wolf head carved into the hilt. Some have a little more blood dried onto the blade than others. I grab the closest one. It's heavier than Kieren's—the only sword I've ever held—but the handle fits neatly in my palm. I test the weight, swinging it around. It wobbles in my right hand, so I add my left to keep it steady. That helps a little. But I'm pretty sure the shaking has more to do with the potential for imminent death than a lack of strength.

Taliesin begins circling me, eyes narrowed. "Have you ever fought before?"

"Once or twice." I'm not sure knocking sticks around with my best friend or a few self-defense lessons count. But the last thing I want is to appear like an easy target. Even if I am.

He smirks like we're playing Liar's Hand and he just glimpsed my cards. "Perfect. Let's see how you do."

I grip the handle as tightly as I can, every muscle in my arms straining at the effort.

"Relax your hold," he advises. "There's nothing to be afraid of."

Except you.

He comes at me fast, his blade swishing through the air. But the swing is sloppy—almost lazy. I barely block it, my heart jumping into my throat. He laughs and dances back.

"Good," he says. "Again."

This time, he's serious. The blows come faster, harder. I block the first two, but the third slices across my arm. I yelp as air hits the wound, and Taliesin backs off, lowering his sword.

"You're not bad," he says, barely breathless. "Better than most first years."

Being scared shitless for your life will do that. "Was that a compliment?"

He shrugs. "Don't let it go to your head."

I drop the sword to the ground and look down at the cut.

"Just one thing." His movement is a flash, and a second later, he's behind me, his blade hovering at my throat. "Never assume the fight is over. Never drop your weapon."

I don't dare speak. Breathe. Move. Gone is the grinning man from this morning. In his place is someone hard. Determined. Dangerous. A knight who has proven his loyalty and is ready to protect the kingdom from . . . me.

"Lots of people want you dead," he whispers into my ear.

Well, that deserves a response.

"Like you?" I mutter through clenched teeth.

"That depends."

So much for his promise to make it quick. "On what?"

"On you." The blade presses harder into my skin. "Now, give me one good reason *not* to kill you."

FIFTEEN

I don't want to die.

Somehow, I doubt that will qualify as a strong enough reason for Taliesin.

"Can't think of anything?" His breath is hot against my skin. The metal blade is cold.

A shadow circles overhead, drawing my eyes to the stormy sky. Maybe I released my own death into the world. Maybe that's why I keep seeing omens.

And I am so fucking over it.

A raindrop hits my forehead with a splat, and something snaps inside me. "You want a reason?"

"I believe that's been established," he taunts me.

"*Fine*. You don't have to kill me." The words tumble out as the rain picks up. The sounds of sparring continue in the distance. If the conscripts won't stop for rain, I doubt they'll notice what's happening to me. "Maybe you've spent so much time taking orders from wealthy assholes, you've forgotten that. But it's up to you. Not them. Not me. *You*. Maybe you want to kill me. Maybe you don't. But you sure as fuck don't have to do it. So, give me one good reason why you *should* kill me."

I wait, ready this time for pain or pity or whatever unpleasant thing happens next. Instead, the sword vanishes. Taliesin backs away, but I don't budge. It's a trick. I know it. He'll wait for me to move and then finish the job. Call it an accident. Self-defense. I don't know how he'll explain how I wound up with a sword in my back, but he's charismatic enough to get away with it.

"Not bad," he mutters.

Metal on metal clashes behind me like a clap of distant thunder, but all I hear is what he doesn't say: *Not bad . . . but not enough.*

When he doesn't strike, I turn to face him—and find Bishop standing behind him, *his* sword at Taliesin's throat. I choke back a gasp as silence falls over the proving grounds. Bishop's presence is enough to command the attention of every soul present. Even the sparring match behind us grinds to a halt.

"Why don't you give *me* a reason, Sir Procrax?" Bishop glides the blade across Taliesin's skin, drawing a thin line of blood like his knight is the one here with something to prove.

"If you kill your only friend, who will put up with your shit?" Taliesin's voice is a little too breezy for someone one spasm away from being headless, but he lowers his own weapon slowly before letting it fall to the broken stones beneath him.

Bishop doesn't respond. Instead, he steps between us, his weapon still aimed at Taliesin. For a moment, they just stare at each other.

"Bishop." Taliesin raises his palms, but he doesn't offer any more reasons. No explanation. Just those empty hands and a single, pointed look.

"Her reason was better." Bishop takes a deep breath and sheathes his sword. "This isn't a game. You should be more careful when someone suggests playing like it is."

His eyes are glued to Taliesin, so it takes me a second to realize he's speaking to me.

I swallow. "I wanted to know what he would do."

"What did I say about trouble?" He glances at me. "You can't avoid it for one afternoon?"

I scowl. "He's the one who gave me a sword."

Taliesin's eyes flick briefly to me, like he wants to say something. Maybe *sorry*. Or something thoroughly arrogant like *better luck next time*. But he only grins.

Bishop takes a step closer to me, and I realize every soul on the proving grounds is still watching us.

His expression could be carved from marble. "Enough for today," he says over his shoulder to the gawking crowd. "Anyone who didn't finish their drills will start again at dawn. Hit the baths."

A few groans ripple through the conscripts, but they scatter toward the bathhouse.

When he turns his attention back to me, somehow his expression is even colder. "What exactly are you doing here?"

"Me?" How am *I* the one in more trouble? I hitch a thumb toward Taliesin. "You left him to babysit. He was showing me around."

"How *friendly*." Bishop is back to glaring at him.

"Except for the trying-to-assassinate-me part." A tremble rolls through my body, and I cross my arms to hide it.

"*Assassinate* is a strong word. I wanted to see what you're made of."

"Flesh and blood. Just like you." I pin my gaze on the small line of blood on his neck.

Taliesin laughs and rubs his thumb along the cut. Blood smears across his skin, but he doesn't even wince.

Bishop isn't amused. "Get cleaned up before you drip blood all over your uniform."

"Yes, sir," Taliesin says, bowing dramatically.

"We'll discuss this later," Bishop adds.

Taliesin straightens, brows drawing together as he searches Bishop's face. Whatever he finds there sends him hurrying to join the others.

Bishop turns and fixes his attention on me. "You're bleeding." His words are clipped. Nothing more than a statement of fact. But there's a flicker of concern running through them like a hairline fissure in a sheet of ice.

"It's nothing." The cut on my arm starts to throb as soon as I say it, and I cover the wound with my hand.

He isn't fooled. "Let me see."

When I hesitate, he stalks forward and holds out a hand.

"Let me see," he repeats.

I surrender my arm for inspection, resisting the urge to roll my eyes. There's definitely a lecture in my future. Probably some warning about finding myself on the wrong end of a sword—as if that had been my idea. Or maybe he'll fire Taliesin from his chaperone duties and leave me to my own devices. That's likely wishful thinking.

But Bishop cradles my arm with a gentleness that surprises me, his hands warm even through his leather gloves. He's quiet as he peels back my blood-soaked sleeve, but his gaze darkens like the storm clouds over us as he examines the cut.

Reaching for his cloak, he pauses just long enough to meet my eyes. "It's clean," he murmurs before dabbing the blood with the thick fabric. His fingers brush over my skin, and a shiver races up my spine, settling with a tingle at the base of my neck.

"Am I going to live?" My dry tone sounds heavy to my own ears.

"Not if you keep trusting strangers with swords." He frowns as the wound continues to bleed.

"Says the stranger with a sword who keeps rescuing me." I pull my arm away from him. It still stings, but I slide my sleeve back down, trying to ignore how his gaze lingers longer than necessary.

"You're welcome," Bishop says.

"I didn't say thank you."

"I'm sure you meant to." He nods at my arm. "We can bandage that inside."

By *we*, I hope he means me. It's bad enough that he had to step in. Again. But being vulnerable in front of a man like him . . . I can't afford for Bishop to know more of my weaknesses.

"He wouldn't hurt you," Bishop says quietly as we turn to leave.

The cut on my arm says otherwise, but I shrug. Taliesin wanted to learn something about me, but I learned something about him in the process. Despite his flirtations and eagerness to fight, he thinks before he acts. He could have killed me. He really wanted me to give him a reason to stop him.

"If he tries something like that again, tell him no."

I snort. "He doesn't seem like the type who listens."

Actually, something tells me that Taliesin makes up his own mind. It's an unusual trait for a knight. I doubt it means he's good at taking orders.

Bishop sighs like he knows this, too. "That doesn't mean you shouldn't try."

I follow beside him in silence.

"We have six pools. You're welcome to use them," Bishop says as we reach the side of the building and he opens the door.

Steam hits us as we step inside. My shoulders relax involuntarily, my body anticipating the heat. Not that I'm about to get naked in front of a bunch of strangers.

"Velesont must love you." Transporting all that water must cost a fortune.

Bishop shakes his head. "Hot springs run under the mountains. We pipe them through."

"Not magic?" I ask, surprised.

"Just good old-fashioned engineering. Something we can always rely on. But the water is full of healing minerals from the mountains." He tips his head toward the door. "You can use them now. You fought today."

"I'd hardly call it a fight." But that's not what's stopping me. I glance down. The last thing I need is people ogling the mark burned across my chest.

"They've seen worse," he murmurs.

I doubt it.

"Maybe another time." Like when all seven hells freeze over.

"I'll get you something for that." He gestures to my wounded arm.

Bishop lets himself into a small infirmary, not bothering to turn on the light as he rifles around in a cabinet. Meanwhile, I do my best to politely ignore the conscripts stripping off their training uniforms only a few feet away in the changing area.

It takes him a while, but finally he holds up a bandage and a small tin stamped with the license of Order Leontia. "This will heal it in a day or two."

"I can do that." I take both from him and nod toward the steam shrouding the baths' entrance at the far end of the space. One of us should enjoy them. "Why don't you . . ."

He adjusts his gloves, not bothering to even look. "It's better not to fraternize."

Maybe he doesn't want anyone to see his own markings—the ones I glimpsed while we were traveling—but if I didn't know better, I'd think Bishop was shy. Somehow, that seems impossible. But before I can test this theory, Taliesin strides by wearing nothing but a towel slung around his hips and the skin the Stars gave him. There's definitely not a shy bone in *his* body.

He winks as he passes us. "Care to join me?"

"Unbelievable," I mutter. "You tried to kill me less than ten minutes ago."

He only shrugs. "Light bloodshed is just foreplay."

"Actually," Bishop says, stopping him, "let's talk now."

"But—"

"Now," Bishop cuts him off. He turns to me, hesitating for a moment. "Feel free to wait wherever you're most comfortable."

It feels rude to stand around in clothes, so I force a grim smile. "I'll be outside."

And I don't care what either of them says, there's no way I'll ever use the baths. There's a perfectly good tub in the privacy of my own room, thank you very much. I'll probably never let anyone see me naked again.

The rain has stopped, but the grounds are even muddier. Swollen gray clouds linger in the sky, suggesting an encore shower is imminent. But the air is crisp, and the mist has thinned enough to show the stone walkways and the training grounds beyond. I slather my arm with the tincture, hissing slightly when it stings. I'm wrapping it when a small voice pipes up: "Does it hurt?"

My fingers slip on the bandage. Looking down, I find a small boy on his knees nearby, drawing in the mud with a stick.

"Only my pride." I crouch next to him. "What are you working on?"

His freckled nose wrinkles with frustration as he drags the stick through the mud. "My letters."

"Shouldn't you be in school? They'll give you parchment." He reminds me of Andry, although he's much younger.

He rakes another line through to form a crooked *F*. "I'm not old enough for classes."

But clearly still determined.

He drops back and sighs, wiping his mud-caked hands on his equally dirty pants. "I can't remember what comes next."

"Here. Let me show you." I pick up another stick and drag it through the sodden dirt to form a half-decent *G*, then add an *H*.

He immediately copies it. His *G* loops backward, and the crossbar on his *H* slants. He grunts, his shoulders falling a little. "Mine don't look like yours. I can't do it."

"It took me forever to get it right when I was learning." If only I was making that up so he would feel better. "I had to go to school and use a pen. I wish I could have drawn in the mud."

"Really?" He eyes me with a suspicion all children reserve for the claims of adults.

"*Really*. You'll get it, too. Try again."

He bites his lower lip and sets to work, eyes darting over to mine like he's cheating off my test. The results are significantly less lopsided and facing the right direction. He looks up from his work at me for feedback. I give him a thumbs-up, and he beams.

I show him a few more letters, and he sets to work, concentrating on each like his life depends on it.

"Let me guess. You want to be a knight," I say.

But he shakes his head and keeps working. "Nah, my sister says that if I learn all my letters and how to read the ancient tongue, I can be a vesper."

"A vesper, huh? That's better than a knight." And a lot safer. "Do you like books?"

He lights up, nodding so hard I'm afraid his neck will snap. "My mother used to read to us. She said books can take you anywhere." But then his face falls. "Do you think they can take you to the Stars?"

"The Stars?" My throat constricts. I guess that answers the question of what he's doing here. "I suppose so."

He smiles again, but this time it's brittle. "Good," he says, a slight quiver in his voice. "I want to see her again . . . but only after I learn how to read."

"Well, then you'd better keep practicing." I show him how to do another set of letters.

He works through a few more before he asks, "What's your name?"

"Arden." I spell it out in the mud with deliberate strokes. "Can you spell yours?"

"Yes!" He slumps forward, biting his lip in concentration as he works.

He manages to get most of a *B* drawn before a severe voice interrupts us. "Breccan, what did I tell you about bugging people? And look how filthy you are." The female conscript who won the first sparring match drops to her knees beside him. Her red hair is still damp from the baths, but she doesn't seem to care about getting dirty. She glances over at me. "I'm so sorry if he was bothering you."

"He didn't bother me at all," I say, meaning it. "I was waiting for someone anyway."

"I'm Shea." She holds out a hand.

I start to take it before realizing mine is covered in dried mud. "Oh." I brush it off before I shake hers. "Arden. I saw your fight earlier. Impressive."

"Thanks," she says with the air of someone who has long since forgotten how heavy a sword is. "I saw your fight, too."

I shake my head. "That wasn't a fight. It was public humiliation."

But she laughs. "No one beats Sir Procrax, except Bishop."

I don't miss the reverence when she says Bishop's name, like he's more than a man or a commanding officer . . . like he's a god.

"My sister is going to be a knight," Breccan boasts, leaning against her.

She ruffles his hair. "And you are going to be a vesper."

A pang hits me squarely in the chest. I push onto my feet, dusting off my pants. "I should find . . ." I stop short of calling the others my friends.

Shea stands up, too. "If you ever want someone to show you some moves, let me know."

"Thanks." She would probably be a less homicidal teacher than Taliesin, and Bishop has better things to do.

"You never offer to teach me how to fight," Breccan whines at our feet.

"Because you are too smart to fight. Mom wouldn't have wanted you to join the army," she adds, but he's already digging in the dirt again.

"Won't he have to?" I ask her in a low voice. "Once he's old enough to attend classes, I mean."

Her eyes shine as she watches him. "Not if I become a knight," she says fiercely. "He stays with the other children now, but knights get their own lodgings. They can have families there. I promised my mom I'd keep him safe."

I know a thing or two about family responsibility.

For a heartbeat, it isn't Breccan sitting in the dirt. It's a younger Andry. If we weren't patrons, this could have been my family's fate when Dad died. How many people's futures hinge on Bishop, because they have nowhere else to go?

"What about you?" I ask. "Is this what your mom would want?"

She's quiet for a moment. "It's safe here."

Something in her voice twists my stomach. "You weren't safe at home?"

"Not anymore. Not after Mom died. Not after . . ." She shakes her head like she's clearing out cobwebs, then smiles brightly. "We didn't have anywhere to go. We had to leave our village. Thankfully, we made it here."

"But Bishop won't make him join?" My eyes stray toward the stairs to see if he's coming.

Her brows knit together. "He doesn't *make* any of us join."

"Okay." I'm not sure preying on children without other options constitutes much of a choice.

"Really," she insists. "Half the kids who show up here leave with only an education. I guess that doesn't sound like much."

Taliesin said they needed to be literate, to know why they were fighting before they joined the ranks. He failed to mention they're given a choice.

"Actually, it seems like a lot . . . I'm just surprised." I can admit it, even if I don't quite understand the economics behind it. "And knights get to learn magic."

She grins. "There's that, too."

And that's the real difference between us. Shea wants magic. I'm dreading the day mine finally stirs in my blood.

The bathhouse door slams open, and Bishop storms out, eyes sweeping across the grounds. They stop on me, his forehead creasing when he spots who I'm with. I brace for whatever sin I've committed now. But when he makes his way over, he kneels down to look at Breccan's handiwork.

"Not bad, but you're missing the tail on that *G*." He points to the letter, and Breccan bends to fix it hastily.

"I'm sorry that—" Shea begins apologizing again, but Bishop waves it off.

"It's not a problem. I've been meaning to check up on you. Things have been busy. I've had my hands full."

With assassinations and omens of war—and dealing with me in general.

"Arden helped me," Breccan pipes up. He glances down at my name in the mud. "Will you come back if I learn to write your name?"

I can't help smiling as I nod. "Yes, but only if you keep working on all your letters."

"I will." He chews on his lip, eyes darting between Bishop and me. "If I do, will you bring me a real book next time?"

Before I can answer, Bishop tousles his hair. "You learn all of your letters, and I'll bring you a whole stack."

Breccan beams, and even Shea looks grateful. For a second, I see Bishop as they do: not as a patron or a commanding officer but as a hero.

Bishop stands, brushing mud off his knees.

"Are you ready to get out of here?" he asks me.

I nod, but not before glancing back to Shea. "You take care of him," I say to her, and she nods solemnly.

The rain begins again as we start back toward Miradores, but Bishop doesn't bother to ask if I want to take a postern. I wonder if he's thinking about the little boy or if he's already moved on to brooding about something else.

My thoughts stay on what Shea said about giving those kids an education.

"Why do you do it?" I finally ask. "Why help them?"

He shrugs, staring into the distance ahead of us. "Someone helped me once. I figure I owe the universe."

He doesn't elaborate, and I don't press.

The rain turns to a steady mist by the time we reach the bridge, fog shrouding the manor from sight. "I'm surprised they didn't build the Bellatorum here," I say, trying to make conversation. "Shouldn't it be defending your estate?"

"That's not how it works." Bishop shakes his head. "Miradores is the shield between Antares and the rest of the world."

I might have laughed at the idea that the nearly empty estate is the kingdom's first line of defense, but the heaviness in his voice calls to the weight I carry in my own heart.

"Miradores or you?" I ask softly.

"There's no difference. The estate is wood and stone, but my family's blood built it. There is no Miradores without Order Marius."

Spoken like a man who's worn duty like armor his whole life.

"And now you're the last one to protect it." I can't imagine how lonely that feels. At least I had siblings to help shoulder the burden.

"Plenty of my extended family would be willing to take up the responsibility."

I nod. This, I understand. Even our most distant relatives had taken to checking in on us after Dad died—hoping to find that we'd failed. It's easier to inherit a legacy than hold one together. "And they all think they could do a better job."

He grimaces. "My cousins are posted to river ports and wine valleys. Places that never see blood. They only *think* they want my job."

All the privilege. None of the weight.

"Then why stay a bishop?" I can't stop myself from asking. "If you remain heirless . . ."

"I have my reasons," he says without explaining what they are.

I've overstepped. Again. I probably hold some type of record at this point. "I'm sorry. It's none of my business."

"No, it's mine." He pauses. "When I became a bishop, I swore my life to the people. I can't just break that vow."

"Doesn't a patron do the same thing?"

He grunts, the sound a cross between laughter and resignation.

"What happens if Calix or Velesont sends someone . . . after me?" I force out the rest of the question.

"Then they'll have to kill me first." His voice is flat, factual, unforgiving.

I do my best to ignore the slight uptick in my heart rate.

"You don't sound worried about that." I wish I felt the same.

"I'm not."

Maybe that's the benefit of growing up around so much violence. Death stops scaring you. I unlock my arms and pick at the bandage. The slow, throbbing ache beneath it is a comfort—a reminder that I survived again.

We're only a few steps away from the kitchen door when Bishop stops and faces me. "You still think I'm a villain in this story."

I search his face for how to answer, but as usual, he's completely unreadable. Maybe that's what he wants me to think. Maybe that's why he wasn't the one to take me to the Bellatorum. Because now . . . "I think you're something else entirely."

His mouth opens like he might ask what that is. Like maybe he's not sure himself. But he doesn't speak.

Neither of us moves. His gaze drops to my mouth, and heat rises to my cheeks in stark contrast to the chill in the air. That invisible string between us goes taut, but I can't look away. The wind picks up, carrying the scent of damp earth and distant pine, and mingles with the warmth radiating from him. A gust whips a strand of hair across my eyes, but before I can brush it away, Bishop raises his hand, reaching toward me.

Only to stop himself.

His fingers curl into a fist. He drops his arm again and breaks the silence. "I'm going to Wintour for a few days."

"What? Why?" He can't leave me here. He was only gone for a few hours this morning, and Taliesin had a sword to my throat by the afternoon.

"You'll be safe," he says as if reading my mind. Maybe he actually can. "The queen summoned me. It might be related to her brother's assassination. I have to go."

"Take me with you." I blurt out the request. Catching the king's killer will at least stop the rumors that I did it. "I can't stand by and let my family bear the risk if—"

"Nothing will happen to them."

"Like nothing happened to the king?" Instantly, I wish I could take it back.

His jaw clenches, but his voice is steady. "Don't worry. I learn from my mistakes. But I need to focus. I won't be able to do that if you're tagging along. This is dangerous work, and you have a way to go with a sword before you're ready to wield one."

He might be talking about the sword, but his words land somewhere else. On the mark hiding under my shirt that I'm also not ready to wield—and probably never will be.

I flush deeper. "Is that why Taliesin tested me?"

Bishop doesn't answer. "I'll be back soon."

What's the point of arguing? I'm an inconvenience to him. Nothing more.

I turn toward the kitchen door, but he doesn't follow.

I can't just sit around and wait for someone to attack me again. I can't wait for someone else to absolve me.

There are a dozen reasons why I might be safer here, but until this is over, my family isn't. Bishop believes he's protecting me, but protecting them is my job.

I turn to tell him that, but he's already disappearing back into the fog.

How many sides are there to a man like him? The same number as there are stars in the sky?

I start after him, but something stops me. Maybe it's the part of me that knows he's right. Maybe it's the side of him I saw today.

Inside, the house is warm and bright. There's a tray of cookies cooling on the table. I snag one, silently cursing Bishop for leaving me while he disappears again.

But I can't stop thinking about Breccan, about Shea, about the strange, fragile hope that survives even here. Maybe I'm wrong about everything in Vennaro.

But if today taught me anything, it's that I can't risk letting my guard down. Especially with a man willing to hold a sword to his *friend's* throat. Not before I figure out why Bishop protected me. Again.

SIXTEEN

"Twelvetide is almost here," Lenora announces one rare sunny morning.

Her greeting is an unwelcome reminder that time keeps moving here whether I want it to or not. Especially since each morning brings the possibility that I'll wake up with Ravenell magic burning in my veins.

"So?" I finish lacing my collar and turn to find her holding a tray laden with pastries and fresh coffee. Clearly it's a bribe, although I don't know what she wants from me. Twelvetide is still six weeks away.

Over the last several days, she's chased me from the kitchen, fussed over my choice to wear pants instead of dresses, and refused to allow me to help with even the simplest task—only to show up with food at every opportunity. I can't decide if she's pleased to have a guest with Bishop away on business so often, or if I'm one more chore added to her list.

She places the tray on a small table by the hearth and pours a cup of coffee. "Bishop always hosts a party for his family and the conscripts." She passes me the mug, adding, "It's a tradition."

Suspicion seeps into my chest, but I accept the bait. "I'm not a conscript."

"No, you are the guest of honor."

I stare at her, waiting for the punch line.

She doesn't blink.

Guest of honor? This has to be her idea.

I set the cup down so quickly that coffee sloshes onto the saucer. "I doubt Bishop wants me there."

His lengthy absence suggests as much. Although each day he's away in the royal city renews hope that he's close to catching the king's killer, which might clear my name enough to prevent further assassination attempts.

A girl can dream.

But even if he does, I'll still have the mark of Ravenell on my chest. Bishop told me I might be able to find answers here. But despite his claim, he hasn't volunteered the forbidden book he took from the shop in Wintour—and I've been too chickenshit to call him on it.

I'd asked Lenora for books, afraid to trespass in Bishop's obviously *sacred* library, but she'd brought mostly boring military histories about the Last War. Nothing about Order Ravenell. Not exactly a surprise. Those books and the dangerous magic in them were destroyed by the first king five hundred years ago. She only blinked when I asked her to check for a book about scions, like she'd never heard of them. The lack of answers, of anything solid to grab on to, has left me restless, especially because I don't even know where to start looking.

Still, the *last* thing I want is to go to a party. My shoulders droop along with my mood. Twelvetide is meant to be spent with family.

But Lenora waves off my concern with a flick of her hand. "You'll need a gown," she says, completely ignoring my sputter of indignation. "More than one, honestly."

"I don't need—" I start to protest.

"You can't wear borrowed clothing all the time," she cuts in. "You need your own wardrobe, starting with a gown for the holiday."

"I'm not sure I'll even be here," I mutter, but she's not listening as she smears butter on an additional bribe.

"Wolf's Keep has a dozen forges but only one seamstress." She thrusts the biscuit into my hands. "She's very good, but she'll get busy soon. Even *soldiers* dress up for the holidays."

That's not a pointed statement at all.

But the thought of visiting a village where everyone is armed to the teeth is not my idea of a great morning. I slouch against the wall. "Can't I just wear one of the old uniforms? They're growing on me."

Lenora actually laughs. "That's Bishop's solution to every problem—put on black and call it a day. You two are quite the pair."

"We're not . . . I mean . . ." I trip over my own tongue. "There's no two. No pair."

The man can barely stand to be in the same house as me, if his constant travel is any indication.

"Of course not." She inclines her head, but her eyes sparkle. "That doesn't change the fact that you need your own things."

I glance down at my scrounged-up wardrobe. Nothing I'm wearing belongs to me. I'm living in borrowed spaces in borrowed clothes on borrowed time. The only thing that's mine is the mark burned over my heart.

I wrap my arms around myself. "The last party I attended might as well have been my funeral."

Lenora softens. It's the first time I've mentioned the night of the Petition, though I'm sure she's heard about it from others. "But it wasn't, love." She reaches over, smoothing my hair back. I wonder if she did that when Bishop was little—if he ever let her. But before her gentle touch can win me over, she's back to business. "Finish up. Vessica's waiting in the kitchen. You two can stop at the post to see if you've had any letters."

Just like that, the conversation is over. Maybe I have it all wrong. Maybe Lenora is the one who taught Bishop how to give orders.

But she pauses in front of the window and gasps. "It can't be."

"What is it?" I jump to my feet. As soon as I look out to the garden, my knees nearly buckle when I spot the oscen roosting on the branch of an overgrown willow.

Lenora taps the glass, but the bird doesn't budge. "I haven't seen one since I was a girl." She leans forward to get a better look. "How auspicious."

"Auspicious?" I repeat, still staring at it, my heart sinking inch by inch. "An omen, you mean."

She lifts her shoulders, shaking her head slightly. "Life is always sending us signs. *We* decide if they're good or bad ones."

I nod, only half listening. Lenora hums that melody I can't place under her breath as she leaves the room, but I never look away from the bird.

I'm pretty sure the escaped pet of a dead king is following me—and there's only *one* way to interpret that.

I continue to the kitchen with a half-eaten biscuit and a growing sense of dread.

Polishing it off in a few bites, I still don't feel better. It's hard to decide what's worse—attending this upcoming party, actually getting a letter from back home, or the prospect of spending the day with Vessica, who always looks like she's deciding which of my bones to snap first.

She's already waiting by the kitchen fire, her mouth set in a grim line. "Ready?" she asks. "The sooner we go, the sooner we're done."

"What if we told Lenora no?" I suggest in a whisper, afraid she will overhear. She can't be far. I don't need a dress, and I doubt there's a letter waiting already.

Vessica huffs as she snatches a scone from the prep table. "Never bite the hand that feeds you."

It's a testament to Lenora's domestic authority that even Vessica doesn't dare upset her.

Before I can concoct another plan to get out of this, Lenora swoops in with a coat and a pair of gloves. "You two will take the postern. I know Wolf's Keep is only a few miles away, but it's faster, and I don't want you walking all the way there in this cold. Besides, yesterday someone tracked half the mud in Vennaro into the house with them."

I'm suddenly very invested in my buttons. I hadn't noticed my boots were muddy yesterday afternoon when I went out for a walk. Then again, apart from soldiers, mud is Vennaro's primary commodity.

But Vessica blinks at the lecture. "Of course we will," she says slowly, like she's not certain why this is a discussion. "You know I hate wasting time."

I bet the ice queen feels right at home traveling by postern.

"Use the one by the gate. It's closer than the bridge," Lenora says, herding us toward the back door.

Vessica strides through it without so much as a goodbye to Lenora, who's too busy fussing with my coat collar to notice.

"Stay with her." Lenora studies me for a moment before sighing. "And try to enjoy yourself. Just not *too* much."

I don't think there's any danger of that, especially given my companion. I glance outside to Vessica. "She's not exactly the outgoing type, is she?"

"Nope. But she'll keep you safe. Bishop trusts her, and so do I." Lenora grins and pushes me out the door.

A blast of wind nearly knocks me down as I step outside. The temperature must have dropped ten degrees overnight. It's as if even the weather is eager for the upcoming holiday and putting on its wintery best in anticipation. I don't care about dresses or parties, but at least visiting Wolf's Keep will give me a chance to get out of the house and see some of the world.

The garden path is slick with dew and scattered leaves. Glancing back, I see Lenora watching from the door, arms folded, like she's not sure we'll come back in one piece.

"Let's get this over with," Vessica says, muttering a few choice words about the cold as she pulls her long wool coat tighter, and we start toward the back gate.

The postern is tucked behind a stand of half-withered evergreens currently under invasion by brambles. Only the top of the arch—etched with nochtimetric sigils—is visible through the overgrowth.

"Why couldn't we use the one inside the house?" I ask when I see its condition.

Vessica frowns, draws her sword, and hacks some of the tangled mess away. "This is the closest postern."

I should keep my mouth shut, but my jaw is practically a broken hinge. "Bishop and I entered directly into the great room the day we arrived."

She pauses, her sword hovering in the air for a moment like she might turn it on me. I take a step away, remembering what Taliesin said about her stabbing him in the back.

"Not every postern is . . . approved," she says carefully.

"Bishop mentioned that when we used his portable one. I don't see why being unlicensed stops us from using the one in the house."

"Of course he told you," she says under her breath, as if she thinks he should have kept this a secret. "Only Bishop can use his family posterns. Just like only your family can use Icaros ones."

"There are no Icaros posterns."

"Hmph" is her only response.

"What does that mean?" If my family had a personal postern at our disposal, I'd know. On the rare occasions that we use one at all, we use the one near the post like everyone else.

But she's silent as she sheathes her sword.

Just another reminder of how small my family is in the scheme of things.

Vessica traces a few of the postern's etched lines, her finger dancing around in a chaotic pattern until sigils begin to glow. The air under the arch shimmers, and I suck in a deep breath, bracing myself. Before I exhale, Vessica is already through.

"Don't wait for me," I grumble. Closing my eyes, I dart forward. My boots skid on flagstone, and I nearly crash into Vessica, who's standing at the edge of a public street with her arms folded, looking like she's been waiting for me her entire life.

"You okay?" she asks, not sounding particularly concerned.

"I'm not dead," I manage, but my teeth buzz from the double blow of the postern's cold and the weather.

"Good enough." She scans our surroundings. "Stay close to me."

Squat buildings line the street, nearly lost in a haze of smoke. The sound of clanging metal rings out all around us. Every other business is a forge, and every structure appears built for defense, as if the lives of each soul in Wolf's Keep revolve entirely around the needs of Order Marius. Houses and shops are packed tightly together, their roofs sloped to shed rain and their windows barred like the village's inhabitants always expect intruders and never guests. The wood used to build is old and battered, but nothing is broken or in disrepair. The streets are wide and paved. Every pothole is filled. The town is rough but ready for whatever the Stars throw at them.

Vessica moves through it like she owns the place, a privilege she's earned as a knight. Although I suspect she had that confidence long before the rank. People nod as she passes, their eyes sliding right over me. But it's better than being stared at.

We head for what might be considered the main street in an average village. Still, normal trades—a baker, apothecary, and grocer—feel like an afterthought here. A sign swinging over the entrance of The Last Drop tavern reads: No Fights. No Questions. No Credit.

The dress shop is tucked beside it, colorful gowns displayed in the windows. Vessica deposits me there, promising to return after a quick trip to the post.

I survive the entire fitting before she returns and taps on the glass like she refuses to even step foot inside. Sliding the receipt into my pocket, I mutter a quick thanks to the seamstress and hurry out to find Vessica studying one of the dresses through the window. It's made from deep blue velvet, cut close to the body, the sleeves slashed with silver and lined in white silk. Severe but elegant.

I clear my throat as I close the door behind me. "You should try it on."

"I have no use for dresses." But her eyes linger.

"Lenora says even soldiers dress up for Twelvetide."

She snorts. "Only the ones trying to catch someone's eye."

I can tell what she thinks about doing that.

"You could wear it for yourself," I say quietly. "Who cares what anyone else thinks?"

Her gaze narrows. "If you believed that, you wouldn't keep covering up that mark on your chest."

I want to tell her that she's wrong, but I can't.

"Here." She thrusts a single envelope into my hand along with a small box wrapped in brown paper. "These were at the post for you."

My heart thunders at the sight of Kieren's sloppy handwriting. The envelope is thin. There can't be more than a single piece of folded parchment inside. But a package? After weeks with no word, I resist the urge to tear it open.

"I can't dance anyway," Vessica confesses as we turn to leave, her tone so conversational that I nearly trip on the threshold.

Before I can point out how easily we can remedy that, the doors of the neighboring tavern burst open. People spill into the street toward the Civicus in the center of the square. There's already a group clustered around, arguing over something posted there. I can't see what, but the energy has shifted since I entered the shop an hour ago. Voices rise and fall like a storm. People are tense, glancing between the Civicus and the street like they're looking for something.

A couple of them spot me and stare.

"They know you're the raven-marked one," she warns me in a low voice. "They all do."

Raven-marked.

I reach to adjust the collar of my coat, eyes darting around like I might catch people gawking in every nearby window. "How? Did Bishop send out announcements?"

"Of course not." She looks offended on his behalf. "The whole kingdom knows. The Quincentennial was a matter of public interest."

For so many reasons, it's hard to believe that I'm one of them. But the thought that people know what's hidden under my shirt . . .

Vessica grabs my elbow. "We should go."

I follow, ducking my head as we weave our way through the clogged street. Vessica doesn't break stride, but she keeps her hand on her sword like she expects trouble.

My eyes stray to the Civicus as we pass, and I stop in my tracks when I see the headline.

ANOTHER MURDER IN DAMALIS

I stare, the shouts around me fading, the people forgotten as the world stops spinning and recenters on that single word. Damalis? How? Thoughts crowd my brain until my head hurts and my eyes strain from staring at the headline. *Who?* A jolt of adrenaline startles me out of my stupor. I move without thinking, pushing through the crowd to get a closer look, two words practically screaming at me even from a distance: *heart removed.* Like the king. When I don't recognize the victim's name, I nearly collapse with relief. But a murder this close to home? Things like that don't happen in Damalis. Maybe that's why Kieren finally wrote to me. I reach into my pocket for the letter as someone shouts from behind me. They're too far away for me to catch what was said, but it sets off a ripple and people turn.

In my direction.

A woman next to me jabs my shoulder with her finger. "It's her! That's the one from the palace!"

"The harbinger," another voice yells, loud enough to carry.

The word bounces from mouth to mouth—*harbinger, harbinger, harbinger*.

I try to back up, but someone shoves me, and I stumble into another stranger, dropping my package on the ground. They shove me until I'm being pushed around from person to person like I'm nothing more than that rising chant on their lips. Hands rip at my coat, my hair—each person trying to take a piece of me. Someone yanks hard enough that my neck snaps back. Another fist catches my ribs. I taste copper and realize I've bitten my tongue. The chant swells until it's the only thing I can hear.

Suddenly, the hands and fists vanish, and I crash, my knees hitting the street with a jarring crunch that rattles me all the way to my teeth. Vessica steps in front of me and draws her sword with a deliberate slowness, allowing each inch of the metal to catch the watery afternoon light.

"Back off," she says, voice flat as a gravestone.

The mob hesitates. No one wants to be the first to test her.

Finally, a man spits at my feet, a gold tooth flashing when he sneers at me. "Go back to where you came from, witch."

I flinch, but Vessica simply whips the sword toward him—and taps its point on his nose. "What was that?" she asks. He stammers something, eyes crossed as they focus on the tip of her blade, but she shakes her head. "I didn't hear you. *What did you say?*"

"N-Nothing," he finally manages.

She presses the flat of the sword's tip to the base of his nose, forcing his head up. "*No*. I distinctly heard you," she says. "You said: *I'm sorry, my lady*. Now, try again. Louder this time so everyone can hear you."

The man's throat slides, red creeping up his neck, but he opens his mouth and shouts the words.

Vessica withdraws the sword as a half dozen guards jostle their way toward us. The crowd begins to disperse, most splintering off in the face of more weapons.

"Make sure that no one follows us," she orders the men. They pull their swords and form a shield around us. I scramble for the package, relieved that only the paper is torn. Vessica grabs my arm, still holding her sword with the other, and drags me down the closest alley.

The crowd gets louder behind us, people shouting and arguing, but we don't stop to see if they've broken past the guards. She doesn't let me go until we reach the postern, and then it's only to slam her hand against it, tracing the pattern with lightning speed.

"Get in," she barks as soon as it begins to glow.

I don't argue, and this time, the cold of the portal is a relief.

We stumble out into the garden at Miradores, breathless, the world suddenly eerily quiet.

Vessica sheathes her sword and leans against the garden wall, closing her eyes.

I hover. What do I say first? An apology for nearly getting us killed? Do I ask about what I read? In the end, I settle for: "Thanks."

Even if she was only following Bishop's orders—and I'm certain she was—she could have left me at the crowd's mercy.

She frowns. "You can thank me by keeping your head down next time and not wandering off."

"Sorry," I mutter, meaning it. "I wasn't thinking."

"You better start thinking," she warns me. "You need to learn to use a sword before you go back to the village."

I manage a nod, but there's no way I'm returning to Wolf's Keep. Even here, hundreds of miles from where the latest murder happened, people think I'm responsible. It won't be safe to leave the estate until the killer is caught.

When Vessica finally looks at me, her eyes are bright. "Are you okay?"

"No," I admit, then draw a long breath. "But I will be."

No matter what it costs me.

SEVENTEEN

Arden,

Thank you for letting us know you arrived.

Your family is safe.

—Kieren

Two lines. Four if you count the pleasantries of writing out our names.

No "I miss you." No "come home." Not even a "don't die."

My body crumples onto the bed, the springs creaking under a weight suddenly too heavy to carry. I don't know what I'd hoped to hear, but *nothing* wasn't on the list.

Tears blur my vision, and I drag my forearm across my eyes before they can make it to my cheeks. Like that might erase the sting before it settles any deeper. I hadn't expected Broderic to reply. He's too stubborn. But Kieren?

We've spent nearly our whole lives together. We have our own language of shared looks and inside jokes. And now it's reduced to two lines that feel as shallow and distant as strangers nodding to each other on the road.

I read it again. And again. Each time hoping the words might shift, soften, reveal something I missed the first dozen times through. They don't. They just sit there, indifferent to the fresh wound they've carved into me.

I fold the note carefully this time, smoothing the crease with my thumb, like gentleness might coax something kinder from the message. I drop it on the bed next to the package, the contents of which are somehow even worse.

An old pair of shoes, a few worn shirts, my comb. A collection of things from a life that's no longer mine. Thrown into a box. Whoever packed it didn't even take the time to fold the clothes.

Lying back, I stare at the ceiling and let my feelings settle from numb to something else entirely. Not sadness. Not even anger. It's the heavy, increasingly familiar ache of being dispensable.

I stay that way for a long time—until the light fades and shadows lengthen. Until I'm sure Lenora isn't going to hunt me down and force me to the table for dinner. Until I convince myself that there's no piece of my heart left to break.

Tucking the letter in my pocket, I go down to find something I can eat that will help put me back together.

It's fine. It's all fine. I don't need anyone.

But I can't shake the urge to burn the box and its depressing contents in the fireplace, just to see if that leaves a mark, too.

The great room's chairs are empty, and the kitchen is deserted. There's a plate of food waiting on the prep table, but, for once, I'm not hungry. Probably because the letter in my pocket feels like a splinter under my skin. The kind that only burrows deeper when you try to deal with it. I guess some pain even food can't soothe.

So, I find the wine instead.

Prying out the cork, I pour wine into a chipped mug and drink it in one go. It burns all the way down, but the taste is dark and rich, almost sweet. I pour a second glass, then take the whole bottle and wander back into the hall.

I've just finished my second cup when I hear Lenora singing. *"Run, gray wolf, the stars are falling . . ."*

Her sad tune grows louder as she moves through the great room. *"Oh lovers weep, war is calling."*

The song isn't exactly a pick-me-up. But it's the possibility of a lecture, even a well-intended one, that sends me ducking into a small parlor near the front door. A room I've never been in nor seen another soul enter. Lenora's voice fades in the opposite direction, but I linger in my new hideout.

The furniture is formal, all gilded wood and ornate silk upholstery. Nothing about it seems to fit with the rest of the estate, especially the polished black piano that looms like a phantom in one corner. But there's not a speck of dust to be found—the only proof that anyone's been here in years. I take up residence on a built-in bench under the bay window, safely tucked out of sight thanks to the heavy curtains hanging on either side. It's the perfect place to hide from the world.

I curl up on the cushion, knees to my chest, and sip the wine. Slowly at first, then faster. Eventually, I stop bothering to pour it into the mug and drink directly from the bottle, watching raindrops race down the window-pane's warped glass until the world outside is painted in deep blues and blacks. Overhead, the Night's Scar is empty save for one bright dot. I sink back, nestling into the cushions like the new star will see me.

I drink half the bottle before heavy footsteps that don't belong to the housekeeper interrupt my sulking. Bishop is home. Yesterday, I might have been excited, might have been hopeful that he would have news. But I have no home to return to, so I take another drink.

He walks right up to me, his arms folded and his mouth flattened into a thin line.

"Celebrating something?" he asks.

I glare up at him, cradling the bottle like it's as precious as a child. "Your glorious return. I thought you'd left for good."

He ignores the gibe at his absence and eyes the label. "You know Lenora will flay you alive if you finish that whole thing."

"She's not my mother."

His mouth twitches, but he doesn't smile. "No. She's worse."

"Find anything in Wintour?" I dare to ask him.

He pauses, and my heart leaps, only to plummet when he shakes his head. "Dead end."

I'm not sure it really matters if he catches the king's assassin anymore. My family has obviously disowned me, which is even more effective than clearing our family name.

"The queen kept you there long enough," I say, changing the topic before I get even more depressed.

He hesitates as if he doesn't want to tell me the real reason he was gone so long. Probably something to do with his unwanted houseguest.

So, I swig again, practically daring him to take it from me. He does, but instead of scolding me, he raises it to his own lips and takes a long swallow before he hands it back. "You shouldn't drink alone."

There isn't a single light on in the room, and in the dark, he's more a shadow than a man. If this house *is* haunted, maybe Bishop is its ghost.

"Not much else to do," I say with a shrug.

He sits on the window seat, the wood creaking under his weight.

"There's always something to do," he says.

I snort. "Like what? No one will let me lift a finger."

"That's not true." He shakes his head. "You could train. Learn how to fight."

"For what?" I ask, voice sharper than any sword he might hand me. "Oh, wait, I remember. All the times people try to kill me, including your friends."

He doesn't even blink. "We have a saying at the Bellatorum: Wolves will bite."

"Yeah? No shit." I sip again, the wine warming my stomach, and pass the bottle to him. "What else do you say? The sky is blue?"

"It means . . ." His forehead creases as he considers how to explain it. ". . . no one hunts what can hurt them back."

Somehow, it doesn't feel that easy. "And if they still do?"

His gaze doesn't leave mine. "Then the wolf chooses to live."

"Profound." He continues to stare. I sigh and swipe the wine. I'm going to need to be a little drunker for this conversation. "You really want me to learn to fight?"

"Vessica told me what happened in Wolf's Keep. It wouldn't be a bad idea if you carried a sword."

I set the bottle on the floor. There's no amount of wine that can convince me *that's* a good idea. "Remember the last time I pulled a knife on someone?"

Like he could forget.

"That's exactly why you should learn how to use a blade," he says in a measured tone, as if slowing it down will help me understand what's at stake. "The only thing more dangerous than a sword pointed at you is having one in your hands that you don't know how to use."

"Well, pretty much everybody wants me dead. Odds are, someone succeeds." Is that the wine talking? Probably. Is the wine right? Unfortunately. "So, I'm not sure training me will matter much."

He looks at me, *really* looks, and for a second, I see something almost like pity cross his face.

"It matters," he says. "More than you know. Most people freeze. You fight back. It would just help if you knew what you were doing."

I pick at a thread on the cushion, unsure what to say.

He stands and holds out his hand. "Come with me."

He's not wearing gloves, and I hesitate, my eyes snagging on his bare skin, on the silvery lines that form patterns unlike any birthright mark I've ever seen. Curiosity wins, and I drop my hand in his to see if something will happen when I touch those lines. His fingers close around mine, and the jolt that goes through me has nothing to do with those strange markings. My skin warms under his touch, heat traveling across my skin. I want to pretend it's also due to the wine, but I'm too drunk to lie—even to myself.

Bishop pulls me upright, releasing me as soon as I'm on my feet, and shoves both hands in his pockets. I reach down to snag the bottle of wine, taking another long pull before following him out.

The house is quiet, apart from the faint ticking of a clock and the occasional creak of a floorboard. I should ask where we're going, but my brain is too muddled from the combination of wine and his touch to care. He strides past the library and takes the stairs two at a time, forcing me to keep up with him. But I stop in my tracks when he continues straight toward the western wing.

He traces a pattern on the lock, then pushes the door open and gestures me inside.

I hold my breath as I step through, half expecting a torture chamber, but it's only a sitting room. Large but not particularly grand, with a bank of east-facing glass doors and cozy, overstuffed furniture littered with mismatched pillows. The sea pounds the stone outside, making the floor shudder like it's breathing. The hearth is dark and cold, but Bishop twists a knob on the wall, and a pair of sconces blaze to life above it, illuminating a large, darker patch of paint over the mantel. Turning, I discover a dozen more dark spots, as if every portrait and painting that once hung in this part of the house has been taken down.

But there are unmistakable signs of life in the forbidden wing: scattered books on a table near the sofa, a pair of boots left next to a tufted stool, holes worn into the threadbare rug. The low ceiling with its thick, exposed beams is angled to the steep pitch of the roof, but the sitting room doesn't feel claustrophobic. It feels like shelter—like coming home.

"What's down there?" I point to the corridor that extends to one side. It's lined with more closed doors.

"Are you sure you don't want to try them yourself?" he asks, scooping a few papers off a nearby table and dumping them in a stack on another. "Maybe you'll get in this time."

My mouth falls open. "How did you . . ."

"The lock is coded to tell me if someone tries to enter."

Of course it is. Because this place is secure enough to be a prison. "You could have mentioned that." Then it hits me. "You were testing me."

"Maybe." He shrugs.

"And I failed," I say flatly.

"No surprise." But he nods to the other rooms. "This was my family's wing. I never bothered to move out."

I don't know what I expected to find. I trail my index finger over the cover of a book, outlining its title. I slowly trace the languid dips and swirls of an *S* and then a *C* as my mind races with the fact that we're alone in the forbidden part of his house.

Being alone with him here feels different. Maybe that's why I'm suddenly too aware of him. Aware of the broad span of his shoulders in the low light. Of the way he seems to fill the space—fill my *thoughts*.

"I'm a little disappointed," I admit, trying to ignore that dangerous realization. "Tell me there's a dungeon hiding down the hall."

"My study, bedroom. The rest were . . ." Bishop picks up the book and adds it to an already teetering pile.

I lift a brow. Somebody hates people touching his belongings.

"I stopped making Lenora clean in here. She has enough to do," he explains, already moving on. "I want to show you something."

He crosses to the glass doors and pushes them open to reveal a large stone terrace. Ocean air snaps at my clothes as I follow him out. Thanks to my blood alcohol content, I barely notice. The balcony juts out over a cliff, its railing slick with moss and sea spray. Bishop grips it, staring at the wild, black water.

"This is where I come when I want to be alone," he says, voice almost lost to the roar of the water below.

I shiver as I step to his side. "Do you bring all your guests here?"

He laughs, but there's a bitter edge to it. "You're the first."

The sky is clear overhead, the rain having finally stopped, and thousands of stars glitter in the darkness, save for in the void of the Night's Scar. A thick mist drifts up from the sea and rolls across the balcony. Bishop shrugs off his coat and drapes it over my shoulders. I want to give it back and insist I don't need anything from him, but it's warm, and I've drunk too much to pretend. Like it or not, I'm alive at the whim of Bishop Marius. But right now? I don't hate it.

We stand like this for a long time, watching the sea batter the rocks below. My own thoughts churn just as violently, my wine-soaked brain compiling question after question that I shouldn't ask him.

When he finally takes the bottle from me, he frowns. "You finished it." He holds it upside down like there might be a few drops left.

"Hazard of drinking with company," I point out. "The wine goes faster."

He snorts. "It does. Hang on."

He disappears inside. When he returns, he's holding another bottle.

"I thought you didn't drink alone," I say as he passes it to me.

"I'm better at giving advice than following it."

"And not used to having company," I guess.

"Taliesin and Vessica—"

"Don't count," I stop him.

"They'll be thrilled to hear that."

I wave it off. "You can't count people paid to follow your orders."

"I suppose it's good that you're here, then. You wouldn't follow my orders if I *did* pay you." He sighs, but I could swear he wants to smile. "But that's why I brought you here, where I never feel alone."

"Because it was your family's wing?" I ask him.

"My father was always gone, even when he was here," he confesses. "My mother loved the sea. This wing used to be reserved for guests, but she wanted to wake up to the ocean."

"And your father wasn't around to stop her from claiming the western wing," I guess.

"He loved her too much to say no." He pauses, looking out into the endless abyss of night and ocean in front of us. "I thought he did it to make her happy, since he was always away on business and never home with us. I used to resent him for it."

"What changed?" I ask.

"I became patron." He sounds sad about it. "Now I understand."

"Tell me about it. I thought my parents made us do everything at home, but once they were both gone . . ." I shake my head. "It's a lot of responsibility."

He glances over at me. "Do you miss it, though?"

"All the work?" My laugh is laced with bitterness. "No. But my family? The land?" *Knowing where I belong? Having a place in the world?* I swallow and nod. "I do. But mostly I feel like an asshole for leaving Broderic to handle everything by himself."

"He'll figure things out." He picks up the bottle and takes a swig. "We all do."

"That's good news, because I don't have anything figured out. If you do, feel free to share," I say dryly.

"I work out most of my confusion on the proving grounds," he says, and I instantly regret seeking advice. "It might help you, too. Unless you'd rather avoid the Bellatorum after what happened in Wolf's Keep."

"I'll go back to the Bellatorum. I made a promise." I can't let fear lock me in this house forever, though I'm not about to join his army, either. "But you have enough conscripts to train, especially with all this talk of war coming and invading the Lost Continent."

"There won't be an invasion." His voice is so quiet that I'm certain I've misheard him.

"Are you sure about that?" I tap my chest. "Everyone else seems to think—"

"No one thinks," he cuts me off, his lip curling slightly. "That's the problem. One supposed omen, and everyone loses their heads."

"Agreed." I lift the bottle.

"And I will not invade." The quiet determination in his voice makes me believe him.

Unfortunately, all the wine inside me has questions. "What if you're ordered to?"

"Duty only matters if you still have a choice," he says. "Once that's gone, it's just obedience."

"Is that why you don't force the children to join the army?"

"People trying to survive don't have choices. They obey. They endure. They become whatever keeps them breathing." He looks out at the sea. "The innocent deserve more than that. They deserve the right to decide who they become."

I pluck a patch of moss off the railing, noticing how several of the balusters are starting to crumble. "I'm not sure the crown agrees."

"The crown doesn't know."

Maybe the wine is loosening his tongue, too, so I ask the obvious question. "How? You must have to report numbers to them for funding and supplies."

Turning, he surveys Miradores with narrowed eyes like he can see it clearly, even in the dark. Then he sighs and takes a drink from the bottle. "I've found ways to make up the difference."

I glance at the house. I don't need light to know what he sees: a few poorly patched windows, plaster in need of repair, spots where the wood framing is soft with rot. A lump forms in my throat. "That's why so many things need to be fixed," I say softly. "Why you don't have a staff. Why the garden is dead."

He's using his own money to take care of those children.

"I let the garden die when my family did." But he nods and passes me the bottle like we're sealing some pact. "The rest is my secret."

"I won't tell anyone," I say, meaning it. Whatever doubts I have about Bishop, this I can respect.

"They'll figure it out eventually." He grimaces like the words taste sour. "Calix keeps sniffing around, asking to inspect our infrastructure. They suspect. Velesont and Leontia, too."

The bottle nearly slips from my hand, and I set it down before I drop it. It's not just about funding. The Bellatorum must be using more resources and supplies, too.

"Your family is the only one not asking questions." He gives me a pointed look.

It's my turn to spill what I know, but I can't help snorting. "My dad used to say that we don't care how many mouths there are, as long as they're fed.

But then, we've never been very good with money or politics." Or maybe one of us might have noticed.

"Maybe that's why the Stars chose you."

His words send my stomach spiraling. I don't know what to say, so I just stand beside him, letting the sea spray slowly soak my hair.

Bishop grips the railing, eyes darker than the sea below. "Sometimes, I think the problem isn't that the estate is falling apart or that it's empty. The problem is that it's not empty enough. Every room feels haunted."

His words tug at the ache inside me, calling out to some part of me that knows what it's like to live with regrets, if not ghosts. My fingers brush one of the pale lines on his knuckle, tracing it without thinking.

Bishop sucks in a ragged breath, and his hand tightens on the railing like he's anchoring himself to it. He looks at me, and for the first time I see the fear that he must usually hide behind that armor.

"You could tell me," I murmur. "What they are, I mean. I won't judge."

He laughs again, but it's softer this time. "You wouldn't believe me."

I think of the mark on my chest, how people flinch when they see me, the way the world seems to speed up every time I attempt to stand still. "Try me," I say.

But he straightens and releases his grip on the railing. "It's late. We should go in."

That's the problem with Bishop. If he lets you past one wall, it's just because he's already building a new one. Maybe the only way to make him stop is to let him past one of mine.

"They don't want me." I reach into my pocket and pull out the now-crumpled letter. Unfolding it, I hand it to him. "I know what I chose, but . . ."

I'm too embarrassed to tell him about the accompanying package.

His lips press into a thin line as he reads it. Then he wads it up and throws it into the ocean below. I whip around like I can catch it.

"Let the past be in the past," he says quietly but firmly.

I spin toward him. "That's easy for you to say."

He still has an estate, a title, a reputation. I don't even have a shitty letter from the person I thought was my best friend.

"No, it's not." His voice is strained. He lifts his hand toward me and hesitates like he might stop himself, then tucks a strand of my hair back. My breath snags as his fingertip traces the shell of my ear, and I have to fight the urge to press my cheek against his palm. "Go to bed. Things will look different in the morning."

But right now, I'm seeing things clearly. Or maybe I'm just seeing *him* clearly. We're both alone because of the choices we've made, only some of which we've confessed. But maybe we're not keeping secrets from each other. Maybe we're just keeping them from ourselves. Maybe that's why we're out here in the middle of the night together—so those secrets can't haunt us in the dark.

I reach for his hand and slip mine through it. "What if I don't want to go to bed?"

It's the wine talking again, but it has a point.

Bishop closes his eyes for a second, and when he opens them again, the blue of his irises looks like sparkling starlight. "Go to bed."

Not an order. A plea.

But still a blow to my ego. "Because you're a bishop? Because you're above . . . the rest of us?"

"A bishop is still a man. We aren't above. We're apart," he explains quietly, but his thumb brushes the back of my hand, stoking the fire slowly building inside me. "The title reminds us of our duty even when we're surrounded by the temptation to forget it."

"And that's what I am—your *duty*." I start to pull away, but he doesn't let me go.

"No," he whispers, finally releasing me, "you're my temptation."

The confession nearly knocks the air out of my lungs. My pulse stutters, then races forward, hammering in the middle of my throat. I can't deny that I've wondered about the rest of him. About what he could do with that warrior's body. About how that silver-blond hair would feel between my fingers or, better yet, between my legs.

"Go to bed, Arden," he whispers again.

Humiliation floods through me, jolting me from the wine's haze, and I inhale sharply. At the sound, his gaze drops to my mouth. It lingers there for a heartbeat that stretches until it aches. He isn't noble. He's fucking scared. Scared of me. Or whatever is happening between us.

That makes the decision for me. It *is* time to go to bed.

"You don't get to call me a temptation and pretend that's noble," I say quietly as I shrug off his coat and toss it at him. "That's just dressing up fear and calling it virtue."

"Arden—"

But I'm already walking away. He's made his choice. There's no time to question mine. "Sleep well, Bishop," I say, flipping him off over my shoulder as I add, "with your ghosts."

EIGHTEEN

I wake with a headache so precise, it feels like someone's drilled a hole in my skull.

The only thing louder than my pulse is the patter of rain dripping from eaves and windowsills. For a minute, I lie there, trying to decide if I'm alive or being tortured in the fifth ring of hell—the one reserved for gluttons. Or maybe I'm in the third, because I'm pretty sure I wanted to fuck Bishop last night.

Not my finest hour.

The memory chases me out of bed. I dress, avoiding the clock and the mirror. I don't want to know what time it is, and I'm too mad to look at myself. But there's a mug of coffee already poured and cooling on the table by the time I step into the kitchen. The first sip is enough to convince me that I'm alive. The second is enough to make me wish I wasn't.

Lenora is gone, but her touch is everywhere—dough rising under a towel, one loaf of bread already cooling on the rack, a to-do list poking out of a novel like a bookmark.

I pick it up, another fuzzy memory of last night returning: Bishop taking a book from me because I touched its cover. Because I traced its freaking title.

No, because it was the fucking book he took that day in Wintour and shoved into his cloak. Likely the same one he told Taliesin about in the kitchen—the night his friend proposed murdering me.

Last night, I'd traced an *S* and a *C* . . . for scions. The book was in his wing the entire time. This is what I get for drinking so much starsdamned wine. Whatever he's hiding, I can't shake the feeling it has something to do with why the stars cursed me with Ravenell magic. That's why he took the book from me.

Maybe he isn't trying to help me at all.

Maybe that's why he called me a temptation and hid behind his title and vow.

Or maybe he's just as fucking confused as I am, too busy wrestling his own demons.

Regardless, I can't trust him. No matter how kind he is or what he's given up for the people in his charge.

He's a Marius, and I am . . . not. I can't forget that.

I creep to the western wing, my headache now feeling like fitting punishment for my multiple lapses in judgment. But it's locked. Maybe Bishop is regretting his choices, too.

So, I head to the next best thing. The library that I've been avoiding like a coward since I thought I saw a ghost. The idea seems almost laughable now. Bishop has one forbidden book. There are probably others. Ones about whatever secrets he's keeping, and probably plenty about Ravenell. Lenora either didn't know where to look or wouldn't touch them.

That's why I was scared away from the library, and I can't keep letting fear make choices for me.

I need answers about the mark the Stars branded me with before it's too late, even if I haven't felt the tiniest tingle of magic stirring in my blood yet. Some nights I lie awake, taking inventory of my own body, terrified I might find it. Magic has never skipped a member of the Icaros bloodline. I'd be the first. That thought used to scare me, but with Ravenell's mark on my chest . . .

I have to know what I'm up against. I push open the door with more force than necessary. It swings wide open, and I stop in my tracks.

The library might as well be a cathedral. But not one dedicated to the worship of the Stars. Nope, this place is all about the books. Three stories rise toward a stained glass dome, each floor filled with shelves, and every inch of those crammed with books bound in leather and cloth. Wide balconies ring the upper levels, connected by a spiral staircase carved from mahogany. The windows are also stained glass, each panel depicting a different constellation. Light pours through them, dappling the main floor's reading tables and benches in blue and gold and crimson. Leather chairs are stationed around the perimeter, their high winged backs ideal for settling in with a book. At the far end, another cavernous fireplace hosts faintly smoldering logs. Even the air smells of ink and old paper.

I step inside, pulling the door closed behind me. The silence feels sacred. I half expect the Stars to smite me for even breathing in here.

Circling the first level, I eye the spines on display. Most are records, military treatises, collections of laws and judgments. The kind of books that Lenora brought me. The next section is labeled with engraved brass plaques. There are ones for philosophy, geography, even nochtimetry. I start with that section. The shelves are meticulously organized, each book lined up like a good little soldier, exactly where it's supposed to be alphabetically. I run my finger along them, searching for anything out of place. In Wintour, I only glimpsed the book he stole. Only caught those two letters in the title: *S* and *C*. Now I know the rest of the title, and I'm hoping the library can tell me what it means.

I select a volume at random. The cover is black, embossed with a pattern of crossed swords and stars. The title is in the ancient tongue, which I can't read. Thankfully, the rest of the text and the inscribed dedication inside are not.

For the House of Marius—that the past
is neither forgotten nor repeated.

Not exactly a sentimental gift.

I flip through the pages, finding them dense with diagrams and footnotes. The text focuses mostly on the ethics of nochtimetry in warcraft. Yawning, I slide it back into place and move on.

The next shelf down is stranger. The books are smaller, some barely larger than my palm. Some have plain, unmarked covers. Others have handwritten titles dashed in illegible scrawl. I flip one open and find patterns and measurements, some only partially finished, all drawn by hand. They're journals of some kind. The text is minimal, more notes than sentences, and, unfortunately, most of it *is* actually written in the ancient tongue.

I'm so absorbed that when I hear faint footsteps behind me, I nearly jump out of my skin.

I freeze, the book half open, and glance over my shoulder. The room is empty, but the air feels charged. Someone is in here. Quickly replacing the book, I scan the upper floors for movement.

But I'm alone apart from the dust drifting in constellations through the morning light. Relieved, I keep searching until I'm interrupted by the sound of a book snapping shut.

I spin and shriek when I find a man standing too close behind me. My hand flies to cover my mouth.

"Wrong shelf," he says.

My heart stays lodged in my throat for a full beat before I realize he's talking about the book. He yanks it out and shelves it along with his, but all I can do is gawk at him.

He's older than Bishop, maybe by ten years. Although it's hard to say, since his cropped hair is still brown with not even a hint of silver streaking it. And while his light brown skin is unlined, there's a heaviness in his dark eyes that suggests either wisdom or perpetual disappointment. Despite his robe, he can't hide the broadness of his shoulders, his build suggesting that he was once a man of action. Probably a knight.

For some reason, he's here of all places. He pushes a pair of wire-rimmed spectacles higher on his nose and looks at me like he's found a rat in the grain bin.

"Lost?" The question carries the edge of reproach, as though the books are meant to be looked at, not touched—or, Stars forbid, *read.*

Not a fucking ghost.

I flush, feeling caught, even though my hands are empty. I have no idea how long he's been watching me. "I was looking for a book."

Please don't ask which one.

He moves closer, his steps soundless on the thick rug. "Yes, that's usually what one does in a library. Just don't disturb the order." He gestures to the books with a curt nod. "They are arranged by subject and author. If you move one, put it back. If you dog-ear one, I'll notice."

He winces like the idea physically pains him.

I nod, fighting the urge to apologize. It's not like he's angry, more resigned to the inevitability of chaos in what's clearly his domain.

"Lenora warned me that Bishop is particular about his books," I say instead. "I didn't mess anything up."

Why didn't she warn me about this guy?

He considers for a moment. "Hadrian. I'm a friend of the family."

That ghosts around the library?

"Arden," I reply, forcing myself to add, "Icaros."

His eyebrows lift a fraction higher. "The initiate from Damalis. Bishop mentioned you were with us."

I wait for him to call me harbinger, or Ravenell, or monster. But he just moves to check that I have, in fact, left the books in order.

"If you're looking for something specific," Hadrian says, already turning back to the shelves as if the conversation is an inconvenience, *"ask."*

I glance at the shelves, weighing his offer. "Are there any books in here about what happened to Ravenell during the Last War?" It's a slightly dangerous request, but one that might prove personally useful to warrant the risk. "Or the original patron families?"

"Plenty." But he doesn't elaborate.

I hesitate. "I was hoping there would be something . . . I don't know." I reach for the most convincing reason of all. "Maybe a way to break a harbinger's curse?"

If I can't figure out what Bishop is hiding, getting rid of this fucking mark might be equally useful.

His eyes narrow. "That's what you think it is?"

For weeks, I've pictured the faces of the people in the throne room and replayed the conversation I overheard between the men casually planning to kill me.

"If it was a curse, you'd already be dead," he adds. "A harbinger is only something people attach fears and hopes to—there's no true power in it."

"So, it's not a curse?" It sure feels like one to me.

His mouth tightens. "It's a challenge. Maybe a reminder."

"And who is being reminded?"

"Everyone," he says darkly, but then he shrugs. "Or no one. Sometimes the Stars just like to stir the pot."

I scowl. "I wish they'd stirred a different pot."

"Yes." He manages a tired laugh. "Most people do."

"I haven't felt any magic yet," I confess. "Maybe the magic skipped me."

Maybe it was all a mistake.

He stares over his glasses at me. "The Kindling can take some time to manifest a single magic. If the Stars have chosen you as a Ravenell, you have access to all magic. I imagine that might take longer."

So much for wishful thinking.

"So, they just doomed me to this fate on a whim?" That's less comforting than thinking they did it for a reason.

He murmurs something in the ancient tongue, then translates when he sees my confusion. "The Stars incline us. They do not bind us."

When I raise a brow, he shrugs, adding, "You'll figure it out."

Well, that's helpful.

"If I find the right book," I say with a heavy sigh. There are a lot of books in here.

Hadrian snorts. "Knowledge is a dangerous weapon. Wield it wisely." He glances at me over the rim of his glasses. "And try not to turn it on yourself."

I came for a book. Now I'm getting a lecture. I might have preferred finding a ghost in the library.

Fuck it. I can't keep avoiding answers, even if it means asking his grumpy ass, and there is one subject left that might give me an explanation for all of this. "Do you have any books about scions?"

Hadrian freezes. "What do you know about scions?"

"Nothing," I admit.

He pins me with a look. "That's not a word you stumble upon."

I swallow so hard my eyes feel like they're going to explode.

Must drink less wine during future pity parties.

"Someone mentioned scions. It sounded . . . important."

He blinks before shrugging. "No one has written about scions since the Last War."

"Half these books must be older than that." I've picked up at least six that are in the ancient tongue, and no one's writing in that dead language these days.

He's quiet for a beat. "The subject is forbidden. That should tell you enough."

More forbidden than Ravenell? I can't quite screw up the courage to ask.

He takes off his glasses and wipes them on his robe. "Who mentioned it?"

"I don't remember," I lie. "Probably just gossip in the village. People mixing up fact and fiction."

"And you believed them," he scoffs, slightly shaking his head. "That's all history is: gossip and lies mixed up with facts. We're just stuck sorting out which is which."

If anyone even bothers. And why would they, when gossip is currency in Antares and lies are easier than facing the truth? "I feel like no one cares about the facts."

"Are we still talking about history?" he asks evenly.

"Maybe not," I admit. "I just wish I knew where I fit in all of this."

"You think a book will tell you who you are?" he asks.

"I don't know where else to look."

"You're looking in the wrong—" Hadrian cuts off as the library doors swing open and Bishop strides in, boots heavy on the marble, coat buttoned up like armor, hair pulled back but wet as if he's just stepped through a storm. There's stubble shadowing his jaw like he didn't bother shaving after a late night. My heart kicks at my ribs as I recall exactly why he was up late. It's annoying how good he looks even slightly disheveled.

Bishop stops cold at the sight of me with Hadrian. For a second, I see something in his face—surprise or disapproval, or maybe just his special knack for being perpetually unimpressed. It stings a little after last night.

Although that might just be my wounded pride.

"For the record, your visitor has not destroyed any of the collection today," Hadrian offers with a meaningful glance in my direction. "That's more than I can say about whoever was in the Florentia section."

"I'm not a visitor," I mutter, but neither is listening.

"Do I need permission to access my own library?" Bishop asks, one eyebrow raised.

"You will if you bleed all over any more of the books."

It had to be the night I overheard him in the kitchen with Taliesin.

"I'll do better." The promise comes out so stiffly, it takes me a moment to realize Bishop is being sincere.

"Next time, get the bandage," I mutter.

Bishop's gaze narrows on me, and I wish I could crawl under the table. But before I can lie my way out of the slipup, he says, "I'm leaving in ten minutes."

Running away again? Surprise, surprise. "And where are you off to this time?"

"Bellatorum," he says flatly. "You can come."

I blink. He's inviting me? "Is this a field trip, or am I being drafted?"

Or are you in the mood to torture both of us?

"Think of it as educational." He chooses the word carefully.

I snort. "So, you're planning to shove a sword in my hands?"

"Only if you want to train," Bishop says with a shrug. "You mentioned that you wanted to go back."

Something in my chest squeezes. He remembered.

"I do," I say. "I need to take some writing supplies to Breccan. Paper and pens. He's trying to learn his alphabet."

Bishop nods. "Supplies are in my study. It's the first door on the right. Try the top drawer in my desk. It's unlocked now," he says, and I realize he knows I tried to get into the western wing again.

Heat floods my cheeks. Fucking Stars, he probably thinks I was there to throw myself at him.

"Ten minutes," he repeats, "or I'm leaving without you."

It will take me five minutes just to get all the way to that side of the house. I race out of the library to his family's wing.

I can't stop myself from checking for the book I saw last night despite my hurry. But it's nowhere to be found in the sitting room, so I continue down the hall.

His study is a surprise. I expected it to be cold and severe, all business, like the man who uses it, full of weapons and secret files. But while those are here—swords racked over the mantel, a trio of battered ledgers stacked on the window ledge, even a dagger stuck point-down into the desk itself—there are also signs of life. A half-eaten apple on a plate, a mug with a ring of coffee clinging to the bottom, a chessboard frozen mid-game.

Dialing on the desk lamp, I peek in the top drawer to find a stack of folders with some type of travel log on top. Dates. Locations. Short entries written in the same tight hand as the notes I saw last night. But there are no writing supplies. I reach for the stack as Bishop appears in the doorway. "Wrong drawer."

Startled, I slam it shut and open the other to find a few notebooks, loose sheets of paper, pens, and ink. "Sorry." I gather as much as I can carry. "I didn't want you to leave without me."

His mouth quirks. It's not quite a smile but not a threat, either. "Ready?"

We're halfway down the stairs when I realize what I saw in that not-quite-smile. Bishop was pleased—which irritates me more than it should. Apparently, I'm the only one who feels awkward about last night.

"Why didn't you tell me about Hadrian?" I ask as we reach the landing.

He hesitates. "My uncle keeps to the library when he visits."

My stomach drops at his lie. Hadrian told me he was a friend of the family. But I don't call Bishop out. Obviously, he won't tell me the truth. "He visits just for the books?"

"He's helping me with some . . . research." He shuffles us toward the great room. "We should take the postern."

The bastard knows how to distract me.

"I'll walk." He gives me an incredulous look, but I shrug. "I know the way. Through the haunted garden, over the death-trap bridge, and head straight into the heart of your childhood trauma."

He snorts, which is probably the closest to a laugh that I'm getting out of him today. "If *we* walk, we'll both be soaked, and the paper will be ruined."

And we'll have to endure each other's presence after the embarrassing finale to last night's bonding exercises. Somehow, that idea sounds even worse than the postern.

"Fine," I say, tucking the writing supplies into my jacket to protect them. "Torture me."

"Your sacrifice is noted," he says, leading me into the great room.

"We're allowed to use this one today?" I ask as he walks toward the wall we came through the first day we arrived.

He sketches a pattern, and an arch shimmers to life. "Consider it a perk of spending time with me."

"This isn't the way to bribe me," I warn him as I approach it.

He rolls his eyes, grabs my hand, and drags me through. When he doesn't let go, the full-body shiver that crests over my skin has nothing to do with the cold.

The postern delivers us directly into the corridor of the Commons, which is teeming with people wearing stiffly starched uniforms. Most of them look anxious or, at the very least, curious. Bishop drops my hand and quickly puts distance between us as he tugs on a pair of gloves.

"New conscripts coming in for orientation," he explains, scrubbing at the back of his neck. "I should, uh . . ."

"Don't worry about me." I cross my arms and force a smile despite the lingering thud in my forehead. At least the hangover is a reminder why I should ignore any and all full-body sensations this man produces in me.

His forehead creases as he gazes down at me. "Arden." He hesitates before continuing gruffly. "We can walk back after . . . since you won't have paper to keep dry."

But I've learned my lesson. Now I just have to pass the follow-up test.

"Whatever." I wave him away. "Go play soldier."

He looks like he wants to say something else, but I walk away before he can.

Breccan is in one of the study rooms, huddled at the edge of a table too big for his small body. He's surrounded by older kids, most of them ignoring him, but his eyes are fixed on a battered notebook so full of scribbles that he's drawing in the margins. The moment he spots me, he jumps up, knocking it onto the ground, and rushes over.

"You came back," he whispers like my arrival is a big secret.

I can't help smiling. "I told you I would."

"Did you bring . . . ?" He squirms like he's nervous to ask.

I hand him the writing supplies. He takes them with reverence.

"Holy Stars." His eyes round as he hugs them to his chest. "There's so much of it. I can write forever."

I wish I had half his optimism. "Use it up. I can always bring more."

He grins. "Thank you, Lady Icaros."

I flinch. "Just Arden," I remind him as Shea joins us.

"I told him to use your title." She scrunches her nose at him. "I'm trying to teach him manners."

Breccan holds out the ink bottle to her. "Can you open this?"

Her sleeve rides up as she reaches for it, revealing a slender silver line on her wrist. She hurriedly pulls it down and breaks the wax seal. So, the marks are some Marius trade secret.

And just another reminder that I don't belong here.

"He'll use every page," she says as she gives the ink back to him. "But he'll share, too. He always does."

Breccan is already flipping open the notebook, eyes wild with possibility.

"Go on." She shoos him off to use his prize. Shea lowers her voice so only I can hear. "Thank you. When I'm a knight, I'll be able to afford supplies myself."

"Don't worry about it. I stole them from Bishop." The color drains from her face, and I quickly add, "It was his suggestion."

"I'm paying him back," she whispers fiercely. "I already decided. After we're in our own quarters, I'm paying Bishop back for every silver he's spent taking care of my brother."

The pride in her voice hits me like a punch. "You don't have to—"

"I do." She cuts me off with a shake of her head. "Most of these kids don't have families to support them. My brother does. This is my job."

I want to argue, but I can't. Not when the truth stares back at me in the shape of a girl with a sword and a brother who clings to hope like it's the last good thing left. If it were Andry and me, I'd feel the same way.

"I just wish the other kids . . ." She trails off, looking at the children seated near us. They're older than her brother but not by much.

"Bishop will take care of them." There are parts of him I don't understand, but, after last night, I believe that much.

"Will you show me how to write your name again?" Breccan calls over. He's already on the second page of his notebook.

"Of course." Then I remember that his sister is here. "If that's okay."

Shea nods. "I was on my way to the proving grounds." She glances at the hall. "If I can get past all these new conscripts."

"They don't have swords yet," I remind her, and she smiles.

She gives Breccan's shoulder a squeeze and mouths her thanks to me before slipping away.

I lose track of time, getting nearly as caught up in Breccan's struggle to perfect his *S* as he does. When I finally glance toward the windows, the rain is heavier against the glass.

"I'd better go," I say, scrambling to my feet. "Keep practicing. I'll come back soon."

Breccan beams like I've promised him the moon.

The Commons is free of new conscripts, and I hurry down the corridor, half jogging when I don't see Bishop anywhere nearby. I reach the front doors just in time to catch Bishop opening them, a folded list clutched in his fist.

His shoulders are so rigid that I can feel the tension from here.

Something's wrong.

"What is that?" I ask.

He glances up, startled to find me standing next to him. "What?"

"That." I point at the paper. "You look like you've seen a ghost."

"The list of new conscripts," he says without offering more explanation for his rattled appearance before he walks straight outside to the crowd gathered in the yard. There's more of them now, standing in uneven rows, their cloaks darkened with rain and boots sinking into the wet gravel.

Bishop scans the crowd, his jaw tight like he's waiting for someone to jump out and shatter his last nerve. His eyes finally land on someone in the crowd, and he curses under his breath.

I follow his gaze to the offending party and gasp, hand flying to my mouth.

He's standing with the rest of them, wearing a new uniform. This one fits so well I already know it was assigned to him. His hair is cropped shorter than the last time I saw him, but his face is set with that stubborn, mule-headed look he gets when he's determined. The start of a beard brackets his mouth, making him seem even older. Or maybe it's the decisions he's been forced to make aging him.

Water runs down his hair and into his collar, but he doesn't wipe it away. He's not talking to anyone. Everyone else looks like they'd rather be anywhere else. He doesn't. He's here for a reason.

Broderic did it. He actually forced Kieren into conscription.

Because I wasn't there to stop my brother.

I must have walked right past him in the hall when we arrived, so wrapped up in my own bullshit that I didn't even see him standing there.

I want to run to him, to scream at him for letting Broderic do this, or cry, or maybe both.

But my heart is in my throat, and I can't move.

Bishop's fist closes around the list, knuckles white as he fumes over his newest conscript. He doesn't look at me as he barks a single name.

My best friend looks right at him. At me. And his face doesn't change. There's not even a flicker of recognition. But I see him, and he sees me, and I already know how this ends.

Someone's getting hurt.

NINETEEN

Kieren doesn't move at the sound of his name, just stares Bishop down from the middle of the muddy courtyard. It takes a second for the rest of the pack to realize he's the one being called out. The others shuffle aside, their faces a mix of confusion, envy, and the kind of wary respect reserved for people who might lift themselves past the dregs.

Bishop speaks again, but I'm already moving. I cut straight through the line, boots squelching in the muck, tunnel vision blurring out everything except the idiot in the conscript uniform.

There's an ugly bruise on Kieren's cheek that wasn't there when we said goodbye. But his eyes—the same warm brown as always—find me, and the entire world shrinks to the space between us.

"What are you doing here?" I hiss, grabbing his arm and tugging him to the side. "Did my brother . . . ?" I can't even finish the sentence. If Broderic forced him out—made him sign up—then my brother should be glad it's not safe for me to leave Vennaro.

He doesn't pull away. If anything, he looks . . . relieved. Like the hard part was getting here, and now he can finally breathe. "Arden." He shakes his head. "No one forced me. It's a long story, but I chose to come here."

Bullshit. Unless . . . he came because of me. My stomach pitches as it hits me.

"You're here because you couldn't leave well enough alone." I want to shake him until his teeth rattle. "You're supposed to be in Damalis, taking care of Andry and Isidore. What the void are you thinking?"

One of us should be there.

"There wasn't much for me to do back home. Not after . . . everything."

"Not after what?" I demand. I want to punch something. Preferably

Broderic, for letting him leave. Although maybe Kieren could do with having some sense knocked into him.

His mouth twists, like he's chewing the words before spitting them out. "Your brother said things were handled once the troops arrived. No need for a guard when you have a personal army, right? I figured I could do more good here."

"Here?" I repeat. "You don't belong in Order Marius."

"I don't belong anywhere," he says bitterly.

The ache in my chest deepens because I know exactly how he feels. I want to say something—*anything*—that will fix this. That will make him see it isn't true. "Neither do I."

"That's why I'm here. I can't just let you face this alone."

Part of me wants to send him away. Tell Bishop to cross his name off the list. Order Kieren to go make a real life somewhere. Because he's not one of the Bellatorum's orphans. He signed up as an adult. He'll be expected to fight, and if Bishop is wrong, if we can't stop war from coming, if the other orders get their way and vote to invade the Lost Continent . . . There are a dozen reasons that this is the worst decision of his life. But I know why he made it, so I pull him into a hug so tight I might crack a rib.

He grunts in surprise but doesn't fight it. Instead, his arms circle me, warm and solid, and for a second, I'm home again. We stand like that, the rain slowly soaking us through, our audience forgotten.

When I finally let go, my hands are shaking. "You're a fool, but you're my favorite foolish, foolish man."

He grins, and the sight is so familiar it nearly guts me. "I missed you, too."

Behind us, Bishop clears his throat. A gruff reminder that we're not alone. I round on him, still gripping Kieren's sleeve like he might slip away. "Did you know about this?"

Bishop's face is stony. "Not until I saw his name on the roster."

The men exchange wary looks, appraising each other in this new setting. Bishop is half a foot taller, and in his fitted officer's uniform he looks like he could chew Kieren up and spit him out. But my best friend doesn't back down. It's a good, old-fashioned pissing contest, and neither wants to lose.

"Well," I say, refusing to let either off the hook, "Kieren's coming to dinner tonight."

Bishop blinks, the muscles in his jaw flexing. "He has orientation."

"Obviously, he'll come after he's done."

He pauses, and if I didn't know better, I'd say he's looking for a way out. "Lenora isn't expecting guests."

"She'll be thrilled," I counter. "Kieren has better table manners than your friends. *He's coming to dinner.*"

Kieren looks between us like he's just realized that what he signed up for by agreeing might be worse than actual warfare. "That's not necessary—"

"It is," I cut him off. "You're not getting out of this just because Bishop is allergic to company."

I'm still deciding how to make this all work when boots splash behind us, and Taliesin appears, eyes lit up like he's won a bet. "Is this private drama, or can anyone watch?"

"We're just discussing dinner plans," Bishop says tersely. "Tell Vessica that we're having dinner with an old friend of Lady Arden's." He glances at me. "If that's okay with you."

Bishop needs reinforcements? Fine. "The more the merrier."

"An old friend, huh?" He claps Kieren on the shoulder, sizing him up like he's a fresh slab at the meat market. "You look like you might survive dinner with us. I give you even odds."

"I'll take those odds," Kieren deadpans, and Taliesin cackles.

Bishop looks ready to murder them both. "Orientation," he calls out, earning the attention of every new recruit in the courtyard. "Line up and follow Sir Procrax." He tips his head at Kieren. "We'll see you this evening."

He sounds absolutely thrilled about it.

Kieren gives my hand a squeeze. "We can catch up tonight," he promises. "Don't worry."

There's little to no chance of that, but I nod anyway.

The other conscripts file into line, shoulders squared despite being half soaked through. Kieren takes his place at the rear, ignoring the curious looks most of the others give him. Watching him fall in with them feels wrong, like I'm letting go of something I won't get back. Taliesin leads them toward the barracks, already shouting information.

Bishop doesn't say anything. He just starts walking, expecting me to follow him.

I do—but this time, my steps are light. For the first time in weeks, I don't feel adrift, don't feel as though I'm slowly drowning. Kieren is here, and while I don't approve of the circumstances, that's all that matters.

We walk back to Miradores in silence. Bishop doesn't try to fill it, which feels like a mercy. At first. But by the time we reach the gates, I'm painfully aware that he still isn't talking.

He waits until the back door closes behind us to finally speak.

"This wasn't in his letter?" Bishop asks. The question sounds bitter after the quiet that preceded it.

"You read it," I remind him. And he threw it into the ocean. Not that it matters now. "I'm as surprised as you are."

"But you're happier about it."

So, that's how he's measuring the situation.

He drags his tongue over his lower lip, and something deep inside me clenches. "I can't give him preferential treatment."

I pull my gaze up to his again. "Why not? You let the orphans decide—"

"He's not a child. He's a grown man. He signed up for a reason." He pauses and gives me an expectant look.

"Things were tense back home," I say, but he lifts a brow. "What? I didn't sign him up."

Bishop closes his eyes and draws a deep breath. "Sure."

"What are you implying?"

"Look, clearly you're in love—"

"What?" It bursts out of me, more laughter than question.

"And you're planning to run away together," he continues, ignoring me. "You should know that if he deserts, it's considered treason."

Ice filters into my veins. Treason is punishable by death. It's the only crime nearly as serious as practicing forbidden magic. "First, there is no plan. Second, he's my best friend. Nothing more. I'm not going to let him do anything that could get him killed." I poke him in the chest. "And you are going to make sure he's safe."

"Nothing more?" he repeats, like this is somehow his sticking point.

"Is that so hard to believe?"

"Maybe. Most women might be moved by such a selfless gesture."

"You know me," I say. "I'm just wandering around hoping anyone with a penis will sweep me off my feet."

He opens his mouth to say something but hesitates.

"Anything else?" I snap, tired of defending myself.

His nostrils flare slightly. "I'll make sure Lenora knows he's coming for dinner."

"Thank you," I force through gritted teeth.

Bishop nods like this settles the matter, but as he disappears into the house, the word *treason* echoes uncomfortably in my head.

Isidore kept all my gowns, so I'm forced to resort to one Lenora dug up. It's at least a size too small, and I've never thought of blue as my color, but tonight feels momentous enough to make an effort. Especially since Lenora has been scrambling around the house all afternoon to prepare for Kieren's arrival.

Pausing at the mirror, I rake a comb through my windswept hair before dusting a little bit of color onto my cheeks and lips. The effect can best be described as presentable, if nothing else. If things go well, this might be the first of many dinners. If they go poorly, I might as well be dressed up for our final supper together.

A quick glance at the clock on the mantel informs me I'm already five minutes late, so I leave it at that. I gulp down a steadying breath, say a silent prayer to the Stars that we avoid bloodshed, and head toward the main floor.

I make it to the stairs only to find Bishop waiting at the foot of them, his back to me. He turns at the sound of my approach, his eyes lifting slowly like he's still caught in his thoughts. But when he sees me, he stiffens. His nostrils flare slightly, and a muscle works in his jaw like he's biting back commentary on my tardiness.

I smooth a hand over the tight waist of my borrowed dress. Clearly, it was made for someone with less appreciation for bread than me. He tracks the movement, his mouth flattening into a grim line.

"Should I change?" I ask, grabbing the railing like I might need to haul myself back in the opposite direction.

He shakes his head, his throat bobbing as he swallows. "No." It comes out so softly that he coughs before he adds, "I didn't expect you to . . . dress up."

Something in his voice summons heat to my cheeks, but I shrug.

It's a good thing that I did, because he's out of uniform. He's traded it in for something simpler that, for once, doesn't include a sword. The jacket he wears is dark and fitted, buttoned high at his throat. It molds to his body, showcasing his muscular form like a subtle reminder that he doesn't need to carry a weapon to be deadly. He looks less like a bishop tonight and more like the man the title was built around.

His gloves are nowhere to be seen. The strange markings on his hands lie exposed and unapologetic—and the realization that he's stopped hiding them from me sends a dangerous flutter through my chest.

It doesn't mean anything, I tell myself firmly, and cling to the thought like a rule I can't afford to break.

Bishop meets me at the base of the stairs and offers his arm. When I don't take it, something tight flickers across his face before he turns away. What did he expect after last night?

"Follow me." He strides forward without waiting.

He leads me past the great room and into the formal dining room instead. The long table is set with polished silver and starched linen, candles guttering in wall sconces that haven't seen this much use in years.

Kieren is already there, flanked by Taliesin and Vessica, and whatever mood Bishop was in darkens more the moment he sees them.

"Thank you for having me," Kieren says to us. He's washed the mud off his boots and slicked his hair back, but he looks nervous to be in the presence of his commanding officer.

Bishop glowers back, and I shoot him a look. Sighing, he offers a grim, "You're welcome." Then he frowns. "Why are you all standing around? Are the chairs broken?"

Taliesin and Vessica exchange glances as they take their seats on the opposite side of the table.

I move for my chair at the same moment, but Kieren beats me to it. Bishop steps in from the other side, already reaching for the back of it, and the two knock hands.

"It's fine," Kieren says quickly, pulling it out himself. "I've got her."

Bishop straightens, jaw flexing, and takes his place at the head of the table without another word. The air is already so thick with tension that I half expect the chandelier to snap from the additional weight and crush us all.

Lenora sweeps in with the main course, beaming like she's hosting a royal feast instead of a standoff. Roasted rack of lamb and a sauce with a fragrance rich enough to make my stomach tense. Or maybe that's just the atmosphere.

"I'll be right back with the rest," she announces as she places it on the table.

"Do you need help?" I ask her, already wanting an excuse to escape for a minute.

"I'm quite capable of serving dinner," she scolds me. "Just enjoy your guest."

She vanishes back into the kitchen, and Kieren reaches for the platter first. He hesitates before serving himself a modest portion.

Bishop waits until he's finished before reaching for the dish. He selects a piece nearly twice the size and sets it on his plate, his eyes never leaving my best friend, who's too busy cutting into his meal to notice.

But Taliesin catches on. He snorts, clearly delighted by the game, and helps himself to an even larger cut than either of them.

I curse under my breath.

"Save some for the rest of us," Vessica mutters.

"Can someone pass me the wine?" I ask quickly, desperate to smooth the moment.

Bishop picks up the red.

"She prefers white," Kieren says easily and picks up the other.

Bishop pours himself a drink instead, setting the bottle down with a heavy *thump*. "She drank red last night."

Silence ripples around the table. Vessica stares at her plate like she regrets accepting Bishop's dinner invitation, but Taliesin seems on the verge of applauding.

"Either is fine," I cut in, leaning to grab the bottle from my best friend.

As long as there's plenty of it.

Lenora arrives with bowls of vegetables and a basket of bread just as I'm sure things are about to come to blows.

I load up my plate, determined to act like this is fine. Like this is normal or that it will be someday—if we all survive this first dinner.

The table goes quiet as we start to eat, but the silence feels strained, like everyone is waiting for someone else to make the first mistake.

Taliesin breaks first, obviously incapable of keeping his mouth shut. He raises a glass in mock salute. "To new friends," he says, "and the Stars that brought us together."

Vessica rolls her eyes. Bishop sighs. None of us raise a glass.

Taliesin takes a drink anyway, undeterred from his fuckery. "So, Kieren, what did you do before this? Raise chickens with Arden?"

Kieren chews a bite of meat and swallows slowly. "There's lots to do on a farm."

"Kieren grew up with us," I jump in. "When my brother became patron, Kieren accompanied him as his personal guard."

Taliesin smiles the way people do when they've already decided they like someone—or intend to test them until they don't. "You ever kill anyone?"

I nearly choke on my wine. "Taliesin—"

"What?" He spreads his hands like this is completely normal dinner conversation. For him, it probably is. "You said he was a guard. It's a fair question."

But Kieren shakes his head. "I wasn't really a guard. No one quite knew what to call me after Arden's father died. I guess 'guard' sounded better than calling me their obligation."

The word sticks. *Obligation.* I'd never thought of him that way, but somehow, I'd missed that he did. Bishop's assessing gaze flicks to me before he looks back to his plate.

We make it through dessert by sheer force of will, conversation skirting safely to weather and rations and away from anything that might draw blood.

"I'll walk you out," I tell Kieren when we've finished, pushing back from the table before anyone can object.

He stands immediately, relief flickering across his face.

Bishop rises as well, but he doesn't look at either of us. "Training starts at dawn," he says to Kieren. "Don't be late."

I usher Kieren into the hall before Bishop can offer more thinly disguised threats. We cut through the kitchen, where Lenora is already scrubbing a pan.

"Thank you for dinner," Kieren says earnestly.

She looks up in surprise and smiles broadly. "It's nice to have a gentleman in the house again."

Kieren flushes, mumbling something polite before I steer him onward.

She waves her wet rag at me. "He can come back anytime."

I force a smile and shove him out the back door.

It swings shut with a *click* that sounds way too final. The only light comes from the windows behind us, gold spilling across the weeds and broken stones, as the stars burn cold and watchful overhead.

Neither of us speaks. The reality is that so much has happened. Now there's too much to say and no easy way to start the conversation.

When we reach the garden, Kieren turns and slowly surveys the place. "It's not what I expected." He kicks a dislodged paver into place and stamps it into the mud with his boot. "Lord Marius could use a gardener."

"Bishop let the place go when his parents died." I'm not certain why I'm making excuses for our host, especially after how he behaved at dinner.

But Kieren nods in understanding. "I guess we let plenty go when your dad died, too."

We pause by the crumbling fountain, which is full of rainwater, dead leaves, and Stars know what else. Something rustles in a tree above us, and then the night settles. I tap the stone, watching the moss flake off. "Maybe we can bring it back to life. There's still plenty of time to plant before winter comes."

Kieren scrubs the back of his neck. "I'm not sure I'm welcome here, even as a gardener."

So, he picked up on that. But I refuse to let one uncomfortable evening ruin everything. "You're welcome as long as I'm here. Don't let Bishop scare you away."

"Arden, I'm not like you. I don't have a birthright. No magic. Not even a family name. I don't belong in a place like this." His words land like punches, one after the other.

"I don't belong here, either," I say, admitting the truth about my own magic for the first time aloud, but he looks unconvinced. I try to shake it off, determined to salvage what I can of the night before he returns to the Bellatorum.

"You really joined up just to see me?"

"I'd follow you anywhere," he says, winking.

"But you'll send me a crappy letter that makes me cry." I smack his shoulder.

Kieren drops his head. "I'm sorry. I'd already decided I was coming when we got your letters. I was so angry when Broderic burned his that I couldn't see straight to write you."

Knowing that makes the letter hurt for all new reasons. Someday, my brother will forgive me. I just need to give it time. "Was he surprised when you told him?"

"No," he says firmly. "But he didn't seem upset that I was leaving. Andry, on the other hand, says he won't speak to me again until he's old enough to come here, too."

That sounds like my little brother.

I hesitate, but only for a second. "And Isidore? She didn't try to stop you."

"No." His smile makes my heart ache. "I think she was glad to see me go."

"I don't believe that." I won't. "Did you tell her how you feel?"

"There was no point. She could barely look at me after that night."

"But if you told her . . ." I have to believe it might make a difference, if only because I can't stand the idea of anyone breaking his heart.

"You're such a hopeless romantic," he says, laughing when I splutter in protest.

I want to argue, but the words dry up. Instead, I reach out and squeeze his hand. "I missed you."

"I missed you, too." He squeezes back. "And that's why I'm not letting you rot in this place."

I pull away and frown. "What are you talking about?"

He glances back at the house, dropping his voice to a whisper. "I didn't come here to be a conscript. I only went to the Bellatorum to see if someone knew how I could find you. Enlisting was the only way inside Vennaro. I just couldn't leave you behind. I need to get you away from all this." His eyes brighten. "We can leave. Have that adventure we always talked about. Just the two of us."

The adventure *he* always talked about. Is that why he's here?

"I can't. My family . . ." I shake my head.

But he keeps pushing. "Your family is safe with the troops there."

"And if I disappear, Bishop will pull them out." I can't risk what might happen if he does. Bishop has more pressing needs than worrying about my family's safety.

Kieren shakes his head. "They reopened the outpost near the eastern border. The one by the Cinderwald."

I blink, trying to process this. The outpost near the ancient forest was abandoned long before I was born. Now we use its land for fields to grow corn, the soil still richer there from the ash that fell when Ravenell's volcano erupted. "We need those fields."

"Broderic only agreed after Bishop promised we could keep using them," Kieren reassures me. "And he said the troops will help with the spring planting."

A permanent outpost. I can't decide if I'm relieved or horrified. Damalis is peaceful. Or it was until the murder last week. Maybe it's for the best.

But there's something that still doesn't make sense. "When did Bishop arrange this?"

"During his visit last week," Kieren says. "His inspection took forever. I thought the two of them were going to kill each other, but somehow, everyone survived."

Bishop wasn't in Wintour. He lied to me. Why not tell me he was going to my home region? Why say he was in the royal city the whole time?

Kieren studies me. "Do you trust him?"

I might have said yes before. Now? Why didn't he tell me? "I want to."

"That means you don't," he says, like he's reading my mind. He still knows me better than anyone else.

I hesitate, trying to put words to the chaos in my head. "He isn't . . ." I'm not sure what to say, because Bishop lied. Not just about going to Wintour. He told me Hadrian is his uncle—after not telling me about him at all. He's researching forbidden books.

"He's dangerous," Kieren says in a low voice, glancing back at the house like Bishop might be able to hear us.

I know that. But he also drank two bottles of wine with me last night and admitted why his estate is run-down. Told me he doesn't want to go to war. He might have rejected me, but he also opened up. A little. "He's . . . complicated."

"That doesn't mean he's not dangerous." His hands grip me more tightly, like he's resisting the urge to shake some sense into me. "When news reached us about the murder, I thought he was going to burn the entire region down."

Cold dashes through me. Bishop didn't tell me *any* of this, even when I asked about his trip. "He was there after the murder?"

"And before." Kieren releases me with a weary sigh. "He stopped negotiating the arrangements for the outpost with Broderic to investigate himself. I suppose it makes sense. I would be on edge if two murders happened right under my nose."

Kieren might be, but Bishop? The night of the Quincentennial flashes through my mind. He was watchful but calm. After the Petition, he knew exactly what to do, where to take me, how to hide me. It's just another reason Bishop and I will never see eye to eye. Death doesn't even faze him enough to warrant him mentioning it.

"And that's why we need to go," he says, jolting me from my thoughts. He pauses for a second like he's screwing up his courage. "At midnight. We can head to the Lost Continent. I already have a contact. He hangs out at The Last Drop in the village. We can be on open sea by sunrise. Before he even knows we're gone."

"You really want to run away?" I ask slowly. "With me?"

Treason. I swallow, and the word begins to churn inside me.

Kieren offers a sad smile that makes my stomach turn over. "That ravenmark isn't going away, and when your magic awakens . . . You can't go back to Damalis. We both know that. But you can't stay here, either."

The words feel too close to the truth, like he's peeled something raw out of me and shoved it in my face. I don't want him to be right—but I'm afraid he is. I'm the one living with this mark and what I might become. I pace in a tight circle, hugging my arms around my waist, suddenly aware of the chilly air.

But the knot of dread inside me tightens. Right now, the mark of Ravenell on my chest is the least of our problems. He's so focused, so worried about me, he doesn't understand the mistake he made. "If you desert," I say, forcing each word past the lump in my throat, "you'll be charged with treason."

I can't let him risk that, but how is it any better than him joining the army?

"Tomorrow, I swear my pledge to Order Marius. Once they put their mark on me, I'll be lucky to take a piss without someone knowing," he says, and the weight on my chest grows so heavy I can hardly breathe. Kieren shrugs as if this is just some boring fact. I want to grab him and shake him, make him see what he's done by coming here, but I just stare as he continues. "They can't track me before then. That's why I need to go tonight. I already have passage arranged."

My legs threaten to give out from under me. He came to the Bellatorum to find me. That's the only reason, or he would already be on a boat to the Lost Continent, off to have his adventure. Not about to commit treason.

"Kieren . . ." I search for the right words through a dizzying rush of panic. It's all happening so fast. Too fast.

He swallows and takes a step back. "I understand if you want to stay. But I don't have a choice. There's nothing left for me here. I thought . . ."

He pauses, and I'm not certain I want to know what other foolish belief led to his recklessness.

Something rustles in the closest bramble, and I jump, looking over my shoulder quickly to make sure we're still alone. My heart thrashes against my ribs. If someone overheard us . . .

No one's there. Still, my pulse refuses to slow.

He moves closer and plants a gentle hand on my wrist, calling me back to the moment. "We could have a life. Not as Icaros or Ravenell or any of that shit. Just us. Somewhere people don't care about the Stars or magic or birthrights."

The thought settles like a warm blanket, calming me just enough to help me see his point. But there's something else. It's not just that people don't care. *Different* stars hang over the Lost Continent. There will be no magic to awaken. I close my eyes, almost dizzy with the possibility.

But when I open them, the stars are still there—cold, distant, unmoved by things as trifling as hopes and dreams—and panic floods back through me.

I fight it. I need a clear head. "Kieren," I say slowly, "maybe you should stay."

I can talk to Bishop. Make him promise to keep my best friend here. No matter what.

But Kieren shakes his head. "I'm only here for you. If you don't want to come, I'll understand." He glances toward Miradores, eyes narrowing like it's the reason I'm hesitating. I don't have the energy to argue. To try to make him see how big of a mess we're in. "But I'll wait for you at the crossroads that lead to Wolf's Keep until midnight. If you don't show, I'll assume you made your choice."

It's so black-and-white to him, but the whole world feels gray around me. What am I going to do?

"I'll think about it," I whisper.

That seems to satisfy him. "I'll be waiting." He takes one step before stopping again. "Meet me at midnight."

Then he turns and slips away, vanishing through the back gate without a sound.

I watch the empty path for a long time, my heart thundering louder than the waves below.

I'm more lost than ever.

I stumble back into the house. Vessica's shrewd voice drifts from the great room, followed by a cheerful burst of laughter from Taliesin. They sound . . . normal. Because they belong to this place in a way I never will. Kieren never will. A gust rattles the windows like it's got a score to settle, jolting me back to reality. There's no time for a pity party. I only have until midnight.

I head away from their laughter to the servant stairs off the kitchen, hoping I find a solution to this mess on the way. But as I climb the first step, I'm no closer.

"You were out there a while." Bishop's gravelly voice startles me, and I grab the handrail to keep myself from tripping.

I turn toward him, clutching the railing as blood begins to pound in my ears. He's standing at the base of the staircase, glowering like my father used to when he caught me sneaking in after dark. Question after question hits me as I stare back at him. If Kieren is caught deserting, will Bishop be the one to execute him for treason? Will he cut him down as ruthlessly as he did that thief in the alley for using forbidden magic?

I shake my head a little as if I can clear my thoughts. "We had a lot to catch up on." I keep my voice light, hoping he can't hear the trembling undercurrent in every word.

A muscle works in Bishop's jaw. "Like what?"

He starts toward the steps, hands balled into fists like he already suspects something. Panic bleats in my chest, and I scramble for an answer that doesn't include Kieren's foolish plan to run away to the Lost Continent.

"Like the fact that you were in Damalis." I swallow and lift my chin. "Why did you lie about being in Wintour?"

That makes him pause. "I didn't. I stopped in Wintour on my way."

"But you were in Damalis most of the time," I accuse.

"Doing my job," he shoots back. "Do you think I like being away from . . . here all the time? Some of us don't have the luxury of staying home."

"This isn't my home." He flinches, but the angry rush of heat surging through me makes each word easier than the last. "You should have told me what you were doing."

His eyes narrow farther. "When I returned, you were heartbroken over the letter your *best friend* sent. It didn't seem like the time to mention it."

I am so fucking sick of people deciding what I can handle. "That wasn't your call!"

"Did he tell you I was there to establish new troops at the eastern outpost?" he demands. "To protect *your* family?"

Just like he promised to do. The reminder ratchets my heart rate up another notch. Maybe I can appeal to whatever nobility or sense of duty made him do that. "Take Kieren's name off the conscript list. He shouldn't be here. Shouldn't be a conscript." There's a battle in his eyes. My chest tightens as I watch him wage it. *"Please."*

He tears his gaze from mine. "It's not as simple as striking his name off a list."

"It is for you," I say, voice breaking. "You do it for all those kids."

But he shakes his head. "Kieren is past the age of majority. He's a man. Not a child. And he signed up at the eastern outpost. His name has already been reported to the crown."

The air empties from my lungs, and I nearly collapse against the railing. The very outpost protecting my family has put my best friend—*my brother*—at risk.

Bishop takes a step closer, worry creasing his face. "He'll be safe here. I'll see to it."

It's too late, but I can't tell him that. "Thank you." I force myself to say it. Force myself to pretend that I'm not shattering to pieces on the spot. Kieren is leaving either way, and if his name is on the crown's list . . .

"And I'll be more *welcoming*." His throat slides as if the promise is costing him something.

I nod, a numb realization slowly spreading through me. My voice breaks as I ask, "Because you feel responsible for my family?"

"I feel responsible for *you*," he says, and a vise grips my chest. Bishop feels a duty to protect me. He made that obvious last night. *Not* Kieren. And if Kieren runs away . . . Which means there's only one way to protect Kieren now. I know what I have to do.

"I should go to bed," I murmur, unable to look Bishop in the eyes. He deserves better than this.

"Arden." My name is soft on his lips, and something splinters in my chest, threatening to crack open. "I want—"

A fresh peal of Taliesin's laughter interrupts us, and I seize the excuse to rush up the stairs, not trusting myself to continue this conversation any further. Something stops me when I reach the top, but when I turn around, Bishop is striding out the back door. It slams behind him.

I stare for a moment. Knowing what I have to do doesn't make it any easier, so I continue to my bedroom.

I have a little over an hour until I need to meet Kieren. I throw a few things into a bag, trying to ignore the traitorous ache in my heart. Bishop will be better off when I go. My family will be safe thanks to the eastern outpost, and once news spreads that the harbinger has fled, things will go back to normal for all of them.

And if Kieren and I are caught, I might be the only thing that protects him when he's charged with treason. I can't stop Kieren from running, but I can say it was my idea. It might be enough to sway Bishop's mercy.

And if we aren't caught, we'll start over. Build a new life together like Kieren said.

I move to grab a few things from the vanity. Lenora has lined up the brush and mirror she gave me since I got dressed for dinner. She's always in here, tidying up and dropping off some small item she thinks I might need, trying to make me feel comfortable. Trying to make me feel like I'm home.

And I'm not even going to say goodbye to her. To any of them.

To Bishop.

My heart twists. A letter will have to do, but when I open the drawer, I find it empty. I used all the paper to write home.

I can't go without leaving some word. They deserve that much. *He* deserves it.

Bishop has paper in his desk, so I make my way toward the western wing, praying he's still outside.

Hoping he isn't.

I crush that bewildering feeling. I can't risk seeing him.

The western wing is unlocked tonight—another small, if confusing, kindness, like the way he stopped wearing his gloves. Like secrets no longer matter. I pause at the door, heart in my throat, but there's no sound inside. I tiptoe in and find it empty. He's still gone.

I hurry down the hall. His study is even more forbidding at night. The lamps are out, and the only light comes from the hallway.

I hesitate at the desk, fingers hovering over the drawer handle like the wood might bite, and listen for footsteps. Sliding it open carefully, I find his travel log. Wrong drawer. But I pick it up anyway. If I had just looked at this, I would have known he was in Damalis. Not that it matters now. But as I go to set it down, a piece of paper falls out. A report of some sort about a murder in Isoldoro. I bend and snatch it, eyes snagging on the information. It's the one I saw reported on the Civicus that day at the Grand Arcade. I open the log to shove it back inside and find myself staring at a list of Bishop's travel. Damalis. Wintour. I skim the log, knowing for the first time all the places he's been since he brought me back from the royal city.

My eyes land on the dates I visited Wintour, and I feel a pang in my chest. That's when everything changed. But it's the date above it that catches my attention. Or the city, at least. Isoldoro. My eyes dart to the report, then back to the log.

Bishop was there.

Not after the murder. During. I crumple into the chair, hands shaking.

It's just a coincidence that a murder took place.

Like it's a coincidence that there was a murder in Damalis while he visited there?

Or one at the palace the night of my Kindling?

Tremors roll through me, my body hot and cold at the same time. It can't be. He wouldn't.

He protects people. But somewhere in the back of my mind, I hear the wet *thwap* of a knife impaling the body of that rat. Maybe I don't know him at all.

But I'm certain of one thing after my time in Vennaro—he had to have a reason.

Fuck, I hope it was a good one.

I leave the western wing on unsteady legs, still clutching the log along with some stationery and hoping I make it down the corridor that leads to my own room before I fall. Or get caught. Or discover some other world-shattering bit of news.

This time when I step inside, my room is freezing, the fire down to embers. I dump the journal onto the bed and stare at it. Three places. Three murders. It isn't proof, but it's more than chance. Maybe Kieren is right. Maybe Bishop is dangerous. He might be responsible for the king's murder.

I change out of my dress, opting for something warmer, but it can't chase away the chill I feel. I have to go with Kieren, even if part of me needs to know the truth. Needs to know if Bishop is responsible for the king's assassination and why.

I pace to the window. The garden is a mess of silver and shadow. The moon hangs low, and a shape shifts on the wall—a flickering silhouette of wings through the glass.

Maybe the king's pet was never watching me at all. Maybe it was watching him.

"If you're really a witch," I whisper to the night, "now would be a good time to say something."

But the oscen doesn't appear. This is *my* choice.

I pull a pen from the drawer. My hands are shaking so badly, I almost drop it. I only write a few lines before leaving it on my pillow. Then I grab my bag, sit on the edge of the bed, and stare at the clock . . . waiting for the house to still. There's only one path that makes sense.

I'm choosing my own fate. I'm done letting the Stars decide.

TWENTY

The weathered stone pillar at the crossroads feels older than the road itself, as if it's been waiting for these kinds of choices longer than I've been alive. I reach the ancient milestone with my heart still lodged somewhere behind me, pounding like it's trying to catch up. Above me, constellations burn as though nothing in the world is out of place. Except for that single star blazing in the Night's Scar—and now me.

I pull my cloak tighter around my shoulders and try not to imagine Bishop standing at the window, reading the note I left behind. He won't find it until morning—after I'm long gone. Thankfully, I have a new problem to deal with: the crossroads are deserted. A sharp jab of panic rises past my already crippling anxiety.

"Because I needed one more thing to worry about," I grumble as my mind begins racing with all the potential disasters keeping Kieren away.

But before I can turn around, Kieren emerges, breathless, from the dark with a pack slung over his shoulder. Relief floods his face when he sees me. He grins like this is an adventure instead of an escape, but there's a weariness in his dark eyes.

"You came." He sounds genuinely surprised as he gives me a quick hug.

"I couldn't let you get into all the trouble without me." Joy surges through the fear I've felt since I left Miradores. A quick burst of sunlight on a cloudy day.

"Let's get going." He grabs my bag and throws it over his other shoulder as if it weighs no more than a sack of flour before I can protest.

We walk side by side toward Wolf's Keep, our footsteps the only sound on the empty road. Kieren fills the silence the way he always does when he senses I'm retreating into myself. He talks about ships and places where no one knows our names.

It's almost enough to keep my thoughts from wandering back to the crumbling estate I left behind or the uncertainty facing us. For the first time, I notice he isn't wearing his sword, and my heart sinks a few inches. "How are we paying for this?"

"I sold some things. The astrolabe. Other stuff." His grin is sheepish. "I know it wasn't really mine."

But I shrug. It's probably better that my brother doesn't have a way to reach him. And Broderic's wrath is the *least* of our problems right now. "It can't have been worth much."

"It wasn't," he says grimly, "but it's enough to secure our passage."

"And what exactly are we going to do once we get there?"

"I don't know." But he doesn't sound worried. I'm glad one of us is optimistic, especially since I keep listening for the sounds of people coming to drag the deserter and the harbinger back. "I figure I can work on the boat, and I hear sailors love Liar's Hand. I can make some money that way."

I question his sources. "Where did you hear that?"

"The guys who taught me how to play this afternoon in the Commons."

I resist the urge to grimace. "I'm not sure gambling is a solid plan."

Especially betting on a game he only learned a few hours ago.

"Life is a gamble." He bumps his broad shoulder against mine. "The only way to lose is if you don't play."

"There are other ways to lose," I point out, but his excitement is infectious. Still, my fingers keep checking the clasp of my cloak, as if the mark below it might burn through the fabric if I stop touching it and give us away somehow.

"And who knows if I can make something of myself on the continent," he says lightly. "Maybe I'll come back with enough coin that Isidore won't pretend I'm invisible anymore."

I don't have the heart to remind him that he'll be charged with treason if he comes back. It doesn't matter if he's moved on to predicting how long we'll be at sea.

I let his voice wash over me, the sound comforting after weeks apart. It's the sound of my childhood. Of afternoons spent listening to him in the fields, the two of us flinging dirt clods at each other when it was too hot to work—and Broderic wasn't watching.

He's technically a guard, but that title never fit him. He was always beside me in those fields, our boots muddy as we navigated every painfully awkward moment of growing up. Like when he caught Coen Hawthorn giving me my first kiss in the barn and made puckering faces at me for weeks behind everyone else's backs. Or when I found him with Hanna Aster by the plow shed two summers later and made the same face behind her back. Kieren turned beet red and chased me halfway across the orchard. Probably afraid I'd tell Isidore.

He stayed by my side the night my mother died, when I couldn't believe the sun would rise in the morning. Held my hand when we lost my father. He's been with me every step. Maybe that's why coming to Vennaro never felt right. He wasn't here. And as terrified as I am of leaving all I've ever known behind, with him, it *will* be an adventure.

"You're quiet again," he says after a few more minutes of him carrying the conversation. "Are you afraid?"

"Yes," I admit. Only a fool wouldn't be.

"Of going to the Lost Continent?" he asks softly.

I know he'll understand. The trouble is, I don't quite understand it myself.

"Not of going, exactly." I search for words that explain the churning dread I can't shake. "But what I'm leaving behind."

Our family. Everything I've ever known. Maybe even Bishop. What if war does come? Or our siblings still pay the price after we've fled?

Kieren considers before he nods, and I know he's thinking about Isidore.

When I fall silent, he does the talking again. He speaks about the Lost Continent like it's a promise—a place without orders or marks or Stars weighing every choice. I remind him there won't be magic there. He only laughs again. "That's why it's an adventure."

By the time we reach Wolf's Keep, he's distracted me. But as we cross the city's threshold, I can't help turning to look back at the road.

"He won't know you're gone until morning," Kieren reminds me, catching my nervous glance.

"Unless he finds my note," I murmur absently.

Kieren stops dead in his tracks.

"You left a note." It's not a question, but his voice pitches up like it should be. "Do you want him to chase after you?"

I roll my eyes, but he waits like he actually expects me to answer him. "Of course not," I say, pulling my hood tighter as a group of soldiers passes us. "That's why I left him a note, so he would know that I left Antares."

My best friend's mouth falls open. "You told him where we're going."

"No," I say quickly.

"There is really only one way to leave the kingdom." Kieren rakes a hand through his hair, glancing around like he expects to be ambushed momentarily.

"And we'll be sailing on the Baron Sea before dawn, right?"

He nods, but his face remains uneasy.

"Trust me, he'll be glad to be rid of me." It's not like Bishop will waste his dwindling resources chasing after us.

Kieren grumbles like he doubts this but doesn't say anything else.

Thinking of Bishop finding my note makes the knot in my stomach clench with each step, my gaze finding the ground like if I don't look up I won't have to face my own feelings—or what I might have discovered about him.

Bishop is a heart collector. He was present when three of the murders took place. Leaving helps me see it in a way I couldn't with him always near me. That's why he took me in. When the rest of the patrons debated whether or not I was responsible for King Ophelian's death, he brought me to his home. He's never been afraid of me—not even for a second.

And there's only one way he could have been sure I wasn't the assassin.

The pieces all fit. Mostly. But the picture is still clear enough to see.

The trouble is that I'll never know why.

It's well past midnight, and most of Wolf's Keep is quiet. Windows are shuttered and doors are barred, but The Last Drop's lights still blaze like it's daring someone to look at it too closely. The smell of stale ale and smoke hits me the moment we step inside, but it's the sight of the man behind the bar that raises the hair on the back of my neck.

"Kitchen's closed, but we have beer," he calls to us, giving me a glimpse of his gold tooth—the one I saw when he spat at my feet yesterday, right before Vessica held a sword to his nose.

Kieren waves that he's heard him, and I let him take the lead. A wolf's head hangs above the hearth, its horns polished smooth by whoever mounted it, its glass eyes dull and watchful.

I tug my hood lower, my pulse skittering every time someone shifts in their seat. I do my best to avoid eye contact with anyone, looking at the floorboards scarred by too many passing boots.

We make our way to a table in the back corner. The man sitting there looks like trouble wrapped in charm—contagious smile and watchful eyes—with sun-worn brown skin and dark hair threaded with silver at the temples. His grin widens as we approach, and a thin scar pulls at the corner of his mouth like it learned the shape the hard way. He leans back in his chair, crossing his arms behind his neck. "You came back," he greets Kieren, his eyes sharpening on me too quickly for someone lounging so casually.

"I told you that I would."

"And she came with you."

"Don't sound so surprised." Kieren pulls out a stool for me before he claims one for himself. "Jude"—he greets him by name—"this is—"

"Isidore." I give him my sister's name before anyone overhears him use mine. Too many people here have read my name in the Civicus.

Kieren's brows bunch together, but Jude nods like he understands.

"Nice to meet you, *Isidore*." He winks at me.

Jude signals for another round without asking, as if he's decided we're staying awhile. The tavern seems louder now, full of shouts and laughter. The noise scrapes against my nerves. I keep my hood up, but I can feel eyes sliding toward us and then away again.

"You look like someone waiting for a knife in the back," Jude says to me. "Relax. If I was going to sell you out, I'd already be richer."

"That's not reassuring," I say.

He laughs. "It should be."

"So, how will this work?" I ask. Jude strikes me as the type who might be full of shit, and I'd rather know that before I set foot on his ship.

He explains the route like it's a game—rough waters, forgotten lanes, places Bishop's patrol ships won't bother watching. "We'll leave at dawn."

My chest constricts, time closing in around me like a fist. That wasn't the plan. We can't be here in the morning.

"Dawn?" Kieren repeats, rolling his small bone token between his knuckles. He leans across the nicked table and lowers his voice. "We need to leave before—" He falls silent as the barkeep places three overflowing mugs in the center of the table.

The man squints down at Jude. "You'll pay your tab before you go," he warns, gold tooth glinting with every word.

Jude beams that easy smile at him. "I'm settling my finances right now."

"Before your boots leave my threshold," the barkeep clarifies. He turns slowly, his head tilting slightly like he's trying to get a peek under my hood.

Kieren edges closer to me, and the man grunts and walks away. My best friend watches him leave before swiveling back to Jude. He leans forward, his voice pitching low again. "We go tonight, or you're settling that tab yourself."

Jude stills, both men sizing each other up. Kieren has a foot on Jude easily and the kind of muscle that comes with years spent on a farm, but the ship captain looks like he fights dirty. I press my lips together, trying to ignore the sinking feeling in my gut. Can we really trust him to get us out of here in time?

"You drive a hard bargain." Jude chuckles and lifts his mug. "One more for the road." He tips his head at me. "Drink up. The ale won't be this fresh at sea."

I manage a few sips as they hash out final details. Their beers are long gone by the time Kieren slides a few gold coins across the table to him.

"You'll get the rest when our feet touch the Lost Continent," Kieren warns him.

But Jude snatches the coins up, eyes shifting around the room, and then stands swiftly. "I'll pay the tab. Meet you outside in five."

As we head for the door, the bartender's gaze catches on me again. This time, he doesn't bother hiding his interest. His gold tooth flashes when he smiles, and my stomach drops. I pick up my pace, and Kieren matches, shooting me a confused glance as I push open the door.

Outside, the night feels colder than it should, but I gulp down the fresh air.

"Once we're aboard," Kieren says, swinging one of our packs higher on his shoulder, the other dangling by his side, "you sleep. I'll watch the door."

"There's no need." Now who's lying?

But he holds up a hand. "You'll rest better." He looks around us. "*Everything* will be better when we get this place behind us."

I'm not sure I'll stop looking over my shoulder until we're on the Lost

Continent. "Do you trust Jude?" I ask him, lowering my voice as a few men stagger out of the tavern.

"Trust might be taking it a bit far," he admits. He glances at the tavern's sign, then back at me. "But he didn't ask who you were. We paid, so we're his cargo now. He'll protect us. I think we're in good hands."

Good seems like too strong a word, but I don't argue with him. There's enough to worry about without looking for more problems. But when the door to the tavern slams shut behind us, I nearly jump out of my skin.

Jude strides up to us, whistling. "Best get going. Tide waits for no one."

The streets thin as we head closer to the water. Stone pavers give way to packed earth and narrow lanes that slope steadily downhill. Houses grow sparse, lights fewer, until the dark opens up and the smell of the Baron Sea rolls in heavy with salt and rot.

The docks skirt the edge of Wolf's Keep, and I keep my head down, counting steps and listening for anything out of place. This close to the water, the wind sends mist up to swallow the stars. Between a series of warehouses, wooden piers jut into black water, ropes creaking and ships rocking restlessly against their moorings. Lanterns flicker low and far apart, their light smeared by fog and spray, and beyond their faint glow is nothing but an endless abyss. Past the last pier, the land rises again in a ragged line of trees, their branches clawing at the sky.

Jude moves with that easy confidence, whistling under his breath like this is any other night.

Kieren leans close. "See? We're almost there."

We're only a few feet from the docks when Jude stops so suddenly that I nearly run into him.

His head snaps toward the dark between the warehouses, head angled as though he's caught a sound the rest of us can't.

Unease prickles over my skin.

"Problem?" Kieren asks.

But Jude doesn't answer. He lifts a hand without turning around. "Stay close."

His hand disappears into his coat and reappears with a knife.

Something is wrong.

The words are on my lips, but it's already too late.

"Run," Jude shouts as the night explodes around us.

Shadows peel away from the warehouses and spring toward us. But I can't make my legs move, even when a figure lunges from between two stacked crates and slams into Jude's back.

There's a flash of metal. Jude swears and ducks just as a sword carves through the air where his throat was a second before.

He shoves me back hard enough that I stumble, my heel catching on a warped plank. Our packs thud on the wooden pier, and Kieren catches me.

"Get to the trees," Jude barks, and his knife flashes again as he drives it into the first man who reaches for me. His scream tears through the docks.

For one panicked moment, I wonder if this is Bishop.

If he found the note. If he's come to stop us, lock me up in Miradores, and drag Kieren back to face charges.

To the left, someone else shouts, "There! That's the witch!"

At the word, my stomach pitches. It's not Bishop.

And whoever they are, they aren't alone. More figures spill from the dark. There are too many of them.

Kieren's grip tightens, trying to pull me away. "Arden."

"Don't say her name," Jude growls, as if it's a lure. He slashes again, buying us a heartbeat. "Get out of here!"

Kieren yanks me forward, dragging me off the pier and onto solid ground. We sprint toward the dark line of trees. My legs scream as the ground slants up into scrub and bramble. Jude is still behind us, snarling curses. The sound of the fight follows us. Boots skidding. Steel clattering against steel.

I slow for a step. We should go back. We paid him for passage to the Lost Continent. Not to die.

"We have to keep going," Kieren pants, grabbing my cloak and urging me faster.

I finally look back when we reach the trees, just in time to see a sword pierce Jude's rib cage. He staggers, one hand going to his side. Something dark gleams between his fingers. Blood. More than a cut. *Too* much.

He catches my eye for one brief second. His face is grim, almost apologetic. Like he knows this is it.

Then his knees hit the planks.

"Jude!" His name escapes me in a choked panic.

"Too late. He's . . ."

Kieren doesn't say it. He doesn't have to.

Boots thud toward us, and he grabs my hand. We run until the dock lights vanish behind us. Branches snatch at my cloak. Thorns scrape my wrists. But we don't stop running. We stumble over roots and half-buried logs until we reach a fallen evergreen, its rotting trunk large enough to hide us.

Kieren shoves me down behind it and drops beside me, chest heaving.

I collapse, lungs burning along with every muscle in my body. My legs shake so badly, I can't tell if it's exhaustion or terror.

"This is my fault," I whisper. These aren't soldiers chasing after us. "If I hadn't . . ."

Kieren grips my hand. "No."

"Yes," I insist, tears blurring the dark edges of the woods. "They're after me. They don't care about you or Jude or anyone else." My throat constricts. "You need to keep going without me."

"There is no way in all seven hells."

"Leave me." My voice cracks on the plea. "Run. They want the witch, not you."

He grunts, rolling his eyes. "No fucking way." He squeezes my hand until it hurts, until it anchors me to the world. "You listen to me." His face is a shadow, but I can feel the steadiness in him, the stubborn warmth that has never truly left me behind. "You're my sister."

The words gut me.

Not because it's a lie. Because it's true in a way that I've never thanked him for and never deserved and never properly earned.

"I'm not leaving my only family," he says with such certainty that it makes my chest ache.

"Kieren, I . . ." There is so much I need to say to him, so much I need to apologize for before it's too late.

I'm searching for the words as a whistle cuts through the night, answered by a low howl. Another howl follows. And another.

Kieren tenses. "We have to move," he whispers.

We scramble up and start running again, moving deeper into the trees. Away from the docks. Away from Wolf's Keep.

But with each step, the howls grow closer.

My lungs burn, unable to get enough air, but I don't slow down.

"They're gaining," I choke out.

"I know." He looks over his shoulder, and his eyes widen. He shoves me forward and starts to turn. "Go!"

I trip, nearly falling, but manage to stay on my feet. "Not without you."

"I'm right behind you," he pants.

I dash toward a clearing ahead, his footsteps thundering behind me. The road can't be far.

The hounds crash closer. Too close.

I keep running, even when my legs want to give out. But it's not enough.

A snarl splits the dark, so near I feel it in my bones. Something hits me from the side. Breath hot. Teeth snapping at my ribs. I scream and kick, and suddenly Kieren is there, swinging his pack like a weapon. He drives the beast back far enough to push me toward the woods on the other side of the clearing.

"Keep moving!" he shouts.

I stagger ahead, tears streaming, my throat raw. I'm barely able to force my legs to keep going.

I reach the trees, stumbling into their cover, but when I turn to him, Kieren isn't there. I spin around, heart in my throat, nearly slipping in the mud, and finally see him.

Kieren is on the ground in the clearing.

A hound has him by the arm, dragging him backward like he weighs nothing. He fights, kicking the animal off as his hands claw at the dirt, trying to find leverage. But the dark is full of movement now as the others close in.

"Get up!" I shout.

One of the dogs looks around, alert. Interested. I can draw them away. Give Kieren a chance to move again. My eyes scan the woods around me wildly, looking for any sign of a path, any clue how close we are to the main road. If we can reach it, we'll be going in the direction of Miradores. They wouldn't dare to follow us there.

I wet my lower lip, pursing my mouth to whistle, to call the hounds after me.

But on the far side of the clearing, lantern light blooms between the trees, and men emerge from the woods. A half dozen of them, and the one holding the light . . .

"Where are you going?" the bartender calls, voice filled with delighted cruelty. "Are you going to leave this one behind for us to kill, too?"

My heart stops.

They can't see me. Not under the cover of the forest. I retreat one step into those shadows.

"We're here for *you*, witch. Not him." The barkeep crouches down with the lantern and presses a knife to Kieren's throat. But my best friend looks up, staring toward the darkness ahead as if he knows I can see him, and mouths the command he's given me twice already.

Run.

I grab hold of the nearest trunk to steady myself. A few steps back and the woods will swallow me from sight. But I can't bring myself to keep running.

If I do that, he dies.

If I go back, we'll probably both die.

The idea lodges in my ribs like it's that blade at his throat.

And then I shake it off, because I am not leaving my family.

Not again.

Tree branches catch at my cloak, the forest trying to stop me as I walk toward the clearing. But I keep going, stepping out of the tree line and into open view.

Fix it. I can still—

The sight of him steals the rest of the thought. Kieren is on his knees in the mud, two men forcing him upright as he fights them like an animal. His bottom lip is split and bleeding. He's close enough now that I can see where the hounds tore his clothing. Far enough that I can still turn and run.

"Arden, stop," he shouts hoarsely. "Run. Don't—"

The lantern light wobbles ahead like a beacon.

Do what needs to be done.

I couldn't make the sacrifice that night. But this? This isn't a sacrifice at all.

It's what needs to be done.

Only one step left. The noise drains away, and there is only stillness—as if the world has narrowed to a single unavoidable path. I step before the barkeep. Lifting my chin, I aim my words directly at him. "Let him go."

That's all it takes.

They close around me. Rough hands grab my arms, yanking me backward so fast my teeth clack together. The man laughs and shoves me down. The ground bites into my knees, wet and cold.

"Witch." He hisses the verdict.

It hits me low and hard, knocking my breath into a gasp.

I drop my head back to find the Stars and sob. "Please."

If my magic is going to wake, let it be now. Please.

"Isn't she polite?" The man above me sneers. He bends over me, so close I can smell the stench of whisky and poor hygiene on his breath.

"Let the *lady* beg," another taunts.

"Enough," the barkeep says, pressing his boot into Kieren's back. His blade is still pointed at him. "I want to see the mark."

"No." The word escapes me in a strangled cry. I throw my weight forward, nearly tearing free of the man holding me. Nails raking skin. Teeth snapping for anything I might reach. He grabs me by the hair, and pain explodes across my scalp as he yanks me back hard enough to make my vision swim.

"Easy," his voice croons near my ear. "We just want to have a look."

His companion steps in front of me and unfastens my cloak. I squirm, trying to aim a knee at his groin, and he leaps back as he snatches it off me. "Vicious bitch!"

I open my mouth and spit at him.

The hand in my hair wrenches me back. "Hold still and this will be over faster."

My stomach lurches violently, and heat floods my throat. I gag, my body revolting against what my mind can't escape as he aims a dagger at my heart. His arm circles my waist, locking me against him, and every instinct in me screams to fight, to flee, to disappear out of my own skin—but there's nowhere left to go. I guess the Stars aren't listening tonight.

"Is this where it is?" he whispers, his knife trailing over the front of my sweater. "That's what the Civicus reported."

"Don't touch her!" Kieren struggles to get to me, but the bartender keeps him pinned.

I can't bring myself to look at him, my whole body shaking. When he walks out of here, it will be worth it. He'll understand someday.

"Open it up and let's see," the bartender orders, voice flat.

A single tear rolls down my cheek, so warm it almost stings in the cold night. The man fists my shirt, and the others urge him on, applauding him like he's a fucking hero. I stare straight ahead, ignoring their cheers, pretending I can't feel his body pressed against mine. Even Kieren's protests fade from notice.

But I can still feel the tip of the blade, sharp and cold through the thick knit. My breath catches as the knife pauses, and then in a blink, it slashes a single, careful cut. His friend leaps forward and rips the sweater and undergarments down the middle to my waist. Cold air slams into my bare skin, and I gasp, lungs burning, more tears falling.

Kieren whimpers somewhere in the distance.

The man before me stumbles back a step, eyes widening at the sight of the raven-mark burned into my chest.

Their gazes roam my skin, and I close my eyes, because it's the only place left for me to hide. Dread fills the hollow silence like it's building toward something inevitable. Just like that night in the throne room. Just like those nobles. These men are no different than they were. Rank, class, status—none of it matters. All men are equals in the face of fear.

I brace for pain. If there's a price to pay, it's mine. Not Kieren's.

For half a heartbeat, no one moves.

Then someone whispers, cruel and hungry all at once, "Harbinger."

A louder voice follows. "It's true. She's the harbinger."

The word spreads on their mouths like rot, like they are all part of a ritual that can't be stopped. I bet most of them don't even know what they're afraid of. Just a superstition they've inherited, passed down generation after generation. The kind that festers and grows in the way only fears can until it makes sense to punish a single person for the sins of an entire group. Fuck that.

I buck, rage cutting through the terror. "Get your hands off me!"

I twist and claw, my nails scraping against wet leather and wool. Someone kicks my legs out from under me, and I go down again, face-first this time. The taste of dirt and iron floods my mouth.

Their jeers become a chorus as they circle me, moving so quickly that they blur into the night. The hounds howl and pull at their leashes as if scenting prey. I lurch to my knees, ignoring the blood in my mouth and my torn shirt. I chose this, but I will not make it easy.

Wolves will bite.

I spring forward and grab a boot, knocking the man to the ground. I shove against his chest and propel myself onto my feet just as someone tackles me. Fingers choke my throat until blackness seeps into my vision.

"Should I kill her?" my captor calls to his friends.

I tear at the hands around my neck.

"No," the bartender's cold voice answers. He moves away from Kieren and takes a single step toward us. "Burn the witch!"

"Nooo!"

But the cry doesn't come from me. It's Kieren. He's on his feet.

The hands at my throat shift and clamp down on my shoulders. I suck in air and moan, "Run."

But Kieren already is.

Just not away.

Toward me.

No.

A blade flashes in the lantern light, followed by the wet sound of flesh tearing. Kieren slows, his body arching, the breath leaving him in a sharp, broken grunt. He stumbles, hands flying to his stomach as darkness spreads and oozes between his fingers.

No.

The word shatters through me.

Not Kieren.

He tries to take another step toward me. He makes it halfway before his knees give out, and he hits the mud hard. His face twists in pain as his breath comes in shallow, panicked pulls.

"Kieren!" My voice breaks, but I don't stop fighting. "Please let me help him. I can help him."

Someone backhands me across the face, and my head snaps sideways, vision bursting into sparks. "Shut up."

In the chaos, Kieren groans, and my insides hollow out. I thrash against the hands holding me in place, kicking my legs out. My feet scrabble against the loose dirt, muscles screaming as I try to squirm free. I can fix this. I just need to get to Kieren. It's not too late. It can't be.

But a meaty arm hooks around my waist and yanks me up like a rag doll.

"You don't look so powerful now," the man says scornfully.

I wrench my gaze back to Kieren. He's on his side now, trying to crawl, fingers digging into the mud and slipping. Each movement is slower than the last as he refuses to give up. He lifts his head, eyes wild as he searches and finds me.

Relief flickers over his face, even now.

"I'm here," I sob. "I'm right here."

I strain toward him, but the arm at my waist snaps me back. My captor seizes my wrist and pins it at a torturous angle behind me.

"Leave him," the bartender says with a casual wave of his hand. "Let him watch."

"No!" I scream, my legs giving out. I sag to my knees, voice choking around the splintering pain in my wrist. "Help him. I'm the one you want. Please."

The word *please* tastes like poison on my tongue.

Kieren drags himself another inch closer. His elbow collapses. He cries out, the sound so helpless that something inside my chest tears open.

One of the men nudges him with a boot.

This time, Kieren doesn't move.

"Should have listened when he told you to run," the man mocks.

I barely hear him as I stare at Kieren. His chest lifts, and air rushes back into my own lungs. He's alive. Breathing. There's still time.

I snarl, but the hand on my wrist tightens before I can dive toward him.

"Get her up," another orders.

The bartender bends and unleashes the hounds. The dogs bound toward Kieren and sniff.

"Get home," the bartender commands them. They back away, tails tucking between their legs, and then retreat into the woods.

The man releases my arm and heaves me to my feet, drags me toward a dead tree at the edge of the clearing. Rope scrapes roughly against my skin, biting into my wrists as one pulls it into a tight loop. Another man stoops to gather fallen branches, snapping them over his knee and piling them at the base of the trunk with slow, deliberate care. The branches are green and wet; they won't burn fast. The fire will take its time.

My heart slams against my ribs. There is no time. If Kieren doesn't get help, if they wait for the fire to catch, it will be too late.

I look at the man binding me, trying to keep my lower lip from quivering and failing. "Please. He didn't do anything. I came back. You have to help him."

He won't even meet my eyes.

"Tie her up proper," his friend says. "We only get one chance."

I blink at the man closest to me. "Why are you doing this?"

He grins, white teeth flashing in the night. "Burning the harbinger to appease the Stars."

"And start a war," the other adds with glee.

I sputter as it hits me. "That's what you want, isn't it?"

This isn't about the raven-mark or superstitious paranoia.

The grin widens. "There's money in war."

They know exactly what they're doing.

I was always going to die—one way or another.

And now Kieren will pay the price.

I sag under the truth's weight. I should have let them execute me that night.

Two of the men force me against the tree, rope biting deeper as they raise my wrists over my head and tie the rope around the trunk. I struggle, twisting in vain, the bark scraping my skin raw.

"Kieren!" I cry again. "Please . . . please don't leave him."

But they don't even look at him.

Kieren tries to lift his head one last time. His mouth moves, his lips trying to form a word and fumbling.

Fire blazes to life beneath me, branches crackling as they spark and ignite.

The flames creep closer, licking at the hem of my cloak as the smoke rises, stinging my eyes and lodging in my throat.

"Kieren," I sob, coughing as my lungs fill with smoke. "I'm sorry. I'm so sorry."

I can't see him anymore, but I want him to know I'm here.

Flames lick my boots, and then—

Steel rings out.

A body hits the ground hard enough to shake the earth beneath me.

Another scream cuts short.

Through the haze, a dark figure surges forward. The flames throw his shadow long, stretching and warping it until it looks inhuman. Metal flashes in the firelight, and hope punches into my chest so hard it hurts.

"Bishop . . ." I rasp, but the rest burns away in my throat.

He moves like the fire isn't there. Like the men aren't there. Like the only thing that exists is *me.*

One of them charges him with his sword raised. Bishop sidesteps and drives his blade straight through the man's chest. There's no flourish, no hesitation—just the sickening certainty of the strike. The body collapses at Bishop's feet.

His gaze darts to the flames climbing my legs, now calf-height, and his expression tenses. He lifts his eyes up to mine, and for a second, everything disappears. I don't feel the icy lick of flames through my pants. Don't smell the sickening stench of burning flesh. There's only the determined glint in Bishop's eyes.

My heart lurches as another man lunges at him. Bishop turns too late, distracted by me, and steel bites into his shoulder. He grunts as blood soaks his sleeve.

"Get him!"

Bishop answers by ripping the sword free and smashing the hilt into the man's face. Bone cracks, and he staggers back as Bishop slashes his throat. He kicks the body aside and keeps moving toward me.

The bartender backs away, eyes widening. "You're too late," he shouts, trying to sound brave even as his voice shakes. Bishop doesn't slow. The bartender holds up his hands. "It's already—"

Bishop cuts him down mid-sentence.

The last man breaks and runs.

Bishop lets him.

Silence crashes down as suddenly as the violence erupted, broken only by the crackle of the fire and my ragged, desperate gasps for air. My eyes water as the acrid stench of burning fabric fills my nostrils. White-hot heat creeps up my legs. I yank at the ropes, but they hold.

"Arden." Bishop rushes toward me.

I can't answer. I can hardly see him through the smoke.

He shrugs off his tunic as he approaches, firelight illuminating his bare chest and the patterns mapped across his flesh. They glow faintly, lines intersecting and branching.

He steps into the pyre.

Flames curl around his boots and lick up his legs, snapping hungrily at his skin, but he doesn't flinch. He just kicks at the burning logs, shoving them aside like unwanted guests.

"Bishop . . . I . . ." I cough, something wild flaring in my chest.

He reaches up and slices through the rope binding my wrists with one clean stroke. My arms collapse uselessly at my sides, and I sag forward. Bishop catches me before I fall into the fire.

"It's all right," he murmurs, pulling off my cloak and tossing it to the side. He guides my arms into his tunic, pulling it over my head to cover my ruined sweater. "I've got you."

He lifts me, and I lock my arms around his neck, press my face into his chest, *cling*.

"Kieren," I whisper. "Please. Kieren."

Bishop stiffens. "In a moment."

He carries me out of the fire, away from the tree, away from death. My vision clears just enough for me to see Kieren sprawled in the mud where they left him.

He lies on his back, eyes open and staring at nothing.

"No, no, no—"

We're supposed to be on a boat. This was going to be an adventure.

Bishop lowers me beside him without a word and backs up a step. But only one step.

I scramble to Kieren's side, pressing my hands to his chest, his neck, anywhere I can think to feel for life.

"Stay with me," I whisper. "Please. I'm here. I didn't leave."

His skin is already cooling.

There's no breath. No pulse.

He was still talking about Isidore an hour ago, like the future was a thing that could be bargained for. He can't just be . . . gone.

I fold over him, a sound ripping out of me that comes from somewhere so deep inside I feel it in my bones. I can't breathe.

I ran.

I turned back.

But I didn't save him.

"Kieren." I cup his face with both hands and cry. "I'm so sorry."

The words aren't enough, but it's all I can manage as my throat closes. Those men came for me, and he was in the way. My vision blurs, tears mixing with ash. He'll never see the Lost Continent. Never cheat sailors at Liar's Hand. There won't be any adventures. No new life in a new world. And he will never go back home to Damalis, fortune made.

This can't be how it ends.

Something heavy thumps behind me, and I whirl toward the sound, expecting another ambush. But it's Bishop. He's on one knee, blinking down at the hand holding his stomach. But all I can see is the blood pouring through his fingers. I'd only seen the one slice into his shoulder. This one is much, much worse.

"Bishop?" I croak.

He sways and drops to both knees in front of me.

Panic slams into me, and I lurch forward, pressing my hands over his bloody ones. I don't know what to do, where to hold pressure. I just push like I can shove the wound back inside him. "I'm going to Wolf's Keep." I'm afraid to leave him, but what choice do I have? "To get a healer . . ."

"No . . . It's too dangerous." His voice is raspy, each word strained.

"There's time." I shake my head, even though something in me knows better. "I'll bring help."

I can't let him die.

His fingers wrap around my wrist. "Arden." He swallows. It takes effort. "Listen."

I press harder against the wound. "Don't say it."

I can't lose him, too.

I don't care that he's a heart collector. Don't care what he's done. All I see is the man who came for me. Saved me. And he's bleeding out in front of me.

He tries to speak again but has to stop. Sucking in a reedy breath, he forces the words out. "There isn't time." He pauses, chest stuttering. "I won't let them take you."

His other hand fumbles for the blade at his thigh. Misses the strap. Tries again.

I grab the dagger and thrust it into his palm. "Here. Just . . . just hold on."

His fingers close over mine, holding the knife between us. They're warm and steady in a way that doesn't make sense.

"It's the only way," he says.

"No," I whisper, shaking my head violently. "No. Not like this. Not you, too."

He smiles up at me with glassy eyes, and my chest aches. "You did what you could," he mumbles. "Now trust me."

He shifts his grip, guiding my hand before I understand what he's doing.

And drives the blade into his own throat.

Cartilage splinters as it slides in, warm blood spilling on my hands.

His grip on mine loosens, and I fling the blade in the dirt.

The sound that tears out of me doesn't belong to my body. It rips through the trees, reaching the stars as his weight settles fully against me.

And Bishop Marius dies in my arms.

TWENTY-ONE

My legs go numb, but I don't move. The fire burns down to embers. The smoke thins, and the forest settles into an uneasy quiet, broken only by the distant rush of the sea and the low crackle of smoldering branches.

Bishop lies in my arms, his body too heavy. The pale patterns mapped on his skin darken like the magic has been poisoned and died with him.

I ran. I thought I had to for Kieren—and for me. I thought it was the right thing to do. I thought Bishop was a monster.

Instead, he came for me. He saved me.

He found that letter—

And now he's dead.

They're *both* dead.

Kieren's hand was warm when he squeezed mine at the crossroads.

Now it's bloody and still in the mud beside me.

My tears run dry before the fire goes out. I can't summon another sob even when I try, as though my body has decided this is as much as it can survive.

I can't keep looking at them. If I do, I'll start screaming again. So, I tilt my head back. Smoke drifts across the sky in pale ribbons, briefly smudging the constellations before the wind tears them apart. The stars look the same as they always have, except for the Night's Scar gaping above me, that single star blazing inside it like an accusation.

Everything I touch dies.

The thought presses in and won't retreat. My parents. My home. Kieren. Bishop.

I squeeze my eyes shut, but the truth won't go away any more than that fucking star will.

A faint vibration hums against my palm, startling my attention back to Bishop. The buzz grows insistent, and I slip my hand into the pocket of his pants and find his astrolabe.

Its faint light pulses weakly, as if echoing a heartbeat that no longer exists, then gutters out.

Bishop planned for this.

Of course he did. He planned for everything. Except for dying and leaving me with the aftermath.

The realization barely registers. I don't have the strength to care who he contacted or why. Instead, I let the astrolabe slip from my fingers and fall into the mud beside us.

Nothing matters now.

My gaze drifts to the dagger lying near my knee. The blade is dark with blood, and a quiet dawning slips in—an ending is within reach.

I pick up the dagger and turn it over with deliberation, watching how the light slides along its stained edge. My grip tightens once, then loosens. Blood has dried into the lines of my palm, cracking when I flex my fingers. Kieren trusted me. Bishop saved me. They're gone, but the dagger is here.

Branches snap somewhere behind me—too loud, too sudden in the quiet—and instinct flares.

If more people are coming to kill the harbinger, so be it.

But it's Taliesin's voice that breaks the night. "Arden."

Taliesin barrels into the clearing like he expects to find a brawl and a punch line, but he stops short. The hand on the hilt of his sword slackens and drops to his side as he turns, taking in the full scene. His gaze lands on me, on the body in my arms and the one beside me, and his throat slides. Without a word, he bends, lifting my fallen cloak from the ground, and drapes it carefully over Kieren's body.

I should have done that.

I left him uncovered, like I left him to die.

"May the Stars welcome you," he murmurs over my best friend, "and may the night be kinder to you than this world was."

He lingers for a moment like he's adding another private prayer before he turns to me, but I don't look up.

It's as though I can't, as though something heavy weighs my eyes to the dirt that's still soaking up Bishop's blood. I can't look at Bishop.

I can't look at Kieren—not when looking would mean admitting that he's gone.

Taliesin kneels in front of me and reaches for the knife. My fingers lock around the hilt like it's the only solid thing left in the world.

"Easy," he says in a low voice. "You don't need that."

He pries it from my hand slowly as if afraid I might shatter if he handles me too roughly.

Light bobs in the trees, and Vessica steps into view a heartbeat later, sword already in hand. Her eyes sweep the clearing, cataloging the damage.

"What the fuck happened?" she demands.

Taliesin shoots her a look. "Not now."

She follows his gaze to me, then to Bishop's body, and her breath leaves her in a single, sharp exhale.

"Stars above," she mutters. "Of course." Her eyes sweep the bodies like a battlefield report.

But when they land on me—on Bishop—something hard strains in her jaw. She doesn't say anything.

Somehow, that's worse.

Taliesin straightens, squaring his shoulders. "Get her back to Miradores."

I shouldn't go back there. Not after I ran from it.

But Vessica doesn't move as she asks, "What about . . . you?"

"I'll handle this," he says more seriously than I've ever heard him, whatever mask he usually wears replaced by grim determination.

Maybe they're used to this as soldiers, accustomed to watching their friends fall and not get back up. Maybe death is a fact they've learned to live with.

She nods, sheathing her sword. Stepping forward, she crouches down so that we're face-to-face. "You need to get up."

I tighten my arms around Bishop's body.

"I can't leave," I whisper. "I never should have left."

That's how this all started. I can't let it end that way, too. Because if I let go of Bishop, this becomes real. If it's real, then Kieren is gone, too.

Her jaw clenches. "We're leaving. Now."

I sink closer to the ground.

"This is where I belong. With *them*." The words come out flat and distant, sounding like they belong to someone else.

Vessica's gaze darts to the cloaked body at my side and narrows with recognition. Her expression shifts slightly. It's not quite pity, but the edge of her annoyance dulls. "You can't help them. Now get up."

I stare at her for a long moment, searching for something—some mercy or reassurance that I can cling to.

There's none.

My arms loosen inch by inch, like I'm lowering something fragile instead of letting go. The cold rushes in, erasing the last traces of his warmth on my skin. Vessica holds out a hand, and I clasp it, allowing her to haul me onto my feet. Instantly, pain ricochets up my legs, and I stagger a step.

Vessica catches me before I collapse. "Be careful. You're burned," she says, glancing down at my boots and the blackened hem. Her gaze travels up to my torn-open clothing and exposed skin above the deep vee in Bishop's tunic, and anger flashes across her face. Her grip locks, like she's imagining throats under her blade. "We'll deal with that later."

I look down to discover my pants scorched and half melted, the skin beneath raw and oozing.

"I'm okay," I mumble, trying to pull away from her.

But Vessica doesn't release me.

"Just let me help you," she says too smoothly. Even now, she is fury packed into a tight, disciplined shape.

She keeps one arm locked around my waist but reaches out to pull Bishop's tunic closed. Her hold on me is a vise grip as we move through the trees as though she's afraid I might dissolve if she loosens it.

I stumble more than walk, each step more agonizing than the last.

Vessica notices. "We can slow down," she offers, "or take a break."

I don't deserve a break. I deserve to be lying dead back in that clearing.

"No." I grit my teeth and push on. "What is he going to do with the . . ."

I can't bring myself to say the word *bodies*, but it echoes in my brain like the men's chant. Another fact of life that I can't escape any more than the raven-mark on my chest.

"He'll take care of it." She shifts her hold on me, trying to support more of my weight.

"Kieren." My heart cracks when I say his name. "Can we bury him?"

"We don't leave our dead in the dirt. I'll talk to Bishop—" She flinches, realizing her mistake. "I'm sure something can be arranged."

I don't press for more. She has her own grief to manage—her own body to bury.

Trees give way to the road. We've cut through the forest at an angle, and the bridge to the estate looms ahead, a heavy mist blanketing it. Beyond, Miradores rises like a gravestone out of the fog.

The door flies open before we reach it. Lenora stands in her nightclothes on the threshold, and her face crumples the instant she sees me.

"Stars preserve us," she whispers. "What—"

"Get Hadrian," Vessica orders, already steering me inside. "Now."

Lenora doesn't argue. She gives me one more horrified look and disappears to fetch him from his chambers off the library.

Vessica leads me upstairs and deposits me on the edge of my bed. I suck in a deep breath, relieved to be off my feet. Right now, even my bones ache from trying to hold myself together. She lifts my left leg gingerly, and I wince.

"Sorry," she mutters as she examines it. "You're lucky. These will heal, but you need treatment."

Luck had nothing to do with it. I'm cursed.

"I'll send for a healer." She starts to leave.

I grab her hand to stop her. "No."

"No?" she repeats like she heard me wrong.

"I don't want a stranger . . ." The words bottle up in my throat and refuse to come out. Just the thought of someone touching me, assessing me, knowing what happened—I can't bear it.

Vessica exhales through her teeth, clearly fighting the urge to argue. "Fine. The Bellatorum will have something. For now," she adds pointedly. "I'll get it myself. Don't move."

As if I could.

She closes the door behind her, and I sit very still, staring at the place where Bishop's blood dried on my hands. My fingers open and close as if they're still searching for someone to hold.

When Lenora returns, she has a basin of water, cloths, and fresh clothes folded over her arm. She moves carefully, watching me with concerned eyes.

"Let's clean you up," she suggests, placing the basin beside the bed and the other items on the mattress.

I don't respond.

She eases Bishop's tunic above my shoulders and hesitates when she sees my torn clothes underneath. Her lips press into a thin line as she surveys the rest of me.

"Let's get you in something clean," she says, easing the ripped sweater off my shoulders. She tugs a sleeping gown over my head, then hesitates. "We need to get those breeches off you, too."

I nod, reaching under the gown's hem to unbutton them. Grabbing the waist, I ease them off, wincing with every inch. Lenora takes the scorched pants and drops them on the ground.

I glance down and shiver.

There are angry, red wounds along my calves, some seeping, others blistering. Lenora swallows and begins cleaning the dirt and blood from my skin like she's done this a hundred times.

She probably has for Bishop and his family, but after tonight . . .

"What will you do now?" I ask suddenly, the words slipping out before I can stop them.

Lenora pauses, her eyebrows furrowing. Maybe in all the chaos, Vessica didn't tell her. She resumes blotting soot from my skin with a damp cloth. "We'll take care of you."

She doesn't know. I have to tell her. Not just what happened but what I did.

"Bishop is dead." The words feel impossible in my mouth, like I'm speaking a language that shouldn't exist. "I tried to run away. They killed my friend Kieren. Bishop died trying to save me."

All this loss reduced to those simple facts. But the words sound wrong out loud, like I'm listing events from someone else's life.

She stills, the rag in her hand dripping onto the floor.

"Sometimes," she murmurs, "the Stars ask more of us than we're ready to give. You'll understand—"

"No." I shake my head. "Don't say that. Don't tell me this was meant to be."

She considers for a second, searching my face like she might find the right thing to say. She settles on, "All right then."

Lenora helps me out of the ruined clothes without further comment, sliding fabric away from burned skin with painstaking care. She wraps a blanket around my shoulders, tucking it close like it might keep me from falling apart. "He'll explain when he arrives."

"Hadrian?" I shake my head. "I don't want to see him."

I can't face anyone else tonight.

But she rises, ignoring my protest, and throws the dirty clothes in the basin. "I'll bring you something to drink. All that smoke . . . Your throat must be raw."

I manage a nod, and she leaves me with my thoughts. I drift to the window without realizing I've moved, my reflection a pale ghost in the glass. The burns smarting my skin are the only proof that I'm not dead.

Moonlight washes over the garden, and in the branches of the nearest willow, a dark shape perches, barely visible against the night. I press a hand to the glass like I can summon it. The oscen cranes its head and stares toward the house. But it doesn't fly away; it begins to sing.

The song is low and strange—unlike any birdsong I've heard before. The thin, aching melody rises and falls and finally settles deep in my bones.

I rest my forehead against the glass as the door opens again behind me.

"Have you come to tell me this isn't my fault, too, Hadrian?" I ask without turning.

But it isn't Hadrian who answers.

"No, I haven't. Because we both know that's not true."

I whip toward the familiar voice, and the world tilts under me.

His shirt is clean, but his pants are burned and bloodstained. He's holding a jar of salve in one hand and a book in the other.

Bishop.

Standing in the doorway.

Talking to me.

Alive.

TWENTY-TWO

The world is still in pieces, but Bishop leans against the doorframe and forces a half smile that doesn't quite reach his haunted eyes. "You didn't scream. Taliesin will be disappointed."

I stare, my skin tightening like I'm wearing it wrong.

Dead. He can't be standing here. He died in my arms.

My thoughts skid, trying to find the trick—the proof that I'm hallucinating. But the fire is still crackling in the hearth, my muddy boots and his bloodstained tunic in front of it.

This isn't real. *He* isn't real.

"Say something," the ghost murmurs, as if I'm some wild beast that must be approached with caution. "You're starting to worry me."

A laugh chokes out of me. Thin, broken, wrong. It scrapes from my throat like something dragged up from the bottom of a well run dry.

He steps into the room, his eyes narrowing with concern, and drops the jar and book onto the bed. They land with a soft *thump*, the quilt rippling from the impact of their weight. Like they're real. But he can't . . .

No.

I'm asleep. I turn and plant my hand on the windowpane to steady myself, but the cool glass sends a shiver racing through my body that doesn't wake me up. Not a dream. He can't be . . .

None of this makes sense.

"You're dead." I need to say it. Even if it feels undeniable and dubious at the same time.

For a heartbeat, the words hang between us.

Then the-thing-that-can't-be-Bishop-but-is-doing-a-fucking-unnerving-impression-of-him lifts his head and meets my eyes. "I was."

A pit opens in my stomach. No, it collapses, the sensation so abrupt it steals my breath, and everything else falls out of focus but those two words.

I was.

But I can still see his death. His body convulsing. The blade slippery and warm in the palm of my hand. Blood so dark it's nearly black soaking into the mud beneath my knees. The copper tang of it mixing with smoke, and my stomach churning. He's heavy in my arms.

I can still feel the ache in my muscles.

And now, he's standing in front of me.

I lost so much today. It's no surprise that my mind is going, too.

I look away, unable to bear it, and my gaze settles on the bed, on the spot where the book has left a dent in the otherwise crisp sheets. If that's real . . . I drag my gaze to him again. The hair pulled back at the nape of his neck is still damp, as if he washed it in a hurry. His face and hands have been scrubbed raw, but soot still shadows the creases of his knuckles, and there's a dark, ruddy smear under one ear. The patterns on his skin have softened back to silvery white scars. His white shirt is clean, the collar open in a way his uniform never allows. But his canvas pants are stiff with dried blood, the bottoms of them eaten away by ragged scorch marks.

I take a slow step from the window, then another before I can lose my nerve. I continue even as something inside me braces as if I'm walking toward a ledge and not a man.

Bishop tenses as I lift a trembling hand out—and stop less than an inch from his chest.

If I touch him, he'll vanish.

That's how it works. Ghosts evaporate at contact. Hallucinations don't survive reality. I can't bear the possibility that this is some cruel trick of my mind. Not after everything else.

His face remains blank as he watches me, but it is his face. His eyes are the same winter blue beneath his dark lashes, his nose still slightly crooked, his mouth set in that impatient line it forms when he's holding something back.

"If you're a ghost . . ." I murmur, my fingers hovering so close I swear I feel the heat of his body. I can't bring myself to move them that last fraction of an inch.

Bishop sighs, the gruff sound sending a jolt to my core, and grabs my hand to close the distance himself.

His fingers are warm and callused. I gasp and pull back out of instinct, but he doesn't let go. He presses my palm flat against his chest. The body underneath doesn't yield. His thumb brushes the back of my hand once. Slow. Deliberate.

Daring me to feel it. Feel him.

His warmth sinks into my skin, and beneath my hand: a heartbeat.

Strong. Steady. Alive.

My own heart stutters, then accelerates wildly, pounding against my rib cage. This can't be happening. It isn't fair.

I yank my hand away, but only so I can dig my fingers into his arm and pinch him.

"Fuck." Bishop grunts like he's biting back a yelp, but he doesn't stop me.

I push his sleeve up, looking for the burns from the fire, for the blisters that had already started to form when he died.

There's nothing there now.

No burns. No scars. Just normal, healthy skin, apart from more of those strange patterns that he hides.

Something fragile flares in my chest. A stupid, treacherous spark I don't deserve. A thousand questions crowd my tongue, all of them desperate and ridiculous and terrifying. But I don't ask them. Instead, my voice cracks around a single name. "Kieren?"

Bishop stiffens. Regret flickers across his face and is gone in an instant, dousing that spark. The finality of that look settles heavily in my bones.

Kieren is dead.

I shouldn't have even asked.

I sure as fuck shouldn't have hoped.

Bishop shifts his weight as if he might step closer, might reach for me. The space between us contracts, charged with the promise of comfort.

But his hands remain at his sides. "He wasn't like me."

Wasn't.

It's strange how a single word can sound so final.

I stagger back a step, needing to put space between us, but my knees buckle. Pain spears up my legs, ripping through tissue and muscle as if the fire isn't finished with me yet. The room lurches sideways.

He catches me before I hit the ground.

"I've got you," he murmurs, lips too close to my ear. Grounding me. Saving me again. I want to hate him for it.

"I'm fine," I say through gritted teeth.

He doesn't bother arguing. He simply lifts me into his arms with infuriating ease, just like he did in the clearing.

But I'm not going to escape this. Whatever this is.

Bishop lowers me onto the edge of the bed and reaches for the glass jar of salve. "Your burns need attention."

I make a weak sound of protest that dies in my throat as he kneels in front of me.

He twists off the lid. The bitter, medicinal scent is so pungent that I can taste it, but his fingers hover above my skin. Waiting.

"Vessica said you didn't want a stranger's hands on you," he says quietly.

Something about the way he says it makes my chest ache. There's understanding there. And beneath it, something fierce. Anger, maybe. Or fear. Or the kind of violence that's better kept leashed.

"Not after . . ." I whisper.

I don't finish.

But he nods. "Tell me if you want me to stop."

My muscles tense in a way that has nothing to do with the coolness of the balm as he kneels at my feet and smooths the salve over my skin. The pain dulls to something manageable, and in its place, there's only his touch.

His focus slips for half a second. Just long enough for something unguarded to surface before he reins it back in. His hands are steady. Controlled. Never lingering longer than necessary. But something reverent burns on his face, in his eyes, in that gentle, patient touch.

He's holding back.

I brush a hand over his forehead, and our eyes lock, something raw and electric passing between us. His breath changes. Mine does, too. He rests his head against my palm, his eyes shuttering, and for one reckless second, I want to close the space between us. Until the grief coiling in my chest strikes. Guilt follows close behind. Relief. Anger. Want.

All of it tangles together until it's impossible to separate.

I choke back a sob, but he hears it.

A muscle tenses in his jaw, and he shifts back again. I lower my hand, but neither of us looks away, the space between us humming with everything we're not saying.

Until I break the silence and admit, "I didn't think you'd come after me."

"You ran," he says, not bothering to look up.

"Why?" We both know what I'm really asking.

He opens his mouth, forming a word that never leaves his lips before he drops his gaze to my wounds, returning to the task at hand with lethal concentration. As if focus is the only thing keeping him from answering.

Part of me doesn't want it to be. The part of me that wants to feel proof that I'm alive.

But I'll never forgive myself for it.

I reach for the book, so I don't reach for him, and clutch it to my chest like it's an anchor.

Like if I let go, I'll shatter and never quite fit back together again. Or worse, make another reckless decision that I can't take back. Because whatever this is—whatever *he* is—there's already no going back.

Bishop finishes bandaging me, but he doesn't stand up. "I expected more questions." He nods to the book in my hands. "About that."

The prompt cuts through the fog in my head, and I glance down at the title embossed on the cover.

Scions.

I almost drop it.

"It's . . ." I clear my throat, suddenly hoarse. "It's the book you stole from the shop."

His expression darkens, lips pressing into a thin line as his eyes flick from the book to my face.

"I knew someone else was there," he says at last.

I let out a brittle laugh. "Why did you take it?"

"I didn't steal it."

I lift an eyebrow.

"I have an arrangement with the owner," he explains. "She lets me take what I want, and I don't arrest her for possessing contraband."

I stare at him. "That's not an arrangement," I say flatly. "That's extortion."

One corner of his mouth twitches. "Semantics."

Something smooths the jagged fracture in my chest. Not relief. Nothing that generous. But the familiar rhythm of this, of pushing back and still finding him here. It feels almost . . . normal.

But it curdles in my stomach, sour. Wrong. I want to spit it out.

Not when Kieren is dead in the mud and I'm here. Alive, warm, and being tended to by a man who keeps saving me even when I don't deserve it.

I lower my eyes to the book again, suddenly unable to meet Bishop's gaze, and swallow. "What does the word mean?"

"*Scion* means . . ." He shifts back on his heels like a little distance might help him think. "It's what I am."

He falls silent after his cryptic declaration. I wait, but he doesn't continue.

"That's it?" I hesitate. Count his breaths. But he doesn't give me anything else. "That's all you're going to say?"

He considers again, rubbing his index finger over his lips like he's drawing his answer out deliberately to fluster me. "Yes."

I blink as this processes, then explode. "That's all I get? You came back from the fucking dead, and your explanation is a single word?"

Such a control freak.

"Do you honestly believe I'm going to accept that?"

He snorts. "No."

He's about to die for the second time tonight.

"You aren't going to answer my questions?" I ask through gritted teeth.

Must not kill him. It will give Lenora more laundry to do.

He pushes onto his feet. "Not tonight."

"Of course not." After all of this, after everything, he's still keeping secrets.

But the others . . . they knew. Taliesin's calmness, Vessica's slip about talking to Bishop . . . I didn't understand in the woods. Didn't understand Lenora's words. *He'll explain . . .*

They all know, and I don't even get a basic explanation.

You didn't scream. Taliesin will be disappointed.

"Everyone else knows, don't they?"

Bishop sets the jar of salve on my nightstand. "Yes."

It's not confirmation. It's a slap in the face.

"Everyone?"

The muscles in his neck bulge like he's biting back what he wants to say to this. "Everyone with access to this house." He crosses his arms, and the thin material of his shirt strains against his muscles like even it is desperate to escape this conversation. "Taliesin. Vessica. Hadrian. Lenora."

My grip tightens on the book, its primary function shifting from anchoring me to occupying my hands so I don't strangle him. "But not me."

He meets my gaze without flinching. There's not an ounce of apology staring back at me.

"You don't trust me." It's not an accusation. It's a fact. And somehow, that makes it worse.

His eyes flash. "Like you trust me?"

He reaches into the pocket of his burned trousers and pulls out a crumpled sheet of parchment. My letter, its edges blackened by smoke.

He thrusts the letter toward me.

I don't need to read it again. The words are burned into me.

> **Bishop,**
> **Don't come after us. Everyone in Antares will be better off without me, especially you.**
> **—A**
>
> **P.S. Your secret is safe with me.**

The ink is smeared where blood soaked through, warping the words until they mean something else entirely. Evidence of the choice I made. Of what it cost.

"And what secret is that?" he asks, eyes skirting to the book.

"Don't you mean which? There are so many." The children he doesn't force into conscription. The reason his estate is falling apart. Being a scion. But I can't bring myself to ask him if he killed the king. "Secret trips. Lying about your location."

"I was in Wintour," he cuts in. "I saw the queen."

Maybe it wasn't a lie, but it wasn't the whole truth. And it's not the only thing that he's kept from me. "Care to explain the others?"

"We will talk about this in the morning," he says through clenched teeth.

But I've gone too far to stop now.

"You hid things. You let me believe . . ." Angry tears clog my throat. I swallow them and keep going. "You let me believe you were helping me."

"I *am* helping you," he growls.

"No, you're helping yourself." A thick silence settles after the accusation leaves my mouth.

Bishop doesn't move. That's how I know I'm right. When he finally speaks, the words strain from him. "But there are things you don't understand."

Something edged hides in the words, like he's still holding back. He glances at the door. I wait for him to try to help me do just that. He doesn't.

"That's not an explanation," I say, voice shaking.

"No," he agrees. "It isn't."

I throw the papers back at him. "You're unbelievable."

He stares me down as they flutter to his feet. "Fine. I'll say it. I want you alive."

I don't know how to respond.

He kneels in front of me again, close enough that I can't look anywhere else. "I want you safe."

There's something I can't ignore in his words.

"And I want you to stop running before it costs you everything." He grips my knees like he'll hold me in place himself before he lets that happen.

"You asked why I didn't tell you about Damalis."

My heart leaps into my throat, and I nod.

"You were pushing to come with me."

I blink. "I wanted to help."

"I didn't want you there," he says plainly.

His bluntness knocks the air from my lungs. "Why?"

He hesitates. "Because it was your home."

Home.

The word hits harder than I expect.

Damalis flashes through my mind in unwanted fragments. The fields and the worn stone walls, Andry's laughter echoing off the hills. Kieren chasing loose cattle with me. The certainty that no matter how little we had, there would always be a warm fire and my family.

Because it was your home.

Like that place doesn't exist for me anymore.

Like I can never go back.

"You don't get to decide that," I whisper, but I already know he's right. I can't go back. Not after tonight.

"No, I don't," he agrees. "But I swore to protect you."

I look away, blinking hard. "You're telling me this now," I say, "because . . . what? You feel guilty?"

"Because if we're going to survive," he says, and the word *survive* lodges uncomfortably in my chest, "we need to learn to trust each other."

"If I had trusted you, maybe I would have told you Kieren's plan. Maybe you would have actually helped me." I let the truth hang in the air, and he doesn't interrupt. "Kieren would still be alive. I wish . . ."

I trail away, but the admission bleeds between us.

I wait for him to argue. To tell me that it isn't my fault. Convince me I couldn't have known how poorly it would end. That the world is cruel and unfair.

Instead, he almost smiles, and the sadness there crushes me. "You'll always wish you'd done things differently," he says quietly. "I do."

The certainty in his voice chills me.

And for the first time, I really see him. Behind the authority, the armor, the careful restraint. There's something old there. A scar opened too many times to ever heal properly.

"How many?" I can barely bring myself to ask.

His forehead creases. "How many what?"

I take a deep breath and force the question out. "How many people did you lose before you stopped wishing?"

He doesn't answer right away. Just stares past me like the question sent him somewhere else. To a different life. A log pops gently in the hearth, and he flinches.

"Too many."

Not a satisfying answer. Or a complete one.

But it's honest.

I nod slowly.

"If I ask you something," I say, choosing my words carefully, "will you tell me the truth?"

His head tilts, and he hesitates a beat. "That depends on the question."

"Figures," I grumble.

Everything with him comes with terms.

"One question." He holds up a hand before I can ask it and adds, "Choose it carefully. I'm not answering more tonight."

I can't blame him. Now that the adrenaline has finally burned out, my head throbs, and my legs ache. The night has already taken too much. Exhaustion presses in from all sides, but I consider what he says.

"Why *did* you come after me?" The question that's been circling me since the clearing.

He glances out the window like he's looking for an answer.

"You left a note," he says after a moment.

This again. "That—"

"Isn't an answer," he finishes for me. He tips his head as if he agrees. "Because I know what it feels like to run."

The idea of Bishop running is so unthinkable that I nearly laugh.

"Because," he adds, lowering his voice like it's a secret, "I know what it costs when you do."

That cost is already burned into me.

Before I can ask anything else, he straightens. "You need rest."

Confession time is over.

I slump into the pillows, frustration warring with relief. Exhaustion finally wins.

I hold the book out toward him.

But he doesn't take it.

"Keep it," he says. "You've earned the answers in there."

Bishop turns toward the door, reaching to turn down the light.

"Wait." The word slips out before I can stop it. "Leave the light on. I don't want to be in the dark."

He nods, not looking back at me. But his hand moves to grip the doorframe, knuckles whitening. He shifts, just enough that I think he'll turn around. He doesn't.

"Try to sleep," he says instead. "Your wounds need time to heal."

I stare at the closed door long after he leaves. Without him here, the room feels too empty and sleep too far away.

My gaze drops to the book resting against my thigh. I don't know if I want the answers inside it, but I can't keep running. From the truth. From myself.

From him.

But when I flip it open, I find the ink faded from time and dense notes occupying every margin. But that's not the problem. I flip the page. Then another.

The whole thing is written in the ancient tongue.

Of course.

Those are the answers I earned.

Just like his trust.

He's not going to give me either until I prove myself.

Even if I already hold his biggest secret in my hands.

The burden snaps the last fragile thread holding me together. Tears come hard. Fast. They rip out of me as though my grief is overdue and they're here to collect that pittance of me that remains. I curl in on myself, letting the book fall to the floor. I can't bring myself to pick it up. To face the truth that even it seems determined to show me.

I let it happen.

Not just tonight.

In Wintour. At the palace. During every moment when someone else stepped in front of me because I couldn't stand my ground.

Kieren paid the price.

So did Bishop.

I won't let it happen again.

No one else bleeds for me.

The tears don't stop. Maybe I don't want them to. Maybe they're the key to my own resurrection. So, I give in to them until exhaustion creeps in and dulls the night into softer focus, dragging me toward the place between here and dreams. I let it take me. But the question I should have asked Bishop follows me there.

Why did he find that note in my bedroom after midnight?

TWENTY-THREE

I only leave my room to bury Kieren's body and begin Interstice, the traditional period before his soul finally rests.

But even the funeral isn't really leaving. I might as well be moving through fog. Hands on my arms to steady me. Lenora murmuring instructions. The hollow *thud* of a coffin hitting packed dirt. The wrongness of newly disturbed ground that's been forced to make room for something that doesn't belong there. *Someone* who shouldn't be there.

And then I retreat again. Back to the room. To the window.

Waiting for birdsong that sometimes comes and then doesn't for days. I stay silent through it all, because if I start screaming, I'll never stop.

I pick at the food Lenora leaves on a tray three times a day without comment. Until this afternoon, nearly a week in, when my stomach declares mutiny, growling so loudly even I can't stand it. But when I finally force myself to leave my room, Taliesin stops me near the stairs and holds out a large box.

"These are Kieren's," he says, not quite meeting my eyes. "You were listed as next of kin."

The words *next of kin* settle heavily on my shoulders. They sound too official.

Too *final.*

"I can see to it if you want," Taliesin says quietly when I don't speak. "Give his things away. There are plenty of conscripts who show up here with nothing. Everyone at the Bellatorum knows what a stack of clothes left in the Commons means."

Because cleaning up after the dead is just a way of life in Vennaro.

Dread bottoms out my stomach. Releasing the dead's worldly belongings is the responsibility of the living during Interstice. "I'll do it," I tell him, but I cradle the box closer to my body. I'm not ready to part with the last remnants of him yet.

Taliesin nods like he understands. "If you change your mind . . ."

I'm gone before the offer fully leaves his mouth.

I don't risk looking inside the box until I'm in my room. There isn't much. Kieren's pack—recovered from the docks. Mine was returned to my room days ago without comment. Folded clothes and almost new boots. A dog-eared copy of a pirate adventure he got ten Twelvetides ago. The little token, its carved pegasus worn down to smooth bone in spots. A leather pouch that's heavier than I expect, though I don't bother to count the coins inside. And two letters. One is mine, its creases worn soft and thin by his hands. Now stained dark where his blood soaked through the paper.

The other is sealed, more blood splattered across Isidore's name and address on the envelope. There's no postage on it, I realize with a pang that destroys any lingering appetite.

I put the box with the one my family sent me from Damalis. Maybe I'll give those things away, too.

I try to ignore them both, try to pretend my heart doesn't stutter every time I catch sight of them. But their presence is like monsters lurking in the shadows. I can't pretend they aren't there. After a few days, I can't stand looking at them anymore. They're nearly as bad as the book Bishop gave me and the answers trapped inside it.

I am fucking sick of waiting for someone else to *give* me answers. Sick of waiting for my magic to manifest. Sick of waiting around for someone else to come after me before it does. The only thing waiting has gotten me is a dead best friend.

I grab the leather-bound volume, determined to find them myself. But I don't go looking for Bishop. I go the other way, down the somber corridors toward the library. The scent of old vellum and lingering woodsmoke from the nearly extinguished fire greets me at the door. Hadrian is working at one of the tables, his face half cloaked in shadow. Something eases in my chest.

Answers are clearly his life's work. I could use some answers.

I plunk the book in front of him, harder than I intend to, and Hadrian glances up sharply. His eyes narrow on the title. "I was wondering where that went."

"Bishop gave it to me." I stick to the facts, afraid that if I offer more, like, Stars forbid, my opinion, I'll break again. "He said it has answers about scions. About . . . *him*."

Because that's what I really need to understand. The man who rescued me. Who told me his deepest, darkest secret.

And has basically been avoiding me ever since.

Hadrian picks up the book and thumbs through it before shutting it again. "It's not where I'd start if I wanted to understand what we are."

"We?" I repeat, blinking at him in the library's dim light. "You're a . . ."

He frowns. "He didn't tell you." There's no surprise in his voice. But he pushes up his sleeve and reveals the same strange markings Bishop hides on his own body.

Hadrian is a scion, too.

Anger floods my veins. "No, he didn't tell me."

Of course Bishop didn't tell me. Because he always decides what I can handle. What I *deserve* to know.

For all I fucking do know, everyone in the house but me might be one of these starsdamned immortals. I might have never found out until Bishop . . .

I shut my eyes, trying to block the memory of him in my arms. Throat torn up. His neck a sheet of black blood that pooled into a warm puddle in my lap while shock held me in place so grief and guilt could sprout. And then he strode into my bedroom and ripped them out like weeds. Like death can be so easily uprooted.

But I still feel what he left behind, digging itself deeper and deeper. I'll never get it out of me, and Bishop just moved on.

He went back to living like nothing even fucking happened.

Hadrian inclines his head as if he can see my blood boiling. "Go easy on him," he says quietly, even though we're the only ones in the library.

I huff. "Why?"

He adjusts his glasses. "Because you don't know what you're asking from him."

So much for information.

But one glance at the notes beneath his hand tells me that Bishop isn't the only one hiding behind books. The paper is crowded with cramped notes and strange diagrams, lines of thoughts crossing and looping back on themselves as if he's trying to trap an answer before it can escape.

"Is that why you're here?" I point to the work in front of him. "You're looking for answers about scions, too?"

At night, when I can't sleep, when I wake still stumbling from that forest to find my bedroom staring back at me, I think about that. About Bishop in that bookstore and the book he stole.

About what he's really after.

"Isn't that what we're all doing?" Hadrian asks. "Trying to figure out why we're here?"

"Is that what Bishop is doing? Trying to figure out what he really is? Is that why he goes out looking for these old texts?" I can't explain why it's important. It's more like it's an itch I can't quite scratch.

He doesn't look up. "He has his reasons."

"And you aren't going to explain them." It's not a question.

But he glances over his glasses at me. "No."

I sigh and shove the book I brought closer to him. "Can you at least read this to me?"

"No."

I stare. "No?"

He taps the cover. "Learn."

I glare down at him. "I don't know the ancient tongue because I'm not . . . How old are you, exactly?"

"Roughly five hundred and thirty-four, but I might have missed a few years."

The answer knocks the air from my lungs, and it takes me a minute to catch my breath. "You were alive during the Last War."

A shadow moves across his face. "Yes."

Five hundred years later, and it's still haunting him. That doesn't bode well for me moving on.

"Were you a scion then?" Something bubbles in my chest, the sensation unwelcome. Curiosity will only get me killed.

"No." He shoves his notes into a stack. "That came after."

I want to understand. I need to understand. Before this sweeps me away and I can never find my way back. I take a deep breath and push forward. "I guess that's why you know the ancient tongue."

"Five hundred years is hardly ancient." He almost looks offended by the idea, but he finally reaches for the book. Squinting, he studies the pages before cursing. "Immortality should come with better eyesight."

"I thought it might give me answers about . . . all of this." I gesture vaguely to where my raven-mark hides under my woolly secondhand sweater. There's a difference between coincidence and the Stars smacking you in the face to force you to pay attention. I can't have just wound up here with Bishop, with this secret, with this mark.

"I can teach you how to read it." He sets the book down and sighs. "It's always better to know how to find answers for yourself. But this text won't have the answers you want."

He rises and crosses to the stacks to put the book away as if the matter is already decided.

I curl my hands into fists at my sides. I'm sick of having truths measured out like I might choke if I swallow them too soon. "I just want to know why the Stars chose you and Bishop."

And not Kieren.

"It's never that simple," he calls while searching through a shelf. He finds what he's looking for and yanks it out. "The Stars don't explain their choices. You know that. They chose a different order for you."

"I wish they hadn't."

He returns and drops another book on the table. "That doesn't matter. You still have to decide what to do about it."

"I'm supposed to rewrite destiny?" Is that what Hadrian is trying to do here? Hide away with old books like he might stumble upon directions for taking back his life? "Pretend they didn't mark me. Pretend . . ." My voice cracks. ". . . that that mark didn't kill him."

"No," he says evenly, "you're supposed to decide who you want to be."

I stare at the cover, at the pegasus painted on the front. I push it away. "I'm not that girl anymore."

Hadrian nods to the book. "That doesn't erase her."

"I'm not an Icaros." I swallow. "It's not my birthright."

No thanks to the Stars.

"Then you're a Ravenell, and by that right, *all* magic belongs to you." He slides the book toward me. "So, what are you going to do with it?"

"Start a farm?" I say flatly.

"That's up to you." He wipes his glasses and sinks into his seat, already turning back to his notes and riddles like he's done with me.

I want my family's magic. Magic that helps things grow. Not whatever power my mark promises me. I want to know why the Stars chose me for this.

He's been looking for answers for five hundred years. What hope do I have of finding any?

"The garden looks terrible," he says, not glancing up from his papers. "Start there."

I scowl at him, but I grab his stupid book.

When I reach the main hall, I don't turn toward the stairs. I keep walking, past the back hall to the kitchen. I pass the great room, where a fire is crackling in the massive hearth. I ignore the untouched piano in the parlor. I don't stop until I'm out the front door, not bothering to pause or consider where I'm going, my feet carrying me where my head and heart have not dared venture before now.

And this time when I reach the garden, I look at it. Really look at it.

Vines claw at one another in a frantic tangle, weaving and choking each other like enemies. There are piles of leaves, all so uneven they must have been gathered by the strong ocean winds and left to rot for Stars know how long. The fountain remains stagnant, filled with brackish water and slowly being reclaimed by moss. Dead trees loom at the edges of the grounds, their limbs twisted skyward, still waiting for someone who never came back.

What a fucking mess.

The oscen swoops overhead and lands in the gnarled branches of a very dead tree.

I glance at it. "I don't know if I can fix this."

And I'm talking to the bird again.

It tilts its ebony head, dipping its beak as though it's commiserating with me.

But I head to the small potting shed tucked in the farthest corner. It's in nearly as bad a shape as the rest of the garden. I try to open it, but the door hinges have rusted shut, so I'm forced to ram it open with my shoulder. There's not much inside other than some old flower bulbs in a worn basket and a few hand tools as rusty as those hinges.

Screw this. Even an Icaros couldn't work like this. I make it a few steps into the garden before the oscen squawks at me.

Like it knows I'm quitting.

"What do you expect me to do?" I squawk back, but I don't keep walking to the house.

I need to do something before I turn that bedroom into my own cage.

Flipping open the book, I skim through explanations and diagrams, looking for something to help me clear old growth. But when I find the pattern—the one that tills the soil and enriches it—I don't have the faintest clue how to actually use it. That was my dad's work. Then Broderic's. The lines have to be formed in the right order, crossing and meeting in the correct sequence, or you risk disaster. Just last year, my brother missed a step and scorched an entire field of corn. The fire was contained, but the soil is still useless. Not that anyone would even notice if I took the garden down to cinders. Except maybe the crown's prodigal bird.

That means falling back on the one thing I know will work: my own damn hands.

The hardest part is picking where to begin. The dead trees and vines creeping over every surface or the skeletal remains of old rosebushes? It all has to go to make room for new life.

Dropping to my knees, I shove my fingers into the rain-soaked dirt. Some tightness eases in my chest as the cool mud coats my hands. Even without tools or gloves or a book with useless diagrams, my hands know this kind of work from years spent doing it with Kieren beside me. They remember it, remember passing tools back and forth with him while we talked about nothing.

And everything.

The memory threatens to swallow me, so I focus on what's in front of me, trying to forget what's gone.

Some of the patches are easy, the soil in them yielding their weeds like they're grateful for the attention. But then I reach the fucking vines. They might have borne fruit once, but now they're little more than brambles.

Their roots are deep, left too long to dig strangleholds in the earth. I rip them out, thorns tearing into my skin. Mud streaks my arms and clothes as I wrestle them, the stinging in my hands building to a smarting throb. Their barbs are punishing me for evicting them.

But that's the cycle of life. The way of things. Like the items sitting in that box in my room.

Someone whistles sharply behind me, but I don't turn around to see who it is.

"Damn, what did those weeds do to you?" Taliesin asks, striding up to watch me work.

"Exist," I grunt, wrenching one free. Dirt scatters across my lap. I brush it off and keep going.

Taliesin murmurs something else before he leaves me, but I don't hear him.

Because the noise in my head is gone. I keep working until my hands cramp and my shoulders burn, until the sun slips past the horizon and the moon casts everything in shadow. And when I trudge inside—dirt under my nails, mud mixing with blood in my torn-up palms, angry and alive again—I finally feel like I found a place I might call home someday.

I just have to fight for it.

By the end of the next day, nothing is fixed, but I've divided the tasks, turning the garden into zones I can work through one at a time. The first one is nearly clear.

Along with my head.

As if every weed ripped from the earth leaves room for new questions and plans and thoughts, but circles back to the same problem.

Bishop is avoiding me.

I hunt him down and find him hiding in his study.

"Yes?" he grunts, not deigning to look up from whatever new crisis he's prioritizing over human interaction today.

"I want to train." The words come out in a rush. I can't let myself rethink this. Not after what happened in the woods. Not after . . .

His shoulders tense, and he hesitates before finally lifting his gaze. But he only looks at me.

Studying me like I'm a fucking mess, too, and he doesn't know where to start.

"It was your idea." Maybe he needs the reminder, needs to see that I'm finally willing to give in and do things his way.

His eyes slide to my arms and zero in on the skin visible below my rolled shirtsleeves.

"No," he says and goes back to his paperwork.

My brain lurches around the single word, and I'm forced to shake my head to reset it. "What? Why not?"

"Your burns haven't finished healing." He reclines in his chair and crosses his arms, jaw setting in a rigid line, perfect mouth ready to deliver his next blow.

Bastard.

I plant my hands on his desk and glare back at him. "I'm fine."

I'm using the balm. I don't even need bandages anymore. Yes, the skin is still raw and pink, and there are a few lingering blisters, but there's nothing to stop me from lifting a sword.

"*They* aren't." He nods toward my arms, then turns back to his work. "And I won't put a blade in your hands until they are."

Heat climbs to my cheeks. "You told me to earn answers," I say. "How am I supposed to do that if you won't even look at me for more than a minute at a time?"

Bishop lifts his head and makes a show of assessing me, his face a mask of that irritating composure. But his eyes narrow when they reach my hands. And he scowls.

I glance down at the bloody cuts and scrapes covering the backs of my hands, at the dirt caked in the webbing of my fingers. Some has spilled onto his very important desk. I draw back and tuck my hands under my biceps but don't apologize.

He remains quiet for a moment, and when he finally speaks, a soft growl laces his words. "What have you done to yourself?"

"I've just been out digging my own grave," I mutter, instantly regretting it when his forehead creases. "Seven hells, I've been in the garden. Is that not allowed? Was it finally becoming the shit pile you envisioned?"

"The garden?" he repeats like he heard me wrong. As if the activity is somehow foreign to him. Considering the state it's in, maybe it is.

I roll my eyes and nod.

A faint wrinkle appears between his brows. "And why aren't you using *gloves*?"

"I couldn't find any." Not that I really tried. But his attention stays on the hands still tucked under my biceps longer than necessary, and I sigh. "It's just dirt. I'll wash them, and I won't touch anything until I do."

He finally lifts his eyes to mine. "Ask me again when you're in one piece."

I choke back a scream and briefly consider throttling him but whirl around and leave instead. Because strangling him won't do me any good. Bishop will always be around to make my life hell . . . even if I kill him.

But the next morning, there's a clean set of tools waiting at the base of the fountain along with several pairs of gloves, all made from different materials and folded neatly.

I stand there longer than I mean to, something clogging my throat. Then, I swallow, pull on a pair, and get to work. But I listen for his footsteps, part of me afraid he'll return to the garden.

Part of me hoping that he does.

TWENTY-FOUR

The winter rain in Vennaro has teeth. It bites spitefully at my cheeks, cold beads of it spilling down the back of my neck and soaking the collar of my thick sweater. It hasn't stopped in the last three days I've been out in the garden. No wonder everybody gave up on tending it.

But after a few days of honest work, the overgrowth in the garden's easternmost zone is almost gone. The ground is visible there again, the dark soil ready to be planted with bulbs and bushes and anything else that stands a chance of surviving if the ground freezes. It's hard to say if winter will bring that depth of cold or just keep spitting rain at us. Much to the oscen's annoyance, the dead tree bordering the garden edge is now a stump.

In protest, my shadow has taken to roosting in its neighbor's branches and watching me. That tree shows signs of the same blight that killed the other. But I can't find a damn thing to save it in the Icaros book. Not that I understand half of what I'm reading. Besides, I've yet to feel even a glimmer of magic waking in my blood.

The oscen dives right over my head when I drag my spade to the stump and lands in the tree next to it with a mournful caw.

"I'll plant a new one," I promise, wedging the spade under a half-rotted root.

I put my weight behind the tool, and the root shifts grudgingly, wet earth sucking at the blade. Leaning into it, I push harder until pain sears through my shoulder and my lower back strains. Until my entire body hurts.

But it hurts less than thinking, so I keep going.

A root snaps, and I stumble back a step. My breath fogs in the cold, and I rest against the spade to catch it. Above me, the oscen ruffles its feathers as if making its feelings on continuing this activity known.

"I'll try to save that one." I tip my head to the tree it's sitting in.

Its beak opens, followed by a caw that's shrill enough to make my jaw clench. Then it hops along the branch, moving closer to oversee the work like it owns the place.

Negotiating with a bird. *This* is what I'm reduced to, but it's better than sitting in my room, waiting for the next time the Stars fuck me over. Or walking Kieren's belongings down to the Bellatorum. Forcing myself to pass them off to strangers. Better than letting go of the pieces of him I can still hold in my hands. And since Bishop won't train me . . .

Even with my burns now nearly gone and only the slightest blisters remaining.

I hope the void swallows him.

I'm lifting the spade, pretending the next root is his beautiful face, when a shadow falls over me.

"You never came for a lesson," Hadrian says.

"I'm not sure . . ." I grunt as I push its cutting edge against the swollen root. ". . . why you're surprised." The damn thing won't budge. I fall back a step, panting, and glance over at him. "Honestly, I'm not sure I want answers."

What good will it do? Scions get to live. People like me, people like Kieren, don't. It's just further proof that life's unfair. That the Stars play favorites and screw over the rest of us. Not that I needed any more evidence of that.

"I assumed as much when you left the book." He tucks his hands into the sleeves of his robe, looking around with a grimace as if he's just realizing that we're nearly in the twelfth month and he should be wearing a coat.

"Let me guess, you came all the way out here to give me lessons in the ancient tongue?" That seems like something he would do.

"I came to make sure you're alive."

My chest constricts, but I ignore it. "You might be the only person who cares if I am."

"You're being looked for. Lenora checked the library," he tells me.

I roll my eyes so hard it almost hurts. "I've been right here. She must not be looking very hard."

"She said you won't come down for meals."

I return to digging at the root. "I've been busy, and I'm sure you all have better things to do than babysit me." I grunt again, wishing the oscen would swoop down and scare him away. Hadrian strikes me as the superstitious type, but the bird has finally quieted, almost like it agrees with why he's here.

Traitor.

"She's concerned," Hadrian says.

He sounds just like Bishop.

"I'm fine." I keep my attention on the dirt so I don't add anything that I'll regret.

But my spade slips, catching on the root, and I trip forward, barely catching myself from falling on my face.

"Clearly," he says flatly.

"I thought this was what you wanted me to do." I abandon the starsforsaken stump and return to my other project: a shallow trench carved for the bulbs I dug out of the potting shed. They need winter's cold ground to sprout roots before they can bloom in the spring. If they're still any good at all.

As soon as I change direction, the oscen flutters down to the stump like it plans to take up residence so I can't keep hacking away at it.

"Oh, have the damn thing!" I shout at it. I collapse to my knees and reach for the basket of bulbs.

But Hadrian shifts to stare at the bird, then goes completely still. "Void above, is that . . ."

I turn a fraction, watching him study it. "It's just a bird."

"I haven't seen one in years."

"A bird?" I shake my head and drop another bulb into the trench. "You need to get out more."

But he isn't listening.

Beads of rain collect on the bird's feathers, but it doesn't budge from its vigil, utterly unfazed as Hadrian moves closer, tracking the oscen like he's seeing a ghost.

"Not since the war," he continues, mostly to himself.

A shiver races down my back, and I straighten, flinging mud from my gloves onto the ground. More than five hundred years old. I still can't wrap my head around it.

But it is like having a walking history book to reference, and I can't stop myself. "Were they hunted back then?"

Have people always been this superstitious?

He's quiet long enough that I regret asking.

"Not until Ravenell fell," he finally says.

I swallow. It's not surprising, but somehow still sad. "I've never understood that," I admit. "We still use nochtimetry."

Hadrian shrugs. "People always choose the parts of a story that serve them and try to rewrite the rest."

"So they blamed birds?" I stare at the oscen's sharp, intelligent eyes. It's only a creature. But I know all too well how easily fear turns a simple truth into a threat. "That's silly."

Hadrian doesn't correct me. He takes another step closer to the stump, and I cringe, waiting for the bird to startle and fly away.

It doesn't.

"Ravenell was never good or bad. People have forgotten that part," he says quietly. "Power hates what it can't control. The other patrons saw Ravenell as a threat to their own magic, so they let everyone believe the worst. It's why, even now, some of them want you dead."

Like the oscens.

An unsettling prickle creeps across my skin. "Where were you during the war?" I ask.

Do I want to know?

His gaze stays on the oscen. "Trying to stop it."

Not what I expected, but it never is with him. With any of the people Bishop has collected in this house. Only Lenora is what she seems to be.

Which means that any minute I'll probably find out she's really an assassin.

"I suppose you succeeded in doing that." Five hundred years of peace with not even a hint of threat until I dropped my blood in a stupid well and ruined it all.

But he shakes his head. "I failed."

I open my mouth to ask what in seven hells that means, but before I can he crouches until he's staring directly at the oscen.

My breath catches as the bird stares back. It doesn't move. Doesn't flutter its wings. Just tilts its head and holds its ground.

"I was there when Ravenell fell," he murmurs.

I sit back on my heels, not daring to interrupt him.

"I tried to reach them." The words are so distant they almost echo, as if he's back there again. "But I couldn't."

The oscen hops forward and makes a soft clicking sound, and I realize I'm holding my breath. He reaches out a hand, and the bird nips him and takes flight, soaring into the low cloud bank overhead.

Hadrian snaps out of his daze and turns to me, but something raw lingers in his brown eyes. "Sometimes, I think I came back to life as a punishment."

"Do you really believe that?" But it's not like I can judge him. Kieren would be here if it weren't for me.

His mouth twists into something that's not quite a smile. "You believe a lot of things after something like that." He looks up at the sky like he might see the oscen soaring among the clouds. "Especially when you jump off a cliff and the Stars put you right back in your body."

The confession knocks every thought from my head. I scramble for something to say, but my mouth won't even open.

Something of the ghost I saw in Bishop haunts Hadrian's eyes now, too. As if the weight of their deaths still lingers like chains around their necks.

Hadrian rubs his jaw with his hand. "There's no need to say anything. It was a long time ago." He pauses, still searching the clouds. "Go on. Ask."

I suck in a breath so deep that it hurts and force out the question. "Was it scary? When you came back?"

Was Bishop scared? His hands were so certain the other night, but the first time . . .

Hadrian finally looks back at me. "I was afraid of what I might become."

"Why? What did you know about scions before?" I ask.

He shifts and squares his broad shoulders, allowing me a glimpse of the warrior he must have been back then. "I lived through the Last War," he says. "I was a child in the one that preceded it. But I knew what scions were capable of."

I blink at him, standing up. "What are they capable of?"

"Scions started the war cycles, fighting to claim the Eternal Throne." He takes a seat on the abandoned stump. "Mortals got in the way."

My eyebrows shoot up. None of this makes any sense. "The king sits on the Eternal Throne. Or he did." Before his death, and then it hits me. "Wait. Is the king a scion, too?"

A faint flutter starts in my chest. If the king is still alive, maybe I can go home. Maybe this can all finally be over.

"I forget how little people today know of their own history." Hadrian shakes his head. "And no, the king was not a scion."

Was. The fluttering stills. He's really gone.

"Then why aren't you fighting for the throne now?" I ask.

"Because the cycle hasn't begun. Yet," he adds, holding my gaze.

I bite my lip and lean against the shovel. "That's ominous."

"In the beginning, the Stars created the Eternal Throne, choosing some of us to become scions and rule from it. But every cycle, the fury rises within us, and we're compelled to fight. To prove which of us is worthy to claim the throne."

"But why?" A bigger question rises in me before he can answer. "How?"

"Scions are gifted with unique birthrights." He taps one of the patterns on his arm. "Most stronger than any magic the patron bloodlines control now. There are different reasons given in the old histories."

The histories that are now forbidden. "And those reasons are?"

He looks up, staring at the oscen circling above our heads. "That our souls are tied to the birth of new stars. Or we're stars that fell to earth. Whatever the reason, we have magic running in our veins when we resurrect."

"Then it's not nochtimetry . . ." My voice sounds too high.

"No." He glances back at me. "Nochtimetry came after. Ravenell crafted it by studying *us*."

"By us, you means scions?"

"Yes." He nods, and my mouth goes dry.

"Those marks," I say breathlessly, hungry to understand what he's telling me, to finally set another piece of this puzzle into the right place.

Hadrian raises his arm and pushes up the damp fabric of his sleeve to show me the lines shimmering faintly like intricate translucent veins etched into his skin. But where Bishop's arms are covered in the silvery patterns, Hadrian has a collection of lines on only one side of his forearm. "Our powers."

"What do they do?" I ask, stepping closer to get a better look.

But he holds up a finger as he stands and moves to the blighted tree. He places his hands on the dead bark, and the markings on his forearm begin to glow, faintly at first, then brighter, growing into a soft pulse that spreads through the pattern on his skin.

The ground shudders. I lock my knees, bracing, my mind flashing to the last time the world shook beneath me. But it's over in a few seconds, and then . . .

Buds sprout from the tree's branches, tiny leaves unfurling from them like trembling wings. The black mold fades from its trunk. It's the dead of winter, and it blossoms like it's spring before bejeweled autumn leaves settle onto its branches.

"How?" I whisper.

He looks at his hands. "It's a healing power."

Something in his tone makes the words sound like a joke at his own expense. Like he can't understand it and never will.

"What else can you do?" I ask. This magic isn't like the birthright the Kindling ignites into nobles born into patron lines. Plus, we still have to study whatever power the Stars saddle us with, have to learn whatever patterns Ravenell harnessed. Patterns that are far easier to fuck up than perfect.

But this . . . What Hadrian has access to . . .

He lowers his arm, and the glowing patterns fade. "I don't know all of what I can do, what every power I've claimed from another is," he says. "The wrong kind of power can become poison."

"Wait," I say slowly. "You *claim* power?"

"When we come back to life the first time, we have only one power. *Our* birthright." He pauses like he's sure I need time to understand there's a difference between the magic the Stars grant patrons and the one they give scions. "When we kill another scion"—he traces a lovely arrangement of arches and lines intersecting on his forearm—"we take theirs as vestiges. Some powers connect with our birthright. Some don't. The vestiges that don't take more time to assimilate before we can wield their magic. Sometimes years."

My mind latches on to the word *years* and refuses to let go. No wonder they live forever.

I think of Bishop's hands. The faint scars I've seen when he removes his gloves. The way he never lets his sleeves ride up. Why he's always wearing that uniform with its high neck. This is what he's hiding.

Power.

I can't even fathom how much.

"That's why Bishop hides the marks," I say. "They would reveal what he is."

"Scions usually cover them," he explains grimly. "They're a map of our abilities."

I understand hiding them now, but . . .

"Wouldn't that have intimidated the other scions back then?" I ask. "Why hide them?"

But he only laughs, the sound thin and more than a little humorless. "Never show your hand to other players."

My pulse stutters like a quiet warning behind my ribs. "How does a scion defeat and collect another scion's vestiges?"

"By killing them." He doesn't flinch when he looks at me.

"But you're immortal."

"All things must end," he says, glancing into the distance like he's looking for his own. "It's the natural order."

But my mind drags me back to the woods, the memory so clear that I can feel the smoke in my lungs. Feel the weight of Bishop's body collapsing into my arms, his warm blood slick on my hands.

And then he walked into my room and shattered my whole world. There was nothing natural about it.

"Scions don't end," I say quietly. I still haven't decided how to feel about that.

"We can," he corrects me. "If you claim our heart in battle, you not only end our immortality, but you also collect our powers. All of them, including the vestiges we've taken."

I stare at him, something clicking into place. The marks on his skin . . . on Bishop's skin. A chill creeps down my neck. Bishop has killed other immortals. He *is* a heart collector. They all are. That's what he didn't admit to me that night. What I couldn't bring myself to ask.

I focus on the fine lines on Hadrian's arms. "You've killed other scions."

His mouth thins to a line. "Yes," he says. "That was a long time ago. I've made peace with it now."

I don't know what to do with that. Peace as a decision. Not absolution.

The oscen circles down and lands on the fountain, clicking its beak a few times.

I shake my head. "Why didn't I know about this?"

"If the crown suspects you're a scion, they execute you."

That's why Bishop is always hiding behind his gloves and uniform. "The crown knows?"

He tips his head, his mouth a flat line. "And the patron of every order. Vespers. The knights charged with hunting down rumored scions . . ."

Literally everyone but me.

"But if there are still immortals," I say slowly as if I can find the answer before I finish the question, "why did the cycle finally stop?"

"No one knows. The last cycle was five hundred years ago." His eyes flick to the trench I've dug. "Before the Last War, when enough scions existed, a cycle started. There was a sign—an omen, and then the fury began."

A harbinger. The word clangs in my chest like a prison door slamming shut. That's why Bishop brought me here. Because if I am the harbinger . . .

"What's the fury?" I blurt out the question.

"The impulse to be the final scion and claim the throne. No matter the cost. Even war."

I gulp. "The final scion? But that would mean . . ."

Bishop and Hadrian would be turned against each other.

He nods like he knows I'm finally catching up.

"If the cycle begins," I ask in a quiet voice, "will you fight him?"

Hadrian closes his eyes and releases a heavy sigh. "I believe we can resist. Most don't."

Noble.

And so beautifully naive.

"But you're still looking for a way to stop the cycle from coming."

When he opens his eyes, something hollow stares back at me. "I have to believe I can."

"And if someone attacks you?" I ask. If the cycle begins, if I'm the harbinger . . .

"I'll defend myself. Try to reason with them first."

Reasoning and swords are rarely compatible in my limited experience trying to combine the two. But I think it answers another question. "Is that what happened when you met Bishop?"

Hadrian's mouth turns up at the corners, as if he's recalling some memory, but he shakes his head. "That is his story to tell."

The weight of our conversation presses down on me, the world once again descending on my shoulders. This is why Hadrian sits in the library, treating books like his friends. Why Bishop got me out of Wintour before those assassins could touch me. Why he brought me to the one place that they never can. Because I might not be the harbinger *yet*. He said it in the council chamber. What if my death is the real harbinger?

A cold weight settles in my gut. Is that the reason Bishop is so protective of me?

Hadrian tugs down his sleeve, and my eyes catch on the hint of a vestige peeking out. What kind of power runs in that thin vein of magic? What magic is worth taking another person's heart to claim it for yourself?

"Do you think I'm the harbinger? Will I really bring war?" I bite my lip, already afraid of his answer.

Hadrian bends down and scoops a bulb from the basket between our feet. "Some things must come to light in their own time." He kneels in the wet grass and places it into the trench, covering it with soil before firming the earth with his palms. "There's a season for all things."

My throat knots. "So, we're just supposed to wait?"

"No," Hadrian says, watching as the oscen lands in its newly healed tree. "We're supposed to prepare."

TWENTY-FIVE

My body is mending, even if my grief is not.

The thin skin where I was burned itches, but the throbbing has softened into something manageable.

And I decide I don't give a fuck if that's good enough for Bishop.

I'm healed.

I dig out one of the old uniforms Lenora brought me when I first arrived. It's tailored too fine for a conscript, its heavy fabric meant for colder months but too worn to belong to anyone alive. It smells faintly of cedar, as if it's been shoved in a trunk no one's opened for years. But it fits me better than it should.

I'd consider it a sign if I still thought the Stars were looking out for me.

I tie my hair back so tightly it makes my scalp sting and stare at the stranger in the mirror. Her eyes are too hollow. Her mouth too tight. But she's standing.

That has to count for something.

The house is eerily quiet in that way it gets when the day's yet to begin. But the smell of baking bread threads through the halls, pulling me forward.

Of course the kitchen is already awake.

And it's not empty. Watery light creeps through the windows, turning the edges of the room pale gold. Lenora stands at the counter, forearms dusted with flour, coaxing dough into shape. Bishop leans against the table with a cup of coffee. He's in uniform, coat buttoned high on his neck like he paused on the way out. Meanwhile, Taliesin's feet are propped on the table, and he looks almost ready to doze off.

All three of them turn when I breach the doorway. I don't remember the last time I shared a meal with them. I haven't even spoken to anyone not passing through the garden or the library.

For a heartbeat, we're all silent, as if none of us can remember what to say to each other.

"You're up," Lenora says carefully. Probably afraid I'll bolt if she startles me.

"I'm up." It feels like admitting I belong among the living again.

Lenora wipes her hands on her apron and reaches automatically for a plate. "Sit. I'll get you something to eat."

"I'm not hungry."

Setting the kitchen on fire might have less effect.

One of Taliesin's boots drops off the table with a *thump* like I've woken him. Lenora pauses to glance at Bishop, whose eyes narrow slightly, the coffee halfway to his mouth.

Lenora puts the plate back down with a sigh before pinning a cheerful smile on her face. "I suppose you're heading into the garden early."

Here we go.

"Not today."

"Then *why* are you up?" Bishop asks with his usual restraint. Although the edge beneath the question suggests he dislikes the answer already.

"I need coffee," I say, striding over to pour a cup. The heat from the ovens washes over my face, but it doesn't reach the place inside me that's frozen solid.

"Me too," Taliesin mumbles, stretching his hands like a beggar.

I pass him mine and get another. If they're worried about my appetite, I'm sure they'll have an opinion on what I've really come down to do. Of course, there's a barrier to my plan . . . and that barrier is still glowering at me.

Clutching the mug, I take a deep breath. Now or never.

"I'm going to the Bellatorum," I announce, "to enlist."

Taliesin chokes on his coffee so violently that he coughs it back into his cup. "Stars, Arden . . ." He sputters, rubbing his chest. "Warn a guy."

"Love," Lenora says gently, "there is no need for desperate measures. The garden is coming along . . ."

A smile tugs at my lips. "I'm not finished yet, but I'll try to have it done by Twelvetide." Before the ground freezes and it's too late to plant spring-blooming flowers.

Lenora's face brightens, and she slaps a ball of dough on the counter. "Well, that's quite enough to keep you occupied."

But I can't waste away in that garden and pretend I'm preparing myself. I want to plant something real. I need to carve my own place in the world. "I'm sure I can handle both." I clear my throat. "And I can't stay here forever."

I'm tired of standing still while a curse decides what I am. My magic can wake whenever it likes. In the meantime, I want a sword in my hand.

Lenora huffs and begins kneading her dough with unnecessary vigor.

But Bishop takes a sip of his coffee. "No."

I'm prepared for his objection.

"See?" I hold up my hands to show they've healed since I started using the gloves he left for me. "All better."

"You are not enlisting," he repeats, his shoulders square as he shifts to full height, as if towering over me will make me change my mind.

But he can't. Not on this. Whatever magic is inside me, I can't be helpless any longer. So, I wait for him to explain whatever new bullshit criteria he's concocted.

"Why not?" I demand when he doesn't.

He fucking shrugs.

Heat erupts on my cheeks, something familiar stirring deep within my gut. "I'm in one piece now."

That was *his* condition.

I glare up at him. He can't power play his way out of this. Learning to fight was his idea. I'm only following his lead. If he changed his mind, there's one reason for it. The same reason those men attacked me. The reason that no one's suggested I go back to Wolf's Keep. "Is this because of the raven-mark?"

"No, it's because we don't make decisions with broken hearts." His voice drops a shade lower, but it does nothing to soften the impact. "It never ends well."

"You told me to come back when I was healed," I snap. He can't actually stop me. We both know it. "Like you still thought it was a good idea."

Lenora takes a tiny step as if she's considering moving physically between us if necessary.

Bishop lifts a hand to stop her, his gaze holding mine. "Learning to fight *is* a good idea." The change of heart makes my head spin until he adds, "But you're not enlisting. I said I would train you."

But I've considered that. It's the last thing I want. I owe him too much already. And joining would give me a place in the world. "I've thought about that. It's not fair to you."

He pauses like he's anticipating my next move before making his own. "I want to do it."

It's not even a believable play.

I scowl and reach for the most obvious argument. "Don't you have better things to do? Like protect an entire kingdom?"

"The last time I checked, you were a citizen of that kingdom," he says coolly. I swear he's got a comeback loaded for everything. "A patron, at that. *I* will train you."

Translation: end of story.

Taliesin smirks behind the rim of his coffee mug, and I consider throwing mine at him.

"You aren't joining Marius. You have your own order to consider," Bishop adds.

Which one? I'm not about to voice that question.

"I don't want your charity." The words spill out in a rush from being pent up inside me for so long.

A shadow crosses his face and vanishes like a passing cloud. "This isn't charity."

Lowering himself to train a patron's daughter? Giving her a room in his house? "What is it, then? It's not like I'm paying rent."

His frown deepens as he sets his coffee on the counter and crosses his arms. "I'm trying to keep you alive."

The answer pierces deep, and I suck back a breath. Because if I'm the harbinger, if killing me starts the cycle . . . that's the last thing he wants.

My throat aches, still raw from nights spent crying into my pillow. I swallow and force myself to nod. I need to prepare. "I'd feel *safer* if you'd answer *any* of my questions."

Hadrian's visit only left me with more of them, and the terrible understanding that I might not have run if I'd known the truth about Bishop.

And then Kieren might still be alive.

But Bishop exhales slowly, clearly searching for a new and unique way to deny me.

"Fine," he says, as if conceding costs him something. "We'll begin today."

"Today?" My pulse jumps a second too soon.

"After you eat." His lips tug at the corners as he speaks.

"I said I'm not—" I start to grumble.

"You'll eat," he cuts me off. "Then we'll train, and you can earn those answers."

The arrangement sounds more like a threat than a compromise, but it's something. So, I gulp down a retort that won't get me anywhere with his stubborn ass and nod.

Lenora looks between us, eyes flashing with triumph. She moves quickly, plate already in hand, and sets it in front of me.

"I guess I know whose side you're on," I grumble. But the bread is still warm from the oven, butter melting in a puddle atop it, and she's left the egg yolks runny like I prefer. My stomach growls in anticipation, earning me a knowing smirk from her.

She pats my shoulder. "I'm on whatever side keeps you safe."

How am I supposed to argue with these people? I pierce the yolk with my fork, sopping up the golden liquid with the toast. The first bite makes me glad Bishop forced his hand. Not that I'll ever admit it. But still . . . maybe this doesn't have to be terrible. Maybe we can find our way back to that tentative friendship we'd started to form before . . .

I down another bite, but I can't quite swallow the memory along with it. Bishop has every reason to be angry with me, but he's given me the benefit of the doubt. I finish my toast, resolving to do the same, even though he watches me eat like he expects me to run away.

When I ask Lenora for another egg, Taliesin snorts under his breath. "Not hungry."

"I thought you wanted me to eat," I say sourly, but I'm not talking to him.

Bishop only smirks back. "Eat as much as you like. You'll need it."

That doesn't sound ominous at all.

. . .

The sky is the color of wet ash when we arrive at the Bellatorum an hour later, the clouds pressing down around the foothills and forming a thick blanket of fog that turns the proving grounds dim and flat. Early winter has brought wind that batters everything between the sea and the mountains with slicing gusts, and the misty rain it carries stings my eyes.

Despite the weather, the metallic clanging of swords echoes in the distance, and neat lines of conscripts move between buildings. The drizzle blurs their faces, but their heads are held high like they don't notice.

If only I could say the same.

I shiver, tugging my coat more tightly to block the rain. At least it isn't snowing.

Bishop leads me toward the far side of the compound, past a line of crumbling plinths and a stone wall half strangled by ivy, toward a trail worn into the side of one of the mountains that guard the rear of the campus. My leg muscles strain as the path steepens, and the ground grows muddier and less traveled the higher we climb. I glance behind us and find most of the buildings below hidden in the cloud bank, only glimpses of their roofs and thin plumes of chimney smoke remaining visible.

"Where are we going?" I glance around. Knowing Bishop, he probably plans to spend the first eight hours providing me with safety instructions and lecturing me on the importance of following the rules.

"Don't you trust me?"

A nonanswer. How shocking.

It's not like we've had a lot of time to work on our fledgling trust since that horrible night. But being here feels like the first step. "I'm working on it."

This earns me a smile, but the bastard still doesn't tell me where we're headed, only, "It's a shortcut."

"Where?" I grumble. "To the void itself?" The steep incline makes it feel like we're high enough to be swallowed by the Night's Scar, just two more stars for it to suck into its abyss.

But we climb even higher, boots crunching when the mud gives way to patchy grass and rock. We're so high above the Bellatorum, even the smoke from its kitchen and smith fires are lost in the foggy haze.

Bishop finally slows when we reach a small cascade jetting from a large fissure in the mountainside above us. The waterfall cuts across our path and tumbles alarmingly out of sight. A series of large stones, just big enough to fit one boot, are set into the crashing water, forming a cross between a path and a sick joke.

I stop and plant my feet on the solid ground that's on this side of falling to certain death. *"Where are you taking me?"*

But Bishop crosses the swiftly moving stream in quick, confident strides before turning to me with one foot on the last stone and one on the far bank, the slightest hint of a smirk tugging at his lips as I creep slowly behind him. He extends an arm toward me when I reach the second to last stone, and I feel a stab of annoyance.

Before I can doubt myself, I grind my teeth and vault over to a slightly smaller stone, nearly as close to the bank as the one he's still on.

I try to look like I know exactly what I'm doing—right as I lose momentum and gravity starts to yank me backward. Panic flashes across his face as my arms shoot out to steady me, the single leg planted beneath me trembling with the effort it takes to maintain my balance barely long enough for me to push off the stone toward the bank.

I'm going to clear it. My heart leaps but falls just as sharply when I realize I'll land in a slick of mud.

One of my boots slips off the bank, dipping into the frigid water, but I right myself quickly. I take a few brisk strides forward, a bit too embarrassed to look back at him.

"I'm not carrying your stubborn ass if you break your leg," he mumbles under his breath as he stalks past me a few seconds later.

I brace for another of his signature lectures, but he only continues along the path, which bends as it meets a tall stone wall covered in so much lichen and bird dross that it might as well be part of the mountain itself. He stops at a gap in it and squeezes through.

As soon as we're on the other side, I realize where we are.

"You brought me to the most sacred place in Vennaro to train?" I ask flatly.

But he continues, climbing the last steep bit of ground between the wall's perimeter and the relatively flat courtyard that leads into the astrolatory.

"Don't worry, we'll train outside unless the rain picks up," he says evenly.

That's probably for the best. I don't need another reason for the Stars to hate me.

The astrolatory rises directly out of the mountain as if its stone grew tired of being earthbound and reached toward the Stars itself. Part of the mountain slope has been sheared flat to make room for it, the rest left raw and jagged. The astrolatory's thick walls are broken only by tall lancet windows carved so narrowly into the stone that they seem more defensive than functional.

I can't see the whole roof from here. Only glimpses of its arched panes, the glass catching the bits of sunlight breaking through the morning clouds. Two stone wolves with elegant, curving horns guard either side of the huge slab door at the entrance.

The courtyard spread before the statues is a wide, bare expanse of paving rock and wild grass hemmed in by the retaining wall that slopes upward to brace the astrolatory against the mountain. On the far side from where we're standing, another passage is worn into the earth. I frown at the wagon ruts that disappear around the bend of the mountain.

"What are those?" I point to what is obviously a freaking road.

He smiles as he ties his hair with a length of leather cord. "That?" He shrugs. "That's the easy way to get here."

I bite my lip to keep from telling him that we might need to take *the easy way* unless he plans on allowing me nap time whenever he drags me up here to train.

Bishop heads into the astrolatory despite his promise to train outside. The threat of blasphemy clearly doesn't faze him. The weather-worn door opens into a narrow vestibule that offers the barest peek of the ceremonial chamber beyond. Though some have gone out, many of the torches flicker with white flames, the sconces carved with nochtimetric patterns to keep the fire alive. But it's the weapon racks filled with swords and daggers—and other deadly things I don't know the names of—hanging on the walls that catch me off guard.

"Void me. What do you do during your rituals?" I ask slowly as he takes down a sword.

Bishop flips it over in his hand like he's testing the weight. "We don't bother with most of that shit, apart from Petitions and Kindlings. The occasional local ritual." He frowns and replaces the sword before choosing another. "Everyone is free to come here, but it's usually empty."

"And we wouldn't want such a perfectly usable space to go to waste." I shake my head. "Have you ever considered building one that doesn't require a two-mile hike to reach?"

He shrugs. "It wouldn't matter. The Stars haven't looked favorably on any of the people who wind up on the Bellatorum's doorstep. Can you blame them for not worshipping them?"

Orphans. Outcasts. People desperate for shelter and food. I hate that he has a point.

"Then why become a bishop?" I blurt out.

He considers for a moment, and when he finally answers, it drips from him. "I didn't do it out of some divine mission, if that's what you're asking." He pauses, his forehead creasing as if he's trying to make sure his answer sounds right. "My brother was the politician, eager to be patron and run things. He was always clashing over business with our father and arguing about any red tape. I just wanted to be away from it, actually doing something. I did it to help people."

I blink, jolted by his casual tone. I can count on one hand how many times he's spoken about his family and still have fingers to spare.

"And that's why you stayed a bishop after you became patron?" I pause, weighing my next words. "You know it puts a target on your back. My brother says people talk . . ."

He tests another sword. "And they would talk more when I never had children. Never produced an heir."

"Don't you want to try?" I blurt out and clamp my mouth shut.

His mouth curves at one corner. "Are you applying for the position, Lady Icaros?"

Seven hells, I walked into that one. I squeeze my eyes shut as if I can hide from my embarrassment. "I just don't think anyone would blame you if you'd given it up to be patron."

He sighs and turns to face me. "Arden, scions can't have children. That ability dies the first time we do."

Oh. My lips form the word, but no sound comes out. I can't believe I actually asked him that. Where is a hole to crawl in and die when you need one?

I scramble for another question. "What are you going to do when you don't get old?"

But he smiles. "I figure I have a few more years to figure that out before people start to ask questions, but you know that everyone expects a patron to get married sooner rather than later."

Something twinges in my chest. Broderic said the same thing, right before we left for Wintour. It feels like a lifetime has passed since that day.

The last thing I want is to dredge up those memories. Not while I'm trying to move forward, while I'm trying to prepare for whoever might want me dead next. I turn the conversation back to him. "Then you weren't called to being a bishop?"

"I do believe in helping people, and I guess if the Stars are real, if they're really watching over us, guiding us," he says, "I think they'd agree with me."

"Well, if they smite me," I say, silently adding *again*, "for desecrating their astrolatory, I'm blaming you."

He snorts. "My brother and I used to fight in here all the time when we were kids," he says, passing me a slender sword. "We'd leave a rock by the back door as a signal, so our mom wouldn't find out."

"It sounds like she didn't approve, either."

"No, she didn't." Something in his smile makes my head swim. He glances around us. "I come up here to think."

I follow his eyes around the stone room. There's a solemnness that invites solitude, and Stars know that Bishop likes to brood.

"How does that feel?" He nods to the weapon in my hand.

Stop being distracted. I don't know all that much about sword fighting, but I'm guessing that's pivotal. I thrust it to the side, turning my wrist like I saw him do a second ago. It's less heavy than I might expect, much lighter than the one Kieren usually carried. I ignore the deep throb in my chest at the thought and focus on his question. "It's . . . good." I search his face for what he's looking for. "It seems like it would . . . kill people."

Bishop raises his brows at my inspection criteria.

It's not like he gave me a lot to go on.

"Is it too heavy?" he asks.

I shrug before lifting the sword a little higher and dropping it. "Honestly, I don't know."

"Here. Hold it like this." He steps behind me and reaches around to adjust my grip. He's not wearing gloves again, and when his palm presses over my hand, a current of energy surges through me and lands somewhere that definitely qualifies as a dangerous distraction.

I swallow hard, shifting forward ever so slightly to put space between us. Something aches in my chest like my body disapproves of the direction I've chosen. I swallow again and try to focus.

"This is a good one for you to start with. It will put less strain on your muscles while you're building them." He's so close that his breath whispers over my ear.

Friends, Arden. Get it together. That's *the goal.* Not a charity case. Or someone who always needs saving. And I'll never achieve these goals if I can't pay attention every time he touches me. How is he supposed to train me? With workbooks?

When he finally steps away, my knees buckle, but I gather myself together . . . until he takes the sword and hangs it up on the rack.

I frown. "I thought that was the right one for me."

"It is." A slow smile spreads across his face—the kind that reveals just how far I'm in over my head. "But training doesn't start with swords."

TWENTY-SIX

"Maybe we should skip to the killing part," I say, my scowl deepening. Rumors must have spread about what happened to those men in the clearing. Not that I'm sorry about it. But half of Wolf's Keep probably wants me dead, so learning how to handle a sword seems like it should move to the top of the training list.

But Bishop is already walking toward the courtyard, forcing me to run to match his long strides. He stops in a section partially sheltered from the wind by the astrolatory's retaining wall and strips out of his coat. Despite the weather, his tunic is sleeveless, putting his corded biceps on full display along with the markings of his power. Vestiges. Proof that he's killed other scions. A lot of them, from the looks of it. The silvery lines travel the full length of his left arm, intersecting in a brutal but somehow beautiful pattern that travels all the way to his knuckles. His right arm is half covered from his hand to just above his elbow.

"Have you—"

I only get a few words into my question before he cuts me off. "No more answers that you don't earn."

The words land like a gauntlet thrown at my feet.

Bishop thinks he knows how stubborn I am, but he's about to discover a new definition of that word. Resolve hardens like steel in my chest.

But he tips his head in my direction. "You'll probably want to lose that coat."

"What?" My eyebrows shoot up. I glance around us like maybe I've had a blow to my head and we aren't standing on the side of a mountain in early winter. Nope. Still here. "It's freezing."

"Suit yourself." And then he sprints across the courtyard, continuing along the slight trail sloping up the mountain beyond the astrolatory.

"I guess we're starting," I grumble. Taking a deep breath, I follow. The path narrows as it climbs, loose rock skittering beneath me, my boots slipping with every stride. My calves start to burn almost instantly, a promise that the worst is yet to come.

I've nearly caught him when he turns and races back down, so gracefully that I consider catching up just to shove him off the side of the mountain. I force myself to continue to the same spot where he turned. By the time I reach it, my lungs are on fire, too.

"Downhill will be better," I mutter to myself and follow him. But he's already on his way back up. Sweat breaks over my forehead. This is why he took off his coat. I pause just long enough to shuck mine from my shoulders and toss it in the general direction of the courtyard. I start back up—just as the bastard flies down past me again. I'm panting when I reach the top, but the cold air feels good on my feverish skin.

If this is his way of showing me how out of shape I am, then . . . well played.

The air is too thin on the mountain, and by the fourth trip, I skid to a stop at the bottom and double over. Bishop is there a second later, a few strands of hair sticking to his forehead the only proof that he's even exerted himself. He studies me, frowning slightly like I've failed the first assessment. "Take your time. This isn't a race. If—"

But I'm already starting back up. If he does it, I will, too. It's the only way that I'll be able to hold my own.

By the seventh lap, my legs are wobbling. Then they start to tingle. When I reach the top for the eighth time, I'm not sure they belong to me at all. Do I even have legs?

Bishop, who is somewhere between four and one million laps ahead of me, stops again. "Sit," he orders.

This time, I listen, but only because my legs are about to give out regardless. At least when I crumple onto the rocky soil, it seems like I'm doing it on purpose.

"You brought me all the way up here to *run*? Are you serious?" I ask in bursts, chest heaving in time with my pounding heart. "When do we start training?"

He looms over me, his silver-blond hair haloed by the late-morning sun. He's not even breathing hard. "I brought you all the way here to see how much you'd argue before you start listening."

I stare at him. "You said you would teach me how to fight."

Not try to kill me with oxygen deprivation.

"I said I would train you," he corrects me. "Fighting comes later—if you don't give up." But he has the decency to wait until I've caught my breath before he helps me stand.

I dust gravelly dirt off my pants, not daring to look at the path back to the courtyard. Because even the descent feels impossible now. Bishop starts down the hill, moving at a slightly slower pace, which I'm sure has everything to do with me, because he's barely broken a sweat.

"What does this prove?" I call after him, trying to ignore the dread pooling in my stomach at the thought of this lasting a minute longer.

"That you're alive," he yells over his shoulder without breaking stride.

Alive. The word hits me like a punch in the gut. I can run because I'm *alive.*

Kieren will never run again.

I shove the thought aside, but it's enough to ignite a new fire inside me. So, I run until my lungs burn, pushing my muscles past their limit. My freshly healed skin chafes, but I don't stop. Not anymore. Not when every time I do, the ache in my chest threatens to swallow me whole.

The sky feels too close, pressing down on me, sitting like a weight on my chest. The pressure is enough that my vision fractures slightly at the edges, my head starting to swim.

Bishop pauses at the bottom, takes one look at me, already poised to start another trip up, and mercifully doesn't. As I finish, he retrieves a canteen from his pack and hands it to me first. I drink most of it, gulping it down like it can quench the blaze in my muscles before I remember that he's with me.

"You're enjoying this," I accuse, passing it back to him.

But he shrugs. "It's just running."

Just running? Like there's *just* seven hells? And I'm pretty sure I might be in one now.

I shake my head, still trying to get a breath deep enough into my lungs. "Is this some kind of test?"

"Isn't everything?" He returns the canteen to his pack.

The sun passes high above, bursting through the rainy clouds and showing itself already headed down toward the western horizon. I have no idea how long we've been running, stopping long enough for me to recover, and then, Stars help me, running more. Hours, if it's already midday. It feels like several lifetimes.

I brace for him to start up the mountain again, but he twists his neck, stretching it like he's preparing to finally move on.

"Is it time for a sword now?" I ask, a fragile bubble forming around my heart.

"Not yet." Bishop bursts it, crossing his arms over his broad chest. His measured tone is anything but reassuring. "Now you're going to work on covering ground while moving *sideways*."

"Nooo." The word escapes as an almost inaudible moan.

"Different muscles," he says, and I swear the ghost of another smirk flashes across his face.

The asshole is *definitely* enjoying this.

Moving sideways over wet stone turns out to be even more difficult than moving forward and back. The wind and rain continue to batter me until the sun is no longer high in the sky.

I look up from my nearly ceaseless shuffle from left to right, right to left, and find Bishop gone. I could stop, but my feet can actually tell whether they're on wet stone or rock without looking now, which is a good thing because I think my brain froze in my skull sometime around midday. And I'm not quitting until Bishop realizes I'm not giving up.

He reappears and tosses me the refilled canteen. "Take a break."

I resist the urge to weep as I unscrew the top. His eyes linger on me as I guzzle the water.

"Are you done yet?" he asks when I finally pass it back to him.

I square my shoulders, ignoring the inferno growing by the second in my calves, in my shoulders—seven hells, in every fucking muscle in my body. "With the water?" I force a flat smile. "The rest is yours."

We both know that's not what he meant.

His nostrils flare slightly before he finishes off what's left in the canteen. My attention snags on the movement of his throat as he swallows, and for one treacherous, *glorious* second, I forget how much I currently hate him. He wipes his mouth with the back of his hand and tosses the canteen with his pack. "Let's get back to it, then."

I suck in a whimper. He won't break me. He can't.

There's nothing left to break.

But when he picks up a loose paving stone and holds it out, I wonder if I'm wrong. I take it from him, nearly dropping it on my feet when he releases his hold on it. Air whooshes out of me, but I readjust my grip, the rock's rough edges biting into my fingertips.

"What is this for?" I stare at it like the stone might actually answer me.

"Swords are heavy."

"No shit." I roll my eyes.

His forehead inches up, but he doesn't lecture me. "Hold it over your head, smart-ass."

That's what I get for asking a simple question. I swallow a whimper as I raise it over my head. Thanks to the gardening, I make it about twenty seconds before my arms start to tremble, just long enough to manage a smug smile. "Now what?" I grit out.

He blinks back at me like it's obvious. "Keep going."

A minute later, I'm regretting that I wasted energy on a smile or words or even breathing.

"Okay," he says, but before I can drop my arms, he continues. "Now walk, one foot in front of the other, to the door and back."

Even my ankles are wobbling by the time I make it to the door and turn, one wolf looming above me on either side. I make it two more steps, and he calls out, "Close your eyes."

I bite back a retort, but only because I don't have the strength with every ounce of me focused on keeping the rock from falling and smashing me in the face. Clenching my eyes closed, I focus on two things: steadying my feet and imagining throwing the rock at him. If I could even hurl it that far.

"You're holding your breath," he says when I finally make it to him.

"I'm still doing it," I grunt, arms quivering so hard that my whole body starts to sway. "Isn't that the point?"

You sadistic prick.

Bishop takes the stone from me. "No, it's the problem."

My arms sag instantly, dead weights attached to my body only by circumstance. "You think I'm weak, don't you?"

That's why he's doing this. To show me that I can't do this. To make me believe I need other people to protect me.

But he shakes his head. "No, I think you're afraid. When your magic finally manifests, it won't be good or evil. It will be yours. A blade isn't wicked because of what some men do with it. Neither is that mark on your chest or Ravenell magic. The only thing that matters is what you decide to do with it."

His words snap the *very* thin thread tethering my sanity.

"Of course I'm fucking afraid! They tried to kill me." The men in the woods. The other patrons. Even Taliesin put a sword to my throat. My legs start to tremble, knees threatening to buckle, but the shaking isn't because of my overtaxed muscles. It's coming from somewhere deeper, a place beyond my bones and blood and pounding heart. Somewhere that can't be touched but that I still feel *everywhere*.

"They did," he confirms with a nod that's all business.

"I suppose that doesn't mean anything to you." I spit the words at him. "People kill *you* all the time."

He doesn't even flinch. Actually, he looks bored. "They try to kill me, and do you want to know how I survive?"

I press my palms to my knees, still struggling to catch my breath, and glare up at him. "Enlighten me."

He points toward the sloping trail. *"I keep going."*

Motherfucker.

The sun is low on the horizon when Bishop calls training and tells me to hit the healing baths at the Bellatorum. I stalk back to Miradores without waiting for him, not bothering to stop.

After today, the last thing I need is a bunch of people staring at me. But when I reach the estate, soaked through with sweat and rain, I see Lenora moving in the kitchen, likely making dinner. The whole house probably smells like bread. My stomach growls as I imagine the scent of butter and yeast, but I ignore it. I'm wound too tightly to face her—to face anyone. She'll ask questions. Innocuous ones like how it went and when am I going back.

I know she means well. They all do. Maybe not Bishop. One day in, and I'm certain that he's no longer protecting me. He's finally decided to kill me.

My entire body hurts. I should want to take a *private* bath or collapse in bed, but Bishop was right about one thing.

I feel alive.

Not that I'm about to tell him he was right about anything. After today, I can't imagine how he'd use that against me.

But I don't want to let go of the feeling, either, so I stalk to the garden. I trudge into the center of it and look at my progress so far. The dead, hanging vines are finally gone from every zone, and I've cleared most of the fallen leaves, too, although more keep showing up from all the damn wind. There are still plenty of brambles and dead rosebushes to deal with.

And of course, there's still the damn fountain, which I do not feel the strength to tackle in my present state of exhaustion. I settle for weeding the patch I didn't finish yesterday.

I fold onto the ground, crisscrossing my legs, and sink my fingers into the soft earth to fist the roots of a large weed. I yank it free and toss it to the side. Then another. And another.

My thoughts drift to my conversation with Hadrian in the garden. It feels like a lifetime ago. Then I think about the book of Icaros magic that I've been secretly reading at night.

I've not felt even the slightest twinge of power since the Kindling. Nothing like how Broderic described coming into his. But maybe that's because I'm too afraid to even try?

My hand hesitates on the next weed. Before I chicken out, I begin tracing the pattern for growth. What's the worst that could happen? It actually works and I have to weed the entire fucking garden again? I'll take it if it means I have another way to be useful.

Down. Left. Half circle looping up. Horizontal line.

I drop my hand into my lap and stare at the weed in front of me, willing it to grow.

Absolutely nothing happens.

Relief and dread arrive as a matched set, the way they always do these days. I grit my teeth and yank the weed free with enough force to border on vengeance.

Fuck the Stars.

Scooting to the right, I attack the next section of weeds.

I lose track of time, the sun melting into a pool of rosy orange when Bishop's shadow falls over me.

I don't bother to look at him. But mostly because it hurts my neck to lift my chin more than an inch. "Did you remember that I earned answers?"

That was part of our arrangement. I'd been so relieved that the torture was over, I'd completely forgotten.

But he snorts. "I answered your questions."

My eyes snap up to him, sharp pain shooting from the base of my skull to . . . everywhere. But I hardly notice because he's smiling grimly down at me.

"What? I never even asked anything!"

"You questioned me about running, if it was time for swords. You questioned everything I told you to do." He ticks each of my sins off on his fingers.

"Are you serious?"

His mouth curves, but his eyes remain shadowed. "Is that one of your questions?"

He's certainly serious now.

My mouth falls open. "Those weren't my questions."

His smile is far from amused. "They came out of your mouth. *You* asked them."

Unbelievable.

Of course he's going to hold every little thing against me. He seems to relish stroking his authority.

But I won't make the same mistake tomorrow.

He lingers like he's waiting for me to apologize or argue with him. I'm not giving him the satisfaction of either. I turn back to the weeds and rip at them like they're his perfect face.

But he's not done punishing me.

"You didn't go to the baths." There's enough disappointment in his voice that I know exactly what his face is doing, but I glance at him anyway.

Actual daggers couldn't be deadlier than his eyes right now.

"No, I didn't." I lift my chin to meet that disapproving glare. "I have a perfectly good working bath in my own room, thank you."

"Dammit," he growls, his eyes shuttering before he sighs. "Your muscles need the mineral water. If you would just—"

I hold up my hand. I am not doing this with him today. Or any day, for that matter.

"I'm really not up for justifying my bathing choices to you, Bishop," I say, confident that will shut him up. "If you were hoping to see me naked, you missed your chance that night on your balcony."

The stunned silence from Bishop almost makes enduring today worth it.

His eyes widen, his mouth moving as he fumbles for a second before he swallows whatever he was about to say. He stalks off, mumbling something that includes my name, "impossible," and a few more choice expletives.

But I can't stop myself from watching him leave, a new and unfamiliar ache stirring in my chest.

TWENTY-SEVEN

Over the next several days, I beat him to breakfast every morning. I keep my mouth shut. I earn answers. Enough that I'm starting to run out of questions. At least ones that I can bring myself to ask him.

I ask him about his order. Miradores. Taliesin and Vessica. The Bellatorum.

He keeps his answers shorter than I'd like, but after every muscle-numbing training activity, he keeps his promise.

I don't ask about scions or harbingers. Or even Ravenell. Those questions sit heavy on my tongue . . . and stay there. Like asking them might cost me this training. I won't risk that. Bishop was right. This is the only thing right now that makes me feel alive.

Based on the number of new ways he concocts to torture me, I'm certain that he still expects me to give up.

I don't.

But grief has turned my body into a stranger. Every inch of me feels too tight. Too tense. Like everything in me is tangled into a single knot that I don't know how to loosen. Training feels like the only way to pull it apart without screaming, but every day the knot is a little more snarled at the end.

He still hasn't given me a sword. Nope. But today, he does *let* me stand on the astrolatory's wall, one foot at a fucking time.

My boot slips slightly on a patch of moss, and my arms circle frantically to keep me from falling. "You do realize," I say slowly through clenched teeth, "that if I go over the side of this, I'll probably roll all the way to the Bellatorum."

"It will be faster than walking." He paces back and forth as if he's as bored with this particular drill as I am.

"What exactly is this teaching me?" Trembles roll through my thigh, growing more pronounced until I'm forced to switch to my other leg.

Bishop's eyes narrow. "Is that the question you're earning right now?"

"Shove your questions up your . . ." I grumble under my breath.

"What's that?" he calls, and I hear a smile in his voice.

"That's not my question," I say more loudly. "Just seeking to understand your wisdom." I drop my voice and add, "Jackass."

He actually laughs at this. But instead of answering, he crosses to the long pack he brought with us this morning. My eyes flicker over, trying to see what he's getting out, but I can't really look without risking my balance, so when he reappears and holds something up, surprise swells in my chest before it crashes.

It's a sword—a wooden one.

"Is that a toy?" I'm beyond caring if he counts that as a question.

"You wanted a sword," he says, holding it higher.

"What is a wooden sword supposed to teach me?" But I carefully lower my foot and plant it over the other's toe. I take it from him, just managing to hold my position on the wall.

As soon as it's in my hands, I swing it over my head like the knights-in-training do on the proving grounds.

Big mistake.

I crash, knees biting into the stone wall. Pieces of it crumble, the sword falling to the ground below, as I barely catch myself from going over the other side and tumbling down the mountainside. My nails scrape against the rock as I dig my fingers between the stones. Sliding the last few feet to the ground, I land on the stupid sword and slump into the wall, bits of moss and dust showering my head and shoulders.

Bishop steps in front of me. "That's why it's a wooden sword."

It's a pretty good reason.

The first time he hands me a sword, and I nearly fall on it. A lump forms in my throat, tears clogging behind it. This is impossible.

"Arden." My name is soft on his lips, like maybe he cares.

But now, *I* don't.

"If you want me to quit," I seethe, voice rising until I'm shouting at him, "just fucking say it."

He takes a single step toward me, stopping when I shoot him a murderous look. "I don't want you to quit. I want you to know why you're here."

"You just want me to fall apart."

"That's the only way you're going to put yourself back together."

I'm still shaking as he hands me water and turns away, like he can give me back a piece of my dignity. I don't know how to pick up the rest of it—the rest of me.

There're too many parts of me that don't fit anymore. And one piece that's gone forever. I collapse around that hole in my chest. Sobs wrench through me, sadness dragging me into a pit that I can't climb out of. Not with this wrecked body. Not while I'm this tired.

Not without Kieren.

Deep beneath the sorrow, in the very marrow of my bones, an ember ignites as if it's been waiting for my grief to spark. "He's dead . . ." I gasp as the strange heat continues to rise, threading through me like I might catch fire. Not now. Not like this. But I can't stop it any more than I can hide from the truth. "He tried to save me, and he's dead."

Bishop crouches, angling his head to find my eyes. "The truth is that a good fighter needs a reason to fight." He meets my gaze and doesn't look away, not even when my breath stutters. The flame inside me shrinks from him like it's afraid of being seen. "You have a reason now."

"That's what I was proving to you?" I choke out through my tears.

"No." A crease appears between his eyes, something of a storm lingering in them. His hand lifts like he might reach for me, but he curls it into a fist instead. "That's what you've been proving to *yourself*."

"Because I'll never prove it to you."

He shakes his head. "I knew you were a fighter when you let the oscen go."

He smiles at me. The first real smile he's ever offered me. The sight douses the smoldering cinders in my blood until I can breathe again.

Something loosens in my chest and tumbles free, leaving a space for the one question that's buried like a knife in my chest.

"Are you the heart collector killing everyone?" The words rush out. The question that's been between us since the night I ran away. The night Kieren died.

He hesitates, like the answer might break me. "No."

He was right.

And I fall apart.

Because I ran away for nothing. I didn't fight hard enough in that clearing. I offered myself up as a sacrifice instead of grabbing a sword. I made a choice, just like I did in the Royal Astrolatory, and it was the wrong one. Again. I don't know how to trust myself anymore. Not after everything that happened.

And Bishop has known that the whole time. He's just been waiting for me to admit it to myself.

I look to him with blurry eyes, but somehow, he's still in focus, still right in front of me like he always is. "How do I do this?"

I'm not talking about training. How do I put myself back together? I'm not even sure I've earned the right to ask that question. Maybe I never will.

But he gives me the answer anyway. "One day at a time." He offers me his hand. I hesitate a moment before letting him help me up.

When I'm on my feet, he brushes a strand of hair from my face, the touch so gentle after days trapped in a cage of pain and guilt that I lean a little closer to him. "Starting tomorrow."

The days grow shorter as the end of the year approaches. During the long evening hours, I split my time. Some of it I spend in the library, poring over old books with Hadrian, trying to learn more about Icaros magic in preparation for spring. Hadrian assures me my *gifts* will eventually manifest. And when they do . . . if I only know Icaros magic, maybe this will all stop. Maybe I can go home.

So, I study. I also help Lenora with the mountain of baking she's taken on in preparation for the coming Twelvetide party.

But during the day, I'm always here, training, with Bishop.

That is, when he's at Miradores, which has been less and less recently.

And every time he leaves, I fight the urge to beg him to stay, not to leave the security of Vennaro, not when there have been so many recent heart collector attacks.

"There's really no other way to kill a scion?" I grind my jaw, throwing all my strength behind my block. Our blades lock with a shriek of metal that makes my teeth clench, but I surge into him, shoulders burning as I try to muscle his sword aside.

Bishop regains his footing far too fucking easily. He raises his sword again, beckoning for me to attack with his free hand.

"Was that a question?" he asks, a hint of a smile playing on his lips.

"I defended, didn't I?" I toss an actual smirk at him.

"Looking for other ways to take me out?" His foot shifts back, and my heart leaps in anticipation of his next attack.

He could go high, come at me from over his shoulder. Or simply thrust. Or throw some other fuckery at me.

Make a choice.

Stars know that it will be the wrong one. After weeks, I'm no better at anticipating his next strike. But I grip the hilt tightly with both hands and swing the sword into first position.

He lifts a brow at my decision. "Interesting."

Shit.

But he's already coming at me, sword arcing over his head and slicing down in a diagonal aimed at the opposite side of my body. Adrenaline seizes me, and I drop my blade lower to counter, but as usual, he's too fucking fast. The tip of my sword narrowly misses the block as his blade stops a fraction of an inch from my leather cuirass. I stare down at it, heart still pounding.

He steps away, bringing his sword to his side. "You left yourself open."

But I can't stop staring at how close his sword came. If this were a real fight, I would be dead.

Again.

I've yet to save myself even once.

He gestures for us to reset, and I shake it off. This is why we're doing this.

"You didn't answer my question," I press, bouncing slightly on the balls of my feet, waiting for him to give me some clue at what he's going to attempt next before I try to defend. "What if you explode?"

"Explode?" he repeats, blinking. "Is that your plan? To blow me up?"

He actually sounds disturbed.

"Yes," I say flatly, giving up and moving into second position. I roll my eyes but keep my sword level between us. "You've figured out my devious plot. There are only a few more steps before I can enact it. I just have to learn forbidden magic and figure out who I'll ask to scrape the bits of you off the floor."

Bishop snorts. "Blowing me up would work. No chest . . . no heart," he admits with a wink. "Add it to your list."

Something entirely unhelpful flickers low in my core. I swallow and tip my head, trying to maintain my balance. "I will."

He lunges without warning. Our blades crash together again, locked high between us, so close I can see my own warped reflection in his steel.

"Are you going to start coming up with better questions?" The silver in his eyes catches the light, his gaze as sharp as his blade—and entirely on me. His breath ghosts over my cheek, steady where mine isn't.

My grip tightens as I lift my shoulder in the barest shrug, not daring to reduce the strength I have behind my weapon. "I think I have it figured out."

"Really?" His forehead jumps an inch, his mouth tugging just a little at the corner. But it's the way that his eyes brighten slightly that sends my heart spiraling in my chest. "I'll tell Hadrian he can stop with all the research."

I lift my arm for my next strike, but he spins behind me in one smooth motion.

There's a sword at my throat. How in seven hells did he do that?

His body is so close that if I lean back, I'll practically be in his arms. But his blade doesn't move, so neither do I.

"Being distracted will get you killed," he murmurs in my ear, and it's everything I can do not to lean against his lips. "You can't let your opponent into your head."

It's not like anyone else could get this close. I doubt that the next person who attacks will have this effect on me.

Just Bishop.

I can't decide if that makes him the worst person to train me or the best.

Facing someone who wants to kill me *has* to be easier than this.

Because this? *This* is dangerous. Whatever it is.

"I doubt my opponent will make me defend for six hours straight."

He shifts ever so slightly, and his chest presses against my shoulder blades, right where my armor dips. The contact sends a shiver through me that has nothing to do with the cold—or the sword at my throat.

I scrounge up what little self-control the Stars have apparently gifted me and ignore the heat blooming where he's barely touching me.

"Are you complaining?" There's a wicked undercurrent in his voice that sends that delicious tremor racing lower.

"Me?" I feign innocence. "I wouldn't dare."

His soft laugh tickles my earlobe, and fuck, I'm distracted again.

He finally drops his sword, but he doesn't move away for a beat, like maybe he doesn't want the distance between us, either. I start to turn just as he finally steps to the side.

So much for that theory.

Before I can even reset my stance, he comes at me again.

I counter by spreading my feet wider, the better to absorb the force of his big swing, but the paving stones underneath me are slick, this morning's rain turning to ice as the temperature drops, and as soon as Bishop's blade meets mine, my feet shoot out from under me, one in either direction.

I go down hard on my butt, my teeth rattling inside my head.

I should have seen that coming.

He slides his sword into its sheath and leans down to offer a hand up. "Ready to hit the baths now?" he asks with the most infuriating half smirk, something wicked blazing in his eyes.

My body warms up instantly as if, despite being nearly frozen, it appreciates that he's practically smoldering.

Not the time.

Not when my shoulders and my ass are having a furious fight for top billing as the body part most likely to kill me.

But the way he's looking at me . . . Void swallow me.

Except I'm pretty sure that this is all in my head. Well, other parts of me are involved, too. But Bishop? Regardless of what he says about his vow being an act, he continues to be a saint.

As soon as I'm on my feet, he releases my hand as if to prove the point.

"It's normal to panic when you aren't expecting an attack," he says with a shrug like I wouldn't have died on the spot if he'd been my actual enemy.

"That's easy for you to say." I snort. It's hard to imagine him *ever* panicking.

"Why?" His mouth twists with genuine curiosity.

"I don't know . . ." I hedge, regretting that I said anything. Somehow, in all this time, we've managed to keep the questions and their answers about everyone but ourselves. It feels safer that way. "I just can't imagine you losing your head." I wince. "Bad choice of words."

He huffs a half laugh, but the smile slips from his face. "Believe me, I've lost my head before."

"Oh yeah? When?" Now that is a better question. If only because the idea of finding out that Bishop, despite his immortality, is only human is too tempting to resist.

He stops, his shoulders setting into a hard square like he's bracing for his own words. "When I died," he admits.

I'm not sure what to say to that. So I reach out, hesitating for just a second before I touch his shoulder gently. Just to let him know that he's still here. In this moment. With me.

"You didn't know what happened?" I guess.

He tries to force a smile and fails. "It was worse than that," he confesses. "I knew what happened."

I blink at this revelation. "You knew? But you weren't even a patron yet." Hadrian said only the patrons knew about scions.

A muscle works in his jaw like he's fighting with himself. When he finally speaks, his voice is strained. "Order Marius controls the scion population."

"I don't understand . . ." I start to shake my head, but then it hits me. "The crown sees scions as a threat." That's why he hides his secret so carefully.

He looks at the ground. "I've done things I'm not proud of."

He doesn't offer more, and I don't press.

"Are you afraid you'll lose control when the cycle . . ." I pause. I know the answer's not *earned* or whatever, but Bishop almost seems to be in a sharing mood today.

He hesitates a bit too long, more unsure than I've ever seen him when confronting one of my questions. "I hope not." His throat slides as if he's trying to swallow his own answer like medicine. He scrubs the stubble on his jaw. "Let's call it early today. I didn't sleep."

By the time we've gathered our things, the sun casts a warm glow, dying on the horizon as the birds come out to sing it to sleep.

"Care to stop at the Bellatorum?" he asks, just like he does every day.

He's stopped directing me to the baths since I accused him of trying to see me naked.

I'm starting to regret that.

"I promised Hadrian I'd look through a few books with him." It's not a lie, but it is an excuse. I've taken to always having one ready.

Bishop snorts, and I shoot a questioning look at him. "What? Are you mocking my scholarly pursuits? I'm a woman with many interests."

"I'm just wondering when you're going to give in, go to the baths, and admit that I'm right that you need the break," he says, his tone so light that I could float away listening to it.

Something clenches low in my belly. Are we . . . flirting?

It's an absolutely ridiculous idea, so I roll my eyes as much at myself as him. "Probably never."

He bumps his shoulder against mine, but he holds it there a beat too long for it to be *friendly*. "That sounds about right."

I should move away from him, but I don't. "When are you going to give up and stop asking?"

"Probably never." He bites back a grin.

"What's funny?" I ask.

He glances at me, letting that smile slip through. There's nothing wicked about it. It finds his eyes in a way that makes my heart hurt. "Nothing . . . It's just nice to have something to count on."

There's something so safe in that smile that my entire body forgets that I've been destroying it for weeks and actually relaxes. But somewhere deep down—in a place I'm starting to build a wall around—I know that feeling safe with him might be my next mistake.

"Do you ever sleep?" a cheerful voice asks the next morning.

I glance up from the rosebush I'm carefully removing to find both Taliesin and Vessica in the garden. I shoot a glare at the oscen. It usually warns me when we have company.

Vessica glides toward the fountain, eyes slightly glazed like she can't believe it's actually working.

Taliesin shoves his hands into his pockets. "It's nice to see you've taken up a hobby other than getting under Bishop's skin."

I fight a sigh and lose. How does he make everything sound like a flirtation? The man could read the Civicus out loud at a bar and get someone to go home with him. Thankfully, I'm immune to his charms. "What do you want, Taliesin?"

I'm certain the visit has something to do with the note I found from Bishop this morning, informing me that he had business in Florentia that couldn't wait.

If he asked these two to step in . . . I'm just getting comfortable with the sword. Bishop doesn't mock me. I'm not sure I can count on Taliesin or Vessica to do the same.

Taliesin leans against the fountain, which I've finally gotten to work after unclogging its small pump. "I thought I might accompany you to the baths."

Okay, that's not where I thought this was going.

I sit back on my heels, brushing dirt off my gloves, and look at both of them in turn. "Did he put you up to this?"

"What do you think?" Vessica asks sourly.

But Taliesin shakes his head.

"It was my idea," he says, spreading his hands, his eyes widening in what is potentially the least convincing display of innocence ever performed.

Vessica sighs with resignation and goes back to fishing fallen leaves out of the fountain.

"I figured you might want a friend with you," Taliesin continues.

Going alone is not what keeps me away from the bathhouse. Not that I'm about to explain myself to him. "I'm not doing anything that involves being naked with you."

"Ouch," he says, clutching his chest. "You wound me. Truly."

The oscen soars overhead as if trying to determine why we have visitors again. It lands on a nearby branch, its beady eyes trained on Taliesin like it doesn't trust him.

He stares back at it. "I think your pet hates me."

"It's not my pet." I'm just the one who let it out of that cage. I guess that's why we're bonded. "It's . . . my companion."

"A familiar?" He laughs, shaking his head. "That doesn't make you sound like a witch at all."

I freeze at the words, and a second later, Taliesin yelps. "What the fuck, Vess?"

He turns, twisting in an attempt to look over his own shoulder—where Vessica's dagger is planted about an inch deep. He glares at her as he pulls it out.

She swipes it from him, not an ounce of concern on her face. "Why don't you hit the infirmary?"

His eyes narrow before he waves a hand at her. Looking down at me, he grins. "If you change your mind . . ."

I nod, trying to keep laughter from bubbling out of me. "Sure. I'll just follow the trail of blood."

Taliesin grumbles under his breath as he leaves, one hand pressed over the fresh wound.

"Thanks," I say lightly to Vessica.

But she doesn't look up from cleaning the tip of her blade. "He wouldn't try anything."

"I doubt that." I snort.

"He wouldn't dare." She lifts an eyebrow in disbelief.

I don't ask her why.

She doesn't offer.

"Is this the part where you say you'll go with me?" This is getting nearly as tiring as my actual training.

But she shakes her head. "You don't need a chaperone."

Exactly. I'm about to say so when she hits me with, "You need to get over that fucking mark on your chest."

My mouth hangs open, the sharpness of her response stealing my own.

"We all have scars," she explains, tipping her head in the direction Taliesin just went. "All of us."

I swallow, the dirt under my knees suddenly very cold. "It's not a scar."

"I know that," she says, and for the first time ever, she smiles at me. It's fucking terrifying. "The question is: do you?"

. . .

I miss him again.

My grip fails for a second, just long enough that I almost drop my sword. Every muscle in my arm burns, and I grab the handle with my left hand, too. But it's not enough. I can't summon the strength, even with two hands on the hilt, and my next slice is weaker. It's aimed so low that I nearly take off Bishop's most important appendage, but he leaps back and easily knocks my sword away.

"Maybe . . . we should call it a day." He draws a heavy breath, giving me a look that sends my very limited confidence crashing.

We've only been here for an hour. That's barely worth the time it took to reach the astrolatory. I clamp my mouth shut like if I keep the pain in, I can leverage it to raise the sword again.

But Bishop slides his own in the sheath strapped to his back. A few weeks in, and I've learned this is his signal that the lesson is over. "You're shaking. You can barely lift your sword."

"I'm fine." But my blade tips down, wobbling in my trembling fingers before my hold on it slips again and it sticks in a patch of grass growing between the loose stones.

His gaze narrows on it.

"I know. Bad form. Proper weapons handling," I grumble, refraining from reciting one of his many lectures back at him. "I'll do better next time. I'm ready now."

"You're lying." He waits like he's daring me to deny it.

I lift my chin, trying to make a weapon out of pride. Because he's right, damn him. I can't lift the fucking sword another minute. "Train me anyway."

"No." He doesn't soften, doesn't show a single ounce of pity. For some reason that makes it sting less when he adds, "We're through here."

Not that I'm about to accept defeat. "If you won't train me, I'll find someone else." I turn to make good on the threat.

I've shown up every day for weeks. No matter how hard it rained or how cold the wind got. Even the day the mountain dropped snow on us like it was testing my resolve, too.

I'm not stopping now.

But Bishop's lips curl into a smile, the one that makes my heart skip a beat for all the wrong reasons. The one that makes me wish he would take me inside and give me a very different kind of lesson . . .

"Try it," he says like he's crossing names off a list, "and I'll personally come down to explain their options to them."

That snaps me right out of my temporary daze.

"Their options?" My voice rises. How does he find new and unique ways to piss me off every day? "Do you really think Taliesin or Vessica will—"

"Yes, I do," he cuts me off.

"You didn't even let me finish the question." I grit my teeth, trying to find the energy to pick the sword back up, to prove him wrong.

"Because you didn't have to," he says, his jaw clenching like it does when he's frustrated.

Specifically, frustrated with me.

But when he finally continues, his tone is gentler. "You can't go like this every day. Take a few days off—"

"Days?" The word explodes out of me. I can't take that much time, not when I should have started this months ago, not when every breath I take is a reminder that I *didn't*.

"Days," he repeats firmly. "Rest. Hit the baths."

"Absolutely fucking not." Something trembles in my voice, something that wants to crack. Break.

"No one will care," he murmurs, taking a step closer. He reaches for my sword, but I lock my grip, refusing to release it. His hand covers mine, and this time, he's the one who won't let go. Not that I try to pull away. "They won't say anything about the raven-mark."

"They don't have to say anything." The truth chokes out of me, working its way around the lump in my throat. I blink against the watery heat that follows. I will not cry in front of him. He already thinks I'm broken. "It's how they'll look at me."

"So?" He lifts a brow. Another step closer.

One more and there won't be any space left between us at all.

"Why don't *you* go to the baths?" I ask, unable to look away from him despite everything.

"That's different." A muscle flexes in his jaw, and my gaze travels to it—to the slight stubble shadowing the strong line it carves. He didn't shave today. That usually means he didn't sleep.

"Not for me." It's little more than a whisper. Part of me is still ashamed that I care. That I haven't learned to live with my birthright. I haven't even tried. "The last time someone saw the mark . . . it didn't end well."

He winces slightly, as if the words hit and stuck like the tip of my sword that's still planted in the grass. "Arden . . ."

But I shake my head, a single tear escaping down my cheek. So fucking weak. "When they . . . That night . . ." I squeeze my eyes shut, trying to keep the rest from falling. "I see their faces when I close my eyes. I can't . . . Not yet."

Maybe someday I won't hide. I have to believe that. I have to believe my entire life won't drain down to the fickle actions of the Stars. Because if I stop, I don't think I'll ever believe in anything again.

Bishop's fingers close over mine, his body shifting just enough that my breath catches. He goes still, and I open my eyes to find him locked in a silent war with himself. The kind that leaves no ground untouched. The battle waging in his eyes makes my core tighten with something I refuse to name. He opens his mouth, and a ragged breath slips free, his full lips parting like he's already losing an argument with himself.

And I can't look away . . . even if I should.

Because he's looking at me like he cares. Not like I'm his responsibility. Or his duty. But someone who matters to him. Heat curls somewhere low and treacherous, and I hate myself more for how badly I want to lean into his grip, to see what would happen if one of us gave in.

If *I* gave in.

Temptation. That was his word for it. I didn't understand it that night. But now? I get it. Get wanting something even though every part of me knows it's wrong. Fighting to hold back when my fingers long to lace through his.

His free hand reaches for my hip, but he hesitates. It ghosts there, close enough that I'm sure I can almost feel him touching me. Far enough that I want to beg him to prove that he's real again. Like that night he walked into my room and put some small piece of me back together. Even if I couldn't admit it to him then.

Even if I won't admit it to him now.

And somehow, I know that we'll keep doing this. Keep tiptoeing up to this line. Keep waiting for the other one to cross it. Both of us stuck in an endless cycle of want and self-denial. Unable to control this thing drawing us together.

But I have to control something in my life before everything I was before him slips away.

So I pull back first, releasing the sword to his grasp.

Bishop sucks down a deep breath, nostrils flaring, and a slight wildness flashes in his blue eyes. But he takes my weapon and nods once, like he understands.

And I hate him for it—just a little. Just enough to maintain this new space I've put between us. Because he'll never break. Never give in. Never step over that line.

And fuck, I want him to. After the weeks spent training, every day. His body pressing against mine to fix my form but reminding me that I'm alive in all the right ways. His gruff brand of friendship making me glad that I am.

"I need to go." His voice is quiet, *strained* like this is costing him something, too. "I have business."

Sadness curves my mouth into the barest smile. "Of course you do," I say softly, adding a silent *again*. It's not escaped my notice that there's a crisis every time we get too close. "When will you be back?"

"I don't know." He turns when I frown at this and picks up the coat he abandoned on one of the stone wolves guarding the entrance. "There's been another one."

I freeze. "Another what?"

But even at this angle, something in his face tells me before he speaks. "Another murder."

The news hits me like a cold splash of water, dousing the embers smoldering at my core. "Where?"

Not Damalis again. Please not Damalis.

His chest heaves as he sighs. "In Ardermare."

It feels like bodies are showing up everywhere but here. As if heart collectors are afraid to step foot in Marius territory and face its wolves. Or maybe they're afraid of facing Bishop himself.

"Do you think this killer is a scion?"

His mouth flattens into a thin line. "You've been talking to Hadrian."

"I've been putting two and two together, because I'm not as oblivious as you both think I am." I cross my arms over my chest, wincing a little when my biceps strain. I hate that he has a point about the soreness. "But yes, I've been talking to Hadrian. Is that a problem?"

Bishop scowls. "I don't think you're oblivious." He pauses. "And I'm not keeping anything from you."

I arch a brow. Except that mouth. Those hands. Stars, I have to get this out of my system before he ruins me.

"I'm not keeping anything from you *anymore*," he corrects himself, misinterpreting my glazed stare. "You've had enough on your mind. Heart collectors don't seem like top priority, since you . . ."

He doesn't finish the thought, but he doesn't have to.

Since I decided to stay.

Since everything became so much more complicated and keeps getting even more complicated every day.

Since Kieren . . .

His name is enough to remind me why I still care. Why I keep showing up here when my body wants to collapse. Why I can't be the one to cross the line. Why I can't let myself be weak ever again.

"I still care who assassinated the king," I murmur, even if I'm not foolish enough to believe catching the killer will restore my reputation anymore. The idea that he thinks I stopped caring, that I just gave up, lands heavy on my chest. "Even if I'm not going home."

He runs his tongue over his lower lip, eyes drifting inward.

"Aren't you going to ask to come with me?" he finally says, like maybe he wants me to this time.

The tightness at my core begins to throb.

Too soon.

I want to ignore the tiny voice that says he's asking me to step over that line. Want to believe I'm ready to give in to whatever this is, to whatever we both know is happening between us.

My eyes find my feet, instead, afraid he'll see right through me. "The ground will freeze soon. I'm nearly done in the garden, but if I don't get the rest of the new plants in the soil before it does . . ."

Bishop tips his head, even as his throat slides. My eyes track the movement. "Don't overwork yourself out there, either," he says. "You need rest."

He's going to be the death of me. "Do you coddle all your conscripts this much?"

He nearly smiles. "No, but they're better at taking orders."

I stare him down.

"Okay." He rolls his eyes. "Maybe the trick is that I can order them *at all*. I'm still trying to figure out how to get you to do a starsdamned thing I ask of you."

I bite back a laugh that threatens to bubble out of me from nowhere. "You could start with please."

"Please?" He snorts, shaking his head. "You would never be that easy on me."

I shrug and reach for my sword, but he holds it back. "I can put it away," I say. "Isn't that one of your very important rules? Put shit back?"

"I'll do it." Our eyes lock, and something tangles in my chest. Fuck, this man *can* see right through me. But he looks away with a smirk, that invisible armor back in place. "I can't have your arms falling off."

I play along and give him the middle finger before reaching down for the pack I brought with me. Maybe it's safer to stick to this. To keep retreating to our sides of the line. To deliver these half-barbed taunts.

I'm trying to survive, after all.

Despite Bishop's insistence that I need to hit the baths, all I want is a cold shower as I track down the mountainside. To wash the grime off . . . and for other reasons.

But I stop at the Bellatorum. The pack on my shoulders feels heavier as I step into the Commons, but I force myself to walk into the closest communal room. This is part of it. Part of letting him go. Setting the bag on a table, I reach in for the items weighing me down. My body screams as I lift the stack of clothes, but it's not the kind of pain the baths could touch.

"He can't use them anymore," I mutter under my breath, but the reminder doesn't help.

I place Kieren's folded clothes on the table anyway, leaving his boots sitting next to them. A boy not much older than Andry eyes them as I turn away quickly.

I don't wait to see if he takes anything.

I'm so preoccupied as I leave, I don't hear my name being called until Shea grabs my shoulder. I tense instinctively, hands curling to fists, and she leaps back. "Sorry!" She gives me a nervous smile. She's out of uniform today, but there's a faint crease between her eyebrows like she's been carrying a thought too long. "I just wanted to catch you and thank you for those books you gave my brother." She glances over my shoulder. "Are you training today?"

"Um, no." I can't hide my surprise. How does she know about that? Isn't the whole point of him dragging my ass halfway up the mountain so we can have privacy?

"Oh." Her face falls a little. "Well, if you ever need someone to practice with . . ."

I have half a mind to take her up on the offer, but then I remember Bishop's threat. "I was training, but only for an hour," I confess. "Lord Grumpiness commands I rest."

"It went that badly, huh?" Her laugh is infectious.

"I think my last slice almost cut his dick off, so . . ."

"That would be a tragedy." Shea cackles, then winces like she's trying not to laugh too loudly. "But I'll keep my condolences ready."

Not as tragic as him never using the damn thing.

I offer a shared grin, but when I shift my weight, the movement sends a warning twinge up my calf.

Shea notices. "Are you okay?"

"I know I'm supposed to act tough." I sigh, glancing around to make sure no one is listening to us. "But everything hurts, and I think I'm dying."

She laughs. "You could go to—"

I hold up a hand to stop her before she says *baths*. "I'm just going to pass out in bed, wake up, and probably help Lenora prep for Twelvetide."

Maybe keep digging at that stubborn stump in the garden before guests start arriving in a few days.

But even as I say it, a flicker of panic hits me. Resting. Cooking. I need to be doing more than that.

"You're coming to the party, right?" I ask, remembering that Bishop said knights were invited, even ones in training.

Shea's gaze drifts past me to the Bellatorum's gate. "I was invited, but I'm not sure if I can bring my brother." Her shoulders droop slightly like she's just remembered the responsibility she carries after a glimpse of something easier.

Another mouth for Lenora to feed and spoil with small gifts? One that probably hasn't had anything home-cooked in Stars know how long? She would kill me herself if I said no. "I think he'd be more than welcome."

She beams, sighing under her breath. "It's been a long time since I've been to a Twelvetide party. The conscripts play cards and get drunk," she quickly adds, "but it's not the same."

"It was my sister's favorite. We got ready together every year." I would let Isidore pick everything out, let her do my hair and dress me up like a doll. It meant so much to her, and I didn't care.

"My mother's, too." Her smile is so wide it creases her eyes before faltering. "I'd give anything to have one more Twelvetide with her."

I know the feeling. Like yesterday when I found a pile of dresses—the ones I'd ordered in Wolf's Keep—on my bed after I finished training and caught myself wishing Isidore would be there to help me choose one. "Come early and get ready with me," I blurt out.

She shifts a little, looking down at her breeches. "I'll probably just wear my uniform. I don't . . . ."

"Bishop's housekeeper made me order all these dresses." I grab her hand. There are three gowns, each boxed and carefully wrapped in tissue paper nearly as delicate as the dresses themselves. Three, which is two more than I know what to do with. Given how different my daily wardrobe of borrowed uniforms and gardening dirt is, I've yet to feel brave enough to try one on. "You can borrow one of them."

She chews on her lower lip before she nods. "As long as Breccan won't be in the way . . ."

"We'll drop him off in the library."

Hadrian will *love* that.

"Okay." She grins. "It's a date."

Her relieved smile stays with me most of the way back to the house, something warm on another otherwise cold, lonely day. But as soon as I reach the bridge, my thoughts ricochet back to Bishop. His hand on mine, the look he gave me before he left, the way he noticed my body giving out . . . and refused to let it.

And now he's trekking off to investigate another murder, leaving the safety of Vennaro's borders—the only region untouched by heart collectors in months. The realization drops in my stomach like a stone, sending ripples of unease through me.

Lenora stops me at the door, fussing as she helps me out of my coat. I let her, my arms too tired to even manage the buttons. When I warn her about a somewhat small guest for Twelvetide, she tuts that I don't have to ask, then forces a plate of biscuits smothered in butter and preserves into my icy fingers before shooing me off to rest.

I head for the library instead.

Hadrian's head appears over one of the upper tier's railings as soon as I step inside. "That better not be jam on those biscuits."

"Good morning to you, too." I devour half of one, tucking it away in two bites, as he clatters down the spiral stairs. By the time he reaches the main floor, I've deposited the plate on the table—safely away from any of his precious books.

He grunts but doesn't immediately order me out.

"Did we get a Civicus today?" I ask.

"It's right there . . ." He waves to the armchairs by the fire, then glances over and frowns. "Taliesin must have stolen it."

It's clear from the tone of his voice that this would be a capital offense if we were all living under his regime.

He takes a seat at the table, pulling a giant stack of papers and leather-bound journals in front of him. "What did you want with it?" he asks as he burrows into his work.

"Bishop left for Ardermare." The words close like a fist around my heart.

I try to shake off the feeling, but it lingers, even though I know he can take care of himself. He proves it every day by kicking my ass during training.

"Nasty business," Hadrian mutters. "It's as bad as Damalis."

So much for shaking it off.

I frown. "And why is that?"

Hadrian scans his notes, responding absentmindedly. "The scion's vestiges weren't claimed."

That's not what I was expecting him to say.

"What?" It doesn't make sense for the heart collector responsible to not collect them. "Is it possible for a scion to kill another scion without collecting their vestiges?"

"It shouldn't be. The power usually just . . . transfers. The patterns disappear from the vanquished and write themselves onto the winner's skin. The body still had its vestiges."

Something tells me that he's trying to protect me from how the process works. Since it involves carving out hearts, I don't push for more details.

He leans back, whipping off his glasses to rub the space between his brows. "But it's the second time the vestiges have been left unclaimed."

"Second?" My voice pitches up.

"It happened in Damalis, too," he says grimly. "We thought it was a fluke. Maybe unrelated. Just . . ."

"Some bastard carving people's hearts out for fun?" That doesn't seem likely. "Or do you think this is a mortal hunting scions? Maybe someone from Order Marius?"

Hadrian peeks out from under the hand he's using to massage his forehead. "You are not helping my headache."

"You aren't helping mine," I say sourly. Except it's not my head that's hurting.

"Yes, but *I* am trying to figure out why it's happening." He jabs his index finger at the nearest of his research papers. "Because if this were just a rogue scion or even mortal, the pattern would make sense. But it doesn't. Only knights and higher know about scions, so Bishop is sure it's not one of his people." He taps the page again as if he knows the answers are on it somewhere. "Which is why I'm back to this."

"And *this* is?" I ask, eyeing the mess.

"The *Ars Astra*." He sounds as if he's naming an old enemy. "Ravenell's corrupted nochtimetry. Their dark work. Unfinished, but still a pain in my ass."

The skin over my birthright prickles. "Dark work?"

He nods once. "There's a passage that keeps resurfacing." He flips a page and reads in a tired voice. "'Our dark work forged by fire to rival the Stars. A vessel of fire to liberate eternal flame and form a crown of rooted magic.'"

I wait for him to continue, to tell me what it means, but he doesn't. "Well, that doesn't explain anything."

His mouth twists. "No. It does not."

"Liberate it from what?" No wonder he's in a mood if all he's been doing is trying to find the answers to shitty riddles.

"That's the problem. I have no idea." He shifts back in his seat to wipe his glasses before reaching for one of the thickly bound journals. "But this text calls the vessel the *revello*."

"Revello," I repeat, more for moral support, which he obviously needs, than understanding. "What's that?"

Blowing out a long breath, he shrugs. "It could be an object. A ritual. Maybe even a person." He scrubs a hand over his jaw. "Ravenell loved riddles and hated conclusions." He curses the name again under his breath before he remembers himself. He winces. "Forgive me."

"I should be asking you that." I sigh. "I wish I could be more helpful."

He waves it off. "Just having someone to talk through it while Bishop is out trying to find the damn thing, whatever it is, is useful."

My stomach flips over. "He's trying to find it?"

"Of course." Hadrian glances up. "It may be what ends the cycle. I believe it was a tool meant to prevent the fury, to liberate the scions from it."

Bishop believes this *revello* can stop the cycle . . . and he's trying to find it. A bubble of hope forms in my chest. If there's a way to stop the cycle, then what does it matter if I'm some mythical harbinger? Maybe I can go home? But another thought occurs to me . . .

I narrow my eyes. "If that's what Ravenell was doing, why would the Stars destroy them for it?"

"I don't know," he admits. "I think we'll understand when we find the *revello*."

"But you don't know what it is?"

"No," he says grimly, pointing to an illustration in one of the open books. "I keep hoping I'll find a depiction of it."

Which is why Bishop was looking through those forbidden books that day in Wintour. "And when you do?"

"If Ravenell was close when they . . ." Something pained crosses his face, but he pushes on. "Everything we've found suggests this *revello* is key to their work. If we can find it or recreate it . . ."

He trails away, but his eyes dart to my collar like he can see the raven burned into my skin beneath.

"I'm not a Ravenell," I remind him.

"The Stars endowed you with their mark. You might be able to help." He sighs and reaches for another sheet of paper. "But not until we get our hands on the damn thing."

I pick up the plate of biscuits, Hadrian's revelation making me feel the need to eat all of them at once.

And then beg Lenora for a dozen more.

Hadrian flings a finger at the door. "No. Jam. In. The. Library."

I back toward the door. "Good luck." *I guess.*

Because, even if it might free me of this curse, the last thing we need in this house is a dark artifact that might be the reason an entire region was wiped off the map.

Like we don't have enough problems.

TWENTY-EIGHT

I land my first strike against Bishop, earning me a question—and a smile that makes my pulse jump.

The impact still hums up my arm, a bright shock of triumph that makes the world sharpen for a heartbeat. I should be gloating. After weeks of bruises and humiliatingly slow progress, a single clean hit against him ought to feel like victory.

But all I can see is the curve of his mouth.

Bishop smiling feels dangerous, like he's slowly erasing some important boundary between us.

But he tilts his head, wordlessly acknowledging the win, and sheathes his sword. His signal that we're done for the day.

The sun is already sinking below the horizon, causing the temperature to drop. The cold works its way under my skin as we walk toward the astrolatory, my muscles stiffening as the heat of exertion bleeds away. Every step reminds me that I've pushed too hard again.

"Go on," he says as we enter. "Ask whatever you've been vibrating over all afternoon."

I have been vibrating, because I've *finally* come up with the perfect question to ask him. I hook the hilt on the rack, trying to ignore the butterfly wings suddenly fluttering in my stomach, and turn to face him. "What's your real name?"

I could have found out as soon as it occurred to me. He wasn't always Bishop. I'm sure there's a record somewhere. Lenora probably even knows. However, for reasons I don't quite understand, I want to hear it from him.

Maybe it's the way Bishop guards his past so carefully. Or the way every answer he gives feels calculated, as though he's deciding exactly how much of the truth he'll let me see. But if I'm going to learn anything real about him, it won't be from records.

It will be from the moment he finally trusts me with it.

But Bishop tenses, drawing a sharp breath before shaking his head. "It doesn't matter." He manages a half smile that is gone too soon. "That part of me is dead."

Well, now I've stepped in it.

"I'm . . ." It never occurred to me that he would care. Not after he told me that remaining a bishop was only a ploy to keep people from asking questions when he didn't marry and produce an heir. "I'm sorry. It's none of my business."

His jaw tenses, and he looks past me for a moment, as if the apology has pierced him somewhere deeper than he usually allows anyone to reach. "Don't apologize. That man died the night I became immortal," he says quietly. "I can never go back."

I want to ask him why, but that skirts dangerously close to the other question I keep circling around but can never bring myself to ask. About *how* he died the first time.

Too personal.

But honestly, I don't think I can handle knowing. The thought of him dying . . .

I experienced that once. And once was enough.

By the time we leave the astrolatory, my arms are trembling in that deep, delayed way that promises consequences tomorrow. Cold has worked its way into my joints and sweat clings beneath my coat despite the winter air. I clear my throat and shoulder my pack higher, ignoring a twinge in my back. "I suppose we won't train much the next two days."

Guests have already begun arriving for the upcoming holiday—some from within Vennaro, others traveling from the various Marius outposts throughout the kingdom. Bishop's responsibility to greet them all is already limiting our training time. Although I suspect he's only doing it to remind them that he's watching their every move.

I've even been warned that he'd prefer I relocate to a more secure section of the house. I haven't had the guts to ask him exactly *where* in Miradores he considers secure enough.

But Bishop slows a fraction, brow furrowing as if he's still stuck in his own head and not following our conversation at all.

"Twelvetide," I remind him.

He scoffs. "I'll take any excuse to avoid my family."

Something hollows out beneath my ribs, a quiet collapse I don't have the energy to stop this late in the day. I won't be with my own family for Twelvetide for the first time in my life.

Likely for the *rest* of my life, and one of them . . .

I swallow the thought like I always do.

"You could invite them here," he murmurs, guessing why I've suddenly gone quiet.

Sometimes I think the man has carved a space in my brain and sits there listening to everything that I'm thinking.

I shake my head. "That's not necessary. There are plenty of people coming already."

And Broderic wouldn't say yes anyway. He still hasn't responded to the message I sent about Kieren's death.

I guess we're both dead to him now.

"Speaking of Twelvetide," he says, drawing my attention back to him, "I'm giving you one of your presents tonight. I know it's early."

"One?" I blurt out. I didn't even consider getting gifts, and Bishop has gotten me multiple? "I didn't get you anything."

And now he knows that.

Why has it become so hard to keep my mouth shut around him?

"Relax." He reaches over and takes my pack as we squeeze through the narrow passage in the retaining wall. But he doesn't hand it back once we're through it. He slings it over his shoulder as we start down the steep slope toward the Bellatorum.

He never lets me carry it anymore.

"It's not a big gift," he continues as we take the large stepping stones across the waterfall's tiered brook.

As soon as I reach the other side, I pause to rub out a cramp in my calf.

Bishop sighs as he watches me. "Actually, it's more of a gift to me."

"Well, in that case," I say dryly, wincing as I straighten.

"Back or shoulders?" he asks, not bothering to mask his frustration. It's become our little game. He expresses his concern and disappointment that I refuse to admit that I'm in pain and would benefit from the steam baths, and I ignore him.

"I'm fine."

He mutters, "Stubborn."

And our game concludes until the next time we play.

But when we reach the paved walkways of the Bellatorum, he continues through the proving grounds instead of heading toward the house. I halt in my tracks.

"Where are we going?" Although it's obvious where he's headed.

Bishop is making a new move.

"Come on," he calls to me. "I told you that I have a surprise for you."

That bastard. I take a step in the direction of Miradores instead, but he adds, "Will you just *trust* me?"

That stops me, because that is what we're supposed to be doing now—trusting each other. I suck down a deep breath and force myself to follow him.

"I know what you're up to," I say as I fall into step beside him.

"In that case, I'll assume you have no objections." He smirks at my stunned expression.

"Oh, I have *many* objections." But where to fucking begin? "I told you—"

"That you didn't feel safe using the baths," he cuts me off.

"I didn't say that!" Not exactly.

He releases a weary sigh that sounds as heavy as my footsteps are beginning to feel as the entrance to the baths comes into view. "I read between the lines." He pauses at the door and turns to me. "No one is inside."

I stare at him like he's spoken in the ancient tongue. "What?"

"I closed them for Twelvetide," he explains, eyes burning so brightly they almost glow. Even the blue of his irises looks silver in the twilight. "You're the only person allowed to use them until the new year. Even a brief soak will help, so just . . ." He glances away from me, adding a gruff, "Happy Twelvetide."

"I didn't get you anything," I repeat, half mumbling. He closed the entire complex. It isn't fair. I shake my head, opening my mouth to say just that.

But Bishop continues. "And they are staying closed whether or not you use them, so I'd consider it a personal favor if you let me do something for you just this once."

I bite my lip, unable to stop myself from smiling. It sneaks up on me before I can suppress it, tugging at the corner of my mouth like a secret I've failed to guard. My lip smarts where my teeth catch it, but the small sting is nothing compared to the warmth spreading through me. He did this for me. But closing an entire facility? It's selfish. The gesture is too extravagant to be a *gift*. But if I can count on one thing, it's that he's every bit as stubborn as I am. He really will keep them closed.

Only a few torchieres are lit, but Bishop switches on more lights, revealing an entirely empty dressing room. Now that we're inside, a different anxiety takes hold of me. It curls low in my stomach, coiling with every step I take into the bathhouse. I push it aside, wandering slowly behind him.

I brush my fingers against the wall as I pass, grounding myself against the smooth stone. The dull pain in my shoulders reminds me why we're even here, but the soreness no longer commands my attention.

Instead, my gaze drifts to the broad line of Bishop's back as he moves ahead, utterly at ease in the empty space he's claimed for my sake.

I don't know whether I want him to leave . . . or stay.

But before I can decide, he pauses at the small infirmary and gestures toward the arched doorway beyond. "The pools are all yours."

"Thank you." I'm so preoccupied with the fact that we're both here, alone, that I nearly forget to say it.

He nods, flipping on a lamp in the infirmary before slipping off his coat. Hanging it up, he reaches toward a tin on a high shelf, the fabric of his uniform straining against his strong shoulders.

It's rude to stare. I force my eyes away from him and take a single step toward one of the polished wooden benches stationed between the walls of lockers lining the dressing room. The space is completely empty, each locker door propped open and ready for use. Not even a single towel left on a hook, though there is a row of neatly folded ones laid across a long heating stone near the pool entrance.

The doorway breathes toward me, steam billowing through and fading to wisps that beckon like ghostly fingers before vanishing. But something stronger tries to tug my attention in the opposite direction. Toward the light glowing in the infirmary. I grab a fresh towel and strip out of my training clothes as quickly as my body allows, glancing over my shoulder every few seconds to see if Bishop is looking.

He's not.

Good. I don't want his attention.

But I check one more time to be sure.

He's still not looking, and I push away a stab of disappointment.

Exhaustion clings to my bones as if they've turned to lead under my skin, and my muscles twinge with even the slightest movement like they're deeply disappointed in my choices. I should already be stripped down and racing toward the promise of relief. The trouble is that I'm not sure I want to go in there alone.

You can't have it both ways.

I wrap the towel around myself as my feet carry me back to the infirmary, not the steam. I knock on the open door, already backing up a few steps as if distance can protect me from making a mistake.

I should just walk away, but Bishop turns to me, his attention on an open file in his hands. His eyes lift, freezing on my towel. I clutch it closed, trying to keep it high enough to shield the raven-mark on my chest as his gaze travels slowly over my collarbone, up my neck, to finally meet mine.

Run.

It's safer.

But I don't want to—not this time.

This time, I'm exactly where I want to be.

But my chest tightens, my ribs stretching to accommodate the ache slowly building beneath them.

This isn't how I survive.

This is how beautiful, desperate mistakes are made. Ones that can't be undone.

But maybe I'm wrong. Maybe crossing the line isn't a weakness. Because this is taking more strength than I have.

The question claws up my throat anyway. I blurt it out before it rips me apart. "Will you join me?"

His breath deepens with concentration, his chest rising and falling in heavy deliberation as if he's willing his heart to slow. But then something shifts, the lines of his face hardening, his eyes fading somewhere distant as he locks whatever he's feeling away.

But it was there. If only for a moment.

"When was the last time you used the baths?" I ask quickly, walking back my invitation before he thinks I'm throwing myself at him again.

That's exactly what you were doing.

I shove the thought into the pit of embarrassment that's growing by the moment. "I assume you don't because of your vestiges . . ."

Now I'm just rambling.

Mercifully, he takes pity on me. "It's been . . . a while," he admits.

"Since you became immortal?" I guess.

A muscle works in his stubbled jaw. I can't stand the idea of him here alone when he could relax—something he never does. He needs this as much as I do, but he shakes his head, closing the folder in his hands like the discussion is over. "I did this for you, so you could feel safe."

Something twinges deep inside me and settles in a place the training has never touched. "We're both adults," I say softly, "and you've already seen . . . my mark."

He glances at the desk, his eyes shutting for a split second before he waves off the invitation. "I'll be in here if you need me. I'll make certain you aren't disturbed."

Alone. Supervised. Trust Bishop to find a way to give me both. He'll guard the door but never cross the threshold himself. Always drawing the same line.

And suddenly the distance between us hurts too much to bear.

I start to leave but can't stop myself from whispering, "I always feel safe with you."

The words are barely out of my mouth before I wish I could drag them back. I'm not sure if he even heard me, and I'm too big of a coward to check. Heat floods my face, the confession chasing me toward the baths—where I must now resist the urge to drown myself, so I never have to look him in the eyes again.

Why in all seven hells did I say that to him?

I should have let the moment pass. Or laughed it off like it was a joke. Anything that might have kept the careful balance between us intact. That might have reminded both of us that we're only training partners and reluctant allies, nothing more.

I swear I hear the stillness stretching behind me. He doesn't speak or follow me.

I can't decide if that's a mercy or a cruelty.

Inside, steam rises in languid sheets that blur the hard lines of stone tiles, fogging the glass ceiling overhead just enough that the starry night winks in and out like it's peering through clouds. There are six pools sunken in the floor, each framed with tiled mosaics of the patron constellations. For a moment, I stand there listening, half convinced I might hear Bishop's footsteps after all, following me into the steam to prove I'm not imagining the fragile thread stretched between us.

But the bathhouse remains stubbornly silent. A trace of minerals hangs in the air, as if the room is holding its breath, too. I force myself to stop waiting and move toward the pool in the center, drawn to the way its dark stone steps seem to vanish from sight.

The air leaves my lungs in a long sigh as I take the first step down. The water carries a pale, milky cast that swallows the light a few inches below its surface. The stone inside the pool is slightly rough. It's a mercy, given that I don't trust my overworked muscles to keep me from slipping otherwise. I lower myself inch by inch to the built-in bench, until the water reaches all the way to my shoulders. A moan escapes my mouth as the silky heat closes around me, the sound way too intimate for a space that's usually shared—and suddenly I'm *very* glad Bishop wasn't here to witness *that*.

I linger there, letting the heat cocoon me, my body easing more with each second that passes, warmth sliding into places I didn't realize were tight. The minerals in the water linger on my skin like a caress.

Void him. He was right.

But there's some tension even the water can't help me shake.

It's not like the invitation meant anything. Surely Bishop knows that. The baths are large and empty. Not asking would have been rude. I don't care that he said no.

It's good that I'm alone.

I close my eyes and relish it. Relish the quiet lapping of the water against tile, the slight hiss coming from the sauna, the airy bubbles that break over my skin where the water is piped in directly from the mountain hot spring.

I'm *glad* that I'm alone.

The speed of my pulse suggests otherwise.

I sink deeper into the pool until the water hits my chin, heat sliding over me in slow, insistent waves. Steam curls around my face as I lower my head back to rest on the pool's edge and close my eyes.

This stolen moment is enough. It's all that I need.

And he knew it. Arranged it. Kicked everyone out.

For me.

It shouldn't fucking matter, but just thinking about it betrays me. The heat loosens something devastating, stripping away the sharp edges I've honed through discipline and routine, anger and grief, and leaves something delicate behind.

I am absolutely not waiting for him. *Not* hoping he'll join me. Nope. I am relaxing. Aggressively.

But if he did come in here . . .

I hover in the space between thoughts, held by the water and balanced on the edge of something I refuse to name.

Because what would be the point?

Bishop is probably absorbed in whatever important paperwork he keeps in the *infirmary*.

Maybe I'll punish him tomorrow. Insist we don't train until he kicks everyone out again and takes full advantage of this glorious heat himself. Maybe in the light of day, I'll be able to remember the lines between us better and see that this is enough. More than enough.

I'm halfway through convincing myself when the echo of footsteps on tile tells me I'm not alone.

This isn't happening. He isn't joining me.

Please, Stars, let this be fucking happening.

When I pry my eyes open, Bishop stands at the edge of the pool, wearing nothing but a towel slung around his hips. I sink lower, my own body covered by the opaline mineral water.

Steam beads on him, a thin sheen of sweat already clinging like a second skin. A low rush of heat that has nothing to do with the water floods through me. One of his arms is fully mapped with intricate silver lines in a pattern that winds over muscle and bone like beautiful scars. The other arm is half marked, the design breaking off suddenly, unfinished and waiting. More lines arc across his shoulders, continuing into the hard lines of his chest, disappearing under the towel before reappearing on his thighs and weaving across his calves. His lethal past written on him in a language my body longs to learn.

This is the guilt he carries. The power he keeps sheathed beneath armor and discipline and that maddening restraint.

I want to strip it all away until I reach the man underneath.

Desire coils tight in my belly, sharp enough that my fingers curl around the edge of the bench, biting into stone, to keep myself from moving toward him. Weeks spent training my body to endure fear and pain and exhaustion—and just looking at him threatens to unravel me.

His gaze searches mine for a beat. Then another. Each moment is punctuated by a tick between my legs. Then another. The storm in his eyes builds with each second, the hunger there flashing like lightning trapped by clouds. "If your offer still stands . . ."

The rasp in his voice empties my brain completely, every word I know scattering. All I can do is stare.

He shifts, glancing around the room. "I'm sorry," he murmurs. "I'll use one of the other pools."

The apology feels like a blade laid carefully at my feet. It's up to me what I do with it.

I open my mouth . . . and close it. One word and this finally begins. One word and it ends here.

I'm still fumbling when Bishop turns just enough for me to glimpse the patterns laced across his back and woven down his spine. More power claimed by a man who protects me from everyone.

Especially himself.

"Wait." That one word slips out, followed by a much more dangerous one. "Stay."

He hesitates for the longest second of my life before his hands move to the knot of the towel. He loosens it with deliberate slowness, raising a brow as the terry cloth starts to slip free.

I turn away, cheeks flushing, and fix my eyes on the far wall, my heart pounding hard enough that I feel it in my throat.

It takes every scrap of restraint I possess not to look when I hear the muffled *thud* of his towel hitting the tile.

In fact, not looking is the *single most disciplined* thing I've done in my *entire* life—and I just spent six hours sword training in winter rain.

His foot slaps the tile on the first step, and I close my eyes, trying to remember how to breathe.

Because I want Bishop Marius.

I can't deny it when he's this close to me. I've wanted him longer than I should have. I'm not sure I'll ever stop.

And there was something in his eyes when he stood at the edge of the pool . . .

Something that makes me certain he wants me just as much.

Presumptuous? Perhaps.

But sometimes you can't lie to yourself anymore.

Because now that he's here, I can't pretend that I don't want his skin against mine or to know what that power inside him would feel like inside *me*. I tried to ignore it, tried to fight this urge that's pulled me toward him since the first day we met. But that's about as simple as resisting gravity.

The water shifts as he settles across from me, the surface rolling out in ripples that brush my skin. The contact is incidental. But the effect?

Fucking *incendiary*.

Like the water is trying to close the careful distance he's still putting between us.

Steam rises around us, blurring the line of his shoulders, the pale geometry of his vestiges slipping in and out of view as he moves. He lounges, draping his arms on the edge, and groans. The sound bolts through me, lodging low in my belly before spreading into an insistent pulse.

I'm in so much trouble.

His head lolls back, his shoulders dropping an inch as if the water has taken off some of the weight he usually carries.

Meanwhile, I'm held together by tension alone, every part of me ready to fall apart.

"I've missed this . . . for years."

The admission catches me off guard. I turn my head slightly to look for cracks in that control he wears like armor and notice how his gaze stays fixed *very* intently on the stars overhead.

"Why not?" I ask. "You're patron. You could close them whenever you want."

He grunts. "That would be an abuse of power."

I arch a brow. "But you did it for me."

"Because you needed it." His voice is rough, coated with something that snags on my fraying nerves and threatens to unravel me further.

Heat climbs up my neck as my embarrassment tangles with tension. "I didn't mean to cause trouble. I was just . . . self-conscious. You didn't have to go out of your way for me."

Bishop shifts forward, the damp tips of his silver-blond hair slowly dripping down his shoulders as he pins his gaze on me. *"Stop."*

The command in that single word sends my pulse thudding hard enough that I'm certain he hears it. I can't move, can't look away, can't even see anything past him.

"It's my job to protect you." The storm returns to his eyes. "But I want you to feel safe, too."

I hold myself still by sheer force of will, because I'm suddenly aware of exactly how close we are, of how little stands between us, of how badly I want to lean into him and let that safety he's given swallow me whole.

Breathe.

But I'm not sure that I remember how.

"So," I say, searching for a change of subject as I trace a pattern on the surface of the water, "if you've been avoiding coming here because of the vestiges . . ."

I shouldn't go there. I can't ask him this.

"I mean, if you were worried about people seeing them, I guess . . ." I stumble along, getting no closer to actually asking.

He studies me for a beat before a knowing smirk flickers across his face. "You're asking whether I've let anyone see these." He lifts a marked hand.

I swallow. "Have you?"

He pauses, and I half expect him to make me earn the answer. But we aren't training now. We're . . .

I'm not really sure what we're doing. Part of it does feel like we're training. Like we're circling each other, trying to predict the other's next move but really just hoping we're ready for whatever blow they deliver.

"Only people I trust." His words are a simple strike, but it's one I didn't see coming.

I wet my lower lip. "So . . . you trust me?"

His pause is brief but deliberate, as if he's weighing the potential repercussions of any admission he makes.

"I suppose I do," he says at last, his eyes lingering. Not on my eyes but my mouth.

The awareness of it prickles across my skin.

"And who else have you . . . trusted?" I try to sound casual, even as my pulse skips. But we both know what I'm really asking.

Bishop turns away, rubbing a hand along his stubbled jaw like he's considering whether to answer or disengage. "Vessica," he says finally.

"Oh." It slips out so sharply that I swear it punctures the tension building between us.

But he continues, still staring at something in the distance. "Taliesin."

I blink. "Oh?"

"Lenora. Hadrian," he says, swiveling back to smirk at my confusion, then adds with feigned innocence, "A few other *friends*. That's what you're asking, right?"

I roll my eyes, but the lightness in his tone lifts some of the weight from my chest.

He looks right at me. "I haven't been with anyone since I died."

So, I guess he's done dancing around it.

And there's really only one reason he would tell me that . . . unless . . .

For a moment, the sole sound in the room is the soft lap of water against stone. I don't realize I'm staring until he splashes me from across the pool. "Don't give me that pitying look. I have hands."

"I'm . . ." I shake my head, trying to think of anything but those hands.

I force myself to swallow, my mouth suddenly bone-dry.

"You could always leave your clothes on." I shrug, going for casual and feeling anything but. "Keep it quick and dirty."

"When I take a woman to bed," he says, voice low and filled with promise,

"I want it to mean something." His mouth curves faintly. The way it does across the sparring ring when I'm still circling and waiting for him to make the first move.

He's not going to close this distance. Not unless I ask for it. Not unless I choose it. A sharp thrill races down my spine, and suddenly, the distance between us is unbearable, like holding a breath underwater for too long. I move before I can second-guess myself, the pool rippling softly as I rise from it.

Water slides off my shoulders, trailing over the mark on my chest, before tickling lazily down my breasts. I don't try to hide my body. Not from him.

I wait for the fear to hit. Of letting him see me. Of crossing this line.

But it doesn't come.

There's only a deep, safe certainty and something trembling under it, something that needs his hands on me.

Something that just needs . . . him.

His nostrils flare as I slowly close that final distance between us. He shifts upright, reaching a hand below the water as the other skims the surface, his fingers flexing slightly.

This close, the heat of his body is unmistakable even in the steaming water.

I lift a hand, drawn to the pale, intricate lines on his shoulder, but I stop myself an inch away, asking a question without words. My heart thunders as his breath catches.

But he doesn't stop me.

The permission settles into me slowly, steadying rather than dizzying.

"It's a crime," I say quietly, "that you hide your power. It's beautiful."

I trace a finger along the vestige on his collarbone, following it to the one right over his heart. Something charged sparks where our skin touches, and a low moan slips from my lips.

"If you want me to stop, say it," I whisper, praying he doesn't as I step between his legs.

He draws a shuddering breath, his chest rising with the weight of that armor he's wearing even now. His throat slides, long and slow.

"Arden." His voice breaks on my name, a hand lashing out to grip my wrist. "I want this. I want you."

He starts to rise, but I plant my free hand on his shoulder and push him back down. Pulling free of his grasp, I wrap my arms around his neck and lower myself slowly into his lap, my knees biting into the stone bench as I straddle him.

We're face-to-face, but Bishop remains still, like he's waiting for me. He opens his mouth and hesitates for a moment. "Are *you* sure?" he asks, the longing in his eyes so deep, I think I might drown in it. What a beautiful way to die. "Because this means something to me, so if you aren't . . ."

And somehow, in the midst of all this chaos and pain and uncertainty, this is the one decision I can't bring myself to question. Not even for a moment.

I brush my hand along the back of his neck, and he exhales slowly, his unguarded eyes proving he's finally removed that last remaining piece of armor.

"Before," he says, "I couldn't. Not before you knew the truth. And then you were hurting . . ."

Understanding clicks sharply into place. He was protecting me. Not himself. Not the secrets he carries. *Me*. He was always protecting me.

I think he always will.

And maybe I'm ready to let him.

My heart aches with a deep, breathless pull that feels dangerously like hope. I can't shut him out anymore. I'm not sure I ever truly have.

Slipping a hand into his hair, I grab hold of him. I might never let go. "Will you just shut up and kiss me already?"

The words snap the last thread of restraint between us, and his mouth crashes into mine. It's not the quiet, tentative brush of a first kiss. No, he kisses me as if he's been holding his breath and I'm his oxygen. There's agony behind it, but it's the sweetest kind of pain. It throbs through my skin and bones and sinew.

Bishop shifts, his strong arms drawing me closer, demanding but gentle, as I fit perfectly against him.

Desire grows roots and spreads, reaching every single nerve in my body. It moves slowly at first, unfurling with the patience of something that's been waiting long enough below the surface to take its time. Then it charges through me, blazing to life everywhere he touches. Aching with absence everywhere he doesn't. His tongue sweeps in and claims my mouth like I belong to him, like I've belonged to him since . . .

The weight of a hundred restrained moments presses into this one. This didn't happen over a few weeks of training. He's been waiting. Enduring every measured distance. Every step he didn't take. Held in check through every touch that lingered too long. I break away, panting against his mouth.

"How long?" I ask, as my eyes search his for the answer.

"Since the fucking bird," he rasps, dragging his lips across my jaw before he plants a kiss behind my ear.

The confession steals my breath, the memory rewriting itself into what I didn't see that night . . . even though I was drawn to him, too. Past that altar, I saw him. Not the sacrifice.

Just him.

And his gaze fixed on mine across the altar, too, as if we'd both sensed something dangerous and inevitable in the same breath, even if neither of us understood it then.

His mouth trails down, the hands on my hips sliding under me, fingers digging slightly into my skin as if he needs to know that tonight I'm the one who's real. Shifting forward, he urges my legs around his waist and tugs me closer. I gasp as my body locks around him like I'm falling.

Falling *hard* and *apart* and *into* him all at once.

His cock brushes against me, and a whimper slips from me like a confession. Any remaining pretense shatters, and I dissolve against him. Bishop cradles my back, lifting me slightly out of the water. "I've got you."

But before his words settle, he leans and plants a kiss over the mark on my chest. I tense as he whispers against my scarred skin, "It's a tragedy that you hide this. That anyone made you think you had to."

My pulse kicks up, and for one glorious moment, I see myself like he sees me. Reflected in the dark mirror of his eyes, I'm not broken or cursed. I'm not the girl he whisked away or the omen people whisper about in lowered voices. That feels like a story told about another life. Because the woman looking back at me isn't hiding.

She's fierce and luminous and *wanted.*

Bishop moves down, mouth capturing my breast and sucking my nipple between his teeth greedily. I cry out with relief as a hint of pain threads through my exhilaration.

He releases it, lips brushing the tender tip as he murmurs, "You have no idea how hard it is to keep myself from looking at these during training." His tongue swirls, circling until my nipple contracts to a hard peak. "How hard it is to even think when all I want to do is this."

His hands glide down my back, pulling me gently closer.

But I don't want tender. I want *more. Need* more.

I groan as his teeth tug my nipple again. "You don't have to be so gentle."

I've denied myself too long for that.

He draws back slightly, a shadow falling across his face. "I don't want to hurt you."

I'd tell him to stop worrying about me, but I might as well ask him to stop breathing. So, I dip a hand into the water, reaching between us to find he's already hard. My hand closes around his cock, and every thought in my head scatters.

I thought his vestiges were impressive.

Bishop groans as I stroke the length of him. Between the silky feeling of him against my palm and that sound, I'm barely holding myself together.

I tilt my head back, savoring this final moment of anticipation. Above us, through the haze of steam, the constellations burn in the darkness like silent witnesses, as if the night itself has been expecting this moment to unfold.

I don't know what waits for us on the other side of this.

Hopefully, a wall. A bed. *Any* and *all* flat surfaces.

But it scares me how much I want him.

How alive I feel in his arms. How he makes me feel safe even as he slowly unravels me.

His mouth burrows against my neck, sucking at my skin like he'll let me take all the time I need.

Every muscle in my body tenses, coiling with my own need. For weeks, I've fought this pull between us. But there's nowhere left to hide. I hinge my hips an inch, the water shifting around us. He accepts the invitation without hesitation, adjusting his grip to rock my clit against his crown, my own hand pressing it dangerously close as he drags me along his shaft. Over and over until my entire reality is centered on where our bodies meet and the sweet, torturous need he's stoking.

"If you aren't ready . . ." His words grate out, scraped from the last of his control. "If it's too much . . ."

"More," I breathe. "*All* of you."

He presses his forehead to mine. "Void take me," he growls, his grip on my ass tightening. "I need my cock inside you."

He's finally issued a demand I'm willing to meet.

"Then take me," I whisper. "Stop holding back."

His hands dig into my hips for a beat, and I whimper, my body betraying the longing I've kept secret from both of us.

I've never wanted anyone like this. Like I'll die if he stops touching me. Every inch of me is desperate for him to lose control.

"*Please*," I beg.

That does it.

Bishop surges up, wrapping his arms under me as he hauls us out of the water. His fingers sink into the soft curves of my ass harder this time. Enough that my flesh smarts in delicious agony. I hook my arms around his neck, a hiss of approval escaping my lips. His eyes flare at the sound, and something in them *snaps*.

He slams into me with one swift thrust, all that self-discipline gone in an instant.

Thank the fucking Stars.

A snarl rips from his chest as he sheathes himself fully. He grasps my hips, pumping inside me until I'm panting. I cling to him, eyes closed, dazed as Bishop unleashes his primal side. The pool swells violently around us, water rippling and spilling over its tiled lip—sweeping away the last of my own restraint with it.

"More," I demand. And I mean it.

More of him. More of the way he's undoing me one stroke at a time.

I can't remember why I've spent so long denying this. He's past every wall I've built now. There's nothing left to guard.

Bishop plunges inside me tirelessly, over and over, each stroke harder and deeper than the last, drawing more moans from my lips.

My eyes flutter open, breath stalling when I find him staring back, his blue eyes wild and that iron control utterly obliterated. His cock drives into me relentlessly, determination clenching his jaw tighter with every stroke as if he can't rest until he urges every last mewl of pleasure from my lips. For a few stolen heartbeats, there is no future and no past. Just heat and breath and release.

"That's it. Come for me," he grunts, urging me to the edge. I go over it willingly, shattering in his arms.

Falling apart in a way I only can with him.

Bishop captures my mouth like he needs to taste my climax, like he can't bear to accept anything less than claiming every part of me. He coaxes me through it, his own body tensing as I clamp around his cock. He drives deeper, harder until he groans into my mouth and buries himself to the hilt and spills inside me.

And when our breath settles at last, he presses a final kiss to my lips. "I've got you." It sounds different this time, and my heart stutters. "I always will."

His certainty finds places I haven't fortified yet, and suddenly I'm acutely aware of everything I'll never forgive myself for. Blood in the dirt and last breaths and the quiet, terrible knowledge that my survival always comes with a cost.

I pull away slightly, just enough for the cold to creep in around the edges of the bath's heat. Just enough for me to see the lines of the raven-mark on my chest—the reminder of what I truly am.

Bishop is looking at me like I'm a beginning.

Why can't he see what everyone else does?

I'm an ending.

With the Stars watching us, I can't hide from that. Even in his arms.

Especially in his arms.

Because if war comes . . .

Fear grips my chest like a vise, painful enough that I can't breathe, as if my body is already counting the cost.

He goes still, concern flickering across his face and whatever he sees on mine.

"Arden." My name is a prayer on his lips.

One I can't answer.

"I'm . . . I'm . . ." It isn't him. I want to tell him that. I need to tell him that. But I can't find the right words. Not after this. Not after I told him I was sure.

"Stay with me." The words strain from him, something running through them. Something that hurts. That wants to fix this. That wants to hold me here with him.

Part of me wants him to reach for me, but he stays exactly where he is, giving me the choice.

That's what undoes me.

I unhook my arms from his neck, pressing a palm against his chest. For a heartbeat, he holds fast, his grip flexing like he might refuse. Then his arms give, easing me into the water until my feet touch the bottom.

He understands the wordless request. Of course he does.

His hands stay at my hips even after I'm steady, only slipping free when I step away. Panic weaves through my chest as I move toward the pool stairs. I choke back a sob as my feet hit the bottom step, and I climb out quickly, water streaming from my skin, my hands fumbling as I grab one of the towels.

"Stay," he says, his command stripped down to something raw that slices through me.

But I don't turn around.

If I do, I won't leave. I know that with a certainty that terrifies me. I wrap the towel tight around myself and move on instinct, on survival, on the need to put distance between me and the version of myself that wants to stay.

I close my eyes, trying to break this connection between us. This thread we've both felt since that first night. The one that I'm suddenly sure will destroy him. If I don't move now—if I don't pull away—I never will.

This thing between us started with blood. It will end that way, too.

When my magic awakens, he'll see that.

"I'm sorry." I can't bring myself to look at him.

I make it to the door when he calls one more time: "Arden."

But he still doesn't tell me to stop.

I throw on my clothes, not bothering with laces and ties, afraid that I'll turn around and find him there.

But he doesn't follow me.

I burst into the night, legs burning as I run the dark path back to Miradores. I don't stop moving until I reach the graveyard on the outskirts of the house, collapsing where the soil hasn't settled yet.

Where I can't pretend that I'll ever be anything other than a harbinger. And there, I make a promise to someone I failed to save.

A promise that I'll protect the one person I can.

TWENTY-NINE

Twelvetide arrives like a savior, delivering me from the latest mess I made.

Or at least delaying the fallout for a few days—long enough for me to get my feet back on solid ground. With the house full of guests, there are plenty of distractions to keep me from running into Bishop.

In the kitchen, heat rolls from the oven in waves, thick with the smell of butter and sugar and something spiced that catches in the back of my throat. Every surface is occupied. Honey tarts shaped like stars cool on racks next to bowls of flour-dusted dough waiting to be shaped and baked into more. Biscuits and cakes and cookies crowd the rest of the table. There are bundles of herbs and pine boughs tied with ribbon and twine stacked wherever they'll fit. A box of other necessities, just delivered from Wolf's Keep, sits by the sink, and cases of wine are wedged beneath the worktable.

Tonight's party promises to be . . . memorable, which I've learned this year isn't the same thing as fun.

But regardless, we have to survive the final preparations first. Particularly Lenora, who is digging in one of the lower cupboards, grumbling under her breath.

I crouch next to her. "Can I help?"

She jerks back in surprise, hitting her head on the top of the cabinet. I catch her before she topples over, helping her onto her feet. But she scowls at me. "Everything is under control, and I have plenty of help."

I bite back a response that won't earn me any points with her, recognizing the pigheaded determination on her face all too well. It's the same look my mother used to get when she'd decided something was her responsibility alone. A trait she passed on to Broderic and me.

Something tightens behind my ribs, but before the feeling can take shape, I reach out to help with the tray of candied nuts Lenora is trying to maneuver onto the last available space on the table. She grunts her disapproval at my help.

In fairness, she doesn't really need it. There are a dozen servants currently in Miradores, half hired help from the village, the other half borrowed from the numerous visitors who have already arrived to turn the estate upside down.

She chirps over her shoulder at one with a cloud of black hair who has inched his way toward the baked goods. "Don't *touch* those cookies. I have everything under control."

He backs up so quickly he nearly tumbles into the kitchen hearth behind him, then edges his way out of the room entirely.

"Are you sure I can't help?" I ask again, stepping aside just in time for two boys to tear through the kitchen. They're twins, judging by their matching faces and curly blond hair. They skid around the central table, shrieking with laughter, and nearly collide with a woman dressed in a fur-trimmed coat that definitely doesn't belong around this much butter and flour.

"Boys!" she calls out, already breathless as she barrels after them. "If you break something, I swear—"

The trio vanishes into the great room, allowing the sounds of more chaos to spill through the door. Deep, important voices having deep, important conversations—or what they think qualifies as such. Someone drops a spoon, a bottle clinks, and an argument breaks out above it all.

There hasn't been a moment's peace since the last of the guests arrived, filling the corridors, claiming the spare bedrooms, and drowning every quiet corner with gossip and talk of politics. Not that I'm sure there's much of a difference between the two topics. *Every* one of them looks at me like they believe *every* rumor they've heard. No one would dare touch me under Bishop's roof. That hasn't stopped the stares and whispers. I've been avoiding it all.

Until the baths.

Since quiet has a way of letting the dangerous thoughts surface, the noise dulls their sharp edges. It's easy to disappear with this many people around.

Easy to avoid him. Easier than admitting that the silence between us feels heavier than my guilt.

But considering that I haven't seen him since I left him in the baths, Bishop is probably avoiding me, too.

It's better this way.

Lenora huffs, shaking her head as she stares at the door that's gradually swinging shut. "Rambunctious boys are the Marius curse." She glances at me, her mouth curving ever so slightly. "Just so you know."

"Okay," I say, not sure why this warning matters to me.

"What I wouldn't give to have just one little girl running around the estate at Twelvetide," she adds and winks at me.

Realization slams into me, and I swallow down a laugh. She's not warning me. She's delivering a hint—and not a very subtle one. So, she doesn't know what Bishop told me . . . about scions not being able to have children. I can't help feeling sad for her, but the emotion lingers just a beat too long before I shove it away.

I retreat to the edge of the room, hands waiting uselessly at my sides. There's nowhere to stand without being in the way, nowhere to breathe without inhaling cinnamon and pine and woodsmoke and something sweet enough to make my teeth ache. But even though I'm grateful for the full house, I have zero desire to make small talk while all of Bishop's distant relatives leer at *the harbinger*.

Lenora pivots back to the box that's just been delivered and actually curses, the sound so surprising that two borrowed servants scatter into the great room before they can be tapped for this duty. She glares after them, whipping off her apron. "They always forget something in the delivery this time of year. I'll have to send someone down to the village."

I gulp. Going into Wolf's Keep is the last thing I want to do, but I did offer to help, and I can't hide at Miradores forever.

"I could—" I say weakly.

The sad look she gives cuts me off mid-sentence. "You will not be going there unchaperoned. Bishop is off doing Stars know what." She shakes her head as she lays out a fresh towel and begins piling baked goods in the middle. "The beggars are horrible this time of year," she explains, blanching as if she's already dreading their hopeful hands. "It breaks my heart."

But there is something I can do about that. "Wait. Will you do me a favor while you're there?"

"Of course," she says slowly, as if she's afraid she's just added more to her crushingly long to-do list.

"Just a second." I race up the narrow staircase hidden by the back door before I can overthink this idea. I grab the leather pouch from Kieren's things, ignoring a pang at how empty the box of his belongings looks without the clothes I gave away a few days ago.

Lenora is waiting for me at the door, and her brows rise when I pass the money pouch to her. "Give this to anyone who needs it."

"Love, you don't have to—"

"Please," I cut her off, a lump forming in my throat. I can do Kieren's Interstice right. I *need* to—since I'm fucking up everything else. "It's not . . . mine."

Understanding dawns in her eyes. She purses her lips and then holds the pouch back out to me. "Go on then. Take it."

I back up a step. "I don't want it."

The lines of her face set with determination. "A woman should have some means tucked away. *Your* friend would agree. He would have wanted you to keep it . . . just in case."

"I can't." I shake my head. That's not how this works, and even if it was, just knowing his things are still in my room . . . "It hurts too much to see it."

"I understand, love. But that's not a problem." She pulls a tea canister off the highest shelf, and a cloud of dust puffs off the lid when she opens it, coins rattling inside.

I take a step closer, curiosity winning out over grief.

"You can keep it with mine. Fifty years, and I've never had to touch it." She lifts her chin like she's proud of that fact.

"You have a secret stash?" Lenora is full of surprises.

"When I came here, I didn't know a soul," she confides. "No one in my family had ever traveled this far west. My brother gave it to me before I left. Told me to hide it, so I'd have a way to get home if I ever needed to."

Something squeezes my heart as she talks about her family. "And you never used it?"

"I never needed to." She snorts like even the idea seems silly now. "But just knowing it was there eased my mind while I settled in here. I still like knowing it's there, but now I like thinking about what I might do with it," she says, lowering her voice as if this is a wicked confession. "Maybe I'll take a trip. I never dared leave Bishop to his own devices before, but he's been very *occupied* lately."

I swallow around the lump that forms in my throat at her suggestive tone. She'll be heartbroken when she realizes nothing is going to happen between us.

We can start a club.

Not that I have any right to be heartbroken. But still . . .

"Is there anything you need from Wolf's Keep?" she asks, slipping on her coat.

I have everything I need at Miradores, a fact that slightly unsettles me. "Nothing." I pause. "Unless the bakery there has some of those crescent pastries."

Despite the never-ending feast she's preparing, that is one delicacy she flat refused to "fiddle with," as she put it.

"You'll have to go to Wintour for those." She shakes her head, adding with that knowing, hopeful smile, "Get Bishop to take you."

I force myself to return her smile. There's no reason to ruin her Twelvetide with the truth.

I've already done enough damage.

The day passes, and I'm still successfully avoiding Bishop. His extended family is another story, and there's no getting out of the party. By the time Shea arrives to get ready with me, Breccan in tow, I've lied to one, considered strangling another, and potentially sold myself into an arranged marriage with an elderly uncle who seems to think my name is Lizabette.

"You look tired." Shea assesses me, clutching Breccan by the shoulders to keep him from being trampled underfoot by the harried servants in the kitchen.

"It's been a long day," I say with a sigh.

She glances around at the turmoil masquerading as party preparations. "I can see that." She bites her lip. "If I should take him—"

Before she can finish the offer, Lenora whirls around and gives Breccan a plate stacked so high with cookies he can't see over the top. "Those are for you." She pats him on the head, earning one of his gap-toothed smiles. "But I'm afraid the kitchen . . ."

"Don't worry," I say as much to her as to Shea. "I know where to take him."

Shea plucks two cookies off Breccan's plate as we steer him through the great room, earning her a "hey!"

"You can't even see where you're going." She nods for me to help him out, and I gladly do.

"You're lucky," I tell Breccan around a bite. "Lenora has yelled when any of us try to take a cookie."

He grins wider at this information, but when I lead him into the library, the smile slides from his face, replaced by slack-jawed awe.

I squat beside him, heat prickling my eyes at the sheer joy on his face. It will be worth it when Hadrian hands me my ass over this later. "I thought you might like to wait for us here."

He bobs his head several times, nearly dropping his plate.

I take it from him and deposit it on one of the tables. "Let's put these over here."

"Good idea," he says, squaring his shoulders like he understands the responsibility he has to the space.

Hadrian might not be happy, but I have no doubt that Breccan will take better care of the books here than any adult living in this house besides him.

"Okay, rules," I say, biting back a grin when he straightens like a little soldier waiting for orders. "No writing in books. Keep the cookies away from the books." I try to think of anything else that is likely to make Hadrian apoplectic. "Don't fold any of the page corners."

Breccan shrinks back like the mere suggestion horrifies him.

He's going to get along just fine with Hadrian.

I take a step away, searching the upper stacks for the latter, but I can't see him, so I call out, "We have a guest in the library. He knows the rules!"

Shea gives me an apprehensive look as I link arms with her, but she smiles down at her brother. "Be good. Follow Arden's rules."

"I will," he promises with a solemn nod.

Footsteps clatter on the spiral staircase, and we all turn to find Hadrian descending, robes flying out behind him. When he makes it to the bottom, he stops dead in his tracks. "There's a child in my library."

"Well spotted." I nod, urging Shea back a step. "This child loves books more than you do."

But Hadrian is still staring at him when Shea and I reach the library door. I push her gently through it and make it one step out before Hadrian bellows, "Arden, there's a child in my library!"

I turn to face him just as Breccan presses a finger to his lips, shakes his head, and whispers, "You're supposed to be quiet in a library."

Hadrian's eyebrows bunch as he stares down at the strange creature I've deposited in his sacred space. But he looks up, mouth twisting into a curious grimace, and waves me away. "Off with you, then."

I'm shaking with barely suppressed laughter as I close the door quietly behind us. But Shea lingers beside it. "Are you sure that we should leave?"

"It's good for him. Hadrian spends too much time with books."

We're almost to the stairs when one of Bishop's cousins steps in our path, carrying a plate of pickled sugar root and onions. The scent is so pungent that I start to cough. He tilts his head, studying us as he plucks a ruby-red strand of onion and pops it into his mouth. "So you're the harbinger."

I flinch, but he squints as though he's trying to spot whatever ominous secret I'm hiding. He shrugs and looks at Shea. "And who are you? Another lovely omen?"

And I thought the vinegar was stomach-churning.

Shea blinks at him and stammers out, "I-I'm training to be a knight," then adds a strained, "sir."

"A knight!" His eyes light up as he licks his forefinger and thumb clean. "How quaint! I command the garrison in Isoldoro. Perhaps we can discuss where your future assignment might take you . . . if you are interested in somewhere more *cultured*."

Because nothing says sophistication like sucking pickling juice off your fingers.

I grip Shea's elbow and aim her toward the staircase, forcing a smile. "We need to get ready. If you'll excuse us . . ."

"I'm starting to understand why my invitation ordered me to leave weapons at the Bellatorum," Shea mutters under her breath as we race up the steps.

"Me too." I suppose it's the same reason that Bishop locked the armory before the first guest stepped through the estate's postern.

But when we reach my door, Vessica is standing there, and my heart stops.

"What is it?" I ask, already imagining about a dozen worst-case scenarios.

Her mouth flattens into a thin line as she looks at Shea. "You didn't tell her."

"Shit," Shea says, turning to me. "I meant to say something. I invited her to join us, but it was so loud down there and—"

"It's no big deal," I cut her off, shoulders sagging as relief floods through me. I thought she was here on behalf of Bishop. That he sent her.

Or worse, that . . .

I bury the thought and force a smile. I could use a few allies around here, especially with Twelvetide's mixed company. I stride forward and quickly draw the nochtimetric pattern on the lock Bishop installed last week—a concession I made so I could stay in my bedroom while the guests are here.

"Do you want to borrow something?" I ask Vessica as soon as we're inside. Pausing, I yank off my boots and toss them next to the fire.

"I'm fine." She smooths her tailored dress uniform as she says it, but her eyes tighten slightly.

"Are you sure?" I throw open my wardrobe to reveal the new gowns and mirror hanging inside. "Because Lenora ordered half the dress shop after that fitting, and you know I'm never going to wear most of them."

The impracticality of it, with the estate needing so much work . . .

"Come on." Shea nudges Vessica toward the wardrobe. "We're doing her a favor."

"You really would be," I insist. I push the gowns apart on the rod, showing her a glimpse of a midnight-blue gown, the color so deep that it's nearly black. It's not quite the gown I caught her admiring in the shop. The neckline is higher, and the sleeves are lined with gold fabric, but it's cut in the same severe, stunning angle. "This one," I whisper.

She tries to shake her head, but her eyes stay on the dress. "I don't need—"

"No one *needs* a ball gown"—contrary to the belief of most of the people currently crowding the estate—"but sometimes you deserve one."

"Are you sure?" She brushes her hand across the silky fabric.

"Yes." I lift it from the rod and shove it into her arms. "And you can keep it. I really don't know what I'm going to do with all these dresses. It's not like I have anywhere to go."

Shea steps forward and begins looking at the others. "You could wear them for Bishop," she says casually.

I nearly choke on my own spit. "What?"

"You two have been training together constantly." Shea shrugs a shoulder, her attention pausing on a sleeveless gown of soft gold silk with a flowing skirt and neckline that's cut unapologetically low. There's a capelet of white fur to wear with it—the dressmaker's concession to my request to keep my mark covered. "The whole Bellatorum is talking about it."

So much for the privacy of training at the astrolatory. I glance at Vessica, who is doing an admirable job of pretending not to care.

"You have to have considered it." Shea holds the dress to her chest and sighs dreamily. "He's . . ."

"He's what?" I ask slowly.

"Beautiful," Vessica supplies with a snort like it's perfectly obvious.

But both Shea and I stare at her.

I mean, she's not wrong.

"What? I have eyes." She holds up a palm like she thinks I'm some kind of feral dog that needs a firm hand. "Relax. He's not my type."

"I'm not jealous," I say a little too quickly, beginning to reach for the final dress. They've left me the most daring option. Naturally. "And it's not like . . . I mean, we're not . . ."

But I can't quite force the lie out. Not after the bathhouse. Not when the memory of his body pressing against mine is still so fresh. Just thinking about it starts a low pulse thrumming at my core.

Shea tilts her head, biting her lip but not managing to cover her smirk. "It isn't? Because it sure looks like—"

A knock at the door saves me from further embarrassment. I have no idea who else wants to join our little party. Taliesin probably sensed three women were in the same room and ran here as fast as he could.

"Nothing is going on with Bishop and me," I say smoothly, the lie easier with my back turned to them.

But when I open the door, he's on the other side.

"I'm sorry." His voice is so low that I recall the sound he made the moment his cock slid inside me, and something clenches hard between my legs. He leans against the doorframe, already dressed for the evening. He isn't wearing a uniform, but rather a dark coat tailored high at the neck and cut close to showcase the powerful lines of his body. It's sinfully brutal despite how it covers his skin and hides his vestiges.

He looks like temptation and salvation collided with each other and he was the glorious result. He takes a single step toward me as if he knows exactly how close my knees are to buckling. How much my fingers itch to reach for him.

Get it together. You have an audience. I suck down a steadying breath. "Bishop, I—"

I stop short, glancing back to where Shea is carefully laying her gown on the bed. Vessica is inspecting hers by the window. Both far too absorbed in their dresses to be believed.

Bishop hesitates when he sees them. He doesn't just pause. He actually falters, looking more frazzled than I've ever seen him.

Not that I've ever seen him frazzled.

Except when I reached below the water and . . .

I shut out the tiny, unhelpful voice that seems determined to force another reckless decision from me.

He braces his hands on the doorframe as if he's choosing how to retreat.

"I'm sorry," he repeats, but this time he adds, "I thought you were alone."

The blue in his eyes burns as bright as the tip of a flame, the heat there warming my own skin—and I know exactly what would have happened if I had been alone.

His gaze flicks past me to the mirror, the discarded boots, the open wardrobe, then back to skim over the mixed and matched secondhand uniform I'm wearing. A muscle strains in his neck. "Are you coming to the party?"

Suddenly, I'm not sure if I should. I don't know how I'm going to survive it, orbiting the room around him, pretending that there's nothing between us.

How I'm going to keep the promise I made at Kieren's grave.

I swallow the raw feeling. "Yes. We're getting dressed now."

He nods once. Then again. He opens his mouth like he's about to say something else, but he leans closer, still clutching the doorframe, his knuckles going white. So close that I remember how his lips taste.

"Tonight . . . I . . ." He stops, exhaling through his nose, and tries again. "Save me the Turning."

I forget how to breathe. Forget how to speak. Every word I know is replaced by this one request to start the new year. *Together.*

"As friends, as whatever you need," he says, already stepping back like he can't stay a moment longer. "I'll wait for you."

His eyes linger on mine for a beat too long to pretend he's speaking only about tonight. Heat pools low in my belly, and when Bishop closes the door softly, I stare at it long enough that Shea clears her throat. The sound startles me, freeing me from whatever spell he just cast.

When I finally turn, Vessica's dark brows lift a fraction, but she says nothing.

Shea, on the other hand, drops fully onto the bed, bouncing once as her grin splits wide. "Soooo," she says brightly, crossing her arms. "How is training going?"

"Fine." I stalk to the vanity, trying to remember what I was doing before Bishop just turned my world upside down.

Again.

I sit and reach for a pot of rouge, stopping when I look in the mirror and find my face is roughly the color of a ripe tomato. I grab the powder instead and dab at my cheeks like it might undo whatever damage has already been done.

Shea squints at me in the reflection. "You can't pretend like that didn't just happen." She leans forward, dropping her voice into a conspiratorial whisper. "Did you kiss him?"

I make a noncommittal noise and start on a second layer of powder. It still doesn't help the situation on my cheeks.

That only winds her up more. "Seven hells," she breathes. "Did you?"

"They slept together," Vessica says calmly, starting to strip out of her uniform. "And Arden broke his heart."

"What?" Shea shrieks—and I yell at the exact same time.

I spin on the stool toward Vessica. "How did you . . . Were you . . . ?" My mind whirls with every possible explanation and keeps landing on the only reasonable answer. "Did he say something?"

She slips out of her pants. "No."

Relief and indignation collide, and I sputter, "Then how did you know?"

"I didn't," she admits.

Void swallow me. Nothing gets past her. Me, on the other hand? "You were bluffing."

"Not exactly." She slips the gown from its hanger, admiring it for a moment. "He's been in a better mood since you arrived. Lighter. Less . . . him." She looks right at me. "But a few days ago, that stopped."

My stomach drops.

"Plus, it was written all over his face when you opened the door," she says so matter-of-factly that I can't scrounge up even an ounce of anger.

Shea flops backward on the bed, pressing a hand to her chest. "Will you meet him for the Turning?"

Of course they heard him ask. It seems they didn't miss anything—even the things that weren't said.

But Turning the Threshold? Taking that step even as friends? "I'm not sure if that's a good idea."

Shea groans with disappointment, but Vessica meets my eyes again and says in a low voice, "If you aren't sure, don't. The door always remembers."

Because once you cross certain thresholds, there's no returning.

Vessica steps into her gown, but it feels like she's stuck a dagger into my back.

Only it's not a training exercise for me.

It's a warning.

THIRTY

The sounds of the party reach my bedroom by the time Shea manages to help me into my gown. Standing in front of the mirror, I wonder if it's safe for Bishop to see me like this after . . .

A tingle races down the back of my neck as if reminding me that's the *entire* point of a dress like this.

Its wine-red color does something dangerous against my skin, as if it's too rich. Too *alive* in a way that draws attention instead of hiding. Especially once my hair is pinned up in dark curls, allowing the collar to rise the full length of my throat. Lace sleeves stretch to anchor neatly to my middle fingers with a little loop that allows free movement of my hands while everything on my front half feels controlled. The same can't be said of the back of the gown. Because while the high neckline shields my chest intentionally, when I turn, the back falls away in a single, uninterrupted sweep of fabric, leaving me bare from the nape of my neck to the small hollow between my hips. The skirt skims my hips and thighs, fluid against my skin with a slit that shows the line of one leg just enough to feel deliberate.

"Don't overthink it," Shea whispers, adjusting her fur stole. "He won't be able to take his eyes off you."

That's what I'm afraid of.

Music and laughter spill toward us as we step out of my room and find Taliesin lounging at the base of the stairs. He's dressed in a suit cut from deep purple wool, shot through with subtle silver thread that catches the light when he moves. He glances up as we start down, letting out a low whistle.

Vessica gives him the finger.

He only smirks and crooks his arm for her when she reaches the bottom.

He offers his other arm to Shea, but she shakes her head, flushing deeply and muttering something about "the library."

"We'll find you in a moment," I tell him, hooking my fingers around Shea's elbow. As soon as we're safely away, I shoot her a knowing look. "You have a thing for him."

Shea sighs, but she doesn't deny it. "He's my superior."

Enough said. I'm not about to press her after just being roasted for my own romantic entanglement.

But when we reach the library, Shea presses her palm against the door to stop me from opening it. "You know it's okay, right?"

My first instinct is to disagree, even though I'm not sure what we're talking about. "What's okay?"

"To want Bishop back," she says in a quiet voice. Not because anyone could possibly hear us.

She's softening the blow.

Before I can tell her she's wrong, she squeezes my arm once and nudges me forward. "Let's make sure my brother hasn't destroyed the library."

"I think we'd have already heard about it if he did," I say. Reassuring her is far easier than reassuring myself.

But when we walk inside, we both freeze. My brain stalls as it tries, and fails, to reconcile the scene in front of me.

Hadrian and Breccan sit shoulder to shoulder as the librarian explains something that sounds too complicated for me to understand, let alone a little boy. But Breccan is hanging on his every word like he's some type of god.

And they're both eating cookies.

In the library.

I stare for a second. "Well, all seven hells must have frozen over."

Shea presses a hand to her mouth to muffle a laugh, but that just makes *me* laugh. Hadrian looks up sharply, crumbs on the corners of his mouth. He swallows, but only so he can frown. "We are in the middle of a lesson," he informs us. "*Someone* wanted to learn the ancient tongue."

"The party started," I say. It's harder to hear the commotion through the library's thick walls.

But Hadrian waves us off without looking away from the book. "We'll join later. When he's finished the lesson."

Breccan beams like he's just been knighted.

"I told you," I murmur to Shea as we slip into the hall. "Those two are a match made by the Stars."

Relief relaxes her shoulders. "I owe you."

I consider telling her that she can repay me by dropping the Bishop talk, but part of me doesn't want her to. Part of me needs to be pushed.

Because that look on his face when I opened the door . . .

This is more complicated than keeping my distance. How am I supposed to do that when we live in the same house?

I'm no closer to an answer when we enter the party. The great room has been cleared of its usual furniture, the space transformed into something like a ballroom. The floor is open, musicians set up along one wall, the long banquet tables pushed back to make space for movement. Pine boughs and dark ribbons are woven across the hearth, candles flickering in the dark branches.

Fur-trimmed cloaks are slung over chair backs, their owners mingling in a blur of dark velvet and wool threaded with silver and starlight blue, even the occasional burst of gold, all catching the firelight from the hearth.

For the first time since Bishop brought me here, the house doesn't feel haunted. It's bursting with life.

And I can't enjoy any of it.

Because I'm expected to make constant small talk—every single member of Bishop's extended family seems eager to chat with me. And every single one of them manages to get a slight in, their comments ranging from overtly rude to almost laughably oblivious. Shea stays with me the whole time, offering polite smiles and pleasantries before excusing us firmly when someone tries to get their hooks in deeper.

We've made a full round of the room, but before we can retire to shove pastries in our mouths, a willowy woman steps into our path. Thin lines pinch the corners of her eyes, her lips twisting into something stuck between a grimace and a smile.

"We heard our cousin brought you here," she says, an icy current running through her voice. But it's the young woman next to her who makes me fall back a step. They have the same calculating eyes. "Lady Perran," she adds in introduction but doesn't offer her hand. "I believe you met my daughter, Livia, at the Quincentennial."

Met is an overstatement—the lone Marius initiate kept to herself. But I force a smile. "It's a pleasure to see you again."

Livia snorts, her dark gaze darting around the room like she's already bored. "You're awfully chipper for a prisoner."

"And well-dressed," her mother mutters.

"Prisoner?" I repeat, and Shea steps closer like she senses trouble.

"You *are* the harbinger." Lady Perran sniffs. "I can't imagine any other reason Bishop would allow you into Vennaro. Of course, we all thought he'd have killed you by now."

My mouth falls open. What had Shea said about not bringing weapons?

My friend takes a full step in front of me. "Perhaps you should ask Patron Marius about that. I'm sure he's dying for your opinion." Shea steers me away before either of his cousins can get in another snub.

"Thank you," I say when we finally work our way to the banquet tables groaning beneath the weight of Lenora's lavish spread. Platters are crammed everywhere, their edges overlapping to make up for the lack of room for all of it, the polished wood of the table barely visible beneath the sprawling feast. Steam rises in lazy spirals from heated serving trays, carrying the mingled scents of roasted fowl, melted butter, and spices warm enough to soften the chill of winter seeping into the room from the constantly opening front door.

I grab a plate and start piling everything I see on it. "Is there a contest I don't know about?" I grumble to her. "Who can deliver the worst insult to my face?"

She snorts. "Do you think there's a prize involved?" She pops a grape into her mouth and deadpans, "I could use the money."

"And I thought we were becoming friends." I polish off a honey tart in two bites, suddenly famished. Which definitely has nothing to do with the constant simpering and ogling.

It's because *he* keeps moving through the room. Never close enough to cross paths. Never far enough for me to miss. But always just within my periphery.

Every time, it's like a shift in gravity. Like I can feel him before I see him.

He doesn't look at me once, apparently immune to whatever invisible thread keeps pulling my attention back to him.

Maybe I imagined that look on his face at my bedroom door earlier. Four honey tarts later, I'm still not sure.

The closer the clock creeps to midnight, the more I find myself checking Bishop's location.

At an hour to the Turning, I spot him near the doorway, talking with a richly dressed man with rings on every finger and a voice that carries like he wants the whole room to hear him.

Bishop's eyes lift and meet mine across the room. Our gazes lock, and then . . . he turns away, continuing his conversation as if he didn't see me at all.

The casual dismissal might as well be a blade slid neatly between my ribs.

I stop looking after that.

When there's less than half an hour until midnight, the crowd moves toward the hall. The borrowed servers appear carrying goblets of sparkling wine on silver trays. Anticipation and dread tangle into a knot in my stomach.

Someone jostles their way through the swarm to us, Lenora appearing a moment later in a deep-green gown, her sleeves rolled up but not entirely hiding their usual dusting of flour. A sprig of holly hangs limply from her bun, and I can't quite decide if it got stuck there accidentally during the decorating, or if she pinned it there hours ago and it finally conceded its bid to keep up with her.

A server appears at the same moment she does and holds out his tray. "Last two."

Shea and I both snag flutes of the sparkling wine.

"Here." I hold it out to Lenora. If anyone deserves a drink tonight, it's her.

But she waves me off. "I still have to clean up after everyone goes to bed."

"Absolutely not." I scowl at her. "You aren't lifting a finger."

But she refuses to accept the drink. Before I can take a new tack, a chair scrapes loudly against the floor.

"Stars preserve us," Lenora mutters as the man Bishop was talking to by the door hauls himself onto the chair and gestures for the crowd to quiet.

"Who is that?"

My question earns a disapproving huff from her. "Lord Perran." She says the name like it tastes bad. Having just met his wife and daughter, I understand. "He's first in line to be patron if Bishop doesn't marry."

The thought of this man's family running the Bellatorum turns the food in my stomach to lead.

Lord Perran clinks a fork against his crystal goblet. "It's time to Turn the Threshold," he calls over the lingering whispers, and a hush falls through the crowd. His chin lifts as if he already hears applause, leaning into the attention like he's been rehearsing for this moment. "It's been an . . . interesting year. Let's choose the right door this time."

Laughter ripples through the crowd, and I don't think I'm imagining that quite a few heads swivel toward me.

I don't laugh.

If this year taught me anything, it's the danger of thumbing my nose at tradition, of what can happen when you make the wrong decision for the right reasons.

I don't know if I'm afraid of choosing wrong—or I'm just afraid of choosing him.

Perran gets his applause, glasses rising to toast with him, and I find myself looking for Bishop again. This time to see what he thinks of his cousin—to see if he finds him as insufferable as I do.

My fingers tighten on the stem of my glass, everyone around me swallowing their drinks. But I can't find Bishop.

Maybe he changed his mind.

Maybe he forgot.

Maybe I need this drink after all. I lift my wine absently and take a single sip right before small hands latch on to Shea's and my dresses.

"It's time!" Breccan shouts, bouncing on his feet and knocking my goblet to the rug.

He's clearly had one too many cookies. Or maybe ten too many, based on how excited he is.

I stare down at the wine seeping into the wool, heat creeping up my neck. "I guess that's what I get for being distracted."

I bend to collect it, but Lenora shoos me off to follow the crowd. "Go on. I've got it."

Breccan clings to both our hands as we're swept up in the tide of bodies surging toward the front entrance. Bells chime faintly as they're lifted from hooks, cold air rushing through the hall as the doors open.

The night is clear enough to see every constellation, but the temperature has plunged to near freezing. Frost whitens the stone, and my breath blooms in pale clouds. The estate is lined with glowing lanterns, their light trembling across the sweeping staircase that leads to the walking path that winds around the grounds.

Breccan tugs us toward a group of older boys ringing bells far too close to one another's ears.

But Shea stops him from running off and whispers to me, "Good luck."

They vanish into the crowd spilling onto the lawn below, leaving me to face the Turning—*and* Bishop—alone.

And when the steps clear, he's there. He's not pacing. Not searching the giggling, frantic mass of people rushing to be the first to turn the new year at the threshold of the back door. He simply waits, one hand resting on the stone balustrade as he stares toward the black sea beyond.

This is my Threshold. Not the walk around the house. Or the door waiting on the other side. *This.*

I can turn around and return to the house. Maybe I should.

It's probably easier than trying to go back to being friends, than telling him that I can't risk more.

It would certainly hurt less.

I don't know how long I linger, overthinking things, before I realize he's turned toward me.

There's something raw and unguarded in his eyes. His jaw tightens like he's holding his tongue, and my own pulse stutters. For a single stolen moment, there is no one else. There are no guests, no party. No silly traditions or any of the pressure that goes with them. Just this man looking up at me like I'm a dream that might vanish if he dares to move.

Bells ring out in the darkness, followed by laughter. The sound rolls through the night and settles into my bones.

Twelve minutes to midnight.

This is my last chance to turn back. To flee to the warm safety of the house. If I do, he won't stop me.

Releasing him from this purgatory I've built for us might be the kindest thing I could do.

The stone beneath me suddenly feels unstable, as if it might tip in either direction if I don't make a choice soon.

The bells chime again.

Eleven minutes.

I don't turn around.

I step down, heart pounding as I continue past him onto the path that curves along the side of the house. But I pause, and he falls into step beside me without a word.

Ten.

The estate stretches in the night, its windows glowing like hopeful eyes as we move along its perimeter. The path feels longer now than it does in the day, giving time for a chill to slip under my sleeves and needle my skin.

Nine.

I shiver as the cold creeps farther in, finding the thin places in my resolve. I fold my arms around my waist, afraid to look at him, afraid I'll stop in my tracks and never figure out whether to go back or move forward.

His coat settles on my shoulders.

He doesn't say anything. Doesn't invite the opportunity for me to refuse him, because we both know I would freeze to death before asking for his help.

Its warmth wraps around me, drawing me back to the baths. I can't resist the urge to clutch it closer. His scent is everywhere. In my mouth. In my lungs. I breathe in traces of woodsmoke, leather, and something darker that lingers underneath it all. Something that belongs only to him.

Eight.

The Turning is about letting go. Leaving the old year behind and stepping into the new one.

I wasn't letting go when I ran from him. I told myself I was cutting the rot away—cutting myself away. Protecting him.

That leaving was strength. That the torture of distance could be a kind of mercy.

That wanting him was the danger, not the choice.

But rot doesn't ache when you hack it away. It doesn't linger in your chest long after you've told yourself that it's gone.

Seven.

Our arms brush, and I move mine a fraction away, my body reacting to the light touch before my mind catches up.

Because the closer we are, the harder it is not to reach for him.

It won't be a decision then. It will be instinct.

And I don't trust myself not to unravel.

Bishop takes a step away without comment, the move easy enough that it hurts.

Six.

Time peels off in ringing strokes. Each chime strips away a lie I want to stop telling myself.

Five.

Is he close to breaking? Is he thinking of my mouth on his skin? Or the way I shook afterward?

Because my mind keeps returning to the way his hands steadied me as I fell apart.

Four.

Light spills from the back entrance ahead of us. The door is open, the smell of wine and food seeping toward us like a friend beckoning us forward.

It would be so easy to step over the threshold together.

The door always remembers.

Three.

Tradition says to make a wish on the final bell. To touch what you want to carry into the new year.

But my hands are empty at my sides.

Two.

I try to think of a wish. But there are only thoughts of him, and that makes wishing feel too dangerous.

One.

The final bell rings out, and my breath catches as everything breaks at once. The night's silence dissolves into cheers. Corks pop as the celebration continues.

As we approach the threshold, I slow, reaching for the door . . . and his fingers close around mine. My hand fits perfectly in his as if it remembers something I don't.

He wears no gloves in the dark where his secrets are safe, and his warm skin feels like a silent vow, his grasp gentle but firm as if to remind me that he's here.

Here without expectation.

Whatever you need.

I think that might be him.

I'll wait for you.

He pauses, leaving space for me.

He doesn't chase. He doesn't have to.

I could pull away.

I should.

But I don't.

His fingers weave through mine, and he tugs me away from the door. Away from the strangers with their prying questions and leering eyes. Away from a decision I'm terrified to make. Away from a page I can't quite turn.

But his hand is in mine, his coat over my shoulders, his taste lingering in my mouth even days later.

And I realize that whatever I thought I left behind the other night is right here.

That I can't run from this any more than I can run from my own heart.

Bishop leads me to the garden, where the sounds of the sea are wild tonight as waves break against the cliffs below. Ocean gusts rattle the branches of the trees, all bare save for the one that Hadrian healed with his magic.

He stops under that tree and turns to face me. Moonlight spills across him, casting a glow over the sharp planes of his face and deepening the rims of his eyes. "This seems like a good place for a new start."

"What about the Threshold?" I glance toward the house.

"The Threshold will wait." His hand tightens on mine, and want courses through me, the small touch enough to remember all the places his skin met mine the other night. Under the stars, I can't remember why I pushed him away. Not when he's looking at me like he'd wait forever.

And he could. Because he will never fade. Never grow frail or wane into something unrecognizable.

Never die.

The thought sends a spark racing through me, like standing on the edge of something vast with no bottom in sight and choosing to step forward anyway.

Maybe that's all I've ever needed—to pull him closer instead of pushing him away. So, I take a single, tentative step.

The surf crashes on the rocky cliff behind me, and something in him seems to answer it, his chest heaving as if he's the one being dragged under.

I open my mouth, not quite sure what I'm going to say, but he cuts me off. "I have your present for you."

"Another one?" My pulse jumps at the memory of the last gift he gave me and how it ended.

"I've wanted to give this to you all day." He glances up, the smile on his face so soft, so boyish, so hopeful that it steals my breath. "But I haven't been able to get you alone. I thought I'd have to sneak it into your boot after all."

There's no accusation in the words, just a gentle acknowledgment that I've been avoiding him. I don't know how to explain why I hid, why I left, why part of me is still screaming to run while my heart is still intact.

Bishop misreads my silence, and the smile falls from his face. "If you'd rather go back to the party . . ."

A laugh bursts out of me. The oscen startles from its nest, wings rustling as it lifts into the night like it knows the moment demands privacy.

He tilts his head, mouth curving again. "I take it you're not enjoying yourself."

"Your family is . . . interesting." It's the nicest thing I can think to say about most of them, but I walk it back. "Not that I've spoken to all of them."

His thumb rubs circles on the back of my hand, and it's nearly impossible to think of anything but that singular touch. "Let me save you the trouble. They're all the same. Wolves circling and waiting for the carrion."

"They're going to be waiting a long time, then," I say, trying to keep my tone light, even as my body grows heavy, each moment making it harder to stand still when all I want to do is crash into him.

"I suppose you're right." He pulls his hand away, and I instantly miss his warmth.

But I was the one who ran. I left him there.

This moment deserves to be on his terms.

His fingers find the edge of the coat still hanging off my shoulders, and for a single, breathless second, I think he's going to pull me in for a kiss. But instead, he withdraws a small box from the pocket and places it in my hand. It's wrapped in white paper with a gold ribbon.

I stare at it, a tiny ripple of guilt coasting through me. "I still never got you anything."

Bishop bites his lower lip like he's trying to hold himself back. And loses the fight. "I think the baths were more than enough."

I flush, looking down at the ground. So little space left between us, but we're both still tiptoeing toward that line.

"I'm sorry," he adds. "I shouldn't—"

"Stop." I cut him off. I clear my throat, trying to find the right way to make this confession. In the end, I blurt out, "I wouldn't change it. I'm glad that it happened."

And there it is: the truth.

Laid before us like the gift in my hand.

"Open your present," he says, a dark current running under the words this time. "I'm not sure how much longer I can wait."

The rasp in his voice tells me that we're not talking about the present in my hands or our relationship, but a need that's more immediate. This desperate, raw connection we share that's begging to reignite. It's getting harder to keep it at bay, even in the frosted garden with a hundred people inside waiting for attention.

My fingers tremble as I pluck the bow, not quite sure what to expect. Under the paper is a simple box, and when I lift the lid, I gasp.

Tears blur my vision as I stare at a piece of myself I thought was gone forever.

My mother's locket.

It's been reshaped by someone with expert hands. I can see the work in it. The hours. The patience. All for something that held no value to anyone but me.

My eyes fly up to find him watching me. "How? I threw it away."

Before any of this happened. Before the Stars marked me. Before he chose to save me.

"It seemed like it mattered to you," he says softly.

My longing eases into a hunger that doesn't feel like it might consume me but rather carry me.

Because he is my safe space.

He always will be, and, it seems, always has been.

"Let me." He lifts it from the box, and I turn, sucking in a jagged breath. Bishop tucks an escaped curl back in place, his finger pausing for a moment at the nape of my neck before he drapes the locket across my throat. The clasp clicks softly, but his hand lingers for a beat too long. "This dress . . ."

Two words. That's all it takes for me to picture it on the floor beside his bed.

I swallow and turn back around, touching the metal at my throat.

Bishop takes the empty box, pocketing it like it matters, and nods. "Look inside."

My fingers tremble as I unlatch it. He's had that fixed, too, and nestled inside . . . a small likeness of Kieren.

"Oh." It comes out on a broken breath.

"So he's always with you," he murmurs.

Bishop isn't trying to replace what I lost. He's protecting what's left.

And I've been holding the line between us, trying to pretend I can control what's happening.

Except I can't.

"I'm sorry." The whisper is nearly lost in the night air, but he tenses. My throat tightens as the words try to find their way out. "I was scared. Scared that the Stars marked me to be the thing that destroys you."

I want it to sound silly. I want him to laugh, but he doesn't.

"Never explain your heart to me." He cups my chin, pinning his gaze to mine like he needs me to hear this as much as he needs to say it. "I see you. I've always seen you, Arden. I think I know your soul better than my own."

The words strip me down until the truth of it is too exposed to deny, and a single tear leaks out of the corner of my eye.

He brushes it away with his thumb. "Happy or sad?"

"Both," I admit. Because on the cusp of this Threshold, I don't want to put up any more walls between us. I want to tear them down. I cover his hand with mine, grasping it so I can pull him forward.

I take a step, then another, towing him toward the house.

"I thought you didn't want to go back to the party," he says, but he doesn't try to stop me.

"I don't."

"Then I have bad news for you, because you're heading right for it." I can hear the smile in his voice, and it lifts my own lips.

I wish it could always be like this. Effortless and light and . . . easy.

But the things worth fighting for never are.

Bishop is worth fighting for.

When we reach the kitchen door, the lights inside are dim. The party has already moved on. The guests have Turned the Threshold without us.

"I'm glad we waited for everyone else to go through first," I murmur. Bishop eyes me warily as I swallow hard and continue. "But I'm done waiting."

I take both his hands and back toward the door. Bishop follows, pressing me gently against it.

"Are you sure?"

"Will you just shut up and kiss me?" I say with a soft smile.

But he pauses and searches my face like he might find a clue that will help him understand me better. "I meant what I said earlier. I will wait. There's no rush."

But there is. Because I only have one life, and even if it's painful, and even if I'm still a bit broken, I need to start living it.

I slide one hand from his. Reaching behind me, I turn the knob, then push the door open with my backside, my other hand still locked with his.

And we step through the door together.

Bishop's nostrils flare as we stumble into the dark kitchen, my back colliding with the wall that leads to the narrow servant staircase. He plants his hands on either side of me, creating a cage I never want to escape from. "Is the invitation to kiss you still open?"

"I think I might die if you don't," I breathe.

His mouth crashes into mine.

There's nothing gentle about the kiss. Only hunger and relief and the sweet edge of finally giving in. His hands grip my hips, shoving aside my skirt as he lifts me off the floor. His jacket hits the ground behind us, and suddenly I'm acutely aware of all the clothing that we're still wearing.

My hands slide to the buttons of his shirt, fumbling to unfasten them, needing to feel his skin on mine, needing nothing left between our bodies, between our souls.

He smirks against my lips. "Can I take you to bed before you start ripping off my clothes?"

"Only if you're quick about it." I tug his lower lip between my teeth, earning a growl.

Bishop hoists me up, and I wrap my legs around his waist, our mouths crushing together as he starts up the back staircase. Every step makes it harder to breathe. Like my body knows what's coming and is already begging for it. We only make it a few more before he pivots and we slam into the wall. He plants his knee between my thighs, pinning me in place as his tongue works deeper into my mouth.

His hands are everywhere. Skimming over my breasts, pushing my skirt to my waist, shoving aside the scrap of lace that's a barrier to what he really wants. He brushes a finger along my swollen sex, snarling with approval at the wetness he finds. "This . . ." He pushes the finger inside me, and I nearly arch off the wall as pleasure bolts through me. "This is all I want for Twelvetide."

That's a request I'll happily accommodate.

I choke back a moan as he continues to pump that single finger.

"What happened to going upstairs before we started ripping clothes off?" I tease breathlessly.

Bishop starts to draw away like he's going to comply. But who needs a fucking bed? I hook my arms around his neck and drag him back to me, unable to wait a minute longer. "I need you inside me. *Now.*"

He doesn't hesitate. Smart man.

He reaches between us, swiftly unbuckling his belt, then his trousers, and a tiny whimper escapes me as he strokes his newly freed cock. One arm circles my waist, hoisting me just high enough to bring us together. He slides inside me, and everything else falls away. His hips rock hard and fast. I lock my ankles around his waist and just enjoy the ride.

"Next time," he grunts, "we'll take our time."

I'm not sure if it's a promise to me or himself, but just the idea of Bishop taking his time makes my muscles clamp around him.

"Void, Arden," he grits out. "Warn a man before you try to kill him."

But seeing him wild like this? Knowing I can push him past the point of control?

I need more.

A smile lifts the corners of my mouth. "Where's the fun in that?"

I squeeze my core again, and a low growl rumbles from his throat. Shivers dance across my skin as he picks up speed, each thrust more urgent, as if it might be the last thing he does. Like he'd spend his final breath right here, inside me.

My back pounds against the wall, and plaster dust showers us. Bishop moves a hand to cradle the back of my head.

"Don't. Fucking. Stop." I gasp each word as he stokes the heat building inside me, already close to the edge.

"Never," he promises, driving harder.

And *I* will never get enough of this. Of him.

My hands unwind from his shoulders, and I slam my palms against the wall behind me, using the hard surface to gain leverage, meeting each of his strokes with my own unbridled abandon.

"More," I beg as fire ignites in my blood.

He clutches the back of my head, his fingers digging into my ass, as he finally loses the last shred of his control. His jaw clenches, his expression stripped raw, that relentless hunger blowing out his pupils until there's nothing left but darkness. The sight sucks the air from my lungs and pulls me under with him, something deep in my chest unfurling in answer as we both come undone.

The last shudders of climax tremble through me as I drop my head onto his shoulder and laugh softly. "One day, we might actually make it to a bedroom."

He chuckles and carefully sets me down on the stairs.

"I love a challenge," he warns, smile widening in a way that makes my chest ache. He rights his clothes, glancing to the dark landing below. "There's still the kitchen table and the—"

"Bishop!" A shout from the other side of the wall interrupts us, and we startle apart. "Are you there, man?"

Bishop shoots me an apologetic look, then starts reluctantly down the steps. My heart crashes into my ribs like it's lodging a complaint, and I quickly smooth my dress into place before I follow. But I freeze when I catch something dark on the wall out of the corner of my eye.

As I turn toward it, a chill crawls down my spine.

Two blackened handprints scar the plaster, faint but unmistakable. Exactly where mine were.

No. It can't be.

I grab my skirt and scrub at them. They come off like ash being dusted from a hearth as Taliesin skids around the corner, his eyes widening at our current condition.

"Can it wait?" Bishop barks, a hint of urgency lacing his words.

But Taliesin grimaces as he shakes his head. "No, it can't," he says, and something in his voice makes my heart stop for a beat. "I think Shea's been poisoned."

THIRTY-ONE

Poisoned.

"What?" I stare at Taliesin, still trying to make sense of what he's saying. Before I can, Bishop barrels toward the great room.

We follow him, Taliesin muttering what little he knows. That she mentioned feeling lightheaded and then went down.

Something twists in my gut. There are so many people here. Too many to keep an eye on. But why would anyone want to poison a conscript? "Maybe she had too much to drink."

But Taliesin shakes his head. "I've seen Shea drink. This is different."

He has to be wrong. She's so young, and then there's her brother . . .

When we reach the party, an unnatural hush has fallen over the guests. They're clustered so tightly together that the mixture of sweat and wine and perfume makes my head throb. Every eye is turned toward a corner of the room as people jostle for a better view. Taliesin grabs my arm as we push our way through the onlookers, but I stop in my tracks when I see her.

She's on the floor, her body unnervingly still except for the shallow rise and fall of her chest. Her face is pale apart from the rouge she borrowed earlier, its pink tint standing in garish contrast to her now waxen skin. Hadrian hovers over her, whispering rapidly to Bishop. I'm close enough to catch one word.

Bellanotte.

Taliesin curses like he heard it, too. He turns and urges the people crowding behind us back a few steps. I start to help, but my attention snags on the little boy peeking from the front of the group. Breccan's face is ashen as he clutches the hem of his tunic, his knuckles bone white. He looks so small against the tide of onlookers as they start to shift that, for a terrible second, I think he's going to be trampled. I break from Taliesin and dart over to grab him.

"I'm here," I say, trying to sound calm even as my pulse ratchets up.

"Is she okay?" he asks with a shaky voice.

The truth is too heavy, so I swallow it.

"She's resting," I lie, hoping I can find a gentle way to break his heart later. "She'll be fine."

He clings to me as I search the room until I find Lenora wringing her hands by the window. Waving her closer, I nudge Breccan toward her. "Get him out of here," I say in a low voice. "He shouldn't see this."

She gives me a curt nod and gathers him into her arms. "Come on, love. I have a few treats in the kitchen."

But before she can whisk him away, the little boy turns shining eyes on me. "I should stay until she wakes up."

Lenora doesn't hesitate as she pats his back. "Bishop will take care of her," she promises. "You'll stay here tonight, and we'll make butter cakes in the morning." She continues her promises, cradling his head as he sobs into her shoulder. She casts a quick look at me, her face lined with worry. "Everything will be fine."

I don't know which one of us she's trying to reassure.

She carries him quickly from the chaos, and I turn back to catch Bishop nodding at Taliesin. The knight leans down and lifts Shea into his arms as if she weighs nothing. Her head lolls against his shoulder, her arms slack at her sides.

But Bishop addresses his guests in an even voice. "She's only fainted. There's no cause for concern."

Several of his cousins exchange disappointed glances, like a corpse would have livened up the festivities. The nearest onlookers part to grant Taliesin just enough room to carry her away, still crowding close to get a good look, their curiosity outweighing concern.

Even I can't help gawking. It's clearly a lie.

Bishop pauses to whisper something to Vessica. She listens, her shrewd eyes never leaving the faces in the room. When he finishes, she sweeps through the crowd with the calculating grace of a predator. Bishop catches my attention and tilts his head toward Taliesin's fading form. I nod in understanding as he stops to redirect his overly nosy relations back toward the party.

I hurry to catch up with Taliesin, and Hadrian trails beside me, clutching a book and a vial of something I hope is useful. "We can take her to my room," I say when I reach him.

But Shea arches in his arms, something foamy frothing on her lips.

"There's no time," Hadrian says, rushing to open the library doors.

Taliesin hurries inside before anyone sees the truth about what's happening.

"You said it's bellanotte," Taliesin says, laying Shea on a chaise near the fireplace. "What can we do?"

Hadrian shakes his head, his mouth drawn in a thin line. "Not much. If it's a heavy dose, she'll keep seizing until her heart stops."

My stomach drops with a sickening jolt. An hour ago, she was laughing with her brother as the year turned. She can't die. The fire dances in the hearth behind her, and suddenly I'm back in the woods. Darkness presses in on the corners of my vision, the slight pulse in my head beginning to throb like my mind wants to shut down. Something warm stirs under my skin before fizzling away.

As if my head can't bear this any more than my heart can. But I can't bring myself to budge from the doors. Instead, I fall against them, unsure what to do but be a human barricade. We should send everyone home. Bishop should have done that. How can he let the party continue like nothing's happened?

Someone pushes open the door behind me. I glance quickly over my shoulder and find Bishop peering through the crack. I move to let him inside. But as soon as he's through the door, his gaze lands on Shea before it flicks to me and lingers for a heartbeat.

I force myself to ignore the tingle that follows that look and say, "We should send the guests home."

"I'm more concerned about her." Bishop strides over to assess Shea.

"It won't be long," Hadrian says grimly. "Minutes at most."

"No," I finally say so loudly that all three of them startle, remembering that I'm here. "There has to be something we can do. An antidote. Look in your stupid books!"

They can't just give up on her. She needs to be here for Breccan. She's so close to being a knight. There's so much left for her to do.

This can't be happening.

Hadrian takes off his glasses, his eyes squeezing shut as if he's running through an inventory of the knowledge he's collected in this room. But when he speaks, I realize he's not looking for an answer. He's trying to find the right words. "That's why they call bellanotte 'the assassin's friend.' A full dose will kill slowly." He glances at Bishop, a look of understanding passing between them. "There's nothing we can do but wait."

I shake my head, starting toward them, but Bishop catches me. He grips my shoulders. "It will be okay."

But it won't be. "We should get her brother," I say, voice breaking. "He needs to say goodbye."

Even if it hurts, I know it's worse when you don't get to say goodbye.

But when I try to take a step, my knees buckle, the darkness chasing me nearly winning.

"She will be okay," Bishop says gently but firmly.

"She's dying!" I try to pull away from him, but he anchors me in place.

"Just tell her," Taliesin snaps as he lingers by her side.

I look between them. "Tell me what?" I grab hold of Bishop's shirt. "What is going on? What is this about?"

"She's a scion. That's why she came here." He pauses. "Why I brought her here with her brother."

"Oh." It comes out as a breath instead of a word. For a moment, I only stare at him, trying to decide if I want to strangle him or kiss him. Then a laugh bubbles out of me.

"I'm sorry. It wasn't my—"

"Secret to tell," I cut him off, rolling my eyes, which does nothing to help my growing headache. "I know. I've heard that excuse before."

He frowns. "It's not an excuse."

"I don't care," I say, surprised to discover I mean it. I release my grip on his shirt, smoothing out the wrinkles. I feel almost weak, the relief sapping whatever was holding me together. "As long as she's going to be okay."

"She will be, eventually." But shadows linger in his eyes, as if he's thinking of his own deaths.

"Is everyone in this house a scion?" I ask with a brittle smile. "Have you left anyone out?"

Bishop's lip lifts at the corner. "Lenora isn't."

"I'm not, as far as I know," Taliesin says. "Unfortunately, there's only one way to be sure."

I snort, afraid an actual laugh will encourage him. "Please refrain from finding out." I press a finger against my temple, realizing this headache could have been avoided if any of them had trusted me. "You could have told me, you know."

Still, I can't muster any real anger this time. All that matters is that Shea will live. That we're all alive. But, with the danger past us, questions rise in its place. "Why would someone poison her?"

Bishop shrugs. "Vessica is trying to figure that out."

That's why he didn't tell everyone the party was over. Because someone here is responsible for what happened. Dread creeps down the back of my neck.

"Maybe it was one of the other conscripts. A rival?" I suggest. There are plenty of them here tonight. "Someone who doesn't want her to become a knight." I've seen her fight. She's hard to beat in the proving grounds, but without a sword . . .

Taliesin opens his mouth, but before he can speak, Shea's back arches. Her arms flail, knocking a book off a nearby table. He lunges to pin her shoulders, holding her down as she continues to spasm. Her eyes snap open, her pupils as dark as the Night's Scar. Then she collapses again.

Hadrian checks her pulse and frowns. "She's fading."

I turn away, unable to watch her die, even if she is immortal. Grabbing the arm of the nearest chair, I sink into it, and Bishop's hand finds my shoulder again, squeezing just hard enough to keep me tethered.

No one speaks for a moment, the room quiet apart from the ticking clock on the mantel, her rattling breath, and the muffled sounds of the celebration happening just outside, life and death divided by the library doors.

Eventually, Bishop releases me and begins to pace the length of the rug, hands clasped behind his back and eyes distant. Taliesin keeps hold of Shea's arms while Hadrian retrieves a blanket and tucks it around her.

I'm the only one rooted in place, listening as her breathing slows. My own pulse does the same as the adrenaline pumping through my blood begins to ebb. I still can't decide if being a scion is a blessing or a curse.

"None of her rivals would do this," Taliesin says. "Maybe it was an accident."

People don't accidentally get poisoned at Twelvetide, but I'm too tired to tell him that.

"Bellanotte is expensive," Hadrian says, adding, "and hard to get. Someone *wanted* her dead. Or they meant to kill someone else."

We all know he means me. I'm the only target that makes sense. I wait for the old fear to hit, but I'm too tired. Tired of waiting for magic that doesn't come. Tired of being a pawn in other people's games. Whatever happens on this side of the Turning needs to be up to me.

Hadrian is still thumbing through a book like the answer is hidden inside, but his gaze flicks to Bishop for a fraction of a second before returning to the pages. "Lord Perran is here."

"He doesn't have the imagination," Bishop says.

I laugh, but it catches in my throat, my mouth suddenly dry as if I've been breathing cold air for too long. When I stand to get a drink, the room sways beneath my feet. I grab hold of the chair as an icy prickle crawls across my skin.

"Arden?" Bishop's voice is oddly distant.

"I'm fine," I say, but the words come out slurred. "Just . . . tired."

"Did you drink anything at the party?" Hadrian's eyes narrow. At least I think they do. The room is full of fog.

"Not really," I mumble, flopping back into the chair. "Just a sip of wine . . . during the toast." Before Breccan knocked it from my hand. "I didn't even finish it."

Bishop is at my side in two strides, kneeling in front of me, his hands bracketing my face. "Tell me exactly how you feel."

"Tired. Dizzy." The words tangle together, slipping away before I can catch them. I flex my fingers, realizing they feel funny, too. But I can't remember the word for it. I hold my hand out like maybe Bishop can see what's wrong with it.

"Her pupils are dilated," Bishop says quietly. He sounds like he's standing at the end of a tunnel.

I want to ask what that means, but my body answers for me. My arms go slack, the room tilting in a way that makes my head swim. Bishop cradles it against his shoulder.

Someone is moving. I don't know if it's me.

"Stay with me, Arden," Bishop murmurs, the words stretching and blurring.

"I'm here," I manage, though I'm not sure that's true. The world softens at the edges, becoming nothing more than sounds. Shouting. Footsteps. Doors opening and closing.

Someone presses a cloth to my forehead. Another voice tells me to breathe. I do, but it doesn't seem to help. My mind drifts away from the party to memories of Wintour. Shopping with Kieren. Watching eyes and footsteps. Someone following. Always following.

A connection sparks and fizzles as the darkness crowds in, erasing all but one word.

Harbinger.

"Get everyone the fuck out of my house." Bishop's snarl cuts through the haze. I latch on to it like an anchor. "I don't care if it's midnight. Empty it."

"Bit of an ask, boss," Taliesin says. "The posterns won't hold up if you try to send a hundred drunk relatives through them at once."

"Start pushing," Bishop growls.

The last things I hear before I black out are the distant, rhythmic clang of the estate's bell and Bishop's heart pounding under my ear.

The night blurs in fevered flashes stitched together by the fiery ache working its way through my skin. There's something soft against my cheek. Sheets, I realize as I sink into a pillow that smells like leather and mint and a hint of icy winter. The room is dark, but I know it's Bishop's, because even now, I feel safe.

A hand strokes the hair from my face, fingers shaking.

"Come back," he whispers. "I need you." The words echo in my head, clinging there even as I start to slip away again.

I drift, sometimes waking to a palm pressed to my chest, counting my heartbeats. Sometimes the pillow is gone, and I'm cradled in his arms.

And when I wake, thrashing violently to vomit, Bishop catches me before I can fall from the bed. He holds my hair back with one hand, the other bracing my shoulders as he murmurs something low and steady I can't quite hear.

When it's over, he draws a quilt over me. "You're safe," he says roughly. "I swear it."

I want to tell him I know that, but the poison steals the words, and I collapse into the darkness again.

Voices find me in a place between dreams and waking.

"The worst is over," Hadrian says.

"We need to know how much she was given," Bishop growls.

"If it was a lethal dose, she'd be dead by now." Hadrian again.

Something slams, followed by a crack.

"She will recover," Hadrian insists. "Let her rest."

Bishop's voice fades along with me.

I wake shivering, sheets twisted around my legs as dawn seeps through the windows. My skin is covered in a sheen of sweat, but I'm freezing. Bishop is sleeping in a chair by the bed, vestiges peeking past his unbuttoned collar. One of his hands rests on the mattress, as if he couldn't bring himself to let go even after I fell asleep. I reach for him, fingers brushing his hand, and his eyes snap open.

"Arden?" he says hoarsely, voice choked with something that isn't just sleep.

"That's me," I mumble, discovering how dry my lips are.

He leans forward, taking my hand in both of his. "You scared the shit out of me."

I try to laugh, but it comes out as a croak. "I'm not that easy to kill."

Someone tried to kill me. It still feels like I'm caught in a dark cloud, but that's becoming clear enough.

"Here." Bishop brings a cup of water to my mouth, but I'm shaking so hard now that it spills down my breasts.

I blink, realizing that I'm in nothing but my undergarments.

"You were burning up," he explains, pulling the sheets up to cover me.

I smile weakly. "Nothing you haven't seen before." But each word is punctuated by the clack of chattering teeth as the fever works its way from my body. "So cold."

Bishop climbs into the bed and pulls me against his chest. I melt into him, his heat a balm soothing the final chills coursing through me. His lips press into my hair, and he murmurs words that sound dangerously close to a prayer as I settle into the cage of his arms.

This time, when the darkness comes, I fall into it without fear.

I come to in stages, increasingly aware of a hammering behind my eyes. When I finally pry them open, my tongue is thick, my skin clammy, and every joint in my body throbs. When I try to roll over, I discover he's gone. The effort at movement leaves me dizzy, so I settle for blinking up at the ceiling as this processes.

The empty space in the bed beside me hurts worse than any poison.

A soft snore draws my attention to the chair by my bed. Lenora is there, her Twelvetide gown rumpled and her head tilted back as she dozes.

I force myself to sit up, and she startles awake.

"Oh, thank the Stars!" She jumps to her feet and presses the back of her hand to my forehead. "No fever. That's good."

"How long was I out?" I ask.

She glances at the window. "You missed breakfast and nearly missed lunch. I kept some soup warm for you."

I try to get up, but the effort makes my head spin. She urges me back down. "Don't rush. You gave us all quite a scare."

I scan the room for any sign of Bishop. "Where is he?"

"He was called away to Wintour." She busies herself fluffing a pillow and tucking it behind my head. "He waited to leave until you were through the worst."

I swallow that information, unsure how to feel about it. I only remember snatches of last night, but he's in every memory. I force myself to go back further and bolt upright. "Is Shea—"

"She's fine," Lenora says. "A bit worse for wear, but up and about. She left with Breccan a few hours ago."

"And the rest of them?" I vaguely recall shouting.

Lenora's mouth flattens into a line. "Bishop sent everyone home."

I manage a weak laugh. "Didn't think he liked them much anyway."

She smooths the quilt bundled around me. “You need to rest. I’ll bring up a tray.”

She bustles out, and I close my eyes, wishing I could sleep for a hundred years, or until Bishop returns.

Whichever comes first.

But sleep doesn’t come.

Because I keep remembering how he looked at me last night. Like losing me might break him.

And he left anyway.

THIRTY-TWO

"Morning. Glad to see you're still breathing." Two weeks later, and Taliesin's now-standard morning greeting is more upbeat than usual. Because everybody wants to be reminded that half the world wants you dead just in case you become an evil witch before breakfast.

"No assassinations to report," I confirm, dropping into the chair across from him.

"Well, I'm sure they're trying," he says a bit too cheerfully.

Lenora plops a plate of scones with thickened cream and jam in front of him. Pausing, she pats his shoulder. "That joke's not getting any funnier, dear."

But, still, it's somehow comforting.

Not just that I survived another night but that someone noticed. Bishop certainly isn't bothering with that. He's been too busy the last couple of weeks, between interrogating every family member who was at Twelvetide to chasing leads on the heart collector, who struck again over the holidays. This time in Florentia.

Or so I'm told.

Bishop is barely home for more than a few minutes between trips, and every time I see him, he's already walking back out the door.

I force myself to put food on my plate. My appetite hasn't been the same since the bellanotte, as if the poison still lingers in my blood weeks later. Sometimes my hands start to shake when I lift a glass to my lips. Other days, there's a tangle in my stomach that tightens at the first bite of a meal. It's a little better every morning, though I'm not sure I'll ever enjoy sparkling wine again.

Although maybe my lack of appetite has more to do with Bishop's constant absence.

"I thought I'd let Shea take a few swings at you today," Taliesin says around a mouthful of scone. He's doing an admirable job of pretending not to care that Bishop's absence has saddled him with the responsibility of overseeing my training. Since Twelvetide, every session feels less like practice and more like preparation for whatever comes at me next.

But I frown at his suggestion, pushing roasted potatoes around my plate with my fork. "I'm not sure I want to train with Shea. What if I can't fight a friend?"

Taliesin snorts. "Well, now you are definitely training with her." He picks up his mug and downs its contents in a single swig. "You have to be prepared to face a friend."

"Why?" I counter. I still haven't eaten a bite. "It's not like Shea is going to hurt me."

"Trusting people like that is dangerous," he warns me.

"I suddenly understand why you're single."

He laughs, shoving his blond hair out of his eyes, but doesn't correct me. Instead, he nods toward my plate. "Better eat that. Shea won't go easy on you."

I cram a scone into my mouth, staring at the seat Bishop usually occupies. I don't bother reaching for a second. Shea might knock me flat on my back, but that still sounds better than haunting Miradores and wondering where Bishop has gone off to this time. Pushing back my chair, I stand up. "Let's get this over with."

Taliesin sighs as he rises, unable to contain his disappointment.

We head out through the kitchen door. The sky is a wash of gray, a familiar dampness hanging in the air. The oscen peeks from its nest but doesn't come out to greet us. Something tells me my absence is being punished. But with the ground half frozen, I haven't spent as much time in the garden, only coming to take my frustration out on the stump I'm still trying to dig up.

"Want to talk about it?" Taliesin asks as we reach the bridge.

"About what?"

Taliesin says, "About the reason you're not eating."

"I haven't been sleeping well."

"Neither has he," Taliesin says, calling my bluff.

"Good," I say, and that's the end of it. We walk the rest of the way in silence.

A few lanterns burn dimly along the paths, but this early on seventh day, the Bellatorum is still quiet. Most of the conscripts must have opted to spend their day off from classes and drills in bed. We're nearly to the proving grounds when Taliesin curses.

Looking up, I find we're on a collision course with Bishop. His coat is unbuttoned despite the cold, and the shadows under his eyes are darker than usual.

"I'll go round up Shea," Taliesin mutters and veers ahead. He doesn't wait for me to answer, just slips into the side entrance, leaving me alone with Bishop in the empty courtyard.

We stand there, neither one wanting to make the first move. Finally, Bishop breaks the stalemate. "You're up early."

"So are you." I take a deep breath. "Where have you been?"

"Business." He shifts his attention over my shoulder like his mind is already somewhere else.

My jaw tightens at the dismissal, but I refuse to give up. "Doing what? Or are you too busy to talk to me, too?"

Something splinters in his wintery blue eyes, but it's gone before I can name it.

"I have responsibilities, Arden."

That's bullshit. "Is this about Twelvetide?"

He hesitates. "It's my duty to find the person who poisoned two of my subjects."

"Subjects?" I repeat.

"I am responsible for you," he reminds me. "You are under my protection."

"Is that why you're ignoring me?"

He exhales slowly. "You don't understand, Arden."

"Then explain it to me."

"I am supposed to keep you safe, not . . ." He stops, pressing his lips into a thin line.

"Not fuck me," I finish for him when he refuses to say it.

He winces. "Not get distracted."

A hollow laugh bursts out of me. "So, pushing me away is your big solution?"

What about the Turning? The baths? He said it meant something. He saved my mother's locket. How can he act like there's nothing between us?

"I have to." He drags a hand through his hair, refusing to look at me.

For a second, I only stare. "So that's it, then?" I finally say. "You're just going to pretend nothing happened between us?"

He doesn't flinch. "I'm a bishop. I swore an oath."

I jab a finger into his chest so hard that he actually rocks back a step. "This isn't because you're a bishop." My voice cracks, and I swallow. "It's because you're a coward. Just like I was that night in the baths. You convinced me to live again, remember?"

He can't take that back now. But his face remains as stony as the nearby statues.

I don't bother waiting for an answer before I turn and hurry toward the proving grounds, the threat of tears stinging my eyes.

When I reach them, Shea is waiting, already suited up in her training uniform. She takes one look at my face and frowns. "What happened?"

"Nothing," I say, ignoring the lump lingering in my throat as I tighten the strap on my left bracer. "Let's just get started."

Shea nods, but she doesn't look convinced, shaking her head before we continue to the weapons rack. She pauses to consider her choice. I just grab the first sword I see. Its blade is longer than I'm accustomed to, but isn't that the whole point of this exercise—to throw me in the water and see if I drown?

Taliesin meets us as we head into the arena. "Ready?" he asks, eyeing me like he expects me to explode.

"More than ready," I growl.

Taliesin and Shea share a look.

"Are you sure you're okay?" Shea asks again as we take our places.

"I'm fine," I snap as Taliesin circles us, pausing just once to assess my grip.

The ground beneath our boots is packed down from yesterday's rain, the broken stones a hazardous mix of jagged rocks, sand, and mud. Cold air gusts through the training pit, carrying the briny scent of the sea.

"Remember, you're not friends when there are swords in your hands," he mutters low enough that Shea can't hear him. He's smiling, but the words are so cold, they raise the hairs on the back of my neck. "Okay. Rules are simple: first to disarm or land a blow to the neck, chest, or head gets the point."

I'm not sure I can take any more blows today. Not after the one Bishop just delivered to my heart.

Taliesin steps away and nods for us to begin. I plant my foot, my sword only half raised when Shea lunges, her blade aimed at my ribs. I block it, barely, the shock of the sudden impact vibrating through my fingers.

Stop thinking about him and fight.

Shea moves for the left, second blow coming before I can reset my stance. I twist awkwardly, only for her sword to arc over her head and slice down, narrowly avoiding my right shoulder. But it's a distraction. Her sword cuts low, and I stumble back, losing my footing as the blade taps my thigh. I hit the ground hard, the air punching from my lungs with a force that rattles my teeth.

"One!" Taliesin calls.

I blink up at Shea as she offers me a hand. I guess Taliesin was right about not being friends in here. Ignoring her extended hand, I scramble back to my feet. People are trying to kill me. This is survival. I need to learn to protect myself—because I'm not sure I can stay in Vennaro. And the last thing I want is to prove that Bishop's right, that I'm so weak he has to protect me instead of . . .

"Taliesin told me not to go easy on you," she says, almost apologetically, as we begin to circle each other.

"Good." I flex my wrist, rebalancing the weight of my sword. "You won't break me."

And neither will he. I won't let him.

This time, I attack first. The high slash is meant to drive her back as I pivot to the side, aiming for her shoulder. She parries every move, like she can anticipate them, and when I hesitate, torn between lunging and feinting, she spins, crossing our swords at an angle that forces mine from my hand.

"That's two," Taliesin says, keeping track like everyone can't see who is winning.

I might be here, but my head is still back in that courtyard. I force myself to focus and close the distance, trying to knock Shea off-balance. But I'm too fucking slow, and she sidesteps. She presses forward, sending me into retreat.

I try to counter with a thrust to her shoulder, but she blocks the move like she expects it. Bishop hates when I do that. The thought costs me. Shea locks our blades and shoves hard enough that I stumble again—and wind up back in the mud.

"Three," Taliesin says, his voice a bit quieter.

Heat floods my face as I push onto my feet, anger rising through me. The trouble is I want to aim it at the person who caused it. Not Shea. We keep sparring. I lose every point until finally Taliesin says, "I think that's enough."

"Still friends?" Shea asks as we hang the training swords up.

I rub the sore spot on my rear. "That depends on how big this bruise is."

"We could hit the baths," she suggests.

Even if I was comfortable, the offer only brings back too many memories.

Before I can tell her no, her gaze catches on something over my shoulder. "I think he wants to talk to you."

I turn to find Taliesin leaning against the wall with his arms folded.

"I'll catch up with you in a second," I say. Shea nods, shooting me an encouraging smile before she leaves me to face my next beatdown.

I force myself to walk toward him, even though I know what he's going to say.

"In a real fight, you'd be dead," Taliesin says. "*Many* times over."

It's a reminder that I don't need. "Thanks for the feedback."

"You lost before you even stepped into the arena," he says, ignoring my sarcasm.

I clench my fists, trying to distract myself from the pressure behind my ribs. "I thought the point was to train."

"The point is to stay alive. You know what gets people killed?" He lets the silence stretch until I'm squirming. "Distraction. Thinking about something else—about *someone* else—instead of the opponent in front of you."

"Or maybe Shea is just better than I am," I say coolly.

"She is." He nods. "But you weren't fighting her today. You were fighting yourself."

I want to protest that it was just an off day, but he's right. My head wasn't in the fight. "I understand."

He leans in, voice dropping as conscripts walk by. "Do you? Because they've come for you on Marius land now. They're tired of waiting to kill you. And next time, you won't get multiple rounds. You won't get a second chance. If you can't be present in the fight, you won't survive."

The words land harder than any of Shea's blows, because they're true. But I'm not about to lose another round. Not after letting Shea kick my ass, and especially not after what happened with Bishop. "I was poisoned at a party," I say. "I'm not sure a sword would have helped."

He smiles, but it doesn't reach his eyes. "Not everyone who wants you dead will be so civilized in their attempts."

"I'm the one who nearly died," I spit back, "and there was nothing civilized about it."

But he doesn't bother with sympathy. "Whatever this thing is with Bishop," Taliesin says, disregarding how I bristle at the mention of his name, "you need to decide if it's worth dying for."

I stare at him, unable to muster a response. Maybe it was once, but Bishop is the one who gave up. Who resurrected the boundary between us. If Bishop wants distance, he can have it. I'm through hiding.

Taliesin pushes off the wall and straightens to his full height. "Keep the personal shit out of the fight. If you can't, go dig a new grave next to your friend."

When I finally find Shea near the entrance to the baths, Taliesin's words are still echoing in my head:

Dig a new grave.

Fuck him.

Except . . . he's not wrong, and I know it. If there's a sword in my hand, I can't let Bishop linger in my head. The trouble is that I don't know how to get him out of there.

"That looks like it went well," Shea says as I reach her.

"I think his lecture hurt worse than your ass-kicking," I admit.

"It sounds like you need to go to the baths," she prods, jerking her head toward the door. "It'll help with the bruises. I know you're self-conscious about the mark, but I promise to kill anyone who says something."

The offer twists into a now-familiar discomfort. The thought of people seeing me, of going back into the place where Bishop told me . . .

I shake the thought away. I can't keep hiding, and there's only one way to stop.

"Sure," I say.

Shea blinks in surprise before a grin bursts onto her face.

"Yeah, yeah. You win again," I admit as she leads me inside.

"It's probably not even busy today," she says when we find the dressing room empty.

A faint hiss of steam drifts toward us through the archway that leads to the pools, followed by the faint echo of dozens of voices from the main chamber beyond.

"Or I could be wrong about that," she says with a frown.

"I don't mind." It's a lie, but maybe if I try hard enough, I'll start believing it.

Shea continues on, then stops in her tracks.

"Let's come back later," she suggests, trying to steer me back outside.

"I'll be fine," I promise, tugging her toward the lockers. But I only make it one more step before I see why she's stopped. Bishop is standing in the infirmary, speaking with Vessica. For a second, I consider turning around.

Then Taliesin's voice rings through my head again.

You need to decide if it's worth dying for.

Coward. I'm not the one running from this thing between us, and maybe Bishop needs to see that.

I square my shoulders before Shea can protest again and walk straight past the little office. Bishop looks up just as I pass the doorway, and our eyes meet for half a heartbeat.

I keep walking.

Let him watch.

Behind me, Shea mutters something under her breath and hurries to catch up. "Well done," she says when she reaches me. "He looks like you ran him through."

I flinch at the thought but quickly arrange my face into disinterest and shrug.

She studies me for a moment before she shucks off her training vest. Laughter and conversation float toward us, and suddenly I'm relieved there will be plenty of people to distract me inside. We strip quickly in the changing area, both of us moving faster than usual.

Steam curls around the doorway as we enter the bathing chamber. Every conversation falters almost immediately.

And I haven't even dropped my towel yet.

"Let's use this one," Shea suggests, acting like she doesn't notice that all eyes in the room are on me. It's the pool closest to the door, which is probably why it's empty.

I force a smile, trying to remember how to breathe with the sudden weight sitting on my chest. I can feel them watching, but I know they aren't looking at me. They're staring at the raven-mark. I lift my chin as I descend the steps, refusing to let their curiosity chase me away. Hiding the mark didn't stop someone from poisoning me. I'm through with living like they succeeded. But when the water welcomes me with a rush of heat, I still sink under it to the neck.

At first, no one speaks. Then the whispering starts, low murmurs rippling through the room like the buzz of insects.

Shea slides into the water beside me. "You don't have to do this," she whispers. "We can leave."

I stare straight ahead. "I'm *fine*."

Apparently, that's my word of the day.

"You don't look fine." She glances around us. "Do you want me to say something?"

"I've endured worse." I shrug. Compared to what happened with Bishop, this is nothing. "And I can take care of myself."

She nods like she understands.

Silence falls through the chamber again, and I draw a deep breath, preparing to tell everyone to fuck right off. But before I can stand up and let them all have a good look at the harbinger, a shadow falls across the pool. Glancing up, I freeze.

Bishop is standing a few steps away. His arms are folded over his chest, the expression on his face carved from ice as he scans the room, looking at every pool . . . except the one I'm in.

The whispering dies instantly.

"Oh shit," Shea breathes.

Perfect.

Ignore me for weeks, but the second people start staring, he's here to play savior.

Water slides down my skin as I rise from the bath. "I think I'm done after all."

Shea looks between me and where he's still glowering like a very handsome gargoyle. "Are you sure?"

"Stay." Something tells me this is going to be ugly. "Enjoy your relaxation."

One of us should be able to.

Understanding flickers across her face. "Okay."

I don't rush up the steps, and somehow the utter silence is worse than the whispering as everyone tries to make a point of *not* looking. I swipe my towel from the edge of the pool and wrap it around myself as I walk calmly back into the changing room, counting each second in my head.

I make it to thirty before he follows. For a second, we just stare at each other.

Then the anger hits.

"I don't need you to protect me," I snap.

His brows draw together. "Arden—"

"No," I cut him off. "You don't get to ignore me for weeks and then show up claiming I'm some huge burden. Stop acting like you're in charge of my life."

"I wanted you to feel safe." He holds up his hands, backing away a step. "That's the arrangement."

I laugh harshly. "The arrangement was to train me to take care of myself, which is what I've been doing while you skulked around the country, forgetting I exist. I don't want your protection anymore."

But he shakes his head. "As long as you're under my roof—"

"I'll find another one," I interrupt.

The words hang there, both of us knowing that's easier said than done. But I can't stay here if he's going to make me feel like I'm nothing more than a mistake he made. One that he's now stuck watching over.

Bishop goes completely still. "You don't mean that."

I didn't, but seeing his face now makes me certain that I don't have another choice. Maybe one of us will always fuck this up. Always retreat when things get complicated. After everything, I don't think my heart can survive that push and pull again. "Watch me." I look him in the eye. "Please leave so I can get dressed."

A muscle tightens in his jaw. "I'm not finished—"

"I am," I cut him off again. He can issue whatever edicts he wants. He can walk away. But I don't have to stand here and listen to his excuses.

He hesitates like he might argue. Instead, he turns and walks out of the bathhouse. The second the door closes behind him, the strength drains out of me. The room tilts the way it did the night I was poisoned, and I sink onto the bench so I don't collapse.

I fold forward, the tears slipping free before I can stop them. Because part of me hates him for not turning around. For sacrificing whatever this is between us and calling it duty. I hate myself even more, because he warned me. That night on the balcony. He implied he would always choose his oath. He proved it every time he restrained himself.

And I was stupid enough to turn a moment of weakness into something more.

When I finally leave, my skin is still damp, the winter air biting into it as I make my way home.

No. It's not home.

Not anymore.

My steps slow as my mind races. Not toward where Miradores looms across the bridge. But to some distant future that I can't quite see. Suddenly, I'm grateful Lenora made me put Kieren's money aside. It's not much, but it's a start. If I'm serious about leaving, I need a plan. Somewhere to go. It doesn't matter where as long as it isn't here. I won't hide behind his shadow just to stay alive. And ever since that night on the stairs, I know my magic is starting to awaken. I can't be here when it fully does.

For so many reasons. Including the one I've been desperately trying to ignore. That I was right when I pushed Bishop away that first time. But I'm not ready to face that yet. Not ready to admit I might be the one who destroys us all.

The bridge creaks like it's greeting me, and I swallow a new wave of sadness at what's waiting for me on the other side.

Lenora's cooking. Taliesin's terrible jokes. Hadrian and his rules.

All of it was beginning to fit together into somewhere I could belong, and now I have to tear it apart.

But stepping through the gate, I find Bishop in the garden.

He's not waiting for me. His coat and shirt are gone. Despite the cold, sweat glistens on his skin, catching on the lines of his vestiges as his shovel bites into the hard soil around the stump I've been fighting for weeks. Its roots rip free, dirt scattering as it topples over with a heavy *thud*.

"What are you doing?" The question is out of my mouth before I can stop myself.

He glances up, sweat streaking the dirt on his face. "Fixing something I should have handled a long time ago."

A pang starts behind my ribs. I fold my arms over my chest, but it does nothing to soothe the sudden ache there. "I don't need your help."

"Yes," he says, wiping a hand across his slick forehead. "You made that very clear."

But he's still here. "Then stop."

"That's not how this works," he says softly, setting down the shovel.

I hold my breath, trying to ignore the urge to move closer. "Is avoiding each other how it works?"

His eyes meet mine as he takes a tentative step in my direction. "I almost lost you."

A hot rush of tears fills my throat, but I swallow them down. "I'm right here."

He shakes his head. "I didn't know if you were going to make it through the night," he continues quietly. "I can't let that happen again. I *won't*."

But I know exactly how he felt that night. I watched Kieren die, and I couldn't do anything.

"We all lose people." The truth catches in my burning throat. "Shutting everyone out won't change that. It's just forgetting how to live."

His jaw locks, the muscle there jumping slightly as he looks over my shoulder.

"Right," I murmur. "Good luck with that." I turn, gulping hard to keep more tears from falling before I can get away.

Bishop grabs my wrist, and then I'm spinning, time reversing in an instant to somewhere before the angry words and broken promises. To that fleeting moment where we belonged to each other—and I find myself in his arms again.

"It's been so long since . . . since there was life in this garden. In this house." He presses me closer. My hands land on his chest, and I'm back in the night that he died, and he's solid. Real again. "Since I felt alive."

His face angles closer, his breath whispering across mine, but he doesn't kiss me.

And I can't admit that I want him to—can't risk it even if there are no assassins waiting around the corner.

"Don't let me disappear again. Don't let me become a ghost." He gives the words to me like that dagger in the astrolatory. Like it's my choice. Like his fate has always been up to me.

Mercy.

Sacrifice.

I think we'll always be tangled in both.

Maybe the knife is the least painful path.

But maybe *I* was never the one who needed saving.

Because something wild beats in his eyes, pounds in his chest. Caged and broken by a life he can't control no matter how hard he tries. Trapped like that bird.

I surge up, bringing my mouth to his, and release it.

THIRTY-THREE

Our relationship isn't a secret. But after the garden, we just . . . don't tell anyone. As if we can steal a little more time before whatever crisis comes next. Since Twelvetide, any moment of peace feels borrowed anyway.

Keeping things quiet might work better if everyone at Miradores didn't seem to know already.

Taliesin gives up his lectures and doubles down on sly comments. Lenora takes to leaving breakfast trays outside our respective bedroom doors like she's not sure where to deliver them. Even Vessica smiles when I enter a room.

Bishop spends half his nights chasing those whispers across Vennaro. The other half, he spends here.

In my bed.

His arms tighten around me in the dim light. "The equinox is coming," he murmurs into my hair, and I go still. "I wasn't sure if . . ."

It's been months since Kieren's body was laid to rest in a plot in the private Marius cemetery, but it still feels impossible to think of his soul being gone, too. To imagine the world rebalancing its days without him here.

Some people never let go, never let the world rebalance. I've seen it happen. "My father waited four equinoxes before he released my mother's spirit," I whisper.

"If you aren't ready, it can wait until the next one," he says, stroking my back. "There is no timeline on grieving."

But that's not what Kieren would want. Not the boy who read pirate stories. Nor the man who died before he could go on his own. His soul deserves to be free. To go on its adventure.

I take a deep breath. We've never discussed this, so I'm not sure he'll agree to my decision. But it's for me to make. "I want to go to Damalis. To perform his Evensong there." The words rush out of me, tired of swirling in my brain and finally ready to be spoken. "We don't actually know where he was born. Our father never told us. Kieren didn't remember, but it feels . . . right."

His hand pauses on my back.

"Damalis," he repeats softly.

"I know that you want me to stay in Vennaro," I whisper. "I know it's safer here, but I need to do this." I brace for the argument I already know is coming. The one that's stopped me from even bringing it up.

Instead, he pulls me closer.

"If that feels right to you," he says, "then we'll go."

Relief loosens the knot in my chest. "You'd come with me?"

"Of course." He brushes a kiss across my temple.

"Thank you."

But he scoffs. "Don't thank me." He shifts his weight, rolling me onto my back. "You've carried this long enough. Let me carry some of it with you."

The offer feels like shelter, and something even more dangerous.

His lips find my jaw as he settles between my legs, and then he works his way to my mouth.

The kiss is gentle.

Until it isn't.

Warmth spreads through me, chasing the cold edge of grief away, as our bodies begin to move and we find life again together.

Afterward, I curl against him, listening as his breath slows to a steady, comforting rhythm.

But I can't sleep.

Wriggling free of his arms, I dress quietly in the dark, grab the book from Kieren's box of belongings, and go to the one place I know someone else is still up.

The library is lit by a single lamp when I slip inside, the fire little more than pulsing embers, allowing the dark to swallow most of the shelves.

But it's not empty. It never is. There's something comforting about that.

Hadrian sits at one of the long tables, the sleeves of his robe pushed back, a sheaf of papers spread before him in careful disarray. His pen moves steadily, as if the hour means nothing.

"Do you ever sleep?" I ask, yawning despite my own insomnia.

He keeps working. "Sleep is for people who've made peace with their questions."

I haven't made peace with mine. The biggest one is still under my collarbone, waiting to formally introduce itself. I shove the thought away and focus on why I came down here at this hour. I'm seeking a different kind of peace.

"He read this until it fell apart." I set Kieren's book on the library table. "I thought maybe there was a place for it here."

There's not much of him left, only a few things to give away before the equinox brings his final rest. The ones I'm struggling to part with.

Hadrian nods and picks it up gingerly, scanning the title. "We need more fiction in here."

I drift closer, curiosity pulling me, despite the ache still lodged in my bones. "Still searching for the *revello*?"

His shoulders droop, but he nods. "I've been retranslating that passage, hoping I missed something." He taps the sheet of paper to his left. "The ancient tongue is tricky. Words have multiple meanings."

"Sounds lazy of them," I say, trying not to yawn.

Hadrian almost smiles. "Indeed. I translated this word"—he points to his notes—"as *liberate*, but it could also mean to hold, seize, or possess."

"That's a lot of possibilities." And probably why they're having such a hard time tracking down said *revello*.

"Too many," he says with a deep sigh.

I'm unlikely to be useful, but as I lean over his shoulder to get a better look at the research, my gaze catches on the page beneath his hand. At the top, an eye has been drawn into the center of a star, likely some archaic reminder that the Stars are always watching us, but my breath stalls when I see what's sketched under it.

An ash-black diagram sprawls across the parchment, its lines elegant but somehow deliberate. They intersect and diverge, vanishing like the artist forgot to finish. It takes me a moment to realize where I've seen it.

"That illustration," I say, pointing at the diagram. "I've seen it before. What is it?"

Hadrian's pen stills. Slowly, he looks up at me. "Where?"

A question for a question . . . That's always a bad sign.

I hesitate, feeling something familiar but unwanted creeping over my skin. "A bookshop in Wintour." I fail to add exactly what I was doing in that bookshop or who I was hiding from. "That illustration was on the cover."

Hadrian is on his feet before I finish speaking.

"Was there anything else on the cover?" he asks, already gathering the papers. "Every detail you can remember."

"The raven," I say, heart beginning to race now. "Fire. And beneath it—this. *Exactly* this."

The color drains from his face.

"We need to find Bishop," he says, "now." He heads straight out the door.

Whatever this is must be dire if he's leaving the library.

I follow behind him, racing to keep up with his longer legs. "What is it?"

"The *Ars Astra*." Each word lands more seriously than the last.

Ravenell's dark work.

Hadrian glances at me, his face still stricken. "If I'm right, the book you're describing . . . It might contain information about the *revello*."

The thing they've been chasing after for all this time, and I had it in my hands. Maybe someday I'll stop being surprised at these little taunts from fate.

He turns right when we reach the landing, heading toward the western wing. I guess there is one person who hasn't noticed us sneaking around after all.

I pause, scrounging up my courage, before I call out, "He's not there."

"Where is he?" Hadrian whirls toward me, looking even more panicked. "We need to reach him. He needs to go after the book tonight."

"He's in my room," I admit, heat flooding my cheeks. Which is a sure indicator of *exactly* why Bishop is there, in case Hadrian hasn't figured it out.

But judging by his deeply unimpressed stare, he has now. "Go." He sighs, calling after me, "And for the love of Stars, make sure he puts his clothes on before he comes out."

I'm already halfway down the opposite corridor, spurred faster by my need to escape Hadrian's fatherly disapproval. The man should reconsider being a vesper.

I burst into the room, the door banging into the wall so hard that Bishop jerks awake. He's on his feet and halfway across the room, stark naked and sword in hand, before he realizes the intruder is just me.

I'm too breathless to laugh.

"Hadrian needs you," I say, panting around the words.

He drops the sword on my bed and reaches for his clothes. "Why?"

I repeat everything that happened in the library as he dresses. When I'm done, I sit on the bed and begin pulling on my own boots.

"What are you doing?" he asks as he buckles his baldric over his shoulder.

"I'm going with you."

He pauses, his red cloak still in his hands. "If you enter Wintour, the palace will know within the hour. And if the queen learns you're there, she'll summon you for an audience."

I grimace. That's the last thing we need.

"She could keep you there for days," he adds.

But he doesn't tell me I *can't* go. "I could sneak in. If we're quick—"

His mouth twitches slightly. "Even I have to answer to the queen, Arden."

The whole point is to retrieve the book without drawing attention. Something that will be easier for him to do alone.

"Fine." I sigh. "Go."

He crosses to the bed and kneels in front of me, cupping my cheek. "I won't be gone long, and then I'll take you back to bed."

That promise might normally be enough to distract me, but I'm growing to hate these little quests. If anyone at the palace ever realizes what he's up to, or worse, why . . . Dread crawls down my spine.

"Just . . . be careful." I burrow against his palm for a second.

His hand shifts, pulling me into a kiss that lingers long enough to make the decision feel worse.

"I always am," he murmurs.

Then he's gone.

I definitely don't sleep after that. I attempt waiting in the library with Hadrian, but his pacing and anxious muttering only make my own nerves worse.

I eat half the food in the kitchen, and Bishop doesn't return.

I try lying down again, but every time the wind rattles the windows, I bolt up, expecting him to walk through the door. When a storm begins, the lightning chases me back to the library and Hadrian's company.

But as dawn approaches, even he's drooping in and out of consciousness in a chair by the hearth. When the library doors finally open just after sunrise, I'm exhausted and more than a little worried.

Bishop strides into the library, and I leap to my feet, relief washing over me. But his expression tells me everything before he even speaks. "It's gone."

Hadrian stirs, pushing his glasses up on his nose as he blinks away sleep. "What?" he mumbles. "What do you mean, gone? Did they sell it?"

"Not the book," Bishop says grimly, pulling off his gloves. "The entire shop."

I blink at him, stomach sinking. That's why he was gone all night. "How?"

He shakes his head. "Cleared out." His mouth tightens. "The windows are boarded up, every shelf is empty. There's no trace of any of it. The building looks like it's been abandoned for weeks. No one I questioned knew where the owner has gone."

"But you were there a month ago." It can't have simply disappeared.

"Longer. It was right after Twelvetide." He collapses into the armchair across from mine and stares into the fire.

"I had it in my hands," I say quietly. "And I just left it there."

Hadrian pinches the bridge of his nose, forcing a smile. "You didn't know what it was."

"And I should have found it." Bishop exhales, nostrils flaring as he glances at me.

I know what he isn't saying. That he might have if I hadn't been hiding from him with the book in my hands.

"There will be other traces of it." Hadrian rises, staring toward the stacks with determination. We leave him there, Bishop following me up the stairs.

I sent him halfway across the kingdom for nothing.

When we reach my room, I pause in the doorway. "I should sleep."

"And I promised to take you back to bed." He moves closer.

Part of me wants to let him do just that. The rest wants to fall asleep standing up.

I fiddle with the hem of his cloak and force myself to be responsible. "Tomorrow?"

Stepping into my room, I shut the door before I can change my mind.

But Bishop knocks a moment later. I shouldn't open the door. I should crawl into bed and let sleep drag me away from the hole of self-recrimination I seem determined to dig.

I open it anyway and find him standing there, holding a paper bag.

"You won't be wanting these, then?" He shakes it, letting the buttery scent of crescent pastries waft toward me.

I snatch it from his hand, and this time I don't close the door in his face.

THIRTY-FOUR

My ancestors named our estate Journey's End. I never understood that before today. Probably because I'd never been away from it for this long. It looks exactly like my memory of it. The same low stone walls separate the fields leading to my family's home, freshly tilled and ready for spring planting. Thin green shoots are already pushing stubbornly through the soil. The same olive trees line the gravel drive. Even the air smells the same. The house's limestone facade glows in the honey-gold morning light, showcasing every crack and weathered patch. As usual, the shutters need repainting and several of the roof tiles are missing.

But everything has changed.

My siblings are waiting by the door. Well, Andry and Isidore. Broderic is nowhere to be seen. As soon as they spot me, they start to wave. Andry jumps up and down like I might miss him. He looks taller. I wave back, something swelling around my heart, a bubble of joy that feels too fragile to last.

Especially, I suspect, once Bishop arrives.

Convincing him to give me some time alone with my family was damn near impossible. He insisted on a sword as my travel companion for the two-mile trek to my family estate.

At least we can compromise.

I grab the sheathed sword and jump out of the carriage before it's fully stopped. The driver slows just enough for me to send him back for Bishop at the outpost. The request is barely out of my mouth before both my sister and brother attack me. I only stop hugging them long enough to fasten the baldric over my shoulder.

"Is that real?" Andry gawks at it. Even Isidore's mouth falls open for a second.

"Can't be too careful." I force a smile, feeling a bit silly to be entering my family home armed.

"Awesome!" Andry stares at it longingly.

Since him with a sword is a very bad idea, I change the subject.

"Where's Broderic?" I glance around like he might jump out from behind a bush.

Isidore sucks air through her teeth. Her hesitation tells me enough.

But Andry kicks a rock with the toe of his boot. "He's with *her*," he says, the final word flat with disapproval.

"Her?" I look at Isidore.

"His fiancée." She twists her hands together, and suddenly I understand her jitteriness.

For a moment, I can only stare. "He's getting . . . married?"

"He proposed at Twelvetide." She gives me a sad smile. "The wedding is this summer, but she's already moved into the house."

He's given up on Miranda, then. That's no surprise. But this . . .

A good match will stabilize the estate. Though I can't help feeling like I've lost my older brother. At least the one who used to climb onto the barn roof with Kieren and me, the one who accidentally burned down that barn when a dare went wrong. The bubble in my chest pops, taking any hope I had with it. I try to keep my disappointment tucked behind a smile as they drag me toward the back entrance. Andry runs ahead, off to get whatever latest obsession he's dying to show me.

"You already started dinner?" I ask, my stomach growling at the scent of baking bread. There's a pot simmering on the stove, and for just a moment, I feel like I'm home.

"Not me."

Before I can ask who, I stop in my tracks, spotting an armed guard in the hall. An ache spreads where the bubble was moments ago. They replaced Kieren. It's not like my best friend was ever truly our guard, but seeing someone occupying that position . . .

"Laurel's personal bodyguard," Isidore whispers. "Her uncle insisted. Because Damalis is *so* dangerous."

Maybe not before my Kindling. I swallow the thought.

Surprise takes its place. Clearly, someone is cooking. I hadn't expected Broderic to land someone so . . . *domestic*.

"And who is her uncle?" I ask Isidore, my fingers trailing along the grooves in the kitchen door where we used to mark our heights.

She hesitates, but she knows what I'm really asking. "Patron Velesont."

I can't help thinking of Patron Velesont's cruel interest the night the king died. How he lobbied to have me executed. And Broderic was in the room when he called for my execution. Now he's marrying into his family?

"Is she . . ." But I trail away as Andry returns.

He's holding a wooden sword. It looks remarkably like the ones issued to new conscripts for training. "Laurel brought it for me. She's always bringing new things home." He waves it erratically, nearly knocking over a vase of daisies on the nearest table. "It's just like the ones Order Marius uses."

He's young enough to still dream of being a hero. I hold out my hand. "Let me see."

He passes it to me. "There are lots of soldiers in Damalis now. Laurel says I can join up if I want."

I'm already sure I won't like her.

"Did she?" I say, forcing a smile. "I have something for you, too. From Kieren."

I reach into the satchel I brought from Vennaro. There are only two pieces of him left.

They belong here with them.

I fish the letter out and offer it to my sister. "It was addressed to you. He must have forgotten to send it."

Isidore takes the folded paper carefully, as if she's afraid it might dissolve in her hands. "There's no envelope." She looks up, searching my face. "You opened it?"

I hesitate. She doesn't need to know why I threw the envelope away. Neither of them do. "I didn't read it."

She stares at the letter but doesn't open it.

Turning, I press the pegasus token into Andry's palm.

"He never went anywhere without it," I whisper.

Andry's fingers close around it like it's something alive.

Something precious.

But it's another thread cut loose so Kieren's soul can move on.

"I'm going to put it in my room." He scrambles down the hall.

Isidore is still staring at the letter. "I think I'll put this away, too," she says softly. "I'll be right out."

I trail behind them until I reach my own bedroom's door. Pushing it open, I find the bones of my childhood wearing different skin. The flowered paper my mother hung is gone, the walls now painted deep crimson. The small daybed I slept in until I left for my Kindling has been replaced by a large canopy bed with thick curtains. There's not a trace of my old life, but I step inside anyway, trying to ignore the slight throb in my chest.

I left this place behind. It was my choice.

That doesn't make it any easier. Not when this room held all my dreams. My mother tucked me into bed in this room. I cried myself to sleep in it when my first love broke my heart. I stared at the moon out that window.

I wrap my arms around my waist, trying to hold the memories in. It's not about the wallpaper or my things being gone. It's about the hole their loss carved in my chest. The one that makes me feel like a little girl standing in the middle of a life that doesn't exist anymore, looking for the bed where her mother used to sit with her. But there's no bed. No mother. There's not really even me here anymore. It's just . . . *gone.*

"What are you doing in here?" a harsh voice interrupts.

I spin around and find a woman standing there. Her brown curls are piled like a crown on top of her head, diamond earrings dangling from her ears. The silk overcoat she's wearing probably costs as much as every stitch of clothing I've ever owned. But it's the sneer she's wearing that tells me she's a Velesont. "I'm sorry. I didn't know the room was being used."

"Who . . ." She trails away with a blink. Instantly, her face rearranges into a smile sweet enough to choke on. "You must be Arden. Broderic told me you might be coming for the equinox."

My mouth is open to correct her when Broderic strides into the room, eyes on the shiny new astrolabe he's carrying. "I suspect that your uncle—"

"We have company," Laurel cuts him off, hooking an arm possessively through his. "Your sister is here. Isn't it wonderful?"

Considering the way she's digging her fingernails into Broderic's arm, I don't think she means it.

My brother doesn't smile when he looks up. "You came."

"I sent word." Not that he responded.

"I suppose . . ." But he doesn't finish the thought.

Laurel's smile is beginning to crack, but she turns the flattery back on me. "You must come to dinner this evening. We'll have a little party."

I shoot a confused look at Broderic. "Tonight is the equinox," I remind him.

"I know that." His tone is clipped.

The words slide through me, hollowing a space in my chest.

"It's Kieren's Evensong," I add. He can't have forgotten, which means . . .

"The guard who died?" Laurel asks, smiling like I've made a joke. "You came for *that*?"

I bristle, heat climbing up my throat.

Broderic has the grace to wince. He withdraws his arm, patting her hand. "Can you give me a moment with my sister?"

"Of course." She plants a kiss on his cheek, eyeing me over his shoulder as she leaves the room like I can't be trusted. She doesn't close the door behind her.

"Did you receive my message?" I ask. Bishop told me he sent it, and it's not as though Broderic is surprised to see me.

No, it's more like he was hoping I would change my mind. He shifts on his feet, pocketing the new astrolabe, and I realize that everything he's wearing is new and much too fine for a farmer.

"You are welcome to perform an Evensong." He finally meets my eyes. "But we won't be attending."

I feel like I'm falling into that pit he's opened in my chest. He can't do this. Not to Kieren. "Seven hells, you're not," I snap. "You have to be there. We were his family."

"No, we were not." Broderic folds his arms over his expensive new vest. "Kieren left this house without word after he stole from me. That is not how family behaves."

I shake my head, feeling a little dizzy. "He wouldn't do that."

"He took the astrolabe. Not that he responded to any of our messages." Broderic's eyes flick away, disgust twisting his mouth.

The astrolabe. Kieren told me he sold it to pay for our passage. Now, the funds are in a tin in the kitchen at Miradores. "He needed money. He wanted—"

"I'm not interested in whatever excuse he gave you. I asked him to return, and he ignored my messages."

The accusation destroys the last of my control. "He was dead! He died in the dirt." My voice breaks as I say it. "Trying to save my life."

Even after what's happened. That should mean something to Broderic.

But he tilts his head and glares back. "None of that would have happened if you'd come home with me."

Each word is a stab to the heart. Before I can summon a response, his eyes pin my gaze. They're the same color as mine, hazel like our mother's, but it's the only way we're alike now. I can't stand looking at them a second longer. Turning on my heel, I march out of my stolen bedroom—and find Bishop standing in the hall. Judging by the look on his face, he arrived in time to overhear our fight. I glance into the sitting room, where the others are waiting. They probably heard it, too.

"Obviously, you won't be able to stay here." Broderic continues as he follows me out, but he stops short when he sees him.

Bishop doesn't move. He just stares back at Broderic until my brother shrinks toward the doorframe. "I've arranged for her to stay at the outpost," Bishop says. "For her safety."

That was his request. I'd only asked Bishop to keep a careful distance, not wanting to distract from Kieren's Evensong.

And now there isn't going to be one.

But Broderic looks between the two of us. "I see."

"Is that a problem?" Bishop asks.

"Arden made it clear months ago that this is no longer her home." My brother doesn't sound as certain as he did a minute before.

"Why don't the two of us discuss this inside your study?" He doesn't wait, striding down the hallway like he knows exactly where it is. Of course he would, after meeting Broderic here to arrange the reopening of the Cinderwald outpost.

Broderic hesitates before following his lead. I consider joining them, uncertain leaving the two alone is a good idea.

The door to the study closes before I can make up my mind.

Resisting the temptation to eavesdrop proves nearly impossible, so I make my way back to the sitting room. My siblings are there with Laurel, all quiet enough that I know they heard our fight.

I take a seat next to Isidore, sneaking a glance to see that she's fighting a smile.

"Will you be staying long?" Laurel clasps her hands, sitting like she has a rod in place of her spine.

I was considering it until now. Bishop said we could stay as long as we want. "We're only here for Kieren. We won't be in Damalis long."

"Dinner tomorrow, then." Before I can protest, she's on her feet. "I'll tell the cook."

She glides out of the room, and I turn to Isidore and mouth, *Cook?*

"And a maid, housekeeper, and footman," she whispers.

"Broderic is okay with all these people in the house?"

She shrugs, opening her mouth, but before she can tell me what's going on, the study door creaks open. Bishop strides into the room. "Shall we?"

"You just got here," Isidore says, grabbing my hand.

But Bishop clears his throat. "I have business to attend. I'm afraid we must go."

I squeeze her hand. "I will see you at dinner tomorrow."

Bishop's eyebrows creep up a little, but he doesn't correct me. No matter what was said in the study, I won't miss my chance to see my siblings. The ones who want to see me, that is. Broderic appears as I stand to leave. His face is pale as he enters the room. Bishop doesn't bother looking at him. He just walks straight out the front door without another word.

"Laurel tells me that you'll be joining us for dinner tomorrow," he says stiffly.

I swallow. "If that's not a problem."

"No." He grits his teeth. "You're always welcome here."

His change of heart is about as believable as his fiancée's simpering.

But I nod. "Tomorrow."

He follows me to the door like he's going to see me outside. He pauses on the threshold, eyes lifting to check that Bishop is a safe distance away. "I thought you were smarter than this." He tugs at his vest, shaking his head. "I can't believe you would get involved with a man like that."

Of all the things he could judge me for . . . I flick one of the gold buttons on his vest. "I could say the same. That must have been some dowry they gave you for your soul."

"Someone had to stay." He turns away, but not before I spot the hatred hiding in his eyes.

This time, when I pause on the gravel drive and look at the house, it doesn't feel like home at all.

The Marius outpost sits where farmland gives way to the Cinderwald. The barracks and officers' cottages cluster like a shield between Damalis and the black forest that grew from the ashes of Calvera. Even the pair of sentries stationed atop the tall watchtower are focused on the gnarled mass of trees beyond, like they believe the stories that the ruined land was cursed when Ravenell fell.

Bishop leads me through the outpost yard toward a stone house situated closer to the watchtower than the barracks. A few soldiers straighten as we pass, then hurry away, stealing glances back at us. It's hard to know which of us has the more dangerous reputation here.

"I thought this was a cottage." It's nearly as big as Journey's End. The *cottage* is made of the same pale limestone as my family's estate, but the structure is in better condition.

"An *officer's* cottage," he says, reaching for the knob with a grin. "It will have to do."

He swings the door open and waits for me to step through. The entry is small but comfortable, with a sitting room on one side and a dining room on the other. A stone hearth dominates the parlor to my right, its iron grate swept clean of ash. Furniture is spread throughout, worn and comfortable-looking but not quite enough to fill the large room. Bishop turns left, pausing to take off his cloak by a table long enough to seat ten.

I hang my satchel on the back of one of the chairs before unfastening my baldric. I prop the sword against the table. "Do I want to know what happened with my brother?"

Neither of us said much on the walk from Journey's End, like we both needed to think after seeing my family.

"Probably not," he says, settling into a chair by the fireplace. "I know we just got here, but I heard—"

A knock on the door interrupts us.

"Whoever it is, tell them I said no," he grumbles, but he's already getting up before I can open the door.

My sister stands on the threshold, teeth nipping her lower lip as she scans the outpost. "Isidore?"

"Good. A problem for you," Bishop mutters under his breath so only I can hear him.

She turns, her smile faltering when she sees he's here, too. "I'm sorry," she says. "I came to bring you this."

She passes me a letter with Patron Ravenell scrawled across the front in elegant script, and my stomach knots. My brother will have plenty to say about that designation. I break its wax seal, fingers trembling slightly.

"The queen has summoned me to Wintour," I say faintly, adding, "immediately. She sent word to Broderic."

Why him? Before I can ask, Bishop moves closer and snatches it from me. "Interesting."

It's never a good sign when he uses that word.

"I received the summons as well before leaving for your brother's," he says. "We should respond that we will come, before she sends another."

That's what he was about to tell me. *Interesting* is definitely the wrong word. *Fuck* is far more appropriate. "No."

"No?" he repeats with a hint of a smile. "Shall I send your whole response, *Patron Ravenell*?"

My sister's eyes widen, and I rush to correct him. "Do *not* call me that. Besides, I'm having dinner with my family tomorrow." Only half of whom want me here, but who's counting?

"I'll tell her we'll come following the equinox, in a few days," Bishop clarifies.

"If the queen summoned you, you should go. You're a patron now!" Isidore interjects. "I'll go with you. It will be fun to see the capital again."

She's desperate to get out of Damalis, and all I want is to linger.

Bishop shakes his head. "It's better for you to stay put," he says. Isidore's face falls, and he hastily adds, "But thank you for delivering this."

She turns, still crestfallen, and looks at me. "I thought we could talk, but if you're busy . . ."

"You can come in." I step to the side. I could use the distraction. "He won't bite."

But she glances over her shoulder at the barracks in the distance. "Actually, I've been wanting to see the outpost. Broderic forbade me from visiting it."

I can guess why our brother did that.

Bishop laughs gruffly. "It seems your brother and I can agree on something." He glances between us. "Just stay clear of the Cinderwald and try not to get in trouble."

Like I have any interest in walking through the forest that separates Damalis from the ruins of Ravenell's home territory.

Isidore lights up like he's given her the keys to the entire outpost, confirming that she's not really here to see me. "We will."

"You aren't the one I'm worried about," he says, his mouth tugging into a smirk, but he grabs my baldric. "And remember to take this."

I roll my eyes. "We're surrounded by your troops."

"The deal was that you'd stay armed *the whole time*." He crosses the room and fastens it over my shoulder. He leans closer as he tightens the straps, lowering his voice. "Plus, it looks good on you."

A thrill rushes through me, chasing heat onto my cheeks. I glance back, suddenly wishing my sister wasn't two steps away.

"Do you actually know how to use that?" Isidore interrupts.

"We don't pass them out like toys," Bishop says dryly, as if he spotted Laurel's gift to Andry at Journey's End.

"I won't be long," I tell him. I want to know what he thinks of the queen's summons. Although, honestly, there are more important things on my mind. I still need to decide what I'm going to say to Kieren tonight. There are so many things I never got the chance to tell him. So many things have happened since he died.

Isidore is quiet, fidgeting with her skirt as we stroll through the yard. "So," she says, finally breaking the silence, "what's going on between you two?"

I raise an eyebrow. "I don't know what you're talking about."

"I'm not a child." She rolls her eyes. "He can't stop looking at you."

So much for hiding it. "He feels a duty to protect me."

"Maybe I can find someone here interested in *protecting* me." She scans a group of soldiers playing a round of Liar's Hand near the barracks.

I grab her sleeve and steer her away. "Try again."

"I really came to see you," she says as we edge closer to the watchtower.

I snort. "And the plethora of soldiers has nothing to do with it?"

"Okay. I mostly came to see you," she admits with a sheepish smile. "It's just nice to get out of the house. Broderic says we shouldn't go into the village."

"There's always the fields." And plenty of work to do.

"He says it's not appropriate for patrons to lower themselves," she explains.

I slow to a stop. "He said *what*? That doesn't sound like Broderic."

"It's her," Isidore says glumly, her shoulders sagging. "He hasn't been the same since we came back from Wintour. Then he met her, and it got worse."

But it started with me. Guilt twists in my gut. I chose not to come home. I left Isidore to clean up the mess here. It might have kept my family safe, but that doesn't mean it didn't hurt them.

"That's why he doesn't want me to come here. He's worried I'll meet a soldier and marry him." Her gaze skips back to where the soldiers are laughing over their cards. He might have a point.

"Is that what you want?"

She sighs. "Part of me. Just to get away from this place like you did."

"You can't get married before your Kindling," I remind her.

"Why? Because I might be marked by Ravenell?" She spins to face me. "I wouldn't mind, you know. It gave you a way out."

I want to tell her about the poisoning. About the assassins. But I change the subject. "How . . ." I take a steadying breath and force myself to ask about what really matters. "How is Andry handling it?"

Isidore's throat slides, her eyes suddenly watery. "Not well. I don't think any of us are."

"Even Broderic?" I can't hide my surprise after his behavior this morning. Not with his new fiancée and the clock ticking down toward a wedding.

"He gave all your things away. All the things Kieren left behind," Isidore whispers, glancing around to make sure no one is near. "He wouldn't let Andry keep anything."

Somehow that doesn't surprise me, considering Broderic is acting like I betrayed him. Like I had no right to come back here, especially for Kieren.

"I wish Kieren would have taken me with him," Isidore admits, and my heart stops.

"That didn't end well," I say in a soft voice. She wasn't there. She didn't watch Kieren's blood seep into the dirt.

Isidore toys with something in her pocket. "Maybe it would have ended differently if I'd been there."

"You can ruin your life with maybes," I warn her.

Her head drops, black hair spilling over her shoulders. She finally looks up with tears in her eyes. "He never told me." She pulls her hand out of her pocket. Kieren's letter is clenched in her fist. "If he had . . . I know Broderic would never allow it."

"Void Broderic." I wrap an arm around her as if I can shield her from this, even as my heart breaks, too.

She collapses against my shoulder. "I knew he cared. I think I might have, too." Each word comes out as a sob. "But I was so, so stupid and silly . . ."

"I can't stop thinking about everything he had left to do. To see. He had plans," I say, holding her. So many plans. All gone.

She lifts her head from my shoulder, her cheeks wet. "I want to come to his Evensong, Arden. But Broderic won't let me."

I grit my teeth before muttering, "Void Broderic *twice*."

Isidore lets out a shaky laugh, and we hug again. Leave it to our starsforsaken asshole of a brother to make us closer than we've been in years.

I'm about to step back when a low growl rolls through the trees, close enough that I swear the ground vibrates beneath my feet. Isidore stiffens in my arms, but I look toward the sound and find we're only steps from the forest. My head snaps back to look at the watchtower, and I find trees.

"Shit." We've wandered too far. The area is more like a small copse than the actual Cinderwald, the new trees planted at the edge bursting with spring buds, but my pulse hammers like it's trying to warn me as another growl, deeper this time, answers me. Something is coming after us.

Isidore trembles violently, pulling away like she might bolt in blind panic.

"Don't move," I warn her. When the next growl rumbles through the trees, there's no mistaking the direction. "When I say, *run*. Don't stop until you see someone with a sword."

Isidore nods frantically, though I'm not sure she actually hears me.

My eyes fix where a shifting shadow moves between the tree trunks, and a branch snaps, the sound like a bone splitting.

"Run," I whisper and shove my sister in the direction of the outpost behind us, reaching for the sword sheathed at my back.

She stumbles, her eyes widening with fear as she sees where we are. I draw my blade, stepping between her and the belly of the forest. Two eyes glow blue in the dark, and the shadow of an enormous wolf steps out from the trees. Isidore screams and bolts toward the outpost, branches clawing at her dress as she pushes through them.

I plant my feet, raising the sword between the creature and my sister. The ground trembles as it pads slowly toward me, like it knows *I* can't afford to run. Not if I want her to escape. Its shoulders nearly reach my waist, thick muscles rippling beneath its silver fur and curved horns sweeping back from its skull. The wolf is a lot bigger than the ones mounted on the wall at Miradores.

Panic shoots through me, but I push it away, gripping the hilt of my sword to steady myself.

"Easy," I murmur, feeling ridiculous as the word leaves my mouth. But I don't want to kill it.

If I even can . . .

The wolf's ears flick forward like it understands me.

"That's right," I breathe. "I'm not a threat."

A warning bell rings out through the yard, and the wolf hesitates. But I don't lower my sword. For one reckless second, I see what I'm leaving behind me. Bishop's rare smiles. Taliesin running his mouth with a grin. Vessica's reluctant laughs. The way Hadrian snorts when I break him with a joke. How Shea and Breccan giggle, encouraged by Lenora. *My life in Vennaro.* The one I didn't plan on having, full of so much joy. I took it for granted, and now I might lose it.

I shove the longing down and grit my teeth. Squaring my shoulders, I raise my sword. The fear burns off, leaving anger in its place. Anger at my brother for being a dick and this fucking giant wolf determined to eat me for dinner. And more than a bit of rage aimed at myself for wandering too close to the forest in the first place.

"I won't hurt you," I say evenly, determination threading the words, "if you don't hurt me."

"Arden!" Bishop's shout cuts across the clearing.

I ignore the surge of relief. I can't afford to think I'm safe.

"Little busy right now!" I shout back.

The massive horned wolf crouches, preparing to spring, as if it senses time is running out.

Seven hells.

I grit my teeth, bracing for the pounce as wind rushes overhead. Wings brush my hair, and something lands on my shoulder with a loud screech.

The oscen's claws dig into my skin. It followed me from Vennaro. Naturally.

I freeze. So does the wolf.

For a moment, nothing moves.

Then . . . the wolf lowers its head.

Slowly.

Deliberately.

And sinks to the ground, ears flattening in submission, its giant, curved horns grazing the grass.

"What are you?" I whisper to the bird as the wolf lies before me, its eyes fixed on where the oscen rests perched on my shoulder.

Bishop skids to a stop a few paces away, then stares. He steps closer to me, and the beast growls softly. Bishop's lips curl like he might snarl back. But the oscen angles its body, spreading its wings, and launches into the air with an echoing cry. It soars deeper into the heart of the Cinderwald, and Bishop brings his sword up as the wolf rises.

At least we'll be ripped to shreds together.

But it doesn't even look at us as it turns and bounds back into the trees after the oscen. The forest swallows both, and my knees buckle.

Next to me, Bishop slowly lowers his sword. "What the fuck just happened?"

I stare at the place where the wolf disappeared.

"I have absolutely no idea."

I turn to check on Isidore and go cold. The little copse of saplings is black as ash now, fused into the Cinderwald like the boundary between the two never existed at all. Right where I stood and let my anger take me.

The magic that's ruined the forest didn't do this.

I did.

THIRTY-FIVE

The astrolatory in Damalis is smaller than the others I've seen in Antares. It's little more than a chapel held together by rough wooden beams and stone. The roof's glass panes are uneven, warped with tiny bubbles that distort the sky overhead. Rows of simple wooden benches face the altar at its center.

Bishop's lips twitch. "Benches?"

"People still come here," I say softly, speaking in the low voice my parents taught me to use in the sacred space when I was a child. "To seek guidance. Or when they want to ask the Stars' favor."

A young mother, her baby nestled in a sling, rises from one of the benches, nodding to us as she exits.

"I suppose I can't blame them," I admit. "Sometimes I still want to believe they're listening."

A lump forms in my throat at the confession. Right now, I need to believe they're listening, too. The last time I was here, the astrolatory was full. My family, along with most of the village, coming to share their final words with my father. Kieren was at my side. He carried my lantern then.

Tonight, I'm carrying his. A tear slips down my cheek as the unfairness hits me again.

I didn't think I would be doing this alone.

Because Kieren was good and true, and he deserved more than the Stars ever gave him.

"I'm with you," Bishop murmurs.

I swallow, guilt mixing with grief that I expected more. Some part of me hoped Broderic would come despite everything. Or Isidore would get over her shock from this afternoon and defy him. That Andry would get his chance to say farewell.

Because they should be here. I'm not sure I'll ever forgive Broderic for this.

Bishop places a palm on the small of my back, nodding to the glass above us where night is slowly bruising the sky. "It's dusk."

We move to the altar. It's splattered with wax from all the Evensongs that came before. Someone has left a box of matches as if they knew I would forget to bring my own. Something about that makes me feel less lonely. I set the lantern on the stone and pick up a match.

"Do you want help?" he asks as I fumble to light one.

"Yes," I say, dropping another match as soon as it strikes.

But Bishop extends his free hand, keeping the other firmly on me like he knows I need the anchor. The lines marking his skin begin to glow, and he lowers a finger to the candle inside the lantern. A small flame blossoms as the wick catches quickly, and a soft glow spills through the glass.

I stare at the light that will guide Kieren's soul back to the Stars, more tears smarting my eyes.

"I'll give you a moment." His hand lingers just a bit longer before he slips outside. He won't go far, especially since I refused to carry a sword into the sacred place. But he seems to understand that I need to do this alone.

I can't look away from the flame, warm as it lights up the space like Kieren's laugh.

Maybe this is how it was meant to be.

Just Kieren and me. Like it always was.

"I'm here." My voice echoes faintly in the empty room. I suck down a shaky breath. With everything that happened, I never quite figured out what to say. Truthfully, part of me would rather face the wolf again than do this.

But that's not what his soul needs to make the passage.

"I'm safe." That's what he needs to hear. But saying it feels like writing a letter I know he'll never read.

"I thought you should know." I laugh weakly, wondering why it's different than the other times. "You were always there when we did this." I never had to face it alone.

He was always there. For every heartbreak. For every adventure.

I just want to share one more moment with him. So, I start there. "You'll never believe what happened today."

My fingers tighten on the edge of the altar. "I saw a horned wolf in the Cinderwald today. They're so much bigger than we thought."

I can almost hear his excitement.

"This one came up to my chest. It was so tall."

Almost see his eyes lighting up.

"Remember when we tried to sneak into the forest when we were kids?" Another dare. "You swore you heard something howl, and we ran all the way back to the barn." The tightness in my chest loosens a bit as I laugh. "I've never run so fast in my life. I didn't run today."

There are so many stories I'll never get to tell him now.

So many adventures we'll never get to have.

"I wish we'd gone together," I whisper. It hurts to admit it, because even though I know it's true, something else is, too. "I'm glad I'm still here."

A sob wrenches through me. "I'm glad I'm alive." The tears begin to fall harder. "I just wish you were here, too."

But I know it's time to let his soul be at peace. I can't keep him here forever. "Bishop came with me. He was there in the forest today." I swipe at the tears. "I'm not alone anymore."

The candle gutters a little, and a small smile slips past the sadness. "You would have liked him. Even if he was an asshole when you met."

I can see the two of them, bickering over something ridiculous. Like what kind of wine I prefer. But Kieren would have liked the way Bishop makes me feel.

Because that's all you want for your family. Not just for them to be safe. Or content. You want them to find the person who makes them complete. The person who sets their soul on fire. The one who doesn't quite make sense, but who divides their life into before and after.

Kieren was my before.

"Thank you," I whisper. "For always being there. For seeing me."

The weight I've carried since that terrible night begins to lift.

"Thank you for being my brother." I swallow as I reach for the lantern.

"Keep an eye on me, though, okay? You know I can't seem to stay out of trouble."

I leave the Evensong at the altar and carry his light with me. The Stars burn overhead as I step outside. Bishop is waiting by the door. He doesn't say anything. He just takes the lantern in one hand and mine in his other. The silence doesn't feel heavy as we walk back to the cottage. It wraps around me like the cool night air, soothing. Peaceful.

A few conscripts pause to bow their heads as we pass, and when we reach the small clearing beside the cottage, I take the lantern again and place it on the ground, so the flame can light Kieren's way back to the Stars. By morning, it will be gone, and his soul will be with them.

I thought I couldn't leave it—couldn't bear to turn away from that light. But now I know there's a life waiting for me in the morning.

Because Bishop is my *after*.

But when I turn, Bishop isn't looking at me. He's staring up at the sky, starlight shimmering in his eyes.

"Thank you for letting me come with you," he murmurs. "I've buried enough bodies, but I've never given an Evensong."

My breath catches in my throat.

"I didn't mourn my family," he confesses. "Maybe that's why my soul will never be at peace." His gaze lowers to mine. "I think it's time that I tell you how I died."

I drop onto the sofa next to him, folding my legs under me. Trying to make myself small enough that I don't spook him now that he's finally opening up. With the queen's summons hanging over my head, who knows when we'll have another chance?

"My older brother was charismatic. A true politician. More so than even my parents were. But that charm came with ambition. When King Ophelian suggested Cassiel survey the Lost Continent . . ." Bishop breaks off, shaking his head.

His brother's name. *Cassiel.* I tuck the information away, adding it to the pieces of Bishop I'm picking up here and there.

"King Ophelian favored expansion?" The king hadn't seemed that serious for the few minutes I met him.

"You're surprised." But he nods.

"He didn't strike me as very forward-thinking," I admit. "He had plenty of people to think for him. And his sister?"

"That remains to be seen. She's young."

I can't help but laugh. "So are we."

He lifts my hand and kisses my wrist, where my pulse jumps. "I lived a lifetime in pain before meeting you."

My cheeks heat. I'm unsure how to respond. Unable to cross some invisible line.

He looks away but keeps holding my hand. "Since the Last War, patrons were meant to balance the throne. Five families, five magics, all of us bound to the crown and one another. It was supposed to be a system where no bloodline could take too much. But now . . . now there are plenty who would *take* the throne if given the chance."

Bishop draws a deep breath. "So while Cassiel was away, my father sent me a letter, concerned about the connections he'd formed overseas. But when my brother returned from the continent . . . I was in Isoldoro. I didn't want to go back home yet. Didn't want to deal with it."

I snort with understanding, not amusement. "But you went."

Because that's what people like us do.

"I delayed a few days. I just didn't want to . . ." He trails away before he continues. "I was too late. When I reached Miradores—only Lenora was spared. She'd gone to visit her cousin for the day in Ardermare. Everyone else . . . the other staff . . . my father . . . mother . . ." His voice breaks, and I squeeze his hand.

Looking at him, I see it all at last. The weight of what he lost. The way he's carried on alone ever since. The way he holds himself apart. Always in control.

"And your brother?" I ask, my heart in my throat, but I don't look away. He needs to know I'm here with him as he faces this.

Bishop turns from me, his eyes shining in the firelight. "I could have saved him. If I'd been faster. If I hadn't stumbled through the house checking corpses for pulses I knew weren't there while my brother fought for his life.

By the time I heard him. Realized what was happening . . ." He shakes his head like he doesn't want to remember. "I got to the balcony as the killer plunged a sword into Cassiel. My brother was looking right at me when he went over the railing.

"And his new *friend*"—Bishop spits the word—"he just laughed and told me I was too late." His fists clench, and he shakes his head as if he's back on that balcony. "I lunged for him. That's when I realized he wasn't human. Realized why Cassiel wasn't able to defend himself."

Bishop pauses and looks me in the eye. "He mortally wounded me, too, left me to die on that balcony in the rain. Lenora found me, just as I . . ." He trails away again. "She kept the secret. Said that's what family does. It took me longer to trust the others."

That doesn't surprise me. He got himself killed before he trusted me. "And Hadrian?"

"He didn't tell you?"

I roll my eyes but feel no lighter. "He said it was your story to tell. Is that a scion thing? Being moody and cryptic?"

He laughs softly, but a hard line settles between his brows. "It's part of his oath."

"You make that sound very official."

"It is to him. It . . ." His eyes close for a minute. "It saved me. *He* saved me."

A chill works its way under my ribs, and I go completely still, afraid that if I move, he'll stop talking.

"Why did you need saving?" I ask as my pulse starts to race like my body is running ahead of me and already bracing.

He pulls his hand from mine and runs it through his silver-blond hair. He doesn't reach for mine again, dropping his to his lap instead. I immediately miss the warmth.

"I was mad with grief. And all I could think about was finding the scion who killed them all"—he pauses again, as if each word is costing him another piece of his soul—"but I settled for *any* immortal who crossed my path." His eyes close as if he can't face the truth. "Arden, I killed them all. Quickly, slowly, but *always* brutally."

My heart pounds in my ears. Once. Twice. And then it just stops.

His vestiges. *Hundreds* of them.

Collected in *revenge.*

The fire crackling in the hearth sounds too loud as I try to digest everything.

How many people never came home to their families? How many of them were like Hadrian? Or Shea?

Over our months together, I'd built him into a man who only drew his sword for a reason. I'd convinced myself that his vestiges were collected from dangerous scions, but the truth is so much worse. He murdered them all.

Because one scion killed *his* family. Because he hated that he'd become one, too.

Some part of me is horrified, and the room tilts, my skin breaking out in a cold sweat as I fight the urge to be sick. But then I think of the bishop who dedicated his life to helping others. Of the man who asks for nothing for himself as he gives everything to those under his rule. I think of Bishop on the proving grounds, drilling Shea until her arms shake because he wants her to *live.* The man who gave Hadrian access to his library and helped him search for answers. Not only for themselves but for every scion, so that none of them would have to face the fury and another war cycle.

I take a few slow, deep breaths. My heart begins to beat again as I remember the way he fights with steel and discipline and his own body, pushing himself when a vestige would settle a match in seconds. I'd assumed it was pride. Or some vow I didn't understand.

It isn't.

It's penance.

It's in every conscript he trains. Every life he refuses to use his powers to take. The scion who killed all those people years ago has spent every day since struggling to make himself into a better man.

And he has.

"That's why you don't use your powers," I whisper.

He nods once. "They remind me that there is a fine line between delivering justice and becoming a monster."

I want to tell him he's not a monster, but I don't think he'll believe me right now.

"Hadrian showed me what I didn't know. Taught me there was another way. That I could have control over the powers I'd claimed—that I could rise above their pull."

"Your vestiges?" I ask.

"I didn't have to claim them." He leans back a fraction. "Not every immortal I killed was innocent. Some of the powers they carried . . ."

"But you claimed them anyway," I finish for him.

He turns to me and holds my gaze. But there's no comfort in his eyes. He's looking at me like a man about to open a window he should keep closed, as though he's preparing for what happens when I'm no longer on the other side of the glass.

I can see it etched in his winter blue eyes—the certainty that I'll never look at him the same way again.

"My birthright is one of the darkest, Arden. It's . . ." He pauses as though he needs to choose his words carefully. "A constant fight to control it. Since the day I came back from the dead, it's been roiling under my skin, waiting for its chance. Grief makes it harder. Rage. Wanting you . . ." He swallows. "My vow is its only cage, but if I'm pushed too far . . . If I ever lose control of it again, that cage will be gone. There's no rebuilding it from the other side."

I open my mouth to ask what birthright the Stars gave him in exchange for being part of their endless game but think better of it. Not when I'm not ready to admit mine might be worse.

But he sees my face. "It's terrible," he whispers. "It's the curse I deserve."

"I don't believe that." My fingers find his sleeve and curl there.

"I didn't even know I was using it . . ." His throat slides. "I don't know how many people like Hadrian I killed. How many of them were scared, untrained, and then I . . ." He drags a hand over his face. "I never gave them a chance. That's why when a scion shows up at the Bellatorum, I help them."

Like Shea.

But something about how he says it makes me ask, "There are other scions at the Bellatorum?"

"A few. Some have already gone. I'm sure more will come." His gaze lingers, like he's searching me for the forgiveness that he can't give himself.

"Aren't you worried that if you train them . . ." Guilt rushes through me and cuts off the question.

But they can't all be like Shea.

"It would be just for me to die at the hands of someone I trust." His voice is firm, but his gaze shifts away. "Too many immortals opened the door to a bishop but let in a wolf."

"You aren't that man anymore." I take his hand, waiting until he turns his haunted eyes back to mine. "You're allowed to forgive yourself."

He raises an eyebrow, but he doesn't point out my hypocrisy.

Still, I push back. "You get to choose—and you've been choosing all this time."

"And when I can't?" The words are a hollow whisper. "When the cycle begins . . ."

The skin on my chest tingles. I close my eyes as if I can hide from it. "It won't."

"I love that you believe that."

I swallow, my heart skipping a beat. "I have to."

Like Hadrian needs to believe the fury can be contained. Like I need to believe I'm not Ravenell. That my birthright isn't dark magic. Like I need to believe Bishop can overcome his demons, too.

He cups my cheek in his hand, and I finally look at him again. "Stars, you're beautiful," he whispers. "*Fierce.* That's why I need you to promise me something."

The way he's looking at me . . . I'd promise him anything.

"If the cycle comes, if the fury overtakes me, if we can't find a way to stop it . . ." He pauses, but something in his voice has me bracing before he continues. "I won't be a monster again."

This is the line he's drawn. It's one I can understand. "I know that."

But he shakes his head. "You don't. You have no idea what I'm truly capable of."

I lean forward and press a finger to his lips. "I'm sorry, but that's bullshit. I know you. I see you." I turn his own words against him. "This thing between us . . ."

Something keeps me from saying it, from naming this beautiful pain in my heart. This feeling I've only known with him. I know it's there—planted inside me—but it needs time to grow. Time to see if it grows in him, too.

"The way I feel about you . . ." I tiptoe to the line but can't quite cross it. "It means you never have to explain your heart to me."

His nostrils flare slightly as I finally lower the finger silencing him. He pauses, drawing a shuddering breath, and whispers, "Endymion . . . My name. It's Endymion."

The name lands like a confession, as if he's just placed something precious *and* dangerous into my hands.

"En-dim-ee-uhn." I drag each syllable out, smiling slightly at how it sounds on my tongue.

"He's still here," he admits, as if he's committing a crime by being anyone other than Bishop, "but I can't . . . The vow isn't just a cover. It was a choice. Penance."

Anger flickers through me. Not at him—but at whoever taught him this was the price of being good.

"If it wasn't . . ." The longing in his voice steals my breath, and I shift closer without thinking. "If I could give you all of me. If I could trust myself . . ." But he shakes his head. "I've never wanted anything more, but I can't risk it."

Something cracks open in my chest, but I nod.

"Keeping my vow was about absolution." His knuckles skim along my jaw. "Now it's a shield. A reminder of the man I need to be for you. To protect you. From all of this." He exhales slowly, and my heart breaks a little more when he adds, "From me."

"I'm not scared of you." I slide over and climb into his lap, taking his face between my hands so he can't look away. "You can't scare me. In fact, I'm afraid you're stuck with me."

The corners of his mouth tug up, and there's something like awe in his eyes. "Is that so?"

This moment feels too fragile, so I try to lighten it. "Well, I don't think my brother wants me back." I shrug like this doesn't matter. I'd rather be wherever Bishop is, but it still hurts. "And you did tell me your name, so . . ."

Things are getting serious.

His fingers sink into my hips, and he drags me a little closer. "Now, about that promise. If I lose control, if I lose myself . . ."

"I'll find you." Fear meets the anger still smoldering low inside me and hardens into resolve.

But he continues. "Stop me. You're the only one who can."

I pull back just enough to search his eyes, my hands still gripping him like anchors. But I'm no longer tethering him; I'm trying to keep myself from drowning. "I can't. I won't be able to."

"You're the only one who ever could."

Sadness floods his eyes as if he's speaking of a future that's set in stone. His face settles into the hard lines that tell me he's already made up his mind. "If it happens, *end* me. The world won't survive my birthright if I ever give in again."

I go completely still, my body trying to decide what to do with this warning.

"No." I squeeze my eyes shut, like maybe when I open them, we'll be lying in bed together and it will be morning and all of this will have been a dream. But when I open them, he's still there. "I can't."

"You can." His mouth twitches as if he's aiming for a smile. But he misses the mark entirely. "I trained you, remember? You know all the mistakes I make."

There's nothing funny about it. I shake my head. "I've never won a fight with you."

And deep down, somewhere that hurts, I know I won't win this one. That I'd save him no matter the cost.

"Say my name. It will bring me to my knees," he whispers, like the idea breaks his heart a little, too. "Only you can do it. Because you're the one who found him . . . found me."

He's not giving me control. He's trusting me.

Bishop reaches up and covers the hands still gripping his face. "Promise me." His thumb strokes the back of my hand. *"Please."*

It's the *please* that kills me, and I don't even try to stop the tears from falling. "I promise."

He tilts his head and nods once. "Good girl."

There's no *thank you*. No hesitation. Just the terrible understanding that neither of us can deny the other.

Because this is what trust looks like in our world. Not vows whispered in candlelight. Not promises of forever. It's a blade placed in your hand and the faith that you'll know when to use it.

Bishop is trusting me with the thing he fears most. *Himself.*

The thought sits heavily on my chest. Not because I'm afraid of what he might become, but because of what's stirring inside me. The mark over my heart burns, hot enough that I almost reach for it.

I don't.

Hadrian said that omens aren't binding. That the stars point the way, but they don't ultimately decide our paths. That the harbinger is a warning, not destiny. I want to believe him, but every day it becomes a little harder to ignore that something's changing inside me. Something that calls to my grief and anger. How much longer until I answer?

The silence between us stretches, loaded with what we refuse to name—what we're afraid we'll become.

And I know what I have to do.

"If it comes . . ." The mark blazes with warning. "If the worst happens . . . ."

His eyes narrow with the look he usually gets right before he gives me an order he knows I'm going to ignore. "Arden—"

"I'll find you," I say again.

His jaw tightens.

"And if I can't bring you back?" The question hangs like a heavy sigh.

His eyes close for just a second. Finally, he nods.

I force myself to speak around the knot in my throat. "Then I'll do what you asked."

A mix of pain and relief flashes across his face before it disappears beneath the mask he wears for everyone else. But I'm not done.

"If it comes," I whisper, "I'm not letting you face it alone. If it comes . . . we'll pay the price together."

He starts to protest, but I shush him. "Try to stop me." I lean forward, pressing my forehead to his. "You don't get to be the only noble one."

"What I'm asking isn't noble."

I draw back just enough that I can look him in the eyes. "Yes, it is." I trace the outline of his lips. "You are noble. You are good, and I . . . forgive you. For all of it. I release you, Endymion."

For a moment, we stay locked like this, and then I whisper, "Fly."

And he does.

To me.

The promise lingering on our lips tastes bittersweet as his mouth meets mine. But he surges to his feet, carrying me with him.

Because wherever this man goes, I *will* follow.

His hands worship every part of me by firelight, each of us searching for and sharing those hidden parts of ourselves. When there is nothing left but embers and quiet breaths, he rests against my chest, a hand still tangled in my hair.

But I lie awake, watching the shadows move across the ceiling, plagued by unwanted thoughts as my mind drifts.

Soon, I have to face the queen. Leave the safety of this moment. Answer questions or prove myself worthy. All with his name sitting on my tongue like a coin I'm not supposed to spend.

I close my eyes and try to sleep.

I don't.

Because deep down, I know Bishop isn't the one we should fear.

THIRTY-SIX

The dining room of the cottage has been transformed.

Bishop's only stipulation about my family dinner was hosting it here. Apparently, he doesn't trust Broderic.

But from the moment Laurel swept through the door, her arm hooked through Broderic's like a leash, it's been a stream of orders. Linens draped dutifully over the long table—pale gold with embroidered hydras at every corner. Because Stars forbid a Velesont sit down to a meal without reminding everyone whose niece she is. The candlesticks have been polished. The goblets shined. Every task carried out by Laurel's small army of attendants.

It's not a dinner. It's an occupation.

Bishop hasn't said anything, but his gaze keeps sweeping the room—counting exits, marking the staff, lingering a fraction too long on the guard stationed by the front door. The same one from yesterday, broad-shouldered and perpetually silent, in his Velesont uniform.

Laurel laces her fingers through Broderic's as she pulls out a chair and gestures for me to sit. "I brought the crystal from my home in Isoldoro," she says brightly, as if I might be impressed. "This seemed like the perfect occasion to use it."

"Why?" I ask. One of the innumerable staff pours water into one of several glasses in front of me. How many beverages does a single meal require?

"We're family." Her smile is so sweet it turns my stomach. "Broderic and I have hardly seen you. And now that you're a patron—"

"I'm not a patron."

"Of course you are. That summons from the queen came to our house." She glances at Broderic for support, but he's staring at the tablecloth like he can read his own future in the embroidery—and he doesn't like what he sees.

Andry saves us, careening into the room with his wooden sword from the yard where he's been badgering conscripts since they arrived. "I learned how to slice," he announces proudly, showing off his new move, eyes pinned on Bishop for approval. The sword comes dangerously close to a decanter of wine.

"Andry, mind the linen," Laurel cries out.

He freezes like he's been smacked. Isidore pats the chair beside hers. Andry sits, and she smooths his hair with the kind of careful expression that tells me she's done this a lot in recent weeks.

Despite the ceremony of it all, there's no food on the table yet. The others drink their wine, clutching the crystal goblets like anchors, but I can't bring myself to even try it with my stomach churning.

The food, when it finally comes, is beautiful and tastes like nothing. I push it around my plate.

"Do you like the lamb?" Laurel asks, looking pointedly at my untouched meal.

A serving of guilt is the last thing I need after today, so I force myself to take a bite and nod.

She beams. "My uncle's cook makes it for the equinox."

Of course. "You'll have to give me the recipe. I'll make it in Vennaro."

"I'll send it to your cook." She laughs. I'm pretty sure at the idea of me cooking. But the laugh is so pretty that I'd bet she's practiced it.

"We should toast," Laurel suggests, nodding to her footman.

He hurries to refill goblets, then fills Andry's small glass as well. Andry, who has never been allowed wine in his life, takes it with both hands and an expression of such grave responsibility I almost smile.

Things must be very different among Velesonts. But Broderic doesn't say anything. I'm beginning to wonder if he's a little bit scared of his fiancée.

I know I am. No one pays this much attention to a family dinner without having a few screws loose.

"To your sister," Laurel says, raising her own glass. "The new patron of"—she falters on the name but recovers—"of an ancient line."

A muscle twitches in Broderic's jaw, and he doesn't lift his own cup.

"We're celebrating," she reminds him in that sugary tone.

Broderic does as he's told. So do Isidore and Andry. Is every night like this?

I bring my own glass up, but I can't force it past my lips. I'm already counting the minutes until this is over. Bishop doesn't raise his glass either.

Across from me, Andry takes an eager gulp. His mouth puckers, face screwing into an expression of absolute horror.

"Disgusting," he announces. Isidore shushes him.

"Laurel, you need sauce," Broderic says, passing it to her before she can reprimand our little brother.

She giggles like he's given her a compliment instead of passing a condiment. "You are so thoughtful." Her hand lingers over his a second too long, something possessive in her touch as if she expects competition to break out over him any moment.

"I want sauce." Andry throws his body halfway across the table, knocking my glass of wine over in the process. Crimson seeps across the pressed tablecloth.

A strangled gasp that's almost animalistic escapes Laurel. I've never heard a person make that sound before.

"Andry," she snaps.

"It was an accident, darling," Broderic says quickly.

Laurel pauses, her face resetting into a smooth, pleasant expression that's more disturbing than the gasp. "Of course it was an accident. I'm sorry, sweetheart." She lays a hand on Andry's shoulder, and he flinches.

But her smile hardens as she launches up to dab the linen like it's a precious family heirloom. "Although, where I come from, children learn manners. Or they eat in the kitchen."

"We've been eating in the kitchen most of our lives, even Broderic," Isidore says, slicing into her meat with unnecessary force.

"Well." Laurel hesitates, glancing at Bishop and me like she's suddenly remembering our presence. She clears her throat, extending her long neck, and simply looks past my sister as she says, "That will change now."

I can see why Isidore wants to escape.

Nothing about this feels . . . normal. The tablecloth, the formal dinner, the rules.

I wait for Broderic to say something, but he doesn't.

I can't help myself. "Tables must be very quiet where you come from."

Her gaze lands on mine, and her eyes narrow to daggers. "They are." She shifts her focus to Bishop. "I'm sure it's the same in Vennaro. The discipline, I mean."

Bishop tears a roll in half without looking at her. "My brother and I once set a tablecloth on fire during a dinner party." He shrugs. "So, I try not to judge."

Andry beams from across the table. "I like him."

Laurel turns the daggers on my younger brother, her fingers clenching her precious tablecloth. But Broderic clears his throat, and she settles into her seat.

I lean to their end of the table, as if getting closer might help me understand what in seven hells is going on with them. It's not love, certainly, but I can't tell which of them has the hook in the other.

Bishop's hand settles on my thigh, calming me, as if he senses that I might say something I'll really regret. I frown, sighing a bit under my breath. I lift my water goblet to my lips. But then his hand slips higher, shifting between my thighs, bunching the fabric of my skirt there so his hand can move even higher. Can *distract* me.

And I breathe in water instead of air. I splutter, eyes widening as I try to cough it from my lungs.

Every eye at the table, except his, swivels to me. Bishop removes his hand, biting back a smirk.

At least we're *all* distracted from the damn tablecloth now.

"I'm really fine," I say, setting my cup down with shaking fingers. "Just *distracted*."

"Yes," Broderic says evenly. "That's obvious."

But Isidore smothers a smile with her hand.

"What are you so happy about?" Broderic asks, catching her, and an argument quickly ensues.

Some things don't change.

"You need more wine," Laurel calls over the argument, motioning for the footman to bring me another goblet.

I murmur a thanks as he pours it, but I can't bring myself to drink any more than I can force myself to eat. My stomach has moved from clenched to actively hostile.

"So," Broderic says, setting down his fork. *"Patron."*

Oh, good. Just the change of subject I've been hoping for.

"Isn't it exciting?" Laurel smiles, wheels turning in her eyes. Married to one patron. Sister-in-law to another.

But Broderic shakes his head. "Arden is an Icaros by birth. The Kindling was bad enough."

"Didn't the queen say not to question the Stars?" Void knows that I have, but he can't seem to let this go.

He finally looks at me. "I think the queen made a mistake. I think . . ."

The table falls silent as though we all know what he was about to say next.

His words land in the tender ache beneath my ribs. *I think the queen made a mistake.* I've been swallowing back that exact sentiment since I received that summons. I haven't been able to say it out loud, even to Bishop.

My brother saying it is different.

Hearing it from him feels like a slap.

"I'm sorry I came home." Clearly, he doesn't want me here.

Broderic's laugh is hollow. "But you aren't sorry that you left."

"Stop," Isidore whispers. "Both of you. Please."

Andry stares at his plate like he can make himself invisible. I hate that. I hate that we're doing this in front of him. I hate that we're doing it at all.

"I need some air," I say, getting up from the table.

Bishop stands, but Laurel rises faster.

"I'll go with her," she says, touching Broderic's shoulder like she's warning him not to interfere. "I've been hoping to have a moment with my future sister."

Bishop doesn't sit back down.

"I'll be fine," I tell him, because his face looks like he's calculating his next move. I can practically hear the math. "Your people are everywhere."

And I might as well get this over with. I wouldn't put it past Laurel to show up in Vennaro with her entire entourage for tea if I don't.

"Stefan will come with us," Laurel adds reassuringly. "We won't go past the gate."

"Very well." His voice is even, but his gaze is hard as he looks at me. "Take your sword."

Laurel opens her mouth as though she might argue, but she hesitates and says, "We'll be back for dessert."

Wonderful. *Another* course to suffer through. I can't wait to see what drama is served next.

I push past Laurel and make for the door. I'd thought it bad manners to wear a weapon at the table, so my baldric is in the bedroom. But I need out of this house *now*. I grab one of Bishop's many others and strap it around my waist.

I'm not sure Bishop really thought through arming me in her presence.

The spring air nips our cheeks as we step outside, but it's pleasant enough that the yard between the cottage and the barracks is packed with troops. The lamps are lit, and smoke drifts from a firepit. There are more than a few groups playing Liar's Hand. Others stroll the perimeter of the gate. It's as if everyone is celebrating the equinox and the blessed arrival of a new season.

"I can barely hear myself think out here." Laurel rolls her eyes. She loops her arm through mine as though we've been friends for years and digs her fingers into my skin like she does my brother. "It's quieter back there."

She glances to where the yard continues in the direction of the Cinderwald.

I hesitate.

"I don't think that's a good idea." I haven't seen the oscen all day. Maybe it's already begun its flight back to Vennaro. I can't count on it keeping me from becoming a wolf's supper.

"Stefan is with us." She giggles like caution is a ludicrous concept. "And you have a sword. You can protect me."

Maybe I'll let a wolf eat *her* instead. Though chances seem slim with Stefan four paces behind us.

"I know about Miranda," she says as we stroll. "I know that's why you don't like me."

I stop myself from telling her that's only one reason. "Broderic made his choice. I respect that."

Not that he'll ever grant me the same consideration.

"I wasn't sure what to expect from Damalis." Her head tips back to look at the night sky. "The stars are brighter here than in Isoldoro. It's . . . peaceful."

From the way the word sticks as she says it, I'm not sure she sees it as a good thing.

"Not used to it yet?"

She shakes her head. "Someday."

We walk until the lantern light from the yard is a glow in the distance and the sounds of revelry fade.

"That's better," Laurel says, letting go of my arm.

I rub the spot where her fingers clutched me. "You wanted to talk. About what?"

"I wanted to tell you that I'm glad."

"Glad?"

"That the queen has recognized you as patron, assuming that letter was any indication. It's wonderful news." She turns to face me, and the practiced charm slips. It's not gone entirely. More like paint beginning to flake after too much wear. "Broderic doesn't see the bigger picture. He never does."

"And what is the bigger picture?"

"War is coming." She says it the way most people announce it's going to rain. "The Stars marked you, Arden. They wouldn't have without reason."

I take a half step back without meaning to. "You think I *am* the harbinger."

She smiles. "I'm counting on it. My uncle is, too."

"Why?" The question barely leaves my mouth before Stefan's arm hooks across my chest, pinning my elbows against my ribs. Another hand clamps over my mouth.

I bite it.

Stefan grunts but doesn't let go.

"Don't scream," Laurel says. "It's worse for your family if you scream."

And then Stefan drags me into the Cinderwald.

THIRTY-SEVEN

Undergrowth crackles beneath our boots as Stefan shuffles me deeper into the forest. Laurel is close behind, issuing orders even now. I work my jaw, trying to find another angle to bite the hand over my mouth again, but it's clasped too tightly.

And I was dreading the dessert course.

Laurel catches up to us, her gown gathered in one hand to keep it out of the brambles. With the other, she fishes a small, flat disc out of her bodice and turns it over in her palm.

A portable postern like the one Bishop has. Fear floods through me, the little food I ate threatening to come back up.

"He'll meet us a few miles east of here," she says to her guard. "Then we'll be done and we can go home."

Something tells me she isn't talking about Journey's End.

The guard slows to a stop in a small clearing, but he doesn't release me. No matter how many times I kick him.

"Keep fighting me and I'll knock you unconscious," he hisses in my ear.

I still. I need to be conscious if I'm going to get at my sword and slice his fucking head off.

Laurel steps in front of me, the look on her face almost apologetic. "I'll have him let you go if you swear you won't shout."

I nod against his hand.

She tilts her head at Stefan. He hesitates as though he disagrees with this choice, but he releases me. The instant my body is free, I tear away from him, drawing the sword at my hip.

Stefan watches me, faintly amused.

But I direct my rage at my brother's fiancée. "You won't get away with this."

"Oh, I will." She turns the postern in her hand like she's admiring a ring. "There's no version of this where I don't. I've been *very* careful. Waiting for this moment. Encouraging Broderic to let you come home. Inviting you to dinner."

She sounds like she's reciting a recipe.

"Poisoning the sauce," she adds, and a fresh bolt of terror hits me. "Your brother. Your sister. Andry. Bishop. Everyone at the table tonight enjoyed the meal except you . . . and me."

Cold filters through my veins. "You're lying."

"I'm not." She holds up a small bottle stoppered with wax. "This is the antidote. Enough for all of them. If you go through the postern without making a fuss, I'll see that it makes it into their dessert wine. They'll be fine."

I don't ask what's waiting on the other side of the portal for me.

"And if I don't?"

She shrugs. "Then they'll all die in the parlor sometime in the next hour, waiting for us to come back from our walk."

Acid rises in my throat.

"At first, it only has a soporific effect," she says. "But once the poison takes hold, I hear death can be quite painful." She shrugs. "Unfortunately, *you* didn't seem hungry tonight."

"Twelvetide," I say, my grip on the sword's hilt growing slick. "The bellanotte. That was you."

"Not me. I was here, accepting your brother's proposal. But as you know, my uncle can deliver anything in Antares. Even assassins."

So much for Vennaro being impenetrable. "It must have been disappointing to wake up engaged and find out your uncle's assassin failed."

"Don't worry. We won't fail this time. A Ravenell cannot rise to power." She shakes her head.

I roll my eyes. "Because I'm so scary?"

"Because Order Velesont *will* be the most powerful order. Nothing can threaten that. We've worked too hard to find ourselves licking another set of boots."

By *worked*, I assume she means schemed against the other orders. Just like they're doing now.

"At least you came home before I had to marry him." She grimaces, and I feel my heart crack a little for Broderic.

The sick feeling rises another inch in my throat, and I clamp my mouth shut.

"You're not going to give them the antidote," I say.

She actually looks hurt. "I will. Why wouldn't I?"

Because she hates them. That much is obvious.

"Once I'm gone, your job is finished. I'm sure your uncle didn't pay you to go the extra mile."

"He's not paying me," Laurel says, an edge in her voice. "He's freeing me. Do you have any idea what it costs to be the niece of Patron Velesont? He would have made me stay the rest of my life if I didn't deliver you. Now, I'm done. I don't have to marry your brother. I won't rot in Damalis, a farmer's wife." She shudders, then brightens. "I can go wherever I want. Do what I please. For the first time in my life."

My gaze flicks to Stefan. He's been silent this whole time, watching me with the patience of a man who's done this before. Probably more than once.

"What's your story going to be?" I ask Laurel. "You walked into the woods with me and walked back without. How will you explain that to them?"

Her face changes, mouth drooping. A tear slides down her cheek as easily as a leaf falling.

"There were three of them," she says, her voice softening and then breaking a little as she starts to cry. "Hooded. They came out of the trees. They wanted Arden. They told me they poisoned our food. They had the antidote. They said—" The words catch in her throat, more tears falling. "They said if I gave them Arden, they'd give me the antidote. I'm so sorry, Broderic. I didn't know what else to do. I had to choose. Forgive me."

She wipes her cheek delicately, and her eyes refocus on me as she grins.

I almost applaud.

"Something like that," she says, no longer performing. Her smile widens. "I've been practicing."

"And him?"

"He'll be very dead when they find him. Three sword wounds from fighting bravely. A hero for buying me time to escape with the antidote."

Stefan laughs.

"That's commitment," I say slowly.

"Let's not pretend. You've been with the bishop too long. You know what he hunts. You know *what* Stefan is," she hisses, eyes lighting up with delight.

A scion.

She really thought of everything. I might be impressed under other circumstances.

"He'll resurrect by morning," she says, "and meet us in Isoldoro. Where we belong. Well, not you. But you won't be there for long."

I stare at the bottle in her hand.

She won't deliver it to them. Everything about her is an act, a weapon honed by her uncle. My family's only chance is if I *take* the antidote from her.

"Okay," I say.

Laurel blinks. "Okay?"

"I'll go." I lower the sword an inch. "Just give me the antidote. I'll take it back. Let me say goodbye. I won't tell them anything."

"Oh, sweetheart, no." Her real laugh is ugly.

"Please." I take a half step toward her. "They're my family."

She hesitates, allowing the smallest crack in her plan, and it's exactly the one I need.

I move, heart hammering against my ribs.

It's the same recovery Bishop drilled into me over and over again in the rain. Step in. Hook the wrist. Twist. My free hand closes over hers, catching her by surprise, and she drops the vial in the brush at our feet.

Stefan wraps his fist around the pommel of his sword, and I point my own at Laurel's throat.

"Don't move," I warn him.

But he laughs, the sound of it as dry as cracking ice.

"That's the spirit," he says. He draws his own sword in no hurry at all. "I've just been waiting for an excuse. Lady Laurel, why don't you head back now?"

Laurel's eyes flick from the sword aimed at her to him. "What?"

Exactly what I was thinking.

"Your uncle will be just as satisfied with her heart. He's always happy when I bring him hearts. You know that. He might prefer her alive, but he'll accept her dead." He flexes his shoulders.

"And how do you expect me to walk away?" she seethes, still staring at my weapon.

"She won't kill you," he says.

I grit my teeth. "Try me."

Laurel's mouth opens. Closes. "But the antidote . . . without it . . ."

Shit. Maybe she meant it. My stance slips, sword wavering slightly. Stefan lunges, his sword knocking mine wide with a *clang*. Laurel darts behind him, eyes wide over his shoulder. I step into guard, waiting for him to strike.

"Just finish her," Laurel orders, "so we can go back and give them the antidote. I'm not interested in killing a child."

But Stefan shakes his head. Apparently, he's done taking her orders. "Three patrons gone in a single evening, in a Marius outpost no less—even Bishop himself. Think how easy it will be to convince the rest of the court to consolidate power and close ranks."

"My uncle said—"

"He'll be delighted."

She looks at the antidote on the ground, a decision moving across her face in stages. The flicker of grief. Real, I think. But then there's recalculation. And finally, acceptance.

She tosses her head back, lifting her chin.

"You made your choice," she says, determination erasing any regret. "Now your whole family dies."

She walks past us without another look in my direction.

I brace as she passes the tree line.

Stefan comes at me fast, swinging low. I parry the first strike, twist out of the second, but by the third, he's got our swords crossed as he pushes mine back. I almost lose my footing against his strength. There's nowhere to go.

He shoves at me, advancing another step. But his heel snags, and he stumbles just enough for me to duck to his left. The forest floor is roots and stones and dips, and the man hasn't trained on it.

I have.

I know where to put my feet without looking.

My blade scrapes along his ribs and tears through his uniform. Not deep. But enough.

He stops smiling.

I dodge his next strike easily, but as I twist away from him, he catches my arm with his free hand. Patterns of silver light erupt over the skin above his wrist—where a vestige hadn't existed a minute before.

And ice shoots up my arm.

Not the cold of touching iron in winter. The cold of touching death. It races from his fingertips up through my shoulder, and the muscles in my arm slacken like dead weight.

Frozen.

My grip on the sword nearly fails.

I jerk away, my arm sluggish and numb.

He grins.

"Heart collector," he says as if it's a job title. As if he's introducing himself at a party.

"You're the one killing all those people," I accuse, switching the sword to my left hand. Fighting with my left is worse. Much worse. But since my right is currently a slab of meat hanging off my shoulder . . .

"Some of them," he sneers. "Want to hear the gory details?"

Not even a little bit.

"Why leave the vestiges?" I demand, trying to buy myself a little more time to recover.

"That wasn't me." He almost sounds disappointed. "I would never leave magic behind. Not when a cycle might finally begin. We're all collecting power, hoping it will. Many of us have stopped hiding these days."

So much for that theory.

"I'd love to chat," I bite out, "but I have scheduling conflicts."

I need to reach my family. Laurel didn't take the antidote. Stars know what she's telling them right now, if she even went back. What's the point if they're all going to die . . .

No. I'm *not* letting that happen.

I roll under his guard and go for his hip. My sword connects, slicing deep.

But he's still a scion, and I'm still me. He recovers in half a breath. Closes the distance and reaches for me.

This time, he gets a fistful of my collar.

Cold paralyzes my neck before I can scream.

It floods down to my chest, and my knees buckle. I hit moss, sword scattering into the leaves. My back hits the ground. The air rushes from my lungs.

He hovers over me, silhouetted by the high moon. "This is the part where most people start crying."

"Fuck you," I say instead.

I won't cry in front of a man like him.

He lifts his sword—

Something crashes through the brush toward us.

He turns just as a blur of silver fur hits him in the chest like a battering ram. He goes down in a heap, two giant paws pinning him to the forest floor.

The wolf snarls, baring her fangs. Her ears are pressed back. The curved horns sweeping from her skull glint in the moonlight, and her blue eyes seem to glow like the man's vestiges.

Above her, a black shape circles the starry sky.

Stefan wriggles, working a hand free.

"Watch out!" I yell to the beast as he slaps his palm against the wolf's flank. His fingers pale as he pours that cold through her. The wolf shudders, wavers for a beat that sends me scrambling to my knees, searching for my sword. But she doesn't let go.

Stefan hits her again. She whines, rearing back slightly. He kicks her off and rolls clear, then rises, panting.

He stalks toward his own fallen sword. I'm still fishing for mine. My fingers close on the hilt as the wolf lunges again. She's slower now, listing to one side, but she throws her body between us.

Something small and silver streaks toward her.

It's a pup, all paws and ears and horn nubs barely bigger than my thumb. He barrels out from the trees after his mother, yipping. Following her into the fight like it's his calling, too.

My heart crashes in my chest as the pup bounds in front of me.

Protecting me.

And the mother turns.

Puts herself between us and our attacker.

A second. Only a second.

Stefan's sword slices through her side.

A haunting yowl roars out of her. Her giant body arches and crumples to the ground in a heap.

My scream fills the clearing.

And inside me, something loosens.

The pup scrambles toward her immediately, whimpering as he noses her side. He doesn't understand. He prods again for her to get up.

A sob lodges in my throat and refuses to move. I've spent months ignoring the cracks splintering me. Every loss. Every betrayal. Every terrible truth I've tried to dismiss. Every time, I've shoved the pieces back into place and refortified my defenses, because the alternative meant admitting what the Stars marked me to become.

But watching the pup nudge his mother's broken body, I suddenly see the wall I've built for what it is.

Not protection.

A prison.

One I've built stone by stone, afraid of the mark on my chest. Afraid that everyone was right about what I am. Including myself.

That I bring death.

But death was already here. It was there when my father died. There when Kieren took his last breath. And death was there every time someone decided another life was worth less than theirs. I didn't *bring* any of it. I just keep finding it.

The fear I built my defenses on crumbles, and the wall starts to come down.

The pup lets out a tiny, angry growl . . . and then bounds to where I'm lying on the ground. He continues to snarl at Stefan. Like he already senses it's his duty to protect me now.

The final stone gives way, my chest cracking open like the floor on the night of my Kindling. Darkness rises inside me in answer. Not foreign. Not frightening. *Familiar*. And for the first time, I don't fight it.

The cold Stefan poured into me evaporates as the truth ignites me.

The mark on my skin burns like steel in a forge, fire surging through my blood and flooding the space below it. Shaping me from the inside out.

Something shifts deep inside me, as if a door I've spent my entire life holding shut has finally swung open.

The forest falls silent.

I plant my palm on the ground and push myself to my knees.

Across the clearing, Stefan takes a step backward.

Then another.

I don't know what he sees when he looks at me.

"What in the seven hells—" he whispers, continuing to back away.

I drag in a breath. "Didn't you hear?" I rasp, my voice growing stronger with each word. "I'm the fucking harbinger."

And I decide *my* fate.

The mother wolf came to help me, but she won't survive that wound. Won't live to see her pup grow. She won't be there to protect him.

So, *I rise.*

I rise because she can't.

I rise because Kieren didn't.

I rise because no power, not even the Stars, will keep me on my knees when I know what needs to be done.

Magic scorches a trail across my neck, my chest, my arms. It doesn't matter. Nothing matters except the distance between my sword and his chest. I close it in two strides—arms shaking, lungs burning, throat raw. Stefan pulls his weapon free from the wolf with a sickening squelch and whirls toward me.

But I'm faster. And *pissed.*

I'm still screaming as I plunge my blade through his ribs. Through bone and muscle and tissue. I throw my weight into it with everything I have. With my whole body. For the mother wolf. For her baby. For every innocent life this world has snuffed out in the name of *power.*

His face goes slack, a waxy gray hollowing his cheeks as his head drops in surprise to the sword I've rammed through his heart.

I let him fall.

Leave the sword rising out of his chest like a gravestone.

My strength leaves me all at once, and I crash to my knees.

The pup scampers back to his mother and curls beside her, crying softly.

There's not enough left of me to stand. I crawl across the leaves to where she's gone down on her side. Her eye finds me, the blue glow dimming as her flank rises in shallow pants.

"I'm sorry," I whisper, tears flowing unchecked down my cheeks. I press my hand to the soft place behind her ear, the way I used to do with our barn cats when they were dying. "I'm so sorry."

Her breath rattles once, and then it stops.

The pup pushes his small head against her muzzle and . . . howls.

My heart howls with him.

I'm still sitting in the leaves with my hand on the dead wolf when I hear the outpost's warning bell.

Then shouts. Bishop's. My brother's.

There's no relief. Only a hollow pang like the bell echoing through the night.

Three figures break through the trees. Bishop leads, sword out, Broderic and Laurel behind him. She's breathing hard, the perfect picture of a woman who's just run to fetch help.

Bishop's eyes lock on me. He goes rigid for a heartbeat. Then he's at my side, hand reaching for my arm, helping me to stand. I let him take my weight. "You're bleeding."

But I don't feel it.

He looks over at Stefan's body, and his mouth twists as his gaze snags on the vestiges visible on the man's arm now. Then his focus shifts to the wolves beside me. The pup burrows into his mother, still howling, but each cry is softer than the last.

Laurel gasps. "Oh, Stars. Arden, I thought—"

She cuts off when I point at her.

"Enough with the lies." I spit the words at her feet. "This was you."

Broderic stills.

"What?" he says after a long moment.

"It was her. Patron Velesont sent her. She poisoned the sauce. The whole table." I stumble over to the grass, my palms sweeping the ground until I find the bottle. "This is the antidote. She offered me a trade. My life for this."

Laurel takes a small step backward, and more lies begin spewing out of her. "Broderic, she's hysterical. She ran into the trees. I tried to stop her."

Broderic looks at me. Then at her. And something sinks inside me. He's actually deciding.

"Broderic," I say to my brother, too tired to raise my voice. "It's me."

That has to matter. Even after everything.

His mouth opens as Laurel turns her hand. She doesn't wait to see which side he lands on.

The postern flares in her palm. She drops it, leaping into the shimmering blue puddle. It winks shut behind her with a snuff of air.

Broderic stares at the empty space beside him.

And keeps staring.

Forcing myself back to my feet, I push the antidote into his hands. My mouth opens and closes, my heart searching for the right words to reach him. I settle on his own.

"You're an Icaros," I say. "*Act like it.* Go save our family."

He blinks down at the glass. Then he's moving.

But he pauses a few steps away and looks at us. "Bishop . . . Arden . . ."

"Go," Bishop orders, reaching for me again.

Broderic dashes in the direction of the cottage. I watch him for a few seconds before I collapse against Bishop.

"Wait." I pull back, panicked. "The antidote. You need it."

He snorts. "I didn't eat much, either. I'm fine."

His eyes do a slow inventory of me—my arm, the loose collar at my throat, the dried blood on my hands. Then they flick past me to the guard.

"I have to," he says quietly.

"I know."

He grips my arm. "Don't look."

I nod.

He moves to the scion's body. I drop beside the mother and her pup, unable to watch.

The pup is so small. His paws are too big for him. One of his ears flops, nearly covering the horn nub in front of it. He shivers, and I press a hand to his neck.

"Hey, little one," I whisper.

A weight settles on my shoulder. The oscen's claws are gentle as it folds its wings against its back. It tilts its head toward the pup.

"Yeah," I say to the bird. "I know. I've got him."

Satisfied, she rises in a flap of wings and lands on a nearby branch.

I slide my hand under the pup's chest as slowly as I can, afraid I'll spook him. He goes rigid, so I keep my voice low. "It's okay. You're safe."

I lift him.

He weighs nothing.

The pup presses his face into the crook of my elbow and begins to shake. I tuck him against me and stand up.

Bishop is rising from the guard's body when I turn. His gloves are off, the silver vestiges on his skin flowing. There's a wet darkness on his palm he hasn't wiped away yet.

He looks at the pup in my arms. "Arden . . ."

But this isn't up for debate. "His mother saved my life."

"That's a horned wolf."

"His mother saved my life," I repeat, voice breaking on the words. "She died for me. I can't leave him here. I *won't*."

Bishop looks at me. Then at the pup. Before his eyes land on the wolf lying in the dirt like she's gone to sleep.

He doesn't argue again.

"Come on," he says. "We need to check on your family."

He wipes his hand on his cloak, then starts to pull his gloves back on, but he stops and looks at the back of his hand, just above the knuckle of his middle finger. A new line of silver is etching itself there. Just one line. Then a second crosses it, and a third, each tracing the shape of something I can't quite see yet.

He yanks his glove back on. Leaning down, he picks up my sword. "Let's go."

The pup squirms against my ribs until I whisper, "Shhh, little one. *No one* will hurt you. I'm your mother now." He settles instantly, nestling against my heart.

Bishop says nothing. Smarter every day.

We walk in silence until we near the lights of the outpost.

Conscripts rush toward us. We pause long enough for Bishop to direct them to the body in the woods. Then we continue on to the cottage, where my brother is feeding our siblings the antidote and explaining that his fiancée was an assassin.

It's over.

For now.

I cuddle the pup against my chest, his fur soft against my skin.

"I want to go home," I say to Bishop.

He nods. He doesn't ask which home I mean.

He already knows.

THIRTY-EIGHT

The pup hasn't moved in an hour. Not since we carried it through the postern to Miradores, leaving my stricken family behind.

He's finally sleeping, curled into a tight crescent on the foot of Bishop's bed, his nose tucked under one paw, the tiny ivory nubs on his head catching the lamplight. Every so often, a leg twitches.

It's the most peaceful thing I've seen in months.

Lenora took one look at us when we came through the postern—a wolf pup in my arms and blood on Bishop's clothing—and didn't say a word. She just marched to the kitchen, put a kettle on, set a saucer of cream on the floor, and went to find old towels. When she came back, she had a jar of salve bearing the Leontian seal and the unflappable face of a woman who's seen worse.

Now in my room, Bishop's sleeves are pushed to his elbows, his hair coming loose from its leather tie, and there's blood on his shirt that doesn't belong to him. He looks like he's been dragged through all seven hells, but he's staring at my wrist like it's offended him personally.

"Stop scowling," I say. "He barely touched me."

"He cut you."

"Barely."

His eyes flick up, unamused.

It doesn't matter that he carved my would-be assassin's heart out. Part of him is still stuck back in those woods where I almost died.

Considering I left a fair bit of my pride back there, I get it.

Between the bits of leaves, dried blood, and the patches where Stefan's icy magic soaked through the fabric, my clothes were unsalvageable.

Bishop doesn't even seem distracted by the thin shift I slipped into as soon as we were alone. Usually, he finds its sheerness inspiring. But he hasn't said a single inappropriate thing. He has, in fact, been so studiously not-inappropriate that I'm almost offended.

He rinses a cloth in the basin and starts working his way up my forearm methodically, studying each wound in the light before he cleans it.

I'm only a little worse for wear. A slender scratch where a bramble caught me. A bruise the size of a fingertip on the inside of my elbow where the guard's grip locked. A welt across my throat, which I refuse to think about.

The frozen sensation from Stefan's hand is gone. Mostly. Just a shadow of a frostbite lingers.

"Tilt your chin up."

I comply, but when the warm, wet cloth touches the welt on my throat, my eyes water. I keep them open and focused on the ceiling, hoping he doesn't notice. And honestly, the pain is mild compared to the fear slowly edging its way back into my thoughts.

"I felt something tonight, something dark," I whisper. "I think it was magic."

He's silent for a moment as he wrings out the cloth. When he finally dips his fingers into the salve and starts working it into the wound, his touch is so gentle I barely feel it.

"I told the queen you were injured and we would see her when you were feeling better," he says at last, changing the subject.

Now who's avoiding my destiny?

I roll my eyes at him. "What will they do when I have my magic?"

He shakes his head and starts in with the salve again. "They will do nothing."

"But I'm a Ravenell. Aren't *you* afraid, at least?" He has to be. He shares my bed.

Bishop takes my hand and squeezes. "Not of you. Never of you," he says, as though he senses that this is the question I really need answered. "And Velesont is only scared of your powers because he can't control you."

Power hates what it can't control. The memory swims to my mind. Hadrian said it before, but it's still true now.

"But, Arden, you've always known who you are, since the very first night we met. No one has ever controlled you," he reminds me. "Magic certainly won't be able to, either."

The words soothe something the salve can't touch.

"Freezing people is a stupid power," I mutter, trying to lighten the mood. "I'm just going to thaw."

"Not if he kept you in place long enough to get what he wanted." He releases a heavy sigh.

My heart.

Bishop takes his time tending the wounds. Finally, he sets the salve aside and picks up my hand. He turns it over, running his thumb along the inside of my wrist where the vestige left that faint, bluish bruise.

"Tell me if you lose feeling in this arm," he says.

"I will." I've never seen him this rattled. Even after that night at the docks, he stayed calm.

"I mean it, Arden."

I use my free hand and trace an *X* over my heart. "I promise."

He releases my hand and screws the lid onto the jar.

"You're handling this well," he says carefully.

I shrug, unable to find the energy to talk about it. "I never liked Laurel."

Now I have a reason to hate her.

"I'll bring charges against her tomorrow," he promises.

"And Patron Velesont?"

"We'll lock down all posterns within Vennaro. Cut off his access. But I can't touch him. He knows better than to get his hands dirty." He says it like the words taste bad.

No, people like him have other people do their dirty work for them.

And if they do get caught, they can buy their way out of it. "He'll protect her."

"That's doubtful," Bishop says, surprising me. "He doesn't protect his people. He uses them."

The pup makes a small snuffling sound in his sleep, rolling so his belly is up and his curled paws are raised toward the ceiling.

"What should we call him?" I ask, desperately needing the distraction.

Bishop pauses. "Excuse me?"

"He needs a name."

Bishop stares at me like he might examine my head next. "He doesn't."

"Everyone needs a name," I say. Then I add, "We won't be able to house train him without one."

"Arden."

"What? He can't just be 'the pup' forever."

"Names are for pets," he points out.

"Exactly."

Bishop's face rearranges into the expression he wears right before he tells me something I'm not going to like.

So, I beat him to it. "He's staying."

"Arden."

"Bishop," I repeat in the same exasperated tone.

"Horned wolves grow to the size of ponies. He *cannot* live in the house."

But I won't abandon the pup. Ever. I made a promise. "Luckily, Miradores is large enough to parade a carriage *and* horses through."

Bishop pinches the bridge of his nose. His head drops for a moment. His shoulders are shaking, very slightly, and after a second, I realize he's quietly laughing.

I don't think at me. Maybe at the situation. At his own life. At the fact that it's midnight, he's still covered in blood, and we're arguing about whether a dangerous beast gets house privileges.

The sight of him laughing steals my breath.

The wolf is definitely staying.

By the time he straightens, he's composed again, but light dances in his eyes.

"You're impossible."

He shakes his head as he begins stripping out of his ruined clothes.

"And I always will be. Maybe you should kick me out," I tease, but even as I say it, heaviness settles through me.

One day, he might need to.

I push the thought away and focus on the fact that Bishop is now half naked. It brightens my mood considerably.

But he doesn't come to bed. Instead, he stands over me, gaze skimming across my skin as he catalogues my injuries one more time.

"I'm going to live." It's meant as a joke, but something tells me he needs to hear me say it.

Finally, he sits beside me and wraps an arm around my shoulders. Drawing me closer, he kisses my forehead.

"I was scared," he murmurs against my skin.

"Me too." I can admit it.

Bishop doesn't say anything else for a few moments. He just holds me.

But I can't stop thinking about the Cinderwald, about Laurel, about the man who tried to kill me. And the one who claimed his life for it.

"You took his heart," I say quietly. "Are *you* okay?"

Bishop raises his other hand to my cheek and turns my chin so I'm facing him. He doesn't hide the pain from me, as though the long night has worn a hole through the wall *he's* built around *himself.*

"Let's talk about it tomorrow," he says, clearly not ready to tear down all his defenses yet. "Tonight, I want—"

He pauses, and in the place of pain is a hunger that sends a dizzying rush of blood to my brain. Along with several other parts of me.

"Tonight, I want this," he says and brings his lips to mine, lingering there as if he's proving to himself that I'm really here. Still in one piece. Alive.

I kiss him back like I am promising something. I don't know what, but it feels important.

He makes a low sound against my mouth as his hand slides up the back of my neck into my hair. Shifting, he grabs my hips and lowers my body to the mattress. My legs close around him on instinct, but I pull away a fraction of an inch. I nod toward the foot of the bed, where the pup is watching. "Not in front of the baby."

His brows lift. "I doubt he'll mind."

"Bishop."

He sighs, but instead of rolling off me, he raises a hand. The vestiges on his arm glow, and a second later, a blast of wind throws open the balcony door. The sounds of the sea below rush into the room, a cool spring breeze following.

"Go outside," he orders the pup.

The pup lifts his head and blinks his wide blue eyes like he's trying desperately to understand Bishop's command.

"He's scared," I whisper.

Suddenly in a new place. His family gone. Unsure if he can trust the people who brought him here.

It's a feeling I understand all too well.

But Bishop waves his hand toward the open door. "Go on. I want to make love to my woman."

The pup's eyes widen to saucers, and he lets out a soft whimper.

"Fine," Bishop sighs. Apparently, even he isn't immune to those eyes. He settles on his back and reaches for me.

I nestle into his arms, his body a warm cocoon from the ocean air drifting into the bedroom. "He tried to save me, too," I whisper, and Bishop stills. "When Stefan killed his mother and came after me, he jumped between us."

I would have died to protect that pup.

Bishop watches the pup settle back at the foot of the bed. "So, you're a little hero, huh?" He groans. "He can stay for now."

"Thank you." I plant a kiss on his chest, right on the vestige that covers his heart. He pulls me closer, and for the first time in a very long time, it feels like everything is going to be okay.

Whatever magic is inside me, whatever the Stars have planned, I'm no longer afraid.

I'm not running anymore. I'm here. Alive. Surrounded by love.

And I'll fight anyone who tries to take it away from me.

EPILOGUE

Shea twists my wrist, and my sword clatters to the ground. For the tenth time today.

But who's counting?

"Yield," she says, already stepping back. The command is more about practicing for her upcoming proving trials than anything else. We've been at it for hours, even though the test is still a week away.

I wave my hand in the air like a white flag. I'm beginning to think I took that scion out in the Cinderwald on willpower alone, especially since I haven't felt even a tingle of magic since that night.

"I would like it noted that you just kicked my ass," I pant, one hand on my knee as I try to catch my breath. And I thought Bishop was finally whipping me into shape.

Of course, he's been too busy tracking down Laurel over the last few weeks for much training time. And when we are together, training is the *last* thing on our minds.

Taliesin claps once, signaling the end of the session. "Nice and clean. You're ready."

His smile is a little too warm. That's not going to help Shea's crush on him.

But Vessica snorts. "Your footwork still drifts left on the recovery."

So much for moral support.

"I knew it." Shea eyes the proving grounds again like she might go back out and work on that footwork until they fall off at the ankles.

I bump my shoulder against hers, lowering my voice. "If you're nervous, it doesn't show."

"That's because I'm hiding it under fear and anxiety." She rolls her eyes.

Just like the rest of us.

Taliesin starts re-wrapping the practice hilts. "You've been ready for months."

But Shea huffs, and I know that she'll be out here again tomorrow, doing this all over again. Probably every day until she wears that uniform. "That's what everyone says right before someone eats sand in front of the examiners."

The sky outside is starting to fade into a pale lavender. If Bishop makes it back tonight, he'll probably be waiting already. "You'll be fine." My stomach growls, interrupting my attempt at encouragement. "I'm going to raid the kitchens before Bishop gets home."

Instantly, I realize my mistake. Taliesin catcalls, with Shea joining in. It's beneath Vessica, but a few passing conscripts join in the camaraderie.

In return, I show them all my favorite finger.

It's the same reaction any time I say Bishop's name. But I can't resist laughing, because somehow, in the last place I ever expected, I found all of them.

Even Taliesin, although I'd never admit it to his face.

"Hey," Shea calls as I grab my pack. "Tell Lenora I'll pick up Brec soon."

"Will do," I promise, slinging the bag over my shoulder and starting the familiar hike back to the estate.

By the time I reach the kitchen door, my muscles are shaking and my stomach is on the verge of mutiny. That's what I get for skipping lunch. Which is easy enough to do right now between Shea's upcoming proving, trying to train a half-feral wolf pup, and Bishop constantly tracking leads.

I'm already imagining the warm bread and fresh butter that Lenora always has waiting when my foot catches and I stumble into the door, twisting my wrist just enough that I know training will be worse tomorrow. I curse under my breath, kick the wayward stone back toward the path, and duck through the door.

The scent of yeast and sugar hits me as soon as I'm inside. I barely make it to the table where both bread and cookies are cooling.

Lenora seems to think I have a bottomless pit in place of my stomach and that it's her duty to fill it. I'll never tell her otherwise.

"Save some for Shea," Lenora calls. "She needs her strength."

I nod but snatch another cookie as she bustles toward the sink to wash up.

"She'll be here for Breccan soon," I say, crumbs spilling from my mouth.

Lenora glances over her shoulder. "He's in the library."

Probably further along in learning the ancient tongue than I am with my studies of the forbidden Ravenell texts.

Not that I'm dragging my feet.

"Is Bishop here yet?" I ask as I head toward the hall.

"Haven't seen him, but he might have slipped in through the front." She returns to her dishes, humming that old lullaby under her breath.

I'm going to have to get an astrolabe of my own, if only to keep track of where Bishop is when he's gone these days.

As I approach the library, my gaze lands on another empty space high on the wall. Another mounted wolf head removed, courtesy of Bishop, who doesn't think it's healthy for the pup to see them. He must have found a ladder to get this last one down. He even named the pup.

Hero.

Although Bishop still pretends we aren't keeping him.

I peek inside the library. Hadrian is standing over Breccan's shoulder, reading something in what I assume is the ancient tongue. He catches me watching and waves a dismissive hand.

"We'll be finished soon." His tone holds the same weariness as usual. He's still trying to piece together whatever Bishop brings home about the *Ars Astra*, which isn't much, but now he's also helping me half-heartedly learn Ravenell magic.

The fact that I'm in no hurry to do so hasn't escaped his notice. I'm about as close to truly manifesting my magic as he is to finding the *revello*.

I nod, but before I can close the door behind me, he calls out, "Bishop is home. He's in a bit of a mood."

That's both the first and last thing I want to hear.

"What did he say?" I ask.

"Nothing." Hadrian shrugs. "He just poked his head in and glowered."

Uh-oh.

"I'll check on him," I promise, but Hadrian is already bent over Breccan's shoulder, tapping something in the book in front of him.

I take the stairs two at a time. Hero is waiting at the door to the western wing with his ears pinned back. He greets me with a low, throaty rumble

I've never heard from him before. The kind of sound a much larger animal would make.

"What's gotten into you?" I murmur, but he's already trotting ahead toward the bedroom.

By the time I walk inside it, Hero is planted in front of the balcony doors, growling at his own reflection in the glass.

"Hero. Stop."

But he doesn't. Instead, he swings his head toward me, then back to the glass. His rumble climbs a notch as he stares through it.

Bishop is on the balcony, his back to the house. The sky beyond him bleeds from rose into deep violet, the sun a thin red line over the churning sea.

"Easy." I lay a hand on Hero's head. "It's just Bishop."

The pup lets out another unhappy growl. I pick him up and deposit him on the bed.

Somebody needs a nap.

We probably both do.

Stepping onto the balcony, I unfasten the baldric across my chest and prop my sword against the wall by the door.

But Bishop doesn't turn to face me. He just stares at the sky above us, like he's watching the twilight descend. His hair hangs loose at his shoulders, a new sword sheathed on his back below his red cloak. He stopped wearing it after Damalis, and part of me had hoped . . .

"Bishop?"

He still doesn't turn.

Something in my belly tightens. The feeling I used to get as a child when the closet door wouldn't stay closed and I knew better than to be afraid.

"Hadrian said you were in a mood." I keep my voice light. Or try to. "What's wrong?"

"Nothing's wrong." His voice is low, almost amused, and for some reason it makes the hair on my arms stand on end.

"Did something happen with that lead in Wintour?" I ask, growing uneasy. "Did you find Laurel?"

He shakes his head. "I found exactly what I was looking for."

The strangeness of the answer unsettles me. Hadrian said he was in a mood. But this doesn't feel like a mood.

This feels like the quiet before the clouds dump rain on my head.

He turns slowly toward me. His face remains in shadow, the dying light at his back catching only the edge of his jaw and the curve of his mouth.

He holds out a hand. "Come here."

I hesitate for a heartbeat. But I've learned that when this man asks me to come closer, it is almost always because he needs to hold me through whatever he can't say.

I cross to him, and he gathers me in his arms.

But there's something wrong in the way he embraces me. His grip is too tight. Almost consuming. His breath stutters unevenly into my hair like he's fighting something but already losing.

"You *are* beautiful."

His hands slide up my spine, fingers digging in as if he needs the pressure to stay here. Then they're at the back of my neck and his thumbs drag forward.

And close around my throat for a heartbeat before releasing me.

"Not very bright, though." The words carry a wicked edge.

I flinch at the sting they inflict. Not quite cutting. He's not making any sense. "What in seven hells is wrong with you? You're lucky I left my sword by the door."

"Oh, did that upset you?"

"Insults usually do." As well as hands around my neck. What's gotten into him?

His eyebrow rises in that half surprise my stubbornness always inspires.

"I wonder . . ." He sweeps a thumb over my lips and angles his head, but I can't bring myself to close my eyes as he leans down to kiss me.

His breath caresses my lips, and I recoil.

He chuckles. "That's what I thought. Pity."

I twist away, something squirming in my belly. My eyes snag on the vestige under his ear, and my entire body tenses, understanding before I do.

I lift a hand toward it, and he lets me, trembling slightly as my finger traces it.

I've never seen it before.

The vestige's pattern extends down, meeting another I don't recognize at the base of his throat, where the lines disappear under his black tunic.

My gaze slides back to his.

He was right before. I'm not very bright.

"Cassiel," I breathe.

His mouth splits into a wide, charming grin—the kind that might break hearts.

I wrench away, and he lets me go.

"You're twins." My lips fumble around the word.

"He always hated that part." Cassiel shrugs as if he can't blame him. "I was born at five minutes to midnight. He was born ten minutes after. When he was mad at me, he used to say that meant we weren't twins."

My older brother.

That's what Bishop told me. It wasn't a lie. It just missed the important part of the truth.

A drumbeat pounds in my ears. All these years, he wasn't dead.

"Why?" There's nothing soft about the question. I'm also not sure I give a shit how he answers.

He's alive. He's a . . .

Scion.

Cassiel doesn't answer. Instead, he points to the sword I left by the door. "You'll feel better if you're holding that."

I edge back slowly, knowing it's a trick. Trying to kiss me. Now this. He's toying with me.

When I'm even with the sword, I squat quickly and snatch it. A scrabble of claws hits the door from the other side, followed by a frantic howl as Hero begins scratching, like he's trying to dig his way through the glass.

Hero knew.

I try to ignore the slight shaking in my hands as I rise and find Cassiel armed. Not with a sword.

A *dagger*. He plays with it for a moment, its slender blade flashing, light catching the gemstones embedded in its hilt. "Do you know what this is?"

I've held that dagger in my hand twice. Both times, it changed my life. Yeah, I know what it is, which is why it seems safer to lie. "No, but I bet you're going to tell me."

"Oh, you are a live one." There's a glint of approval in his eyes, and I tighten my grip on the sword. "This dagger was forged by Ravenell during the Last War. I feel like I've been looking for it for eons. But I suppose not as long as some."

A deep cold settles through me as I look at the dagger. Now would be a very good time for my powers to truly manifest. Hero howls again through the door. But it's too late. For my magic. For me.

"The *revello*." He draws out the word, then winks at me. "Interesting fact: During the Last War, this dagger killed the final scion standing in the way of the throne. Stole all his powers and trapped them in the blade. That's what ended the cycle. They've left that out of our history lessons. The crown kept it locked away very carefully. I had to get creative to get my hands on it. Although your stunt during the Kindling was quite helpful."

A vessel of fire to liberate eternal flame . . .

I swallow, still staring at the dagger. All this time, and this is what we've been looking for—a knife I held in my own fucking hand. "That wasn't a stunt."

"I suppose not." He flips it, the hilt landing in his palm. He holds it out to me. "I bet you'd use it now, *Harbinger*."

But I don't bother trying to take it from him.

"Clever," he says, closing his fingers over its hilt again. "The *revello* ended the last cycle, and now it's going to start a new one."

"No." It slips out of me before I can stop myself. "You can't."

If the cycle begins, Bishop . . .

"But I can. The throne has been held too long by the unworthy." But he pauses, tilting his head as if he's considering the situation. "There is another option."

Something in his voice sends a tingle of warning down the back of my neck.

"You could take the *revello* from me." He reaches behind his head with his free hand and draws his own sword. "Stop me from using it one last time."

One *last* time. My eyes widen. "So, it was you killing those other scions and leaving their vestiges."

Another heart collector claiming lives like trophies in the name of power.

"There was some trial and error involved," he admits. "But I think I finally understand how Ravenell used the knife to steal power, after following my brother and retrieving the last clue in a quaint little bookshop in

Wintour. The *Ars Astra* can be so useful if you can reconstruct enough of it. You see, it isn't about how you kill a scion with it. It's about *which* scion you're killing."

My stomach bottoms out. Bishop. He's come back to kill Bishop. That's why he's here. Why he spared Hadrian. He came back for his brother.

"You aren't touching him," I snarl, my foot sliding as I bring my blade up, angling the tip toward his throat. But my fingers are slick on the hilt, my pulse pounding so hard I can feel it in my wrists.

Cassiel barely shifts as he raises his sword, the dagger gripped in his other hand. "That's the spirit." He circles the tip of his sword in the air. "Let's see what he taught you."

He's taunting me.

I drive forward, thrusting straight for his chest. He knocks my blade aside easily. I pivot on instinct, whipping the blade over my shoulder, coming at him with a high slice. He slips left, and I miss.

"Not bad," he crows. He still doesn't bother advancing on me. "What else did he teach you?"

Stars, he loves the sound of his own voice.

Thinking means death, so I don't think.

I move.

I press him before he can speak again, slashing a high cut he meets with his own sword. Next, I aim a low sweep toward his thigh. The dagger flashes down, deflecting the edge with a sharp *clang* that jolts up my arms.

I overcommit on the next strike, thrusting for his shoulder, putting my weight behind it.

But he's too fast. Too strong.

He shifts on his feet, lazily rolling his wrist, sword arcing slowly like he's bored. "Ready to give up? I have more exciting things planned for you."

I spit at him. "Never."

He's too much like his brother.

And that's exactly why I can beat him.

I let my shoulders sag just enough. Allow my blade to dip as I retreat half a step.

Cassiel moves to attack, and that's when I see it. The extra weight on his back leg.

The instant he drives forward, I plant my feet, then explode sideways. My boots skid across the stone floor—out of his reach.

His brow flies up in surprise.

I whip my shoulder and wrist into line as hard as I can, my blade whistling through the air just as Cassiel spins. It makes contact, and my heart soars, then plummets as only the tip of my blade slashes a thin line in the sleeve of his tunic.

That was my opening.

But he recovers faster than I do.

His sword snaps down, forcing mine wide. In the same instant, his dagger flashes toward my ribs.

I leap back to avoid it and slam into the stone railing. His sword sparks as it hits a spot a few inches from my face. I roll to avoid his next strike, throwing myself back into the center of the balcony.

Cassiel turns slowly as I regain my footing, like he isn't in a hurry. Almost like he's enjoying himself. "Or we could come to some type of arrangement," he suggests with a smirk. "You could . . . leave my brother. Come with me. I'll show you everything he's too scared to share. Tell you what you *really* are."

My stomach turns at the rotten words. "You can't be serious."

"I'm always serious." He flips his sword grip in his hand.

Just like I've seen Bishop do a hundred times. My heart squeezes, but I keep my eyes on his blade.

"So, what will it be?" Something wild flickers in his eyes. "Live at my side or die by his?"

That's not even a choice.

I square my shoulders and angle my sword between us, both hands on the hilt. "Carve out my heart," I say, my voice steady. "You'll find his name written there."

His smile widens. "I really do understand what he sees in you. Unfortunately, this is bigger than the three of us. You'll understand someday."

He moves before I can react, his sword slamming into mine and driving it to the side. I throw my weight behind my blade, trying to force it back into blocking position, just as he hooks the toe of his boot around my ankle and swipes me off my feet, face first.

I crash onto the stone floor, spots of light swimming in my eyes. My sword spins away from me, toward the edge of the balcony. I can't reach it. I try to suck down a breath, but my lungs won't fill. I gasp for air as Cassiel steps over me, the *revello* glinting in his hand.

He grabs the back of my shirt and yanks me to my feet. His arm wraps around my body like a vise, pinning my back against his chest, and he presses the cold blade of the dagger to my throat with his other hand. The move is so sudden, the ground tilts beneath my feet.

"That damn pup of yours won't shut up, so, if I know my brother, and I *really* do, he should be here any . . ." He pauses as the door to the balcony bursts open. ". . . moment."

"Arden!" Bishop skids to a stop just inside the doorway, breath catching hard when he sees us. Hero is right behind him, baring his teeth.

For a second, Bishop only stares, the color draining from his face. "You're . . . alive."

"Surprise." Cassiel digs the blade deeper into my skin, cutting a thin slice that stings as the air hits it. I whimper, and Bishop zeroes in on the sound. He takes a single step forward.

"I would think that through, if I were you," Cassiel warns him. "Unless you're ready for me to cut her pretty throat."

"We can talk this out," Bishop says quietly, raising his hands like he's approaching a wild animal.

"Oh, we are going to talk," Cassiel promises. "Just like me and my darling Arden have been while we waited for you, but first, we need to deal with this little matter. Do you want to kill her, or should I?"

I'm going to die.

No.

Absolutely fucking not.

In this moment, I am not a harbinger. Not a Ravenell. I'm just a girl with every reason to live.

Every reason to fight.

I drive my elbow back blindly, but he anticipates it and wrenches me closer.

He clicks his tongue in my ear. "Careful, or you'll slit your own throat." He turns his attention back to Bishop, who's edged slightly closer. "I thought we were clear on the rules. I am in charge. I know that must kill you."

"Why?" Bishop asks the question I couldn't get an answer to.

"I'm not without justification." He flourishes the dagger for effect, and for a second, I draw a long breath, but then its blade is back at my throat. "You took something that belonged to me. It only seems fair I take something of yours."

"She doesn't belong to me."

"Doesn't she?" Cassiel nuzzles my hair, and I fight the urge to gag. "She trusts you. She knows what you are. At the very least, that means you belong to her."

Bishop's nostrils flare wide like he's barely reining himself in. "The power is corrupting you. You can stop this."

"I could, but I don't think I will. You see, there's a clarity that comes only when you stop fighting it." Cassiel drops his chin to my shoulder, and I cringe. Everything about his touch feels wrong.

"What do you want? The patronage?" Desperation edges Bishop's voice. "You can have it back. We can lie. I'll help you . . . just let her go."

"He can be quite sweet when he wants to be," Cassiel whispers to me, his warm breath tickling my ear. "But I have my sights set on something bigger."

Bishop stares back. "The throne."

The dagger feels colder against my skin, and every muscle in my body locks.

"Why stop there? It's a big world, little brother." Ambition drips from his words. "You could join me. We could take the crown together. You just have to stop fighting your power. Give in to the fury."

"There is no cycle."

"Oh, there will be. Can't you feel it? We're so close." He kisses my cheek, and Hero lets out another warning howl.

Bishop snarls and lunges forward a step. But Cassiel wags an index finger, never losing his grip on me. "Uh-uh. You know what Mother always said. We must share our toys."

Cassiel trails the tip of his blade down to where the mark hides beneath my shirt. "I think the Stars want their raven back."

Bishop stills. "Don't. Please. I'll do anything." He draws a shuddering breath, eyes wild. "Take me. You can have my vestiges. All my power."

"No," I beg, shaking my head.

"What star-crossed love." Cassiel sighs. "It's really too bad that she has to die. Arden, any final words you'd like to share with Bishop?"

Cassiel presses the tip of the blade between my breasts, just enough that I feel the point. I don't bother struggling. Don't look down. Don't beg. I won't give Cassiel that satisfaction. That's not how my life will end.

Instead, I find Bishop's gaze, and time slows down.

I stay with him. Drown in his eyes as the *revello* pierces the fabric of my shirt and meets skin. Cassiel pushes it in a fraction of an inch, just enough to make me feel it. The pressure is strange, like my body doesn't understand what's happening.

Bishop lunges toward us as a burst of white heat hits me.

A vessel of fire . . .

I gasp as the air empties from my lungs, and time shoots forward as my lips form the only thing left to say: "I lo—"

The dagger claims the rest.

EPILOGUE

Bishop

This is *not* how her story ends.

"Any final words . . ." The rest of what Cassiel says is lost to the blood roaring in my ears.

The hold I keep on my power slips, my thoughts scattering as my magic swells. I reach for it as Arden looks at me like I'm still her safe place.

Fuck me, that hurts.

For one second, I think my brother might change his mind and carry her off. Power strains against flesh and bone, hungry to tear its way out of me and take my brother apart before he can fucking try.

He's not walking off this balcony with her.

He isn't walking off this balcony at all.

I surge forward. Magic ripples through me as Arden opens her mouth to speak, fumbling for words. "I lo—"

My brother plunges the blade into her heart.

Her eyes widen as it pierces her chest, and then Cassiel shoves her forward.

Into my arms.

She sags as I catch her, head lolling back, body failing. Her gaze skitters, searching for a second before it finds me. She smiles for one heartbeat, and then the light in her eyes is . . . gone.

And my world ends.

I'll follow you.

I feel it happen. Whatever binds me to this body rips in half and follows her.

I fold around her, knees giving out and slamming into stone. I clutch her to my chest like I can force her soul back into it. The dagger's hilt digs into my ribs.

I press my lips to her forehead. She tastes like salt, skin still slick from fighting. She didn't give up for one moment.

I can't fail her now.

I let my eyes close. Let myself memorize the warmth of her skin.

One final kiss.

One last vow.

Then I lower her to the stone, and I stand.

Below us, the sea slams against the cliffs and breaks. Again and again. Like it doesn't know how to stop, either. Somewhere behind me, Hero lets out a low growl.

The balcony's stone railing is at my brother's back—the same one he went over the night I lost everything. Cassiel smirks. "Did you miss me?"

I study him like he's already dead.

There is only the echo of her unfinished words in my ears, and the unbearable silence where her heartbeat should be.

Cassiel's smile sharpens. He thinks I'm broken.

I draw my sword without looking away, something ancient and hungry bleeding into the edges of my sight. This power freed won't stop for mercy or reason. Not even love. It will devour whatever is in its path, like a star collapsing and swallowing everything it touches into a blinding void.

And for a minute, I let it take control.

"*There* it is." He tilts his head, watching me like I'm a wounded thing. "For a minute, I thought I was wrong. That my friend didn't finish the job that night. You put on an admirable show of being mortal. Then again, you've always been good at hiding, *Bishop*. I wondered if you'd awakened yet, but I couldn't be sure without coming home . . . Aren't you glad to see me?"

He's speaking to me like we're still brothers. Whatever I was before is gone. Killed alongside her.

I raise my sword. "Let's have a fucking party."

I fly at him. Our blades meet with a *crack* like splitting bone, the impact vibrating up my arm. Cassiel twists, regains his footing, but I'm already swinging again. Power leaks into every strike. But I rein it in, keep it barely leashed. I won't give in. I won't be like him.

I won't choose the easy path.

But I don't stop.

Strike. Again. Again.

Until time slows. Until I can't see my brother anymore.

Only her—falling heavily into my arms.

"I needed a vessel," Cassiel grunts, throwing his weight behind a parry. "No hard feelings, I hope."

His sword catches my cheek and slices my skin. "You killed her," I snarl, not feeling the cut. "I'll fucking *end* you."

Cassiel rolls his shoulders like we're still kids playing knights.

"Attachments are a liability during the cycle. I've made certain *we* have none. You're welcome."

Like he's done me a favor.

Then it hits me.

He's removed all our attachments, starting with—

"That night. *You* killed them." My throat tightens. The words tremble out, then explode. *"Every one of them."*

"That's a long story." He laughs.

He fucking laughs.

"I will rip your heart out with my bare hands." I mean it.

"The cycle must be released," he says, as if this justifies it all. "You have to feel it. We *all* do."

I don't care about the cycle. Or what he thinks we're meant to become. Her blood is still drying on my fingers. He can preach to the Stars themselves.

I slam him into the rail, and stone cracks behind his shoulder. Our blades grind together over our heads.

"Why are you so afraid?" he grits out. His free hand finds my shoulder.

Bright blue flame echoes from his palm, searing through leather into flesh. My skin peels back in black sheets.

Pain fractures my control, the scent of charred flesh fills my nose and mouth, and I shove away from him.

I stagger back, blade still raised. The power inside me roils, and I reach for it. Just a little. Still trying to hold it in check.

"That's what you're running away from, brother." Cassiel grins. "All that *power*. Locked in a box because you're too *good* to use it."

"I chose a different path."

"Always the noble son." Cassiel sighs. "Aren't you tired of pretending?"

I lunge. He meets me. Steel sings.

"You should be thanking me," he says, blade locked against mine. "You'd have kept protecting her until she was old and frail and your love for her became a fucking joke."

"You're not walking away from this."

"I'm not?" He pushes off. "Honestly, brother, I didn't come for you. I came for an *answer*. Not your head."

I drive forward, snarling through clenched teeth. "What . . . answer . . ." I bite out each word as I swing again and again. Steel meeting steel.

"One only she could give me." His eyes flick past me to where she lies in the dark. "I had a theory. That's all this was. A theory about a girl whose star split the Night's Scar at her Kindling. About a brother who fell for the harbinger and didn't have the *nerve* to tell her what she might *really* be. What a new star in the sky means, according to the *Ars Astra*."

For a half second, something leaps in my chest, but I crush it. I will not bargain with her death.

"Are you done punishing me yet?" he demands, a wild glint in his eyes.

"I will make you pay for this with your last breath," I vow, "and then I'll let you wake up so I can kill you again."

Cassiel lifts a brow, snorting. "You have it *bad* for her."

"Don't talk about her," I roar and come at him. "Don't even think about her."

He meets me, but he's slower now. The fire took something out of him. I see it—shoulders heaving, jaw set, sweat at his temple. He's wearing down.

That's all I need.

I press. Drive. Force him toward the corner where the rail meets the wall. Our blades catch. I twist, nearly pinning him, but his free hand lashes out and seizes my blade. Blood gushes down it. Blue flame races after, searing through my palm, and I drop my sword.

I leap back, but he has his sword at my throat before I can recover mine.

"If she wakes up, I'll take good care of her," he murmurs, breath ragged.

"Let her ride my cock if she behaves. But after I have what I want from her, I'll bury her heart next to yours."

The threat lands, and something inside answers for me. Something that won't allow him to take her. That doesn't care about paths or oaths.

Something that wants blood.

The power roars within me—the *real* power, the one I've kept caged since I came back from the dead—and for one terrible breath, I let it free.

Cassiel leaps back, dropping his sword to the ground. It melts, pooling into nothing more than molten metal. We both stare as the puddle shrinks, consuming itself, then disappears entirely. Like its very existence has been sucked away.

"*There* you are." His voice is almost giddy. "I knew it was in there. Why *lock it away*?"

I don't answer. I can't. If I let this blinding power loose in the world, there will be nothing left when I'm done. The monster will take everything.

He sees *that*, too. And smiles.

He steps back and grins as if he's already won. "You're going to be glorious," he says. "When you finally *let go*."

Cassiel is at the railing. He nods toward her body. "Keep it as a reminder that I can take anything from you. *Anyone*."

I could void the whole damn world. What's the point of it without Arden?

"Can you feel it?" He pauses and tips his face toward the darkening sky. "The cycle is beginning. Let's call it a day before the fury makes us kill each other."

"I'm not like you," I grit out.

"You will be. *All* of us will be." He pauses, just long enough for the words to sink in. "Only one can take the throne. Best of luck."

And then he leaps over the railing.

I don't hear his body hit the water. Hero races to the balcony's edge and howls after him. But I wait. Longer than I should. Until the sky above us is bruised with twilight, and only then do I fall to the ground beside her. Rock bites into my knees as I reach for her, blood trickling down my cheek, shoulder smarting. The wounds will heal soon enough. All of them except the one in my chest where my heart used to be.

My hand shakes as I reach for the dagger still buried in her chest.

"I'm sorry," I whisper and pull it free. There's no rush of blood, only the sickening wet sound of steel leaving flesh. I fling the weapon across the stone and press a hand over her heart, searching for a miracle.

Her skin is cool under my palm. She's heavy in my arms, and her head lolls against my shoulder, boneless in a way that shatters whatever control I had left.

"No." I gather her into my arms, my breath coming out in choked sobs. "No, no, no, *no*. Wake up. Please, wake up. You *need* to wake up."

I drag air into my lungs, the world blurring around me. "Just wake up, Arden. Don't leave me. *Please.*" My voice cracks on the *please*. I keep saying her name. Like if I do, she'll finally answer me. "Please don't leave me. *Please don't leave me.*"

Hero appears at my side and lies down beside Arden, but I can't see beyond my own grief. I pull her against me tighter, as if I can love her enough to make her heart beat again. To make air fill her lungs. I cling to a dream that's been ripped away from me.

"Arden." I press my lips to her forehead. Cold. Too cold. "Come back to me."

A shadow passes over my head, and the oscen lands on the ground beside me. It blinks its curious eyes at me and lets out a shrill caw like it's trying to tell me something.

"I know she's fucking dead."

Dead. The word undoes me.

Cassiel was wrong. She's not going to wake up. She isn't a scion.

Something wild and fierce claws at my chest as I raise my face to the night sky, as I curse at that one lone star in the swath of darkness. At the lie I let myself believe.

But *I* was wrong to hope. Wrong to think the Stars might bend for once.

That star that split the Night's Scar fooled us both—only I wasn't willing to risk it. And I never even told her.

Because part of me wanted her to be like me. To be immortal.

A selfish thing I thought I'd carved out for myself.

I wanted to love her forever.

I look at the dagger lying where I flung it. All of this to start a war.

For power.

To claim a throne.

As if any of that matters. Only a man who'd never met the other half of his soul could think it did.

"I should have told you the truth." My voice is hoarse, my throat raw. I embrace the pain and beg for more than I deserve. "Wake up, and I will. I'll tell you about everything. Never leave a moment of my day out. I'll tell you what I thought when I first saw you. What I think every time you fall asleep in my arms. Every stupid thought I have. Every terrible joke. You'll hate it, actually."

I bury my face in her hair, drink in the faint lilac scent that always lingers on her. I try to memorize it even as panic tears through me at the thought of forgetting. But I can't force the air past the pain long enough to fill my lungs.

"I'll spend the rest of our lives making it up to you. Just wake up."

I'm no longer scared of the fury. The cycle. Any of it.

I'm only scared of losing her. Of never getting to tell her that I love her. Of facing my darkness without her light.

"I needed a reason to fight. To really fight. I have one now," I whisper. "You're my reason."

And I don't care if she is the harbinger.

If this tears apart the entire world.

If war is the cost of hearing her heart beat again . . . I will bleed for her. For this.

Some loves make the world bearable. Hers made it worth living in.

"I love you," I whisper into her hair. "I love you. Come back."

Silence.

And then—

A faint thump.

Another.

Hero sits up, head tilting, as if he hears it, too. But I go utterly still, afraid any movement, even breathing, might steal that sound from me. I close my eyes and count the heartbeats as they grow stronger.

"Whatever comes, we face it together," I whisper. "I'm not afraid anymore."

The rhythm beneath my palms steadies into a fierce beat, pounding its way back to the world.

Faint red shapes thread across her skin, barely visible. But it isn't a birthright. It's vestiges. Hundreds of lines mapping themselves on her arms, over her hands, across the strip of collarbone visible under her bloody shirt.

I look up. Search for her star in the Night's Scar. But as the sky overhead darkens, it's as if the night has dropped a veil.

Her star fades, winks out, then blazes back to life.

And the Night's Scar splits like an unhealed wound torn open once more, and behind it . . .

Stars.

Hundreds of them.

Thousands.

They were never gone.

They were hidden.

And something grips me. Something ancient and primal, rising from the cage I've been holding shut. It demands blood.

Demands I pick up that dagger and carve out her heart.

The power inside me strains, snapping its fangs, digging its claws, and for a single, terrible breath, I see myself reaching for the dagger.

I see myself reaching for *her*.

I shove the beast back down with everything I have left. Slam the cage shut. Lock it from the inside. The effort tears something in my soul that won't heal as fast as the rest of me.

Not her. Never her.

She gasps, chest heaving under my hand, drawing breath in long, ragged pulls.

A small, whining bleat splinters the air beside us, and Hero shoves his nose against her shoulder, whimpering. Slowly, her eyes flutter open to meet mine.

But I find no salvation there.

There's something else—something *wrong*. Her gaze skids around the balcony like a trapped animal's, and when it lands on me, it lands like I'm prey.

"Arden." My voice is wrecked. "It's me."

She jerks upright, wrenching out of my arms.

"Stay away." She's on her feet faster than a woman who just died should be able to manage. She snatches up her fallen sword. The point sways toward me, then steadies. *"Stay away from me."*

I stand slowly. "It's Bishop. Arden, it's *me*."

Her face crumples even as the blade stays level. *"What's happening to me?"*

She's looking at me like she's sees every reason she has to live—and trying not to drive her sword through it.

"Arden—"

"I d-don't want this—" Sobs tremble from her, the sword shaking in her hand. "I don't want this, Bishop. Make it stop. *Please, make it stop*—"

Something is rising inside her. Not the same beast clawing at my cage. It isn't the fury. I don't have a name for it, but I can feel it calling to my own blood.

And she's in there with it. Alone. Holding it back with nothing but her own will.

But her will is the only thing that's ever mattered.

"Look at me." I take a slow step forward. "Look at my *eyes*, Arden."

She does.

The sword lowers a fraction. Lifts. Lowers again. A sob breaks out of her. "I'll kill you. I can't stop myself. Don't come any closer—"

She lunges.

I'm faster.

I catch the flat of her blade in my gloved hand, twist it out of her grip, and crack the pommel of my own sword against the side of her head in one motion. She blinks once, mouth open like she's about to yell at me, and then she collapses.

I catch her before she hits the stone.

"Fuck, you're stubborn." I scoop her into my arms, pausing only to kiss her forehead. "I'm sorry. I'm so sorry. We'll figure it out. I swear we will."

I carry her stubborn ass off the balcony, Hero bounding behind us, back to where she's always belonged. Here. With me. With *us*.

And I don't care if I'm walking toward war. Toward a fight I never saw coming. No matter what it costs me.

She's worth dying for.

Because if any soul can defy the Stars, it's hers.

ACKNOWLEDGMENTS

I owe endless gratitude to my editor, Liz Pelletier, for always having my back. Thank you for being there through all the late hours and nervous breakdowns, for having faith when mine wavers, and for transcending the role of editor into that of friend. Let's do this again (I'm afraid you're stuck with me)!

Thank you to Louise Fury for always living up to your name. Thank you for opening that book I gave you the night we met and reading it. Even after all these years, I think we're just at the beginning of our beautiful partnership.

Becca Syme—I don't know where I would be without your support and friendship. Somehow you always make me see the bigger picture even when I can't. Thank you so much.

A special thanks to Adrian Paul for kicking my ass while teaching me how to use a sword. The book is immeasurably better for your lessons.

Huge thanks to my editorial team. Hannah, thank you for your limitless patience. Thank you to Mary, Nancy, Rae, and Stacy Abrams.

Thank you to Melanie, Heather, Hannah Li-Paz, Justine, Curtis, Katie, Molly, Joanne, Cai, Madison, and everyone at Entangled for everything you do. A story doesn't become a book without you. Special thanks to Meredith Johnson for making the world go round and to Beth Metrick for always finding a way to make miracles happen. Thank you to Bree Archer, LJ Anderson, Beth Kessler, and Elizabeth Turner Stokes for turning *Harbinger* into a work of art. A special thanks to the team at Macmillan for making magic happen.

Thank you to my foreign and film agents for helping me bring my stories to readers all over the world, and thank you to booksellers and librarians for helping readers find them.

I'm grateful for the incredible work Recorded Books does to bring these books to life.

Special thanks to David and the crew at The Fury Agency, Isabelle Knight, Shelby Lynn, Ashley Hazelwood, and Abby Mahkne.

Writing can be a lonely business. I am so blessed to be surrounded by the love and support of my author friends. Miranda Lyn, this book wouldn't be here without you. I think we both know that. Thank you. Rebecca, thank you for always taking time out of your crazy schedule when I need you. And thank you to all of my author friends—your talent and generosity inspire me every day.

I wouldn't be here without my readers. Thank you for staying up late with my stories and loving my characters as much as I do.

To my family: You are the reason I can do all of this. I don't know where I would be without my siblings, my parents, and my mother-in-law. Thank you. I'm blessed to have given birth to three of the kindest, coolest, and most creative kids in the world. I'm prouder of you with every passing day. Thanks for believing in me.

And to Josh, I thank the Stars we found each other. I write love stories because you showed me what true love is. Thank you for always reading, always showing up, and always believing. I love you.

FOR BONUS CONTENT

SCAN HERE